Children of the Resolution

The First Carl Grantham Novel

GW00570435

Gary William Murning

Children of the Resolution—Gary William Murning

Contents © Gary William Murning 2010

The right of Gary William Murning to be identified as the author
of this work has be asserted in accordance with the
Copyright, Designs and Patent Act 1988.

*All rights reserved. No part of this publication may be
reproduced, stored in or introduced into a retrieval system, or
transmitted, in any form, or by any means electronic, mechanical,
photocopying, recording or otherwise, without the prior permission
of the author. Any person who commits any unauthorised act in
relation to this publication may be liable to criminal prosecution
and civil claims for damages.*

ISBN 978-1-4466-5020-2

**In memory of Geoff S.
Without whom there would
never have been a
Johnny Jameson.**

Prologue

During those daily visits to Carl Grantham, I learnt more about humanity than I ever thought possible—not in any way so well formed that I might readily articulate it. No. My time with him was subtler than that. Nonetheless, between his lines and sometimes on them, I found an understanding of what it was to be apart, to be within and absorbed... to be included and yet, as we all are, I suppose, ineffably alone.

I had been told by my friend Andrea that he might not be up to talking to me. He was still fairly weak and if he was feeling as down as he on occasion had been, the interview might well be over before it had even started. It had been a bad and unexpected bout of pneumonia, and this on top of his existing condition had apparently highlighted a vulnerability he'd thought he'd succeeded in side-stepping. I was therefore anxious about the welcome I might receive, hoping for the best but, as my mother had always taught me, expecting the worst.

It was a bright day in late April when I walked tentatively onto Ward Seventeen of the James Cook University Hospital, the watery but welcome sunlight filtering through the filthy fourth floor windows and lending a dubious cheer to the otherwise dreary surroundings. Andrea had told me that Carl Grantham could be found at the far end of the ward's main corridor, in a six-bedder with "a beautiful view of nothing worth mentioning", and so I strode purposefully past the nurses' station, crowded with gossiping nurses, wondering if I would be able to recognise him from the description Andrea had given me.

Thin and long, hair cropped short and greying. Handsome as a dying poet.

Carl Grantham sat in his bed, dressed in pyjamas and dressing gown (which didn't seem to come naturally to him, judging by the way he constantly fidgeted and rearranged them), staring out of the window at the sky, a forgotten book in his lap. I knew him immediately. It could have been no one else. Not usually so precise, Andrea had been bang on the

3

button. He was the only one in that room of coughing and farting men, most of them much older than Carl's forty-one years, that fit that description—fit it perfectly, if I'm honest.

I stood unnoticed in the doorway for a moment, composing myself. I was still worried about how this would go (knowing that the strength and validity of my dissertation depended on it) but not as worried as I had been. He didn't look the type to turn round and tell me to bugger off. Granted, he might ask me to leave, but he would do so politely, I was sure.

He turned and looked over at me as I approached, and I felt my shoulders drop—a soft sigh escaping as he smiled rather sadly at me, any worries I might have had quickly dissipating.

Holding out his hand as best he could, he said, with Stanley-like formality, "Marisa Donne, I presume. Andrea told me I should expect you. Please, sit down."

"'Educational reform'," he said, holding the words in his mouth like a boiled sweet. He spoke softly, his voice raspy and at times rather weak. "That covers a multitude of sins." That smile, again. Tired and somehow lost. "You have a particular area of interest?"

I nodded, glad of the opportunity to explain further. "I'm concerned more with the lessons that can be learned from looking back at past examples of educational reform, specifically reform as it applies to the integration of children with physical disabilities into mainstream schools."

Carl nodded. "Andrea mentioned that. And you think my childhood experiences might help you get a better picture of what worked and what didn't?"

It was difficult to be sure, but I thought he might be testing me. "I don't know," I said, truthfully. "I'd like to think it would—but for all I know, you might have sailed through school without taking anything relating to my area of interest away with you. I doubt that, of course, but it's possible."

He seemed to like my answer. He closed the book in his lap—*H.L. Mencken on Religion*—and looked out of the window, again. "I'm not sure how much help it'll be to you, but I'll be happy to share everything I know." He pointed at the thin notebook I'd brought with me. "That might not be enough."

Chapter One: In the Place of Old Times

I wasn't the big boy they said I was, that was what that first day taught me. I was a leaf in a stream, tossed about on the current of adult opinion and action. They "knew best". They had seen more and done more. They had been *educated* into believing, as I one day might, that this was the road down which we had to travel. The "big boy" had to go to school. That was just the way it was. He had to go to school and he had to learn his lessons, but—oh yes, there had to be a but—he couldn't go to *that* school. Oh, no. *That* school, the one where all his neighbourhood friends would be going, was unsuitable.

Mam and Dad took me in—the car journey seeming to take forever. I sat on the back seat, looking at the scenery passing by but not really seeing it. I should be *memorising* it, I told myself. I should be mapping it all out in my mind like a secret agent so that I could find my way home the minute the teachers' backs were turned. But it was too late now. Something had changed forever—everything *felt funny*—and all the *memorising* in the world wasn't going to fix that.

I'd never known Mam and Dad to be so quiet. Dad was concentrating on the road, he'd told us, but I didn't believe him. He knew these roads like the back of his hand, and would usually delight in telling us every few minutes—battling with Mam for superiority as she pointed out landmarks like Newport Bridge and the General Hospital—so I could only guess that he, like Mam, had other things on his mind.

I didn't want to think about that, though. I wasn't a big boy. I was little and I was scared and I *just didn't want to think about that!* I shouldn't have to. I should have been at home playing, pretending I was Neil Armstrong like I had been yesterday—when the world had been a very different place.

It had been safe and warm, that was what I now understood, if only in a very peripheral, difficult-to-grasp way. I had been loved and protected, Mam and Dad the binary stars at the centre of my small but perfectly comfortable solar system. I only had to look around to know where I was

5

and know that they weren't far away, that, whatever happened, they would be there, making the right decisions for me, carefully explaining the world in all its difficult-to-comprehend shades. Everyone else didn't matter. They did, but they didn't. All the doctors in their white coats and half-moon reading specs, tapping me with their hammers and flexing my ankles so severely that they sprained, all the grandparents and aunts and uncles, solicitous and looming—they had roles of range and a certain merit, but they weren't up there with Mam and Dad, and they could never hope to be.

But things changed. That's what I now had to try to assimilate. Mam and Dad, I didn't think they would ever change. Not in their hearts. Not in any way that mattered. They would always love and care for me, always bend over backwards to keep me from harm (*even if I did a murder or something*, I thought.) But it wasn't them that I had to worry about, because, I was coming to realise, Dad wasn't a big boy, either, and Mam wasn't a big girl. They were scared and small, being made to do things with which, I now know, they at the time hadn't felt comfortable. The world and the people in it exerted an influence, and sometimes Mam and Dad could do nothing about it, however much they might want to.

It's for his own good. Carl needs the best education possible if he's to excel and compete—and a mainstream school just wouldn't be able to provide the specialist support he needs. Trust me. It's not like it's a boarding school. It's a wonderful place. The name says it all. Sunnyvale School. He'll love it there, I promise you.

"I hate it."

"Now I don't think you do, Carl," Mam said as we drove up the drive to the school's main entrance. "You haven't had time to hate it."

"I don't need time. It looks like that film."

"What film?"

"The one in the prison camp with the German Nasties."

Dad chuckled and Mam shot him a warning glance. "You've got to admit, love," he said. "It is a bit dismal."

"It's nothing of the sort." Mam thought it was *dismal*, too. I knew she did. "That's just the weather. You wait—you wait until the sun comes out. It'll look loads better."

Dad stopped the car, pulling on the handbrake so hard I thought it was going to come loose. I did hate it. I hated it so bad it made my throat ache. But I didn't say anything—we none of us did. We just sat there in silence for a few minutes, the rain pattering against the windscreen, the distant windows of the classrooms—each a separate building connected by roofed pathways—illuminated from the inside. They made me think of my friend's dad's aquarium, strange, glowing tanks of bizarre looking fish that all too often ended up floating on the surface, dead and having to be fished out with a little net.

I imagined a big hand coming down and lifting the roof off one of the classrooms—a net fishing out the lifeless form of one of my future classmates—and then Dad said, "Time to gird our loins and get on with it, I think. No use putting it off."

A grey-haired, bespectacled woman dressed in a nurse's uniform that wasn't *quite* a nurse's uniform was waiting for us in the milk-sour lobby. Dad had lifted me out of the car and put me in my pushchair (this was a time before I got my first, bright red wheelchair), and as he wheeled me towards the woman I would come to know as Mrs. Attenborough, I felt myself becoming smaller as she loomed ever-nearer. She looked mean, with little hairs growing on her chinny-chin-chin and a pencilled-in frown—but when she saw us, she smiled and became a totally different and much nicer person. It was a good trick, and I was momentarily impressed.

"Let me guess," she said, going down on her haunches in front of me. She had big knees. "You must be Carl. Yes?" I thought about shaking my head, just to see what would happen—but instead nodded. "Excellent! It's very nice to meet you, Carl," she said, shaking my hand. "My name's Mrs. Attenborough and I'm one of the people who'll be looking after you while you're at Sunnyvale."

I was about to tell her that I hated the place, but Dad skilfully cut me off at the pass. "He's a little nervous," he said.

Mrs. Attenborough got to her feet again, smiling and shaking first Dad's and then Mam's hands. "Understandable," she said. "But there's really no need. He'll love it here once he settles in. Won't you, Carl?"

I shrugged. My throat was aching again. Mrs. Attenborough was nice, but I didn't want to be left here with her and her knees.

"Can we go home, now?" I asked Mam.

"Home?" Mrs. Attenborough said before Mam could answer (a bit rude, I thought.) "You've only just got here, pet. There's still so much more to see and do." She took my pushchair from Dad and started wheeling me away, Mam and Dad trotting to keep up. "Come on. Let's have a look around, shall we?"

"Then can I go home?"

***

I didn't take in all that much of what Mrs. Attenborough said as she showed us around the school. I was too preoccupied with the strange and overwhelming sights with which I was presented—big kids in big pushchairs that, I was told, were *wheelchairs*, other kids with bits of metal strapped with leather to their vine-like legs, others who seemed normal enough until they looked at you, when it became obvious that they couldn't see properly. One boy, a lot older than me, couldn't keep his arms or legs still; they moved about with a will of their own, like some weird monster out of that Sinbad movie I'd seen.

I looked but I could never have understood. Not really. I felt no sense of belonging. I shared no affinity with these injured souls because I wasn't like them. I was different and didn't belong here.

As Mrs. Attenborough led us into what she said would be my classroom, I breathed in the sick-smell of poster paint and tried to push it all away. I was a secret agent, again, *infiltrating* enemy territory, and it was of vital importance that my cover shouldn't be blown. I tried to think of everyone around me as unsuspecting foreigners—but it didn't work. There was only so much the very able imagination of this five-year-old could manage, however much television he'd watched.

The tables and chairs in this classroom were so much smaller than the others we had seen—smaller and painted gaudy shades of red, green and blue. The walls were decorated with "A is for Apple" posters and pictures that my "classmates" had painted (badly), and the large French windows at the south end of the room let in more light than would have seemed possible on such a gloomy day.

Mrs. Attenborough and her knees seemed to be enjoying themselves a little too much. This wasn't anywhere near the fun she clearly imagined it to be—and when I looked up at Mam and Dad, their fixed, unsmiling faces strongly implied that they agreed with me. Dad had again taken possession of my pushchair and me, but this was cold comfort—for by now even I realised that it couldn't last. Sooner or later (probably sooner), I was going to be wrenched away from them, and there would be nothing any of us could do about it.

My teacher, who Mrs. Attenborough introduced with a little flourish of the hand, was called Miss Porter—and I thought right away that it was going to be hard not liking her, because she actually seemed quite nice. Young, with long, shiny black hair, tall but not tall enough to make my neck ache really bad, her smile wasn't something that had to be switched on like Mrs. Attenborough's. It was just there, honest and real and permanent.

"Hello, Carl," she said, very softly, her voice almost hypnotic. "It's very nice to have you with us." Turning to the other children in the room, she added, "Children, this is Carl. I want you to say hello to him and make him feel welcome."

A chorus of hellos rang out and I felt my throat start to ache and tighten again. It couldn't be long now, that much I knew. They would be going. They'd told me as much. They would be going because I was a "big boy", but they would be there waiting for me when I got home with chicken rissoles, baked beans and chips.

And, sure enough, the time came—just as I'd known it would. Mam and Dad said goodbye to me, Mam trying her best not to cry, and I felt the depth of my predicament slowly start to truly pull me down. This was when things really started to get bad. I knew that, now. They were going, bustled away by Mrs. Attenborough, they were gone—and I was suddenly more alone than I'd ever known, sitting at a red table with a bunch of odd-looking kids I didn't even like.

That was when I started crying.

Miss Porter was very patient with me, even though she had eight or nine other kids to teach and look after. She knelt down beside me, her arms folded on the table-top, and talked to me in that soft, precise manner of hers, assuring me that things weren't as bad as they seemed and that, before I knew it, I'd be *looking forward* to coming to school.

That seemed silly to me, and I was quick to tell her. Biting back a smile, she said, "It's like this, Carl. You're a big boy now..." I was getting *really* sick of that one... "and big boys and girls go to school during the daytime so that they can learn lots of fun things and—"

"Every day?" I said.

"What?"

"Do we have to come *every* day?"

Miss Porter smiled. "No," she said, apparently relieved that she could finally give me some good news. "No, you don't have to come every day. You have the weekends off and... here, I'll show you." Getting up, she took a calendar off the wall by her desk and returned with it—kneeling down and taking a pen from behind her ear. Putting a little cross in the days of that month when I'd be coming to school, and a tiny circle in those I wouldn't, she said, "See? These are the days you'll be at school, and these are the days you won't be. Not so bad, is it?"

I looked at the calendar. I looked up at the smiling, pretty face of Miss

Porter. I looked back down at the calendar.

And then I started to cry again.

The day went a lot more quickly than I ever could have reasonably hoped, and by the time it came for me to be lifted into my seat on the school bus, I'd even managed to make my first friend.

Tommy Blackbird had a bouncy limp when he walked and a wasted right hand that curled in on itself at the wrist. He smiled like he wanted to be everybody's friend, but so far looked as friendless as me—so I suppose it was fairly inevitable that, on the journey home, we would find ourselves chatting away at the back of the bus, both of us glad the day was over.

"Miss Porter said you've got a bad leg like me," Tommy said.

I didn't know how to answer Tommy. I liked him, but it was a daft thing to say and I didn't like the idea of Miss Porter being daft. It was fairly obvious to me that, while my legs certainly didn't work the way they were supposed to, they were nothing like Tommy's. Thankfully, as I would quickly learn, having a conversation with Tommy didn't always mean that one had to actually *say* anything. He was an independent chap, and he could manage perfectly well on his own, thank you very much.

"She looks like Marie Osmond," he continued. "Don't you think? Just like her only a lot prettier and not a moron like my dad says Marie Osmond is."

I nodded noncommittally, wondering if Mam really was doing me chicken rissoles for tea. I loved chicken rissoles. I'd been looking forward to them all day. I didn't mind if she didn't do the chips and baked beans, as long as there were chicken rissoles.

The cigarette smoke from our driver—a big woman who talked like a man and said "bugger" a lot, even when we could hear—made Tommy cough and he stopped talking for a minute until he had it under control. "I don't mind it, really, though," he finally continued. I couldn't remember what he'd been talking about last, but I was quite sure it wouldn't matter. "School," he clarified, spotting my confused frown. "It's warm. I like being warm, don't you?"

~

Carl had been talking for a good half an hour, filling in details for me, backtracking when he recalled something he'd forgotten to mention. He seemed to grow in confidence as his story gathered momentum, and I couldn't help feeling that he was more comfortable visiting these times than even he might have expected. As he talked, his words found a rhythm all of their own and, even though it wasn't difficult for me to see that he was growing tired, it was clear that he wanted to continue.

"I settled pretty quickly after that, I think," he told me. "It's surprising how quickly kids adapt. They're far better at it than adults—far better at it than me, anyway."

"Me, too," I admitted. "My friend Andrea... you know Andrea... she's always trying to get me to do different things. From going to a new club in town to bungee jumping. And all I want to do is—"

"Stay in with a good book and a bottle of wine?" He was smiling and I couldn't help but smile back.

"Pretty much." I didn't want this to become about me. As much as I liked Carl, this was about my dissertation and I needed to be sure that I kept him moving in the right direction. He had insisted that it was important that I understand the "pre-integration climate" if I was to ever grasp the whole sense of promise and revolution that came with the new philosophy, and I'd agreed with him. This, however, meant that it was probably going to be a longer job than I'd originally envisaged. The fewer distractions and diversions the better.

Glancing down at my notes, I said, "So how did Sunnyvale feel in those first few months? You say you adapted, but how did it compare with, say, your out-of-school life?"

"Very different," he quickly answered. "I didn't like overlap. I didn't like my parents attending open days, for example. I could never have understood why at the time, but it was as if I was afraid that my home life might become somehow tainted by it if it got too close. Sunnyvale was... I thought of it as old, something from bygone times. In reality, I'm not sure how long it had been there—but... it had the feel of a sanatorium for TB patients, you know, even down to the French windows and the south-facing perspective. Everyone there, the teaching and nursing staff, they all, as I remember it, worked with the best of intentions, but even before I had something with which to compare it, it always seemed stuck in a time warp to me."

"And what about the fact that you were going to a different school to the one your friends at home were going to?" I said. "That must have at least seemed a little odd."

Carl shrugged, looking suddenly rather more tired than I liked. "I don't think it occurred to me, much. Certainly not it any way I could have easily expressed at the time. Maybe on that first day..." he trailed off and nodded to a glass of water on his bedside locker. "Would you mind?"

Leaving my notepad and pen on my chair, I held the glass for him so that he could sip water through the straw. "I'll come back tomorrow," I

11

said. "You're tired."

~

Tommy wanted a duffel coat ("because they are warm") and some marbles for Christmas—which seemed to me a very reasonable request—whilst I was leaning towards clackers and a spud gun. I also wanted my own record player so that I could play my Elvis LPs, and possibly a carpentry set, but I wasn't banking on them.

We were sitting at the side of the playground, me in my new red wheelchair, watching some of the bigger kids play football. It was funny, because some of them were also in wheelchairs and every now and then the ball would get stuck underneath one of them and there'd be this chaotic scrum of people trying to kick it out. Tommy seemed to especially enjoy this—but, then, Tommy enjoyed just about everything.

"They lock them in, you know," he said, out of the blue.

"They lock who in?"

"The kids in the school next door. They lock 'em in."

"Why?"

"What?"

"Why do they lock them in?"

"Dunno. They just do."

I sat and thought about this for a while. I didn't like the idea of being locked in. It was bad enough having to come to school and *not* be locked in, I couldn't imagine what that added indignity would be like. But I wasn't entirely sure that I believed Tommy, anyway. I was already finding out that he was more than happy to make things up as he went along, telling me stories about the time his dad fought Ali and won, how he'd once played professional football with Georgie Best, and this had all the hallmarks of being another of his fibs—especially when it occurred to me that I'd seen them outside at playtime, as free to move around as we were.

"That's not what I mean," Tommy said. "I'm talking about at night and stuff like that. They don't let them go home. They lock them in and make them stay there, eating bread and water and cockroaches."

"Cockroaches?"

"And beetles. My dad says they're *delli ink wents* or something and it's no worse than they deserve. He says they should put more of the little sods away in places like that. The world'd be a saferer place."

I gasped, my eyes wide.

"What?"

"You said 'sods'. That's a swear word."

"No it isn't."

"It is. And you said it."

"Well, if I did," he said with a shrug, "you did, too."

I'd never thought of that, and this seemed to give Tommy an inordinate amount of satisfaction. He chortled to himself and pointed at me as if I was the funniest thing he'd ever seen. "Don't worry, pal," he finally said. "I won't tell if you don't."

I would never have told, and I was quick to assure him of this—before returning once more to the matter of the school next door. It was separated from our school on the other side of the driveway by nothing more than a drystone wall no higher than Tommy's shins... and I had an idea.

"Can we do that?" Tommy wanted to know. He looked rather worried. I wasn't sure why, but I thought that that was a good thing.

"Yes," I said, with a confidence that belied the fact that I thought we probably couldn't. "They haven't told us we can't, anyway."

"That's not the same thing, though."

"Yes it is."

That was something else about Tommy that I was quickly learning; he trusted me. He might ask a lot of questions and express doubts, but if I said a thing was so, it wasn't long before he believed it as if it were something his dad had told him. He nodded thoughtfully to himself and chewed the side of his mouth, staring into space as he worked through it, slowly, in his head—the football game now forgotten. I knew he'd go along with it. It was just a matter of being patient and letting him arrive at the obvious conclusion in his own good time.

"It's not like we'd be leaving the school or owt, is it?" he said. "We'd still be in our school, just looking over the wall at them, right?"

There was no one over this side of the school, which was good, since it meant it was far less likely that we would be caught and get told off. The driveway was quiet, no cars coming or going, but we nevertheless crossed carefully—determined not to get run over by some unforeseen speeding vehicle. On the far side, we moved over the grass, Tommy pushing me, towards the low brick wall and the oak trees that overhung it.

The other kids seemed oblivious to us—distantly playing away on their field without a wheelchair or a caliper or a crutch in sight. Tommy and I watched them in silence, and I wondered if they really did get locked in at night or if their school was actually better than ours.

It was just a little wall, but I still couldn't get over it.

Tommy was growing impatient. There was nothing *happening* and he just couldn't stand it. "You think they'd at least come over and say hello," he said.

"They haven't seen us," I told him.

"Yes they have. They're just ignoring us because they're snobs."

I wasn't sure what "snobs" were, but I vaguely wondered if that was why they got locked up at night.

"We could shout them," I said. "If they ignore us, then we'll know for definite they're snobs, won't we?"

"Good idea, old pal," Tommy said, patting me on the back. "Go on, then."

"What?"

"Shout them."

"I thought we'd do it together. That way it'll be louder and they'll hear us better."

Tommy had a look on his face that I couldn't quite work out—but I thought I knew how he was feeling because, yes, I suspected I was feeling the same way, too. We'd come this far, and it would have been stupid to turn back now, but nonetheless I wished we were still on the playground watching the big kids play football. Maybe if we'd asked nicely they might even have let us join in. As it was, we were facing an unknown that was bigger than both of us, and I for one didn't like it. What if they were bad kids? If they did get locked in at night, there had to be a reason. What if they were bad and they did something to us? There was no one around to stop them and my kung fu was a little patchy. They could beat us up and rob us of *all our worldly possessions*. And there would be nothing we could do about it, except scream a lot.

"Shall we go back and watch the football?" Tommy said. "This is boring."

I nodded, glad that he had been the one who'd suggested it. I didn't want to look *yella*, after all, especially when it had been my idea in the first place.

Before we could get back across the drive, however, a cry rang out. "Oi, you!"

I didn't want to turn round and reply. Christmas was nearly here and we had the party to look forward to and the holidays and the presents and this really wasn't what we should be doing. The wind had picked up and it seemed to carry with it a warning; *turn around*, it said, *turn around and it will change your life forever. Nothing will ever be the same for you.* Maybe that didn't happen. Looking back, it's difficult to say. But in my heart, in the memories of that time that I've carried with me ever since, that was how it seemed. The voice called out and we stopped in our tracks, that sense of dread growing ever more insistent, and before I could say anything to stop him, Tommy had turned my wheelchair around and we were heading back towards the wall—back towards the wall and the gang of children that was already gathering there.

There was about four of them—all of a similar age to us and looking, as lacking in wheelchairs and crutches as they were, as much of a mixed bag as our other schoolmates. One looked neat and tidy, another like she'd been dragged through the dirt, whilst the other two merely looked reticent and a little dim. The neat and tidy one seemed to be the one to watch, however. If there was a ringleader, he was it. His hair parted cruelly down the middle, shoulders unnaturally squared, he managed to make himself look taller than he actually was—and I felt Tommy shrinking beside me, his bad hand going behind his back.

"What?" I said, as belligerently as I could muster.

"You were looking at us," Mister Neat and Tidy said.

"So?"

"We don't like people looking at us, do we, Chris?" he said to the scruffy girl by his side.

"No," she agreed.

"Especially people like you," he added. "People with *diseases*."

"We haven't got no diseases," Tommy told him—and I nodded quickly, hoping that this would lend his statement a little additional weight. "We've got *disabilities*—that's summat different, and if you don't know that, you're stupid."

"Are you calling me stupid?" Mister Neat and Tidy said, taking a step towards the wall but stopping short of stepping over it.

"No," Tommy quickly replied. "I'm saying you're stupid if you think *diseases* and *disabilities* are the same."

"I don't."

"Then you're not."

"Good."

We seemed to have reached something of an impasse. The scruffy lass looked at her two quieter friends, obviously growing bored with the whole scenario. She scratched her bum and looked back over her shoulder at the rest of her schoolmates, running about on the field and generally appearing to be having a much better time than she was. I thought she might walk away. I was hoping she would because, judging by the flaky patches of skin on her neck, if anyone had a disease, it was she, and I for one didn't want to catch it. But Mister Neat and Tidy wasn't done with us, yet, and so she remained by his side, ever faithful and patient.

"Don't alter owt, though, do it, Chris?" Mister Neat and Tidy continued. "We still don't want you and you're *disabilities* looking at us. We don't like it cos you're weird and we don't like weird people."

"We aren't weird," I said.

I expected it to be a straightforward exchange of the "no we aren't", "yes you are" variety—but it didn't go that way at all. Mister Neat and Tidy looked directly at me and something changed. I didn't know what, and to this day I'm unsure how he came to switch so completely and quickly. Maybe he saw something in my eyes, I don't know, or maybe he was, like his Chris, growing bored of such a pointless exchange. Either way, his reaction was quite unexpected.

First stepping over the wall, he then sat down on it and stared at me. "You're different, though," he said. "That must be right horrible. I wouldn't want to be you."

I didn't know what to say to this. I didn't really understand what he was saying—even though, on the surface, what he was saying wasn't all that difficult to understand. It was like there was more to it than first appeared, and even though he now seemed to be trying to be friendly, I wished he wasn't. I liked him the other way best.

"What do you do in there?" he asked, nodding at Sunnyvale. "Play games and stuff?"

"Only at playtime," I said. "Mostly we learn to read and do sums, that kind of thing."

"Fuck off!" Mister Neat and Tidy said in disbelief. It wasn't the first time I'd heard someone say "fuck off", but it was certainly the first time I'd heard someone as young as him say it. "*You* can't read and do sums."

"Oh yes he can," Tommy chirped up. "He's the best in our class. Our teacher said he's a genesis."

"Genius."

"A genius."

"What's one of them when he's at home?" Mister Neat and Tidy said. Chris and her two friends had finally wandered away and it was just the three of us now.

"Someone who's dead, dead clever," Tommy said, sitting down on the wall beside him. "He should be on the telly, on some sort of quiz or something, that's how clever he is. He's so clever that he even knows how to spell really long words like... like... like *house*, don't you, Carl?"

I nodded and, as I'd expected, Mister Neat and Tidy called me on it. "Go on, then," he said, in a not unfriendly manner. "Let's hear it."

Pulling a face that I hoped made it look more difficult (and therefore more impressive) than it actually was, I spelt it slowly and deliberately, knowing it probably wouldn't matter if I made a mistake, since Mister Neat and Tidy undoubtedly couldn't spell it, anyway, but still not wanting to.

Mister Neat and Tidy looked at Tommy, evidently impressed. "He's good."

"I told you."

We chatted for a while longer, and whilst it wasn't exactly the most settling conversation I'd ever had, it was pleasant enough. Mister Neat and Tidy's real name, he told us, was Eric—and even though Tommy and I would never speak to him again, I would always remember him as being the first person from my peer group to make me think—*really* think— about just how different I was... just how different we all were. At the time, and as amiable as he became, he was someone I could never have imagined myself thanking. His role that day had, to my undeveloped mind, been a dubious one, and I gave him no credit. He had served only to cast a cloud over the run-up to Christmas, and it's hard to imagine my ever liking him for that.

Today I wonder, though. Today, I can't help but think that maybe Eric did me a favour. I was different. I suppose I'd known that for quite some time—ever since we'd had the conversation with the doctor about how I was going to die—but Eric had underscored that in a way that showed just how bad difference could really be, or how bad people could believe it to be if they didn't really understand it. He also helped me see, in my way, that being different didn't mean that I wasn't intelligent. I was clever, and sometimes being clever could be *really* useful.

Chapter Two: The Ghost of Emiline Brown

I got in early a few evenings later, hoping that I might meet Carl's parents and maybe get their perspective on his school years, especially those first days, which, as detailed as Carl had been, still seemed a little foggy to him. They had visited that afternoon, however, and, knowing that he was helping me, had decided to leave the evening free for him to continue telling me of his experiences. I didn't know if they were merely being considerate, or if they'd seen some positive change in Carl as a result of our conversations and were therefore eager for it to continue, but I wasn't entirely comfortable with it. I couldn't help feeling that Carl was working to keep us apart—as if I, like Sunnyvale, might somehow taint his other life if our paths crossed.

He was reading his H.L. Mencken book again and I briefly considered showing my ignorance and asking him who this Mencken chap was. It wasn't relevant, though (*I must keep it relevant,* I told myself), and I therefore simply asked, "So you didn't die, then?"

I think it was obvious to him that I wasn't in the best of moods. Closing the book, he looked at me and smiled. "No, I didn't," he said. "At the time, they thought there was only one type of Spinal Muscular Atrophy. What is today referred to as Type I. Type I is always fatal in early infancy, or was thought to be, at that time. That's what they originally believed I had."

"But you didn't."

"No. I had Type II—towards the milder end of the Type II spectrum, actually. We didn't find out until I was about seven, but as it turned out, I wasn't under the death-sentence we'd originally been led to believe. I could expect to live well into adulthood, old-age, even."

"Must have been a huge weight off your parents' shoulders," I said. I couldn't help myself. I had to try to bring his parents back into this.

"I can't even begin to imagine," he said, eyes downcast and difficult to read. "I was a kid. Death was very much an abstract concept to me, even

18

with the things I'd experienced. Mam and Dad had always spoken openly around me, and encouraged the doctors to do the same, but I didn't 'get' it, not really. They did. They had to listen to every cough for about seven years thinking it might be my last. I'm still surprised they managed to keep things so normal for me."

"They sound very special."

"They are."

"I'd like to meet them some time."

Carl nodded to himself, smiling again as if he'd just figured something out. "You will," he told me. "I promise."

Andrea, who worked in the hospital in a voluntary capacity, was on duty. She came in and chatted with us for a while, bringing two cups of tea and a plate of Ginger Snaps, and only when Carl told her to take a hike, we had work to do, did she leave to go about her business. She smirked at me as she left. I knew she'd give me a hard time later; for the Andreas of this world, poor, misguided fools that they are, such enthusiasm could never be for the accuracy of the dissertation alone. There had to be more to it than that.

"Was that not a smart move?" Carl said.

I shrugged. "Andrea sees subtexts everywhere," I told him. "It's not something that can be easily avoided."

Carl had this habit of picking at the skin on the index finger of his left hand. I'd noticed him doing it the day before and he was doing it again now. It was not an easy habit to analyse, but it seemed to suggest intense concentration—maybe even a slight discomfort. I gently nudged him on, away from the subject of Andrea and her subtexts and back to the matter at hand.

"You were telling me about Christmas yesterday," I said. "How nice it was to not have to go to school and how magical it all felt."

He nodded, slowly. "It did," he said. "But, then, it didn't take a lot to get me in the Christmas spirit when I was six, understandably. It wasn't just the presents, either. It was the whole feeling of it—being with my parents and family, everyone pretending that times were wonderful even if they weren't. So much of it seemed to be about me."

"It was a happy childhood?"

"It was the best. My parents didn't have it easy. They had a mortgage and bills to pay, on top of their worries about me, but I was always loved and looked after. I don't remember ever being unhappy. Not really. I must have been, of course. Life couldn't have been that perfect. But I don't remember it."

"School was different, though," I said, gradually herding him back in the direction of Sunnyvale. "Yes?"

"I tolerated it, and returned after Christmas only reluctantly..."

~

Monday morning, the first of the New Year, there was a whole school assembly in the hall. The decorations had been taken down, little tabs of crepe paper remaining on the walls and ceiling in places, and the whole school seemed gloomier than ever. People, pupils and teachers alike, smiled at each other and chatted, but you could tell their hearts weren't really in it. Everyone wanted to be back home. Even our headmaster, Mr. Dixon—with his shiny bald head and his floppy jowls—even he seemed preoccupied as he walked to the front of the hall and took his place. I distantly wondered if he'd had a good Christmas, too. If he'd got lots of presents and if, like me, he just wanted to stay at home and play with them, or whatever it was headmasters did with their Christmas presents. He certainly looked pretty fed up, clasping his hands behind his back and rocking on his heels—staring down at his shoes and breathing in noisily through his nose as he waited for complete silence. And when he spoke, his voice even harder to hear than usual, his words languid and considered, it only seemed to make everything feel even more cloying and grim.

"Today's assembly is going to be rather short," Mr. Dixon said. "We will say a prayer, sing a hymn and then each of you will return to your classrooms where your teachers have something very important to discuss with you. This is not, naturally, how I would have hoped to begin a new year—but I'm sure you will all understand why it has to be this way once the facts are made fully available to you."

I didn't have a bloody clue what he was going on about, but it all sounded a bit scary—and Tommy agreed. "I don't want to be here," he whispered. "I don't know what's going on, but I *definitely* don't want to be here. He's going to tell us tell we're going to get locked in like them next door. You wait and see. I bet you any money."

"They don't get locked in," I told him—looking over at Miss Porter and thinking, in spite of my insisting that it wasn't so, that he might be right, after all. Miss Porter was dabbing at her nose and eyes with a paper tissue, glancing about anxiously as if she didn't want us to see her. I was getting a really, *really* bad feeling about this. We should have all been talking excitedly about the toys we'd got for Christmas, not sitting around here like this, as if we were waiting to be sent to jail or something.

As he had said we would, we sang a hymn (*Give Me Oil in My Lamp*), said a prayer and then filed back to our classrooms in uncharacteristic silence. We all knew that something bad was going to happen—or already had—and now it was merely a matter of preparing for the aftermath, whatever that might entail. It felt like my first day all over again. I had no control over this. It happened however I felt about it because, when you got right down to it, life was what adults did to children. We just had to put up with it.

Back in Miss Porter's classroom, we all went dutifully to our places— glancing at her as she positioned herself behind her desk, standing and staring out of the window while she waited for us to settle down. I noticed that Mrs. Wallace, one of the less scary nurses, had joined us, positioned by the door like a sentry. Tommy nodded in her direction and mouthed "uh oh" to me and I knew that he was working through all the possibilities just like me. There was a plague or something going around and we all had to have these big needles stuck in us so that we wouldn't catch it. We'd all been poisoned and had to have our stomachs pumped. The Martians had landed and we weren't allowed to go home because it was too dangerous. These and many other thoughts passed through my fertile mind, truly predicting nothing but nonetheless guaranteeing that when Miss Porter finally spoke, it was bound to be an anticlimax.

"I need you all to be very brave boys and girls today," Miss Porter presently said, doing an admirable job of keeping her emotions in check. "Because..." she glanced over at Mrs. Wallace, who nodded back at her encouragingly... "because I have some very sad news to share with you."

Bugger, I thought (I'd learned that of our bus driver), *the bloody buggering Martians* have *landed.*

But that wasn't it. What Miss Porter had to tell us was—to her mind, at least—far graver than that. She perched her bum against the front of her desk, staring down at the floor like Mr. Dixon had. I wondered what it was with adults and floors. Could they divine something in the parquet that we couldn't, or did they merely do it because they'd seen another adult do it ages ago and thought it looked so good they just had to copy it? It was weird, but if Miss Porter was doing it, I could only suppose that it had some worth. She wasn't the type to do something for no reason, I was sure.

"You may have noticed," she continued, "that not everyone is with us today." I looked around. Tommy looked around. The whole class looked around. If anyone else knew who was missing, me and Tommy certainly didn't. We looked at each other and shrugged. I for one was actually a little relieved; this wasn't going the way of the Martians or the big needles, after all. Or it didn't appear to be.

"Emiline!" a girl I didn't like called Karen shouted out. "Emiline Brown isn't here, Miss."

I vaguely recalled a girl with pale-pink National Health glasses and pigtails. She had a way of rolling her head from side to side when she got excited that made her look like a loony. When I noticed her (which was rarely), I usually ended up feeling embarrassed for her... or by her.

"That's right, Karen," Miss Porter said, as if Karen had just got a dead hard sum right. "Emiline isn't with us, and I'm afraid she won't be coming to school anymore because... over Christmas, Emiline got very poorly. You know how she had fits, right?"

News to me.

"Well she had this *really* bad fit and poor Emiline died and went to Heaven."

Something occurred to me and I put my hand up.

"Yes, Carl."

"She won't be coming back to school?"

"No, pet, I'm afraid she won't."

"Not ever?"

"No. She's in Heaven, now."

I knew a bit about this dying business, because I'd been meant to do it when I was about two and still hadn't got round to it—but no one had mentioned the bit about not having to go to school when you died. It was a massive oversight on the part of Mam and Dad, I thought. I couldn't believe they'd let me down so badly. If I'd only known, all this one add two equals three and "see Spot run" stuff could have been avoided!

"Is Heaven like London, miss?" one of the other girls said, and me and Tommy sniggered.

"No, sweetheart," Miss Porter said, glancing at Mrs. Wallace—just to make sure she was doing this right. "Heaven is where you go when you die, when it's time for you to be with God and Jesus."

"And she can't come back?"

"No, love. And we won't see her again until we die and go to Heaven, too."

It seemed to be finally starting to sink in. Karen started to snuffle and Mrs. Wallace went over to make sure she was all right—her nurse's uniform that wasn't quite a nurse's uniform shushing and cracking as she bent down. I heard Karen say something about how her goldfish had died and how they'd flushed it down the loo—her conclusion seeming to be that you got to Heaven via the toilet, and that if that was the case then everyone's poo must go to Heaven, too. It was a fascinating idea, but I didn't have the luxury of thinking about it for long because Tommy was kicking me under the table.

"What?" I hissed.

Tommy didn't say anything, just nodded in Miss Porter's direction. She'd turned her back on the class and her hands were up near her face. Her shoulders hitched, and it was pretty clear—as preoccupied as I was with the problem of all that poo in Heaven—that she was crying. I didn't know what to do, or even if I was meant to do anything at all. Staring at Tommy, bewildered but also a little exhilarated by the unusual turn of events, I felt sorry for Miss Porter. If it made her feel bad to tell us about how Emiline had died and everything, she shouldn't have to do it. Someone else should have done it for her. Mr. Dixon in assembly should have said, instead of making us sing *Give Me Oil in My Lamp* (although, I had to admit it was a good song—not exactly up there with *Burning Love*, but good nonetheless.) It wasn't fair and I wanted to make it better for her but didn't know how.

Tommy was apparently better informed than I, however. He got up out of his chair and bounced over to her—putting his arms around her when she bent down and giving her a huge hug. This didn't stop her tears, as Tommy no doubt hoped—in fact, it even seemed to make her cry more—but she seemed to welcome his effort, and I couldn't help but hate him a little bit for that.

When Tommy returned to his place, I refused to speak to him. It wasn't just that I'd fallen out with him over his shameless attempt to get into Miss Porter's good books (when everybody already knew that *I* was her favourite), it was more that the morning's sombre mood was finally beginning to have a real effect on me. I couldn't stop thinking about what it must be like to be dead. If it was all angels with harps and God and the Baby Jesus, why did Miss Porter cry? It didn't make sense. Not really. Not unless death was a bad thing.

Later that morning, I tapped Miss Porter on the arm and asked, "Miss? Is there really a heaven?"

Try as I might, I still can't recall her answer.

As seemed befitting, it was cold and grey that lunchtime—the mood in the hall as we ate our meal of leathery beef, tepid, lumpy mashed potato and plastic carrots was sombre and unusually respectful. Knives and forks clinked and scraped, crockery crocked—or whatever it is that crockery does, apart from smash, when it's banged together—and only a monastic murmur could occasionally be heard. If I'd known what a wake was, that was the comparison I would have made. But I didn't—and so only thought of it as "boring" and "unhappy", desperate for it to end again so that we could get on with the already difficult business of being kids.

It was times such as these that made me especially grateful to have Tommy as my best friend. He could be annoying, there was no doubt about that, and sometimes I wished that he'd have a fit and bugger off to Heaven, too (though I would have felt very sad and guilty, for an hour or two, if he had)—but he had his uses, and today he proved this yet again. At the time, I couldn't have known where it would end, but even if I had I doubt I would have said anything to shut him up. It was too much fun.

"I thought it was just my eyes at first," he whispered to me as I forked around with my leathery beef. "It was just after I'd given Miss Porter a cuddle." I still hadn't decided if I'd totally forgiven him for this. Whatever he had to tell me was probably going to be the deciding factor. "She smelt dead nice. Like flowers and... I don't know. Something nice, anyway. I wanted to cuddle her all day. But I couldn't and so I didn't, and when I didn't, that was when I saw it."

"What did you see?" I was duty-bound to ask. Not to do so would have been like not responding with "who's there?" to the opening of a knock-knock joke.

"Well," he said, determined to drag this out as long as possible. "I wasn't sure, at first. The wind was blowing a lot outside and them roses over by the windows near Miss Porter's desk was wafting about a bit, so I thought it might be me eyes seeing things like, or that it might be a shadow, you know?"

"Off the roses?"

Nodding enthusiastically, Tommy said, "But it wasn't."

"It wasn't?"

"Nope." He looked characteristically pleased with himself.

"Then what was it?"

Tommy leaned in closer. I could smell gravy on his breath. "It was *her*," he told me, looking around to make sure no one else was listening—and seeming rather disappointed when he saw no one was.

"Her?"

"Yes—*her.*"

"Her who?"

I hated it when he looked at me as if I was stupid. Everyone knew I was loads cleverer than him, but still he insisted on doing it—admittedly not very often, but enough to make me want to stab him with my fork.

"You know who," he said.

"No I don't.

"Think about it."

"Just tell me."

"You'll kick yourself."

I shrugged and started putting more salt on my mashed potato. It was too salty already, but it wasn't as if I was planning on eating it or anything.

As I knew it would, the act worked and Tommy leaned in closer still. "Emiline Brown," he told me. "I saw Emiline Brown."

There was a part of the playground that went round the side of the school hall and led to some steps up to the classroom were Mme. Crook taught me and a couple more kids French, and it was here we positioned ourselves after lunch to discuss *The Strange Case of Emiline Brown.*

Tommy hadn't got the duffel coat he'd wanted for Christmas, so he sat on the bottom step hugging himself through his powder-blue bomber jacket, shaking his head at the sheer scale of the peculiar events with which we were now faced.

"She was glowing and sort of wobbling," he told me. "But it was definitely her. I'd have recognised her anywhere."

"But she's dead."

"Aye, I know. But that doesn't change owt. It was still her. Standing there and glowing and wobbling and pointing."

"She's was pointing, too?"

"Yes. Didn't I tell you?"

"No."

"Well she was. Glowing and wobbling and pointing."

"What at?"

"Eh?"

"What was she pointing at?"

Tommy thought about this for a while, sniffing his top lip and looking up at the cloudy sky. "Hard to be sure," he said. "She was wobbling, don't forget, so her finger was sort of moving about a bit. Like this." He demonstrated. I could see what he meant. "At first, it looked like she was pointing at Karen—but that didn't make sense because no one ever points at Karen. Then I thought she might be pointing at Miss Porter, but that would have been rude and Emiline wasn't rude, was she?"

"I don't remember."

"Me neither." He sighed with the burden of it all. "Anyway," he continued, "it was neither of them."

"It wasn't?"

"Nope."

"Who was it, then?"

"Dunno. I'll tell you what, though."

"What?"

"We better find out quick."

"Why?"

"Cos it probably means someone else is gonna die."

As long as it wasn't me, I didn't care. I'd decided that, on balance and in spite of it being a sure-fire way of getting out of going to school, dying didn't sound all that good, after all. Tommy assured me that Emiline's ghost (for that was what it most assuredly was) certainly hadn't pointed at me or him, so we could rest easy and, you know, just get on with enjoying trying to work out who *was* going to die.

"It's got to be someone she didn't like," Tommy insisted. "She wouldn't do it to a friend, would she?"

"Unless she was trying to warn them."

Tommy smacked the palm of his good hand against his forehead. "God. I never thought of that. I bet that's it. A *warning*. Who was her friend, then?"

The truth was, I didn't know. Emiline was the kind of girl who people only truly noticed once she was no longer there, and if she was looking down at us from Heaven, I was sure she'd be surprised by her sudden popularity.

"Great," Tommy said. "So what are we supposed to do now?"

It seemed perfectly obvious to me. I smiled and Tommy's eyes opened a little wider.

"What?" he said.

"I don't know why I didn't think of it sooner."

"Think of what?"

"Let's tell the girls."

~

"That was a bit cruel," I said, nevertheless smiling at him. The picture he was painting of these two little boys, sitting on and by the steps, trying to find a way through the complexity of the subject had touched me and I couldn't help but feel that my own subject, the whole disability integration thing, was possibly going to be more complicated than I'd expected, too. I'd understood that every child was an individual outside of its disability, of course, but it certainly hadn't been central to my dissertation. Instead, I had been intending to focus on the more obvious, physical requirements of ramps and suitably wide doorways—only superficially grasping that disability integration brought with it more demanding problems.

"What can I say?" Carl said. "We were boys."

~

Jenny Jennings—the first girl we told about Emiline Brown's ghost—ran around the playground, screaming, shaking her head from side to side, as if trying to rid herself of the image we had there planted. Tommy and I sat by the edge of the playground, fascinated by the sight and utterly dumbfounded. That wasn't supposed to happen. I hadn't expected that kind of reaction, at all. Okay, so I'd known we'd probably scare her a bit. That's why it had seemed like such a good idea. But this? It was just dead weird.

"She's historical," Tommy told me, and I nodded. "Someone should slap her."

"Do you think that's a good idea?"

"It's what they do on the telly when someone gets like that."

He was right, of course. I'd seen it, too. When some *girl* started doing some screams there was always someone on hand to give her a right good slapping. It worked wonders—and the girl always thanked the person who'd done the slapping once she'd calmed down. I never really understood this, but it had been on telly—and if it had been on telly, it had to be right.

Nevertheless, I said, "I'm not going to do it. She might hit me back. She's got a right temper on her, her."

With a resigned shrug of his shoulders, Tommy got to his feet saying, "Well, I suppose I better do it, then."

At that precise moment, however, Miss Porter came running out of the school hall onto the playground. Chasing Jenny Jennings, she finally managed to catch up with her—grabbing hold of the terrified girl and kneeling down on the tarmac before her. We couldn't hear what she was saying from where we were, but it was obvious that Miss Porter was speaking to her soothingly, as she had to me on my first day. I could almost hear her in my head, working hard to find out what was wrong and make it better...

... find out what was wrong...

I wasn't sure I liked the sound of that. It made me feel a bit sick, and I was just about to tell Tommy that I thought that now might be a good time for us to go somewhere else when Miss Porter finally made her breakthrough.

Jenny's screams had now worked their way down to sporadic sobs and hiccups. She shuddered and nodded, and I knew it was probably too late. We were *doomed*, Mr. Mainwaring.

With a painfully slow turn of the head, Jenny Jennings looked at us.

"We're dead," Tommy said.

Maybe Emiline had been pointing at us, after all.

We waited before Miss Porter's desk, the only ones in the classroom apart from her. She stood with her back to us, letting us stew whilst she read something in a little paperback book she always kept in her handbag. I thought it might be a Bible, but it didn't look big enough.

She sighed and Tommy glanced at me, making a face that suggested that he didn't quite get, whatever he'd said about us being "dead", just how much trouble we were probably in. I turned away from him—ashamed not by what we had done, but by the fact that Miss Porter knew about it. I wouldn't be her favourite now, I thought. She'd see that I wasn't really clever and hardworking. I was lazy and bad, just like everyone else—only I usually hid it better. She'd see and she'd tell all the other teachers, and the nurses, and...

... Mam and Dad.

I didn't want them knowing about this. It wasn't so much that I was afraid of them playing war with me—I could cope with a telling off. I just didn't like the idea of them being disappointed in me. They looked at me with love and pride in their eyes, and I didn't want that to change.

"It's been a difficult day for us all," Miss Porter finally said—putting away her book and turning to face us. "We've had to deal with something that just feels so wrong that we can't even begin to put it into words." I wondered if she was actually talking to us. "And we each find our own way of making sense of it." She looked directly at Tommy and me. Her eyes were red and puffy. "That's why I can't really be angry with the two of you."

Must've been our lucky day.

"What you did was wrong."

Bugger.

"There's no escaping that. But I know that it was just your way of trying to understand everything that's happened today—and that isn't easy for any of us."

She came round to our side of the desk and perched on its edge.

"What the two of you did to Jenny was wrong," she repeated. "I think you both know that, now. Making up stuff like that. It was always going to scare her, now, wasn't it?"

Tommy and I nodded, albeit reluctantly.

Miss Porter sighed. I think she wanted to go home, just like me. If she'd had her way, she would probably never have come in today—knowing what she now knew about what she'd have to contend with. It made me feel sorry for her.

"I'm not going to say anything more on the subject," she said. "I want you both to promise me that nothing like it will happen again, apologise to Jenny and that will be the end of it. Will you do that for me?"

Understanding on some level that we were both getting off extremely lightly, we nodded—this time rather less reluctantly.

Outside again, on our way to find Jenny, Tommy sniffed indignantly.

"What?"

"Don't alter owt," he told me. "Whatever she makes us say, I still saw her."

Chapter Three: Leaving, but Not On a Jet Plane

I wasn't feeling my best the following Monday. The weekend had been spent working on notes for my dissertation, drinking too much cheap wine whilst ignoring intermittent, futile appeals from Andrea to take a break and, laughably, go out on the pull, and to say it had taken its toll was to understate it. This meant so much to me. I'd put so much work in over so many years to claw my way through my "mature" education, working part time jobs and borrowing heavily, that I really didn't want to mess it up now. My dissertation had to contribute something significant. It had become about more than personal achievement; I wanted to write something that would make a difference.

Carl patted the bed as I sat down on the chair beside it. "You look like the one who should be in this," he said. "You okay?"

"I'm fine," I said, smiling unconvincingly. "I've just had a busy weekend."

"Andrea told me. Apparently you need to get out more."

He seemed to enjoy the irritation I was always quick to exhibit when the subject of Andrea came up, and I suppose I piled it on a little for effect, enjoying the way in which he chuckled along with me as I told him about her latest efforts. It would have been all too easy for us to sit there all evening, talking about nothing in particular and generally having a nice old time of it, but, thankfully, Carl was the one to point out, this time, that we had work to do.

He understood that this meant as much to me as it did to him, and I was grateful for that.

"That's how it was at Sunnyvale," he told me, referring to the steady, sheltered day-to-day predictability of it all that we'd been speaking of the Friday before. "I don't really remember much more than what I've told you, other than those last couple of months before Resolution School opened. It became normalised, I suppose. Going there was just what I did and I probably even quite enjoyed it most of the time. I started to grow up there, I even saw my first vagina there," he added with a comical twitch of an eyebrow.

"Whey hey."

Looking out of the window, he continued. "I learned a lot there, but I was still ultimately glad when I found out I would be leaving."

"And this was when?"

"About the spring of seventy-six, I think."

~

Mrs. Aspel was nothing like Miss Porter had been. She was nice, but a lot stricter. And older, too. Habitually dressed in her much more teacherly twin-set and pearls, she didn't like our talking too much when we were meant to be working—and if my voice rose above the background murmur, she would only have to quietly say my name for me to get the message. Her authority lent the class a sense of calm that Miss Porter's never had—there was never any doubt that Mrs. Aspel was in control—and during my couple of years with her, I'd learned to appreciate this. When I wanted to read my book in Mrs. Aspel's class, there were no loud noises to distract me. I liked that.

Today, a Monday morning, she stood at the front of the class waiting for *complete* order. A few of my fellow classmates took a little longer than was usual—the excitement of the weekend still clinging to them, disinclined to let go—but once they had complied, Mrs. Aspel clasped her hands behind her back and started pacing about the classroom, as she liked to do when she was talking to us.

"As you all know," she said, "Carl is leaving us at the end of term and starting a brand new school in September."

This was the first I'd heard of it—and judging by the way in which Tommy looked daggers at me, it was also the first he'd heard of it. I shrugged at him, but he just turned away.

"We will all be very sorry to see Carl go, I'm sure," Mrs. Aspel continued. "But I'm just as sure that we are all excited for him."

She smiled at me while the class mumbled noncommittally.

"Anyway," she told us, pacing with renewed vigour. "In a few minutes, Carl's new teacher will be visiting to meet him and have a little chat. Her name is Mrs. Shires and I want you all to be on your best behaviour. Is that understood?"

A multiform "yes" echoed around the classroom, and I suddenly felt more isolated than I ever remembered feeling in my entire life. It was like my first day all over again, only somehow worse because now I had friends who, if Mrs. Aspel were to be believed, wouldn't be going to this new school with me. I looked at Tommy and whispered his name, but he refused to look at me—very deliberately talking to Jenny about the book he was reading. I knew he was snubbing me, but this wasn't my fault and I wanted to tell him that. I didn't want this anymore than he did (although that was soon to change) but I hadn't had the opportunity to object because *this was the first I'd heard of it!*

I sat there silently, staring at the book I was reading—something with pirates and sea monsters, a story that, only moments before, had completely captivated me, as rubbish as it was, but which now left me cold. It was kids' stuff, I told myself. Real-life was more complicated than sailing the seven seas and fighting monsters. In real-life, you could hurt your friends without doing anything and get the blame for things for which other people were responsible.

It wasn't fair, I thought. It just wasn't *bloody* fair.

There was a gentle knock at the door; so quiet I almost missed it. In a book, I thought, they'd say something about how there was an "air of expectation"—but it wasn't like that at all, really. Most of my classmates were already bored by this. It had nothing to do with them. Someone they possibly liked a bit was leaving, but so what? It wasn't as if he was someone important, or something really unusual was happening to him. People left places all the time. Yawn.

Normally, Mrs. Aspel would have merely called out "enter!", but today it seemed that our honoured guest was getting the full treatment. She actually got up off her chair, walked to the door *and opened it.* Anyone would have thought that this Mrs. Shires was the Queen or something, the way Mrs. Aspel acted.

I was just glad she didn't curtsey. That would have been really embarrassing.

They exchanged pleasantries, Mrs. Aspel saying something really lame about the bad weather, and then Mrs. Shires was brought over to meet me—smiling at the other kids as she came, saying hello here and there.

I liked her right away. She had a good smile (Mrs. Aspel's always looked as if it might make her face crack) and wasn't too tall. In fact, she was short—which was always a bonus, in my opinion, when you had to spend every day looking up at people.

"Carl," Mrs. Aspel said, with great formality, "I'd like you to meet Mrs. Shires. Mrs. Shires is going to be your teacher at your new school."

Mrs. Shires immediately knelt down beside my desk, and told me how pleased she was to finally meet me. She had, apparently, heard a lot about me.

"What you reading?" she said, Mrs. Aspel leaving us to it as Mrs. Shires lifted the front of the book so that she could see the title. "Ah. *Paul and the Pirates*. Is it any good?"

I wrinkled my nose. "Not bad," I said. "It's about this boy who gets kidnapped by these pirates and they go on this adventure and..."

"What?"

"That's where it gets a bit daft."

"Why, what happens?"

"Paul, the boy, he teaches them all about being good and having good manners and stuff."

"Not very believable?"

"They're pirates," I said, grinning.

Mrs. Shires laughed and then said, "So what would you rather be reading?"

I thought for a moment before answering. Mam and Dad had got me a book at the motorway service station the last time we'd been up to Newcastle to see the doctor. That had been good. "I like the Enid Blyton Famous Five books," I told her. "They're good."

"An adventure fan, eh? I'm impressed. Those books were written for kids a little older than you."

"I'm advanced for my age," I told her. "That's what Mrs. Aspel says."

I could tell Mrs. Shires found this amusing, but she tried very hard not to laugh. "And you clearly are," she said. "I'll have to make sure we have plenty of Famous Five books in the library at the Resolution for you, won't I?"

I nodded, and then asked, "The Resolution has a library? All of its own?"

Mrs. Shires made herself more comfortable, folding her arms on the desk and leaning forward. I could feel Tommy watching me, but I didn't look over at him. None of this was my doing.

"Oh, yes," Mrs. Shires said. "It's got a library, all right. It's got a library, bright, new classrooms, open plan design—that means with only a few doors—so it'll be easier to get around in your wheelchair... it's even got its own swimming pool."

"A *swimming pool?*"

"Well, a hydrotherapy pool, really—but it adds up to the same thing, right?"

I nodded again. "I do me hydrotherapy at the North Tees Hospital now," I told her.

"Well there you go, you see," she said. "You won't have to go there when you go to the Resolution. You'll be able to do it without leaving the school."

Mrs. Shires remained there, talking to me for another quarter of an hour, telling me about all the things I would learn at the Resolution and how good it was going to be. She mentioned the schools next door to it—Swallowfields Primary and the Almsby Comprehensive—where I would be going "in due course".

"It's a very new idea," she told me. "And you're one of the first. We'll be just like Captain Cook, sailing into uncharted waters together. It'll be an adventure."

She made it sound like a Famous Five story—and I liked her, I really did—but that didn't alter the fact that Tommy still wouldn't look at me.

"Was Captain Cook a pirate?" I asked her.

Tommy wasn't going to make this easy for me. At playtime, he sat with me on our steps by the side of the school hall—his face somewhere down around his ankles and flat refusing to accept that I hadn't known that I was going to be going to a new school in September. He laughed a little bitterly when I tried to convince him, yet again, that I was as surprised by the news as he and that, in fact, I didn't actually want to go, even if it did have a swimming pool. This, of course, was an outright lie—I now couldn't even begin to imagine staying at Sunnyvale for the rest of my school years. It seemed, having heard from Mrs. Shires just how modern and "ground-breaking" the Resolution was, that Sunnyvale was nothing more than a place for kids who had no place else to go. I did. I had the Resolution. After that, I had the Swallowfields Primary and the Almsby Comprehensive. And after *that*? Who could say? I was sad to be leaving Tommy behind. Of course I was. But I was nonetheless glad that it was him that was staying and not me.

"You're a bloody liar," he told me. "You knew all along, I know you did. You knew all along and you didn't tell me because you're *sly*."

Being called sly by a friend was about as bad as it got when I was nine. It stung to hear Tommy say that, but I was determined to rise above it. He was upset. That was all this was about. His best mate was going to another school and he was being left behind. It was only natural that he should hit out in this way. What he needed was a little understanding—calm reassurance that that wasn't the way it was at all.

"Well if that's what you think," I said, "sod ya. If you won't believe me when I'm telling you the truth, I'm glad you're not coming to the Resolution. I'll be glad to see the bloody back of you."

"And I'll be glad to see the bloody back of you, too!" Tommy was struggling. He wanted to say something else—hurl more insults, no doubt—but his voice was getting all squeaky and strained, and I think he was afraid that he might start crying.

He took a deep breath and stood up, limping a few paces away from me before coming back and sitting down.

"Why can't I go there as well?" he said, more calmly, now.

"I don't know. I think it's because I live closer to the new school and you live closer to this one."

"You reckon?"

I nodded. "It's about five minutes by bus from where I live."

"That's good, then, isn't it?"

"I suppose. It's still scary, though. I'll hardly know anyone."

"Some other kids from here are going," he told me.

"I know."

It was cold and I wanted playtime to be over. This conversation was getting weirder—I was *feeling* weirder, beginning to wonder if I did actually want to leave Sunnyvale, after all. I was safe here. Protected, almost. The teachers and staff, as peculiar as some of them could be, were generally nice—and whilst Mrs. Shires had seemed nice, too, there was still so much I didn't know about Resolution School.

"Was it really a surprise to you?" Tommy said, as the bell went for us to return to our classroom.

Nodding, I said, "I don't think even my mam and dad have been told about it, yet."

"Because they would have told you, right?"

"Exactly."

"So they're going to get a surprise, too, then."

"They'll be glad," I told him. "They don't like me travelling all this way every day."

Tommy was behind me, pushing my wheelchair. I could hear him thinking. Tommy was just about the loudest thinker I ever met.

"I'm sorry I called you a liar and sly," he said.

My last day at Sunnyvale was hot and bright—the school for once, it seemed, living up to its name. The holidays were upon us and everyone was looking forward to being able to play every day for a whole six weeks, without ever once having to worry about school. Everyone except me, that was. When I thought about the summer holidays, I also invariably thought of the uncertainty of what awaited me at the far end of it—the new challenges and, quite possibly, the monumental failures.

Mrs. Aspel had decided that a "breaking-up" party was called for, but we all knew that it was really a "goodbye Carl" party and I for one wished she hadn't bothered. I mean, it was nice and everything—but I wasn't really sure that leaving Sunnyvale was a cause for celebration. I hadn't even *seen* the Resolution, yet. For all I knew, Mrs. Shires' library might be nothing more than a few tatty paperbacks on a shelf—her hydrotherapy pool a puddle in the playground. Until I'd had chance to breathe in the newness of which she'd spoken, I was determined to withhold judgment.

Or that's what I occasionally told myself.

The party took the form of a picnic on the field outside our classroom—with sandwiches and cake and even jelly. Mrs. Aspel had made a real effort, and it seemed churlish not to at least *try* to enjoy it.

Tommy was devouring a fistful of cake—utterly unconcerned by the mess he was making. Looking up at me, he winked. "Guess where I'm going for me hols," he said.

The joke was getting old now. He'd told me where he was going about a dozen times already, and seemed intent on telling me a dozen more. Nevertheless, I played along.

"Dunno," I said. "Where are you going for your hols?"

"Butlins." Getting stuck into his chunk of cake, his good leg twitched with the sheer expectation of it all and he told me, once again, that he was going for two weeks. "We go there every year," he said. "It's usually freezing cold, but I don't mind that cos there's always lots of stuff to do indoors where it's warm. Last year..." he took a drink of pop to swill the cake down, "... last year we saw Morecambe and Wise there. Well, it wasn't really Morecambe and Wise, but it was these two blokes who was just like them—only funnier. Or that's what me and our dad thought. Mam reckoned they were just copying and that wasn't good. I don't see the problem meself. There were still funny."

He rabbitted on like this for a while longer, eating his cake and drinking his pop whilst I looked from my classmates (in various stages of cake) to the expansive school field. I'd never realised before just how big it was. How big and, truly, how small. When I'd first arrived there—*millions of years ago*—it had seemed to go on to the ends of the earth but, I now saw, it actually stopped short just before it got to the council houses.

Mrs. Aspel was looking at me and smiling. She was sitting a few feet away from me on a blanket on the grass, her legs tucked under her. She didn't look like Mrs. Aspel much at all today, truth be known. She seemed cooler than usual, not so worried by us not being on our best behaviour. I supposed that had something to do with it being the end of term and everything. Maybe she was going to Butlins, too.

"A penny for them," she said to me, in a voice that was quite playful (for Mrs. Aspel.)

I shrugged, very aware that Tommy was also waiting for my response. The way he'd suddenly stopped cramming cake in his gob suggested that he was expecting something suitably profound. Not wishing to disappoint, I said, "The field's a lot smaller than it used to be."

Both Mrs. Aspel and Tommy looked at it, frowning and, I imagined, trying to remember how big it had been the last time they had really taken notice. Tommy seemed to find this especially difficult, frowning severely as he sniffed his upper lip—but Mrs. Aspel was quick to nod.

"Ah, yes," she said. "I think I know what you mean, Carl. It's a matter of perspective."

"Perspective?"

"Perspective," Tommy told me, authoritatively.

"That means where you look at something from and how all the things you see fit together," Mrs. Aspel explained. "That tree over there." She pointed. "You and I have a different perspective on it. And that's what's happened with the field. It hasn't got smaller—you've got bigger, pet."

Now that she mentioned it, I thought I knew what she meant, because it wasn't just the field. It was everything. Nothing was as big and scary as it had once been (except for Godzilla in the rubbishy Jap movies on telly.) The world had seemed to have shrunk, in all its generalities and detail, but it was all down to *perspective*. Even the shops in Eston were considerably less impressive than they'd once been.

Jenny wanted to know if Mrs. Aspel had ever been up in an aeroplane, and she (Mrs. Aspel) turned away from us to tell her all about her experience of air travel. I wasn't as jealous as I would have been if it had been Miss Porter turning away from me, but I was still mildly annoyed. Maybe that was about perspective, too.

Tommy looked sad. I knew how he felt. This wasn't such a big, bad place after all, and as glad as I might sometimes feel about going, it would be odd not seeing him again. He was the best mate I'd ever had, and I wanted to tell him—but didn't, in case he thought I was a fairy or something.

"We can be pen pals," he said, as he got stuck into another chunk of cake. "I'll send you a postcard from Butlins and you can tell me stuff about your new school and everything. It'll be fun."

"You'll forget," I told him.

"No I won't," he insisted. "I never forget important stuff like that."

"Important stuff like what?"

Grinning at me, he said, just as I had expected, "I can't remember."

As we drove out of the Sunnyvale School gates later that afternoon, the day still warm and full of promise—my forehead tingling from the afternoon I'd spent in the sun—it struck me that I really was off on the adventure of which Mrs. Shires had spoken. I had made promises to return some time in the not-too-precise future to pay them a visit and let them all know how I was getting along, but I think I knew even then that that would never happen. I was leaving Sunnyvale School for the last time— and I wasn't sad. Not anymore. I wasn't sad because that was that and I was going to be like that Captain Cook bloke that Mrs. Shires had gone on about, sailing into uncharted waters and everything.

It was going to be good, I told myself. Dead good, in fact. It might be weird to begin with, but my *perspective* would change and I'd soon see just how brilliant (compared to Sunnyvale) it really was.

Resolution School was a new beginning; I think even then I understood that. But that didn't mean I had to forget where I had come from.

I will write to Tommy, I told myself.

~

"And did you?" I asked him.

I'd stayed later than expected, the nurses showing a flexibility that I thought might have had something to do with Andrea's limited influence, and whilst Carl was sounding a little croaky, he still seemed anything but tired. I nevertheless made a mental note not to drag the evening's session on for much longer.

"Once or twice, yes," Carl said. "Then... well, I suppose we ran out of things to say to each other. Tommy and I never really had that much in common, I suppose. And the older we got, the more evident that became."

"So you never went back there? You never saw him again?"

Carl shook his head. His breathing seemed a little more laboured than usual and I underlined my mental note not to drag this on too much longer.

"No," he said. "Going back there was something that just never came up. It never occurred to me or anyone around me once I got to the Resolution." A little light went on at the back of Carl's eyes—distant, but bright nonetheless—and he lifted his chin a little higher, looking at me directly and smiling with a warmth that had nothing to do with me. "I *did* see Tommy again though. Christ, I'd forgotten all about that."

"Not at Sunnyvale, though."

"No. It was at a regional sports event up Gateshead way. I was entered in the electric wheelchair racing events and while I was hanging around with my mates, this kid comes bouncing up to me. I didn't recognise him right away, even with the hand and the bouncy limp, but as soon as he said my name, I knew who he was.

"He'd grown up," Carl continued. "I suppose we both had, but it seemed more evident in him."

"When was this?"

"I'm not sure," Carl replied. "Two, possibly three years later. He'd really changed—seemed quieter, more considered. Gentle. We chatted for a while and he told me that Sunnyvale had closed. Or they'd moved it or something. The school he was now at sounded similar in concept to the Resolution and he was being integrated into a mainstream school." Carl shuffled himself about, trying to get comfortable before continuing. "I suppose once one school started, they all jumped on the proverbial band wagon.

"Anyway, I asked if his new school was warm enough for him." He smiled again, fondly. "I remember that bit vividly because he just didn't get the joke at all. It was as if he'd left the old Tommy back there on the steps at Sunnyvale, probably with the old me right beside him—talking about the ghost of Emiline Brown without ever realising they were ghosts themselves."

I pulled a face and Carl laughed. "Too deep for me, mate," I said. Closing my notebook and putting it in my bag, I got to my feet and said, "Might be a good place to stop. You're clearly getting tired and rather too fanciful for my liking. A good night's sleep will do you the world of good."

"I was just starting to enjoy myself."

"That's what I'm worried about. Facts, dear boy, that's the business I'm in. I can't be taking the risk of you dressing it up with your ghostly imagery. It's a dissertation, not an international bestseller. Dry sterility is the order of the day."

In the short time I'd known him, Carl had quickly become someone I'd grown comfortable with. I liked him. There was no escaping that. He was not a man without faults, but he'd lived long enough to know what they were and, it seemed to me, he would always be quick to admit to them. That was rare, and even as I told myself, yet again, that this was about my dissertation—and *only* my dissertation—I suspected that I would continue visiting him even if it turned out he had no more information to offer.

Carl Grantham wasn't just a project. He was becoming a friend.

Chapter Four: Poppies

It had been the hottest summer anyone I knew remembered—a summer of drought and discomfort that even this boy of nine had found difficult to cope with at times. On the beach at Sandsend with Mam and Dad and my cousin Mark, between sessions in the dingy, I had sat in a deck chair with a large towel draped over my head to keep the sun off, reading a book and thinking about September. One minute I looked forward to going to the Resolution, the next I wished I was returning to Sunnyvale. I didn't know what I wanted, and this on top of the extreme heat probably made me a pain to be around. I really was becoming a "big boy", and I wasn't too sure I liked it.

My first day at Resolution School bore no unyielding resemblance to my first day at Sunnyvale. I was too aware of what was going on. Going in on the school bus, sitting next to the escort—a kind, enthusiastic lady in her fifties called June—I was sure my anxiety showed, as cool as I tried to look.

June made it easier, though. She lived near the school and had watched it being built, so she told us all about it as we picked up the other kids—in far more detail than even Mrs. Shires had.

"Does it really have a swimming pool?" I said.

June nodded quickly and put her hand on my arm. "Does it ever!" she told me. "They took me and the other escorts round to have a look last week, and we saw it. You are going to *love* it. Everything's shiny and new, and the front doors open by themselves and—"

"The doors do what?"

"Oh! Didn't I tell you about that? They've got these sensitive mats in the floor or something. In front of the doors. And when you go on them—*whoosh!*"

"Whoosh?" I wasn't sure if "whoosh" was a good thing.

"Yes, *whoosh*—the doors open just like magic."

"Electric doors," I said. I knew all about them. They weren't magic. They were good, but they weren't magic. And "whoosh" definitely struck me as a bit of an exaggeration.

"The teachers are smashing, too," she told me. Everyone else had stopped listening, so I felt I had to keep talking to her.

"I've met mine already."

"You have."

"Yes."

"And was she nice?"

"Yes."

"Told you, didn't I?"

"She's called Mrs. Shires."

June continued talking and I sort of listened—hearing her say something about having met Mrs. Shires herself and how she had known immediately that she was a very nice lady with "a real passion for the job". I missed most of it, however, preoccupied with the fact that we were getting close to the school. The tension and excitement on the bus became palpable, and I thought back to the summer holidays—how Mam and Dad had brought us round this way to have a look at the Resolution when we had been taking Mark home once. From the outside and from a distance (which was all I had to go on), it had vaguely reminded me of the Hinton's supermarket that had been built near where I lived. It even had a loading bay! New, unweathered red brick, aluminium framed windows and freshly laid tarmac. That had been the overwhelming impression as Mark, sitting beside me in the back of our Ford Escort estate, had commented on how small it looked—small but *nice*—and I now wondered as we drove along the road that led to the school entrance if that would be how it was today. Would it still seem small, or would it be as big as Sunnyvale had seemed on my first day there?

I was learning not to trust the early morning September sunlight. It was a low, temporary thing that so often betrayed—weak and watery, and yet solidly associated with the new school year. Driving into the car park, it streamed in through the windscreen and caught me square in the eye, dazzling me and causing tears to well. I blinked rapidly, desperately afraid that June or someone might think that I was going to cry. This wasn't Sunnyvale. I didn't cry now.

"That sunlight really got you there, didn't it, love?" June blessedly said as a tear escaped.

"Just a bit," I said—laughing, just to make absolutely sure there was no confusion.

"Not to worry," she told me. "It'll probably be raining by lunch time."

I wasn't sure I liked the sound of that. It seemed too much a reflection of the way in which the day might yet go. I looked at June as we pulled into our parking space, hoping she might have something more encouraging to add. She didn't, though. She merely sat there a moment, smiling, and then, once the bus stopped, jumped into action.

I had a wheelchair all of my own waiting for me, with my name on it, even, and June was quick to find it and get me settled, all comfy and excited. She seemed as keen as me, and as she handed me over to one of the auxiliary nurses, she ruffled my hair and wished me luck. I smiled, but I hated it when adults did that to me. Now it was all messed up and I didn't even have a comb.

"A little bit thoughtless," the auxiliary said to me, "but I think she meant well. Here, let me fix that for you." She squatted down in front of me like Mrs. Attenborough had that first day at Sunnyvale, flattening down my hair with her hand where June had ruffled it up and telling me her name was Mrs. Alexander. Despite the fact that her name also began with "A", she was nothing like Mrs. Attenborough. She had better knees, for a start. Not so big and imposing. But there was more to it than that. I didn't know what it was, exactly, but it was as if Mrs. Alexander knew me better than anyone at Sunnyvale ever had. She knew right away that I liked my hair nice.

"I bet you don't know how you feel today, do you?" Mrs. Alexander said as she got back to her feet. "Nervous, excited—a little scared, even, yes?"

I nodded, shrugging to show I was okay with that, though.

"Well, Carl," she told me, bending down and speaking to me in a whisper. "I'm not going to make any promises or tell you how wonderful it is. I'm going to let you see for yourself. Then you can tell me what *you* think. Deal?"

"Deal."

I vividly remember the poppies. Hundreds of them—thousands, it seemed. Velvety and deep, their striking shade of red touching me in a way that I would only understand years later, looking back and considering the poignancy of that moment.

"Beautiful, aren't they?" Mrs. Alexander said, softly.

We were by the window in the library—which was, indeed, as

impressive (by my then limited standards) as Mrs. Shires had suggested—looking out at the grounds. I said that, yes, they were, and then added, "There's loads of them. Did someone plant them or did they just grow?"

"Just grow, I imagine. They're wildflowers. Once they start cutting the grass and maintaining the borders, they'll probably disappear for good."

"Really?"

Mrs. Alexander nodded. "A crying shame, if you ask me."

"Me too," I agreed. "They should leave them alone. They look better than Livingston Daisies or anything like that."

"Livingston Daisies are quite nice, too—in their own way."

"Don't make you stop and look like all those poppies do, though."

Mrs. Alexander stared out of the window. "No," she said. "I don't suppose they do."

The tour of Resolution School—my *new school*—was far more memorable than its equivalent on my first day at Sunnyvale... or maybe it would be more accurate to say it was more memorable for its impressive qualities rather than the choking feelings of abandonment and isolation I'd experienced that first day at Sunnyvale. Mrs. Alexander wheeled me around with a cheerfulness that was wholly sincere. There was no sense that she was trying to sell the place to me. She didn't have to. It positively gleamed with its own sense of uniqueness and promise. Everything under one roof, no doors on the classrooms, it seemed ultra-modern and spacious—light spilling in through the large windows but somehow not intruding. From the library, Mrs. Alexander took me along to see the Home Economics area. A cosy, homely place with an impressive kitchen and a separate section set aside for craft and needlework. Mrs. Alexander explained that this side of the school was for the seniors, so I would only really come over this way for Home Economics or to use the library—and then took me along to show me what would, in time, simply become known as "the corridor".

"When you're old enough," Mrs. Alexander said, squatting down beside me, again. "Next year. This is where you'll come to go over into Almsby for some of your lessons." With one wall of painted brick, the other wall and the slanting ceiling of the corridor was made wholly of wire-reinforced glass. It was painfully bright on such a sunny day, and as I squinted through the glare, the corridor seemed to go on forever—stretching away to that other place that I couldn't quite imagine being for me, even though I knew in my heart of hearts that it was. "See that little recessed area?" Mrs. Alexander continued. "Between the two sets of doors at the far end?

That's where the lift is. You'll use that to get up to the art department, the maths rooms and the Home Economics area."

"Another Home Economics area?" I said.

"Another *school*," she reminded me, and I nodded—seeing her point. "Almsby has about a thousand pupils, so it's not like they can all come over and use ours, is it?"

"But I can go over and use theirs?"

"Eventually, yes." She stood up again, putting a hand on my head (being careful not to mess my hair.) "But I think we're getting a little bit ahead of ourselves, aren't we? I haven't finished showing you the Resolution and we're already talking about your next school."

"Hardly seems worth stopping," I said, grinning what I was learning to think of as my "most charmingest grin".

Mrs. Alexander laughed along with me and really meant it. "Come on, you," she said. "Best till last. Let's take a look at the pool before Mr. Johnson's first assembly."

"Who's he?" I said. I thought I knew, but it didn't do to take anything for granted where these things were concerned. Just that morning, both Mam and Dad had told me, separately, to speak up if I didn't know or understand something. *Don't sit there like a lemon, mate,* Dad had said. *No one ever gets into bother for asking polite questions—but if you do, be sure to let me know about it, okay?* Whilst Mam had kept it much more succinct. *You'll never learn anything if you don't ask, love.*

"Mr. Johnson?" Mrs. Alexander said. "He's your new headmaster. He's a lovely man. You'll like him."

Important Lesson Number One at Resolution School: even Mrs. Alexander couldn't get everything right.

It was a hydrotherapy pool. What more could really be said? However much of a step up it may have been, and as impressive as it actually was by the standards of the day, I couldn't help but feel, as I sat with the other kids in the school hall waiting for the apparently late Mr. Johnson to arrive and start speaking, just a little bit let down. I'd expected something Olympic-sized with diving boards and stuff and what in reality I'd got was a poky little thing of about twelve feet by twenty—if that. Matters weren't entirely helped when I'd spotted a cord hanging down from the ceiling over one corner of the pool and asked Mrs. Alexander what it was for. "That's in case someone gets into trouble and we need to call for help," she'd explained—and the very idea of "someone" getting "into trouble" sort of took the already dulling shine off it a bit. At first, I'd thought she'd meant someone doing something wrong and getting told off, but I quickly realised that she hadn't meant that at all; the cord was in case someone hurt themselves or—even better—*drowned*. The question that struck me most forcibly was: If it was dangerous enough to need an emergency cord, should we really be going in there in the first place?

My mind continued to work at this until, a whole ten minutes after the last of us had taken our places in the hall, Mr. "You'll-Like-Him" Johnson arrived.

Mr. Johnson was no Mr. Dixon, that much was obvious. He wore a pair of brown corduroy trousers that looked as if they'd seen better days and a shirt of a lighter shade of brown with no tie, whereas Mr. Dixon was *always* in a suit, however hot the weather. His beard in need of trimming, Mr. Johnson didn't look much like a headmaster at all, in fact—although the way he looked around at everyone with his bog-brush chin held high, I don't think he knew this. Someone should tell him, I thought, but I wasn't about to offer the information myself—not to him, anyway.

I was determined not to hold his scruffy appearance against him, however, even though I myself, a mere pupil, had made quite an effort. Mr. Dixon had always been a bit distant and unapproachable, and I thought that maybe this more "casual" look (I was still inclined to be generous towards him) would mean we'd actually be able to talk to him and ask him things. It was all too easy to jump to conclusions and this, after all, was a fresh, new start. I'd give him until tomorrow and then see what I thought.

"Today is a very special day," Mr. Johnson said, pausing dramatically at the end of the sentence to look round at everyone. "My name is Mr. Johnson and I am to be your headmaster while you are at Resolution School—a position I consider to be both an honour and a privilege. There are few opportunities in life of such importance and validity and when they come along I believe in seizing them and holding on tight." Another dramatic pause as he looked at us—individual by individual, it seemed. "Opportunity. It's a word we hear quite a lot these days, isn't it? And, do you know what?" One of the little kids down the front actually responded with a "what?" Mr. Johnson smiled and spoke directly to the little girl in question. Probably a good sign, I thought. "I'm not sure any of us actually know what it means. Oh, we *think* we do—and in terms of dictionary definitions, we more than likely do. But opportunity is more than just the sum of a bunch of words in the dictionary. Opportunity is the offering of possibility—a gift to be gratefully taken and cherished. And that's what we all have today, with our new school, with Resolution School. A gift to be gratefully taken and cherished."

Mr. Johnson seemed very pleased with this—very pleased with *himself*. He strode back and forth before us, arms folded behind his back, fingers twitching excitedly, and I thought for a moment that he'd forgotten we were there. He smiled, and then turned to look at us.

"We are fortunate," he said. "We have to remember that. There will be difficult times ahead—for pupils and staff alike—but we must always bear in mind that this is a rare and privileged opportunity, a chance to show the doubters how it should *really* be.

"And with this in mind," he said, taking a few sheets of foolscap from one of the other teachers, "it only remains for me to introduce you to your individual teachers and, as they say, get this show on the road."

For the next quarter of an hour, Mr. Johnson very formally introduced the teachers to us, calling out the names of the pupils who would be in each teacher's class before moving onto the next. It was fairly monotonous, until it was the turn of Mrs. Shires, and then Mr. Johnson's speech really started to take effect. This *was* exciting. Mrs. Shires stood at the front of the hall, small but looking like she meant business, and I suddenly understood just how important this really was. Mrs. Shires had told me when we had met at Sunnyvale that there had never before been a school like the Resolution. And she was right. I knew she was. You just had to look at the place to know she was.

When the time came for my name to be called out, Mrs. Alexander came over and collected me—wheeling me to Mrs. Shires and the other kids that had gathered around her. Mrs. Shires looked a little annoyed by something, but when she saw me, she smiled.

"Ready for that adventure?" she said.

Our classroom was a lot smaller than any of the classrooms at Sunnyvale had been—but it had a concourse nearby and its very own quiet room. I liked the quiet room right away. It was dark and, as its name suggested, quiet, done out in dark shades of blue with padded seating around the walls, and I thought that I might spend a lot of time in there, reading a book or something. The classroom proper, I suppose, could have been a bit of a disappointment, but its small size just served to make it seem safer, somehow.

Finding a place at one of the tables with Mrs. Alexander's help, I sat and waited to be told what to do—looking at my classmates and finding myself in the unenviable position of, once again, not knowing a soul.

They were a pretty mixed bunch, but I was fairly used to that. A few years at Sunnyvale had seen to that. A boy in a wheelchair across from me—his hair in his eyes and his head pulled into his neck as if he was expecting a fight, bear-like and oddly imposing—kept looking at me and glancing away every time I met his gaze. He looked like trouble (or maybe, I thought, that was just what he wanted me to think), so I instead turned my attention to the others, trying to figure who might be a potential friend and who might not. It was a bit of a puzzle.

"That's Andrew," the kid sitting next to me said when he spotted me staring at a twitchy looking boy with really thick glasses. "He's got bad eyes. Then there's Louisa next to him. Her eyes are bad, too." He pointed to a Paki girl. "Ananda. She's from India and she's got asthma and eczema like me. My name's Patrick, by the way." I knew about asthma and eczema because some of my cousins had it. I didn't know it could get as bad as Patrick's, though. His skin was raw and scaly, and if it hadn't been for him being so nice to me, I might have sat beside someone else next time.

"Mine's Carl," I said.

He shook my hand. "Good, isn't it?" he said. "The school, I mean. Better than the last place I was at, anyway."

"Same here," I said. "The pool was smaller than I thought it would be, though."

"Know what you mean." Patrick studied me for a moment. "That Mr. Johnson don't half know how to yap on, doesn't he?"

I liked Patrick, in spite of his scaly skin and the fact that he smelt a bit. He reminded me of Tommy—though I got the feeling that Patrick was a much brighter button than Tommy had been. And when he said that about Mr. Johnson, I couldn't help but grin.

"Didn't understand half of what he was saying," I admitted.

"Me neither."

"He seemed pleased with it, though," I added.

"Too pleased, if you ask me," Patrick said. "He thinks he's god's gift. The kind of bloke what kisses the mirror."

It was a fascinating image and I chewed it over for a while as Mrs. Shires arrived with a girl in a wheelchair who she introduced as Kelly. Kelly was all it took to distract me from my thoughts. Looking at her, I said to myself, *Now* that's *disabled.* Her arms moved about with a life of their own, her legs following suit, her face contorting as she struggled to turn her head to look at us—and I wondered how tiring it must be to move about like that all day. Did she ever rest? How did she sleep? I'd seen kids like her before, of course, but I'd never had one in my class. I tried to imagine how she had a wee, then stopped. It didn't seem polite.

Interesting, though.

Once Mrs. Shires had found a place for Kelly, with a little help from Mrs. Alexander, she turned to look at us all for a moment. She could look a little stern, at times, could Mrs. Shires, I was learning. There was an intensity about her that could be easily misunderstood—but I thought I had a handle on her. Just because she sometimes looked pissed off, it didn't actually mean she was (although I was soon to discover that she looked almost the same when she *was* pissed off, which meant it could all get a bit confusing sometimes.) Mrs. Shires' face could be as hard and introspective as a concrete slab, but the minute she caught you looking at her the smile came and all was well.

Or that was how it was today.

"I expect you're all feeling the way I am this morning," she said, finding her chair and sitting down with a sigh. "I feel as if I haven't had a moment to think. My head's all over the place."

We all nodded—except for Kelly, who sort of wobbled her head about and made a squeaking noise like a hamster caught in lawnmower.

"I've had to meet and talk to so many new people that I thought my head was going to explode," she laughed, looking at the bear-like kid in the wheelchair across from me. He slowly lifted his eyebrows and continued staring out the tabletop. "Johnny Jameson, isn't it?" she said, her voice a notch quieter. He grunted and looked at her.

"Yer-yer-yes, miss," he finally said.

Yer-yer-yes? What was all that about?

"How are you finding your first day, Johnny?" she asked him.

Shrugging, he said, "All right, I ser-suppose. Bit b-boring."

Now I may have been wrong, but I was beginning to think that this Johnny lad might have a stutter. All the clues were there, but I still wasn't completely convinced; it seemed such a cruel quirk of fate to be in a wheelchair *and* have a stutter that it hardly seemed possible.

"Yes," she said. "I know what you mean. Sitting around in the hall while everyone got sorted into their classes was a bit of a drag, wasn't it?"

"I liked that," Johnny said. "It was the bit before it that ger-got on my nerves. Swallowed a der-der-dictionary, I reckon."

Mrs. Shires and Mrs. Alexander both coughed into their hands, but I don't think they fooled anyone. Synchronised coughing among adults—teachers especially—only ever meant one thing, in my vast experience.

"Thought he was never going to sher-shut up," Johnny continued, encouraged by the coughing. "Practly give me a headache."

Mrs. Shires apparently decided that ignoring this was the best policy—

for today, at least (and always assuming Johnny would let her.) She made herself more comfortable on her swivel chair and said, "So where do we start?"

"Anywhere ber-but another speech."

"Yes, thank you, Johnny. I think we've got the message."

"Sorry, miss." He wasn't in the least bit sorry. I couldn't help but like him.

"That's all right." She paused a moment to gather her thoughts. "No speeches," she said, "for fear of upsetting our friend Johnny, but I would like to tell you a little more about Resolution School and what we—all of us—are aiming for, here. That okay with you, Johnny?"

"Be my guest."

"Integration," she said. "I know it's a long word but can anyone tell us what it means?" No one's hand went up. Today, it seemed, was not the day for risking a good guess. "No? Carl. What about you? You like reading. What do you *think* it means. It doesn't matter if you're wrong, just have a go."

Everyone was looking at me—Johnny peering out from under his fringe and, I thought, smirking. I didn't like being put on the spot like this, it carried too many intrinsic risks, but I couldn't have Mrs. Shires thinking that I wasn't willing to at least try to rise to her challenge. Even if it meant marking myself as the class clever kid, I had to say something.

"It's got 'in' at the beginning," I said. "So I think it might have something to do with bringing, you know, things *in* together or something."

Mrs. Shires nodded thoughtfully and it seemed that I was on the right track. Other than this, however, there were no more clues as to just how well I was doing—and I was a little wary of continuing. Maybe it would be best if I just quit while I was ahead, I thought. That way I could appear to have done what was asked of me without seeming *too* clever or, perhaps marginally worse (depending on one's point of view), getting it wrong and falling flat on my face. Everyone was looking at me as if I was the fount of all human wisdom, though—even that Johnny lad—and the pressure was just too much.

"I've heard people use it a lot when they're talking about this school," I told Mrs. Shires. "So I think it might be about the three schools. Bringing us all, you know, in together, like."

Clapping her hands together quietly, Mrs. Shires said, "Well done. Nicely worked out, Carl." She turned her attention back to the whole class. "Integration is, more or less, about bringing things together. Bringing *people* together. Making one thing a part of the other. And that's what Resolution School is about. The whole idea behind it is to give you the chance you deserve to learn in as normal an environment as possible with kids who don't all have disabilities—because I'm sure I don't need to tell you, you're really no different to the kids in Swallowfields or Almsby, now, are you?"

I wasn't sure. I hadn't met any of them.

"Or if you are," she went on, seeming to spot a mistake, "you still have so much in common that it doesn't really matter."

Mrs. Shires was nothing like Mr. Johnson. When she got to the end of her little speech, she didn't sit back, looking all pleased with herself. She looked at each and every one of us in turn, just to make sure we'd fully grasped what she'd been saying, before positioning herself to continue.

"Resolution School," she said softly, leaning forward. "Does anyone know what 'resolution' means?" There was no way I was going to raise my hand or volunteer anything for this one—and if she thought I was, she had another bloody thing coming. She could try putting me on the spot again, if she wished, but I would simply sit there, mum, lips tight as a duck's bum.

Blessedly, she seemed to know better than to pick on me a second time. When no one spoke up, she merely smiled and settled back in her chair. "Okay," she said, "the word 'resolution' is a good one for our school. It means to have determination—to decide to do something and really go for it. Captain Cook, a local lad, as I'm sure you all already know and someone we'll be learning more about over the coming weeks, Captain Cook had a ship called the Resolution—originally a North Sea collier called *Marquis of Granby*. Cook said that it was the fittest for service he had ever seen. And that's what our school is going to be. The fittest for service we have seen. We'll serve it well and it will serve us well. We'll be determined. Determined to succeed and determined to make the most of it we can. That's *our* resolution."

No doubt about it, this really was going to be an adventure. Everything was in place and all we had to do was cast off and pray that the wind was with us. The sea would be choppy, at times, but we'd ride it out and all would be well.

Johnny looked up at me and sniffed derisively. I doubted he'd have agreed with me.

Break time was the biggest shock. Nothing could prepare me for what was awaiting us outside when the bell rang and we were granted, albeit temporarily, a kind of freedom.

There were almost as many kids on the playground as there were poppies on the field. Kids of all sizes and ages—some in sort of smart-looking uniforms, others, younger, in ordinary clothes like us. Patrick wheeled me out—Johnny not far behind with a boy from our class called Peter Holmes who seemed to walk and talk in slow-motion (Patrick would later tell me that Peter had been hit by a car when he was little and damaged his brain.) It was overwhelming, and the four of us simply stopped and stared—not knowing quite what we should do next.

"There's a lot of them," Peter Holmes drawled. I wouldn't have minded betting he could do a bloody brill John Wayne impersonation. "Can we go back in?"

"Why?" Patrick said.

"They might not be nice to us."

"Course they will. And if they aren't, Johnny can tell 'em where to go, right, mate?"

"Only if yer-you promise to go with them."

Nice one. I was really beginning to like Johnny *a lot*, but it was hard to imagine ever being his *actual* friend. I didn't think he wanted friends, because friends probably weren't very cool, but I was still determined to give it a try.

Patrick, who must have known Johnny before coming here, I thought, laughed and said, "I know you don't mean it."

"I do so mer-mean it."

"I think he does," Peter droned, looking more uncomfortable than ever.

"I mean it ler-ler-like I've never meant owt before," Johnny said, before glowering at me. "And I der-don't know what you think you're looking at, teacher's per-per-pet."

"I'm... I'm looking at you." It was the best I could come up with at such short notice. I was determined not to let him intimidate me, but it wasn't easy. He was such grumpy-looking bugger.

"Well don't."

"Why?"

"Because I said so."

"And what if I do?"

"You'll find out."

"I'm scared."

"You sher-sher-should be."

"Sher-sher-should I?"

This was the first time I ever took the Mickey out of Johnny's stammer, and as it turned out, it would also be the last.

Turning the colour of a Strawberry Mivi ice cream, he pointed to a distant, deserted spot of playground. "Meet me there, after lunch," he said.

"Why?" I thought I knew.

"We'll ser-settle this," he said, so grandly that it had to be something he'd heard on telly. "We'll settle this with our fer-fer-fer-fists."

A fight, I thought. And on my first day, too.

The promise of fisticuffs with Johnny at lunchtime could have seriously overshadowed that morning's break. It played on my mind somewhat, it must be said—my never having had a fight before and not really knowing how such things worked. Did we both pick seconds like they did in duels in films and stuff, or would it be more primitive than that? Such considerations could certainly have spoiled what was turning into an utterly fascinating morning, but they didn't. I thought about it, looked at all the *girls* collecting around me, and cast it ably to the back of my mind.

They were from Swallowfields, mainly, but there was also a few of the younger Almsby girls among them—their uniforms looking far more interesting than those of the few Almsby boys who were wandering around the playground. The air buzzed with questions and I, ever the little gentleman and wearing my most charmingest smile, did my level best to answer them—breathing in deeply and then not, because whilst most of them smelt quite nice, one didn't. This particular rotten apple (which I managed to narrow down to one of two) whiffed like she'd let off half an hour ago and forgotten to leave it behind. She (whichever one she was) made me think of that kid in the Charlie Brown cartoons—the one with the smelly cloud that followed him about everywhere. Only in this case, the cloud was invisible.

"Do you know Mrs. Shires?" one pretty girl with a slight overbite and fashionably short hair said. Her name was Angela, she told me, getting rid of Patrick and pushing me around the playground herself.

"She's my teacher," I answered—wondering if it was going to be like this every day. Looking round, I did a quick head count; by my estimation, and whilst it ebbed and flowed a bit, there were about six girls tagging along with us.

"She used to be my teacher, too!"

Later that day, when Mrs. Shires ribbed me about all the girls she'd seen me with at playtime, I would put on my gravest face and make her laugh by saying, "They only like me for my brains."

"Don't knock it," she would tell me. "A few brains go a long way, take it from me."

~

I really didn't know Carl. Suddenly quite solemn and introspective, I got the feeling that we'd so far only scraped the surface and that no matter how long I knew him, there would always be things he wouldn't share. He was deeply private, that much I'd already discovered, and any attempt to delve into his present was largely greeted with a swift change of subject. Not that this was any real concern of mine. I didn't want to pry, merely wished to understand just how much of the story he was telling me he might be holding back. Was this everything, or were there hidden layers of complexity that he would always suppress? When he told me about the curious girls that had hovered around him on the school playground, was there a deeper subtext that I was missing and which he would never expand upon? I could see the growing psychology behind the young Carl (for example, I found it difficult to imagine him ever being attracted to a girl who wasn't able-bodied), but I was sure my assessment was superficial and tainted by expectation.

"You were popular with the girls," I said, smiling and trying to bring him back out of himself.

Carl looked up at me. It almost seemed as if he'd forgotten I was there.

"At school. You were popular with the girls."

"For a while," he said. "Yes, I suppose I was. I was a slick little sod in my flares and with my hair down past my ears."

"You had *hair?*"

"As difficult as it is to believe, yes, I had hair. I had hair and flares and my most charmingest smile and all these people telling me that I could achieve anything I set my mind. So being popular with the girls was to be expected. That's the way the 'new frontier optimism' said it would be. We—some of us, at least—thought that anything was possible."

"And the optimism was misplaced?"

"Isn't it always?"

Chapter Five: Johnny on the Haggerlythe

I would have liked it, I think, I wrote, my hand already aching and slow. *Being Captain Cook. Because it would mean I was the boss of all those people and we could sail of looking for new places and even find treasure, maybe.*

I stopped, repositioning my arm and looking over at Johnny, who was whispering something to Patrick. Me and Johnny had been the best of mates since the rather anticlimactic fight of that first day. We'd parked our wheelchairs side-by-side, facing each other, exchanged a few ineffectual punches and slaps, grunted and groaned for effect while Peter, Patrick and Angela cheered us on (quietly, so as not to draw the attention of the dinner ladies) and then shook hands and made up, agreeing that it had been a draw and that no rematch was necessary. Looking up at me now, he grinned, and I grinned back—before returning to my composition, feeling Mrs. Shires' eyes on me.

I don't think I would have liked being away from home all that time though. My arm wasn't in the right place and I moved the book slightly to see if that would help.

"Evel Knievel can jer-jump just about anything," I heard Johnny say to Patrick. "Don't care what ner-no one says, he's the best there is. Yer-you name it, her-he can jump it."

Patrick wasn't convinced. He shook his head a little resentfully and rolled his eyes, and as I tried to move a bit closer to the table so that I could write more easily, I heard him say, "What about the Wembley crash last year?"

"What about it?" Johnny said. "He ger-got to the other side, der-didn't he?"

Mrs. Shires was watching me from the far end of the classroom—about ten feet away. I could feel her eyes on me even when I wasn't looking at her, and I therefore now had two reasons to be uncomfortable. Moving my book once more, I started writing again, hoping that if I looked busy she might forget about me and turn her attention to someone else. I didn't know what it was I'd done wrong, but for her to be staring at me so intensely it had to be bad.

Finding new countries would be good, I continued. *And people different to us. It would be a bit like coming to Resolution School. Doing something no one else had done before. The same but probably more dangerous.* I thought about the hydrotherapy pool and its emergency cord and added in capital letters, *PROBABLY.*

My arm was uncomfortable again and I tried to reposition my book without Mrs. Shires noticing. Johnny had now involved Peter in the Evel Knievel conversation and I remember thinking how bad an idea that was; Peter had had enough bother with cars—I was quite sure he didn't want to be thinking of Evel Knievel and his wrecked motorbikes. I had bigger problems with which to concern myself, however. I had to get this composition finished—and I *really wanted to*, because it was fun to become James Cook for a while. I shuffled the book around and tried writing with my elbow on the table more. My arms didn't work as good as they should. They weren't as weak as my legs, but they weren't exactly strong, either— and as I struggled once again to find a more permanently comfortable position without aggravating Mrs. Shires anymore than I already had, I could have almost got annoyed with myself. This was stupid. All I bloody well wanted to do was write a few lines about what it would be like to be Captain Cook in my book and not piss Mrs. Shires off and I couldn't because my arms wouldn't do what they were supposed to do. It really wasn't fair.

Mrs. Shires whispered something to Mrs. Alexander and then came over to me. As she kneeled down beside my table, I told myself that this was it. This was when I got my first real telling off in the Resolution. I'd have put money on it having something to do with the fight I'd had with Johnny, and I was just about to tell her that I was sorry and that it wouldn't happen again when she spoke up.

"You're not comfortable, are you?" she said in her most gentle voice, and I felt my heart slow to a less alarming rate. I shook my head and she asked me what the problem was.

"I'm not sure," I told her. "I think it's the table."

"Too far away from your wheelchair?"

"It feels like it, but I don't think it is."

Mrs. Shires studied for a few moments—sitting back on her heels and looking at the table as, I imagined, she tried to figure out just what was causing the problem. I felt like I should say something. Tell her that it would be all right once I got used to it. Johnny, Patrick and Peter were all looking at us and I really didn't want to make a fuss. It was embarrassing.

"What's wrong, Miss?" Patrick said.

"We have a little problem with Carl's table," she told him. "Johnny." She looked up. "How do you find yours?"

This was better. Now it wasn't just me. We were all solving a problem together.

Johnny shrugged. "Not bad," he told her. "Could ber-be better, but I'm not having as much ter-trouble as Carl is. I've been wer-wer-watching him."

"Me too," Mrs. Shires said, sitting even further back on her heels before beckoning Mrs. Alexander over. "I'm just going to have a word with the boss," she told her, getting to her feet. "I won't be two minutes."

While Mrs. Shires was gone, Patrick, Johnny and Peter got it into their heads that, with a little thought, we would be able to solve my table problem ourselves. Patrick drummed his fingers on his workbook and chewed his pencil, whilst Johnny frowned hard enough to give *me* a headache. Peter looked under the table, just in case the answer wasn't as obvious as we'd thought, Mrs. Alexander smiling at our efforts. Even Kelly seemed to be having a go at working it out—her arms and legs a lot stiller than usual.

"What if we chop off some of the legs?" Peter said in his habitually considered way.

"Then it would smack him on the knees every time he parked himself at it," Patrick pointed out, Peter nodding thoughtfully. "No, what he needs is summat like one of those storage trays turned upside down and sorta tilted."

"Like an easel," Johnny said.

"Exactly."

"That's a ster-stupid idea. It'll just keep slipping away."

"Worth a try, though."

Before we could give it a go, however, Mrs. Shires (already looking a little hot under the collar) returned with Mr. Johnson. Explaining the problem to him in detail, more detail than I would ever have thought possible, in fact, Mr. Johnson listened, looking far from interested in "our little problem". He clearly had somewhere better to be.

"The angle's just all wrong for him," Mrs. Shires said, Mr. Johnson making a grumbling sound at the back of his throat that could have meant anything but probably didn't. "It isn't so much a height problem. It's more to do with positioning. Carl can't find and maintain a comfortable position to work in."

Mr. Johnson looked around him—seeming to be searching for

something in particular, although it was difficult to imagine what. He curled his top lip in and sucked the edge of his moustache, Mrs. Shires' neck becoming pinker and pinker the longer she waited. Mr. Johnson's whole posture suggested that he wanted to get this little problem solved as soon as possible—not because he particularly liked me or wanted to help, but merely because he wanted to be away from the irritation it was causing him.

Spotting what he wanted, his face lit up. Taking a grey tray from one of the nearby work units, he emptied its contents onto a tabletop, turned the tray upside down and set it on the table before me.

"There you go," he said. "That'll do."

Mrs. Shires looked a little flabbergasted. She took a stagger-step back, laughing in a short little burst that implied a complete lack of belief in what she was seeing, and started to say something.

Patrick beat her to it, however. "I thought of doing that, sir," he said.

Mr. Johnson beamed—deeply satisfied. "Great minds think alike," he said to Mrs. Shires. "You have a young genius in the class."

"Johnny thought it was a stupid idea," Patrick added.

"That isn't really going to help him all that much, though, is it?" Mrs. Shires said, recovering from the shock of the sheer absurdity of the proffered solution. But before she could say anymore, Mr. Johnson was gone. Mrs. Shires glanced at Mrs. Alexander in disbelief, but Mrs. Alexander looked away—not wanting to be any more involved in this than she had to be.

Mrs. Shires' neck was bright red now—and the colour was beginning to leach into her face. She looked at the tray. She once more looked in vain at Mrs. Alexander. She looked at me, trying my best to smile at her reassuringly. And then she was gone. Out of the room like a shot—in hot pursuit of Mr. Johnson.

Nobody said anything. It was perfectly clear to everyone in the room that Mrs. Shires wasn't best pleased and, I think, we were a little afraid for her. She was quickly proving herself to be the best teacher I'd ever had. She knew I was clever and pushed me that bit harder because of this. I resented it on occasion, but on the whole I realised it was for my own good. It wasn't just a job to her, and I hoped she didn't do something stupid. I didn't want to lose her. I don't think anyone did.

Johnny—consciously or otherwise—did his best to take our minds off it, though. He was excited, he told me, Patrick and Peter, looking forward to the trip to Whitby that Mrs. Shires had planned for us later in the month. "Don't care about all the Captain Cook stuff," he told us. "I'm m-more interested in seeing where Draclia was. That'll be dead good."

Johnny loved his horror movies—old, atmospheric Bela Lugosi flicks, or busty, bloody Hammer horrors, it didn't matter, he sucked them up with all the enthusiasm of his vampiric idol. Granted more televisual freedom than most (though I had, citing Johnny's excellent example, managed to get my parents to let me to stay up for the double-bills on BBC2 on Saturday nights), he took great pleasure in scaring the kids in our class who hadn't watched the latest orgy of blood and guts with, I now knew, his much exaggerated retellings. He was utterly shameless, but now it didn't matter so much because I was in on the joke. In the middle of his latest reinterpretation, a group of us huddled around the seats on the middle of the playground, Angela (who was now my girlfriend—whether I liked it or not) cacking her knickers along with the rest of them, he would look at me and wink, and I would know that he was coming to one of his big set pieces.

"My ber-brother saw *Exorcist* last week," he would tell everyone a few weeks later. "He reckons it was the scariest thing he's ever seen. She's with her boyfriend, right, and this big tongue comes out of her fanny and rips his cock and balls off." Even I was disappointed when I finally got to see it, on video (that boon to horror-loving minors the world over!), a few years later.

Now, Johnny said, "I heard he still comes ber-back, sometimes. To see old fer-friends and stuff."

"Dracula?" Patrick said.

"No, Andy Pandy. Yer-yes, Draclia. Who else do you think I was talking about?"

"Well excuse me."

"Should think so, too."

"He wasn't real, though, you know," Patrick told him. Johnny glowered like someone who had practiced glowering in the womb—which doubtless wasn't too far from the truth. "Well, he wasn't. He was just some character invented for a book by this bloke what was called Brad Stoker."

"You ber-believe that?" Johnny said, incredulously.

"Course. Why shouldn't I?"

"Because it's a pack of lies. Ther-that's just what they wer-want you to believe."

"Who?"

"The per-people who don't want you to know the truth."

Patrick didn't seem to know how to respond to this. He sat forward and held his well-chewed pencil aloft, as if he had just found the proof that totally annihilated Johnny's position, and then sat back again and shook his head—looking immensely relieved when Mrs. Shires finally returned.

Judging by her face (although it wasn't always easy *to* judge by her face, as I've already mentioned), things had not gone well. Her neck and face were now redder than ever and her jaw was so tightly clenched her teeth must have been aching more than mine had the time I'd got an abscess. She walked over to Mrs. Alexander and sat down, deflated and, I thought, tired out. She said something in a whisper and Mrs. Alexander nodded noncommittally. I felt uncomfortable for them both, but I didn't really know why.

I'd hate to be a teacher, I thought.

When she'd finally calmed down, Mrs. Shires came over to me. Taking the grey storage tray from the table before me, she started replacing the things Mr. Johnson had emptied from it. "Don't worry," she said, "we're working on getting you a new table—or something that'll help you write more easily, anyway."

From the way she said it, I wasn't holding out much hope.

~

This didn't feel particularly convincing, to me. I'd listened to the episode, dutifully making notes, trying my best not to let it show on my face, but it just didn't seem possible or even likely that such problems should not have been immediately addressed, or that the "honeymoon period" should so quickly have come to an end. It was a new school, the first with such a philosophy, in the region at the very least, and Carl's representation of those early months didn't quite seem to dovetail with that. Was this merely his biased interpretation, I wondered, with little resemblance to the reality? An attempt to push points he felt strongly about at all cost? Or was this the way it had really been?

I'd stopped taking notes and Carl had apparently noticed. The man in the next bed, in his sixties and nosy as hell, kept glancing at us as if trying to work out just what our relationship was. I fired him a quick, slightly belligerent frown and he returned to the Tom Clancy novel he was reading.

"Go on," Carl said. "Say it."

"Say what?" I felt unusually flustered. As if I'd been caught in a lie.

"You don't buy it."

I sighed, resigned to the fact that I'd been foolish to even think that I could hide my true feelings from him. He was just too bloody perceptive.

"It isn't that so much."

"It isn't?"

"Well maybe it is. I don't know. I just..." *spit it out, you silly cow*... "it just seems a little odd, to me. I mean, did it really start to go wrong so early on? Are you sure you aren't mixing up your dates?"

"Positive." His reply was adamant to the point of being curt. He seemed to realise this, however, and, when he continued, his tone had a softer edge to it. "I spoke to her about a year ago. Mrs. Shires. I was... well, never mind, that doesn't matter. The fact is, I found her online and we exchanged a number of emails discussing this very subject."

"When it started to go wrong?"

"Yes. Although I suppose it might be more accurate to say 'if it had ever been right to start with'."

"Explain."

Carl put his head back against his pillows. He wasn't tired. I was learning to recognise even the subtle signs, now. No. He was merely getting himself comfortable, settling into the ideas as much as the pillows before sharing them with me.

I turned to a fresh page in my notebook.

"The concept was very simple," he said. "Mrs. Shires was one of the original eight teachers recruited to set up the school and the whole ethos could really be boiled down to this: the teachers would be provided with whatever they needed to 'level the playing field' for the kids—physical aids and adaptations, that kind of thing—so that they could then be taught, no excuses, like kids in a mainstream school. Not *too* idealistic, in my opinion, but what do I know."

"Absolutely nothing," I said, and his eyes twinkled. "So what was the problem?"

"Some people walk, others talk. There was a lot of well-meaning talk behind the Resolution, from what I've been able to discover, but not a whole lot else.

"There were problems from day one that revealed a serious lack of understanding, too," he continued. "My table problem was a prime example. The furniture for the children was issued using the same criteria as that used for able-bodied children in mainstream schools. The table heights had no reference to the very specific needs of many of the children. Also, the cupboards were arranged floor to ceiling, which was ludicrous when you bear in mind that the whole point of the place was to allow us, the children, to act as independently as possible. That seems pretty minor, I know, but it was such a basic thing to get wrong—and a clear indicator of just how superficial the thinking and planning behind the school had been."

"The responsibility for which you lay at whose door?"

"I'm not into apportioning blame," he said, grinning, "but since you're pushing me, I'd have to say that whilst I'm not familiar with the process or the individual players that led to the Resolution being built, it's always struck me that it had more to do with political advancement, on some level, than a genuine wish to create a better way of doing things."

"A career move?"

Carl shrugged. "I may be being rather too cynical," he said. "Some of the failings were undoubtedly the product of naïvety and a genuine enthusiasm for the idea, as were most of the successes, but, yes, people still have the Resolution on their C.V., I'm sure of it. I know it, in fact."

"Know it?"

"Yes."

"Care to share?"

"I'm not going to do all your work for you." He smirked. "That's why God created the Internet."

"God? I thought it was Tim Berners-Lee."

Nodding, Carl said, "Almost. He invented the protocol that opened it all up. As good as a god, nevertheless. Certainly the only one I'm willing to believe in."

"Even after the Resolution," I teased, "you're still willing to put your faith in man?"

"In some men," he corrected.

"And the same applies to women, I assume."

With a slow, deliberate nod of the head that I couldn't quite interpret, he said, "Naturally."

~

The excitement had been building for days—the anticipation of being away from school for a whole day and going first to Staithes, where Captain Cook acquired his love of the sea, and then to Whitby almost more than we could bear. Johnny tried to look cool in his cagoule, combat trousers and trademark baseball boots as he and I sat at the back of the bus in our wheelchairs, Patrick and Peter in the seats in front of us, but I could tell by the way in which he kept peering first out of the left window and then the right that he was looking forward to this as much as the rest of us.

Mrs. Shires was at the front of the bus, Mrs. Alexander driving. I couldn't hear what they were saying and couldn't really have cared less. Johnny was in full flow and even I, well aware of his tendency to elaborate on the facts, was enthralled.

"Nobody has a clue," he was telling us. "Not one single clue."

"About what?" Peter drawled.

"About Captain Cook," Johnny said. "Oh they ther-think they know all about him, Mrs. Shires and people like her." He was talking in hushed tones, now. We all leant forward in our seats, so's not to miss a single word he had to say. "But they don't know the first thing about him."

"And you do, I suppose," Patrick said. He'd been especially wheezy today, and I wondered briefly if asthma felt like a chest infection. Did Patrick go around feeling all tight and rattly, his lungs itching inside, or was it different to that?

"I know more than they der-do," Johnny insisted. "Because I der-don't believe everything people tell me. I ther-think about stuff."

"So what do you know about Captain Cook that no one else does?" I said, wanting to hear just where he was going with this.

"Lots of things," he told me, a conspiratorial glint in his eye. "But the most important thing is that he was a vampire, just like Draclia. That's why he liked Whitby so mer-much."

At the time, I could never quite understand Johnny's fascination with vampires. Not in any way that ultimately satisfied me. His love of horror in general, I could grasp, because I found it equally thrilling—but vampires held a special place in his heart that never made sense. Now, however, I think I know. Now, when I contemplate this little puzzle, I recognise the vampire for the eternal creature that it is, and can't help but feel a little pang of sympathy for Johnny. Every child must find— must be *allowed* to find—his own way of making sense of the way in which the adult world impacts on his life. Johnny Jameson had his way and it was quite different to mine—but, then, Johnny had Duchenne Muscular Dystrophy, and I didn't. We were both aware of the implication of this difference, but still I didn't then associate it with his love of vampires.

"Captain Cook was a vampire," Patrick said, scratching at an already sore-looking patch on his neck (*If Johnny picks up on that,* I thought, *this could get* really *interesting.*)

"Got it in one."

"That doesn't make sense," Peter said, every word a precise effort.

"Course it makes ser-sense," Johnny said. "That's why he acted so funny on his last voyage. He was drinking too mer-much of William Bligh's blood and it was fer-fucking his head up." Mrs. Shires had told us all about how William Bligh had served under Cook on the Resolution, and also made it quite clear that Bligh wasn't the nasty piece of work that all the *Mutiny on the Bounty*-type movies would have us believe. Johnny didn't buy that, however. This was one occasion when—cheerfully contrary soul that he was—he would choose to remain faithful to the celluloid version and cast Bligh in his own stories as "a right fer-fucking headcase".

"It was bound to her-happen," he told us. "Anyone who knew what Bligh was like and what was ger-going on could her-have predicted it. He was a right greedy fuck, Cook was—and he liked the way Bligh's blood tasted. What with him being a nutter and everything, it per-probably had a bit mer-more meat to it, you know?"

It seemed to make perfect sense to Peter—but, then, he *had* once had his head caved in by a car.

Patrick, on the other hand, seemed to be having a bit more trouble with it.

"What I don't get," he said, "is, if Cook was a vampire, how come he could go out in the daylight?"

Johnny didn't miss a beat. "Because real vampires can," he told us. "Even the real Draclia could survive... *can* survive in daylight, ber-but that Bram Stoker bloke had to mer-mer-make him weaker than he was fer-for the story to work."

"Bollocks," Patrick said. I could tell he had a few doubts about his doubts. Johnny could be very convincing.

"I'm telling you," Johnny told him. "It's fer-fact. Don't ask me how I know all these things."

"How do you know all these things," Peter asked him.

Johnny shrugged. "I just do," he said. "Because I ther-think about ther-things and don't believe everything I hear." He paused and sniffed gravely. "One thing I'll ter-tell you for nowt, though," he said.

"What?"

"What?"

"What?"

"Whoever der-der-decided our school should be called the Resolution was a rer-right sick fuck. We're the undead, just like Cook. Ter-trust me, I know."

Staithes ("our first port of call," Mrs. Shires punned) was Time Warp City Centre. A tiny fishing village at the bottom of a steep road, it looked as if had been resisting the call to fall into the sea for the past four hundred years, and apart from the odd television aerial, it struck me as little changed since Cook's day. The gulls screeched overhead like banshees from one of Johnny's horror movies, forewarning of trying times and lingering loss, and the winter waves bashed against the sea wall with all the enthusiasm and dedication of a squadron of kamikaze pilots. We sat on the bus, staring out at it all through partially steamed windows, waiting for Mrs. Shires and Mrs. Alexander to decide whether we were actually going to get out—the drizzle threatening to turn to rain proper.

Johnny sighed beside me.

"Don't know wer-why they've brought us here," Johnny said. "I wouldn't mind ber-betting we've already ber-been here longer than Cook was."

He had a point. Whilst the place had a certain old world charm to it—a spookiness at this time of year, even—there was little there to hold the attention of a ten-year-old. Houses, waves and few boats in the harbour, and a sense of extreme isolation, even though it was actually anything but remote. This together with the rain, which continued to fall heavier, made for an unattractive mix.

I had no doubt that Johnny could have made it a lot more appealing if he'd set his mind to it. It was the perfect setting for one of his horror stories. He didn't appear to be in the mood, however—sitting in his chair with his chin on his chest, looking about as fed up as it was possible to look. Peter said something to him about how he didn't fancy the cheese sandwiches his mam had packed him for his lunch and Johnny just shrugged. It was none of his concern, that shrug said. He had more important things on his mind.

What could have been so important to make a ten-year-old look the way Johnny had that day? I have often wondered. Did he brood—as I imagined I would, had I been in his baseball boots—on what was to be? The one thing that he and no one else could change. Or had there been something else bugging him, something that even I knew nothing about?

A couple of weeks after starting at the Resolution, me and Johnny had been in the quiet room during a wet lunch break. I hated wet lunches because it meant I didn't get to see Angela—and whilst I wasn't exactly sure I wanted to be her boyfriend, she was fun and I missed her—so I was a little sullen and bored. Johnny had been talking to a dinner lady who had joined us (to make sure we weren't up to any mischief, I expected) and I listened with half an ear as Johnny filled the poor woman in on a few facts.

"Carl's different to me," he told her. "It looks like what he's ger-got is the same, ber-ber-but it isn't, because he won't keep getting worse but I will."

The dinner lady—in her fifties and called Nora or Dora—didn't know quite what to say. From the way she blinked more rapidly and cleared her throat, it was plain to me that she understood the implication of what Johnny had said. The matter-of-fact delivery had concealed nothing; Johnny was in effect dying, and he didn't, that day, seem especially bothered by it.

Now, however, as Mrs. Shires decided that she could tell us all we needed to know about Cook's relationship with Staithes from the bus, I wondered again if it was as easy as he most of the time made it look. It was true that, for a while, I'd thought that I was going to die—up until we'd gone back up to Newcastle and the doctor had told us they'd got it wrong—but that was different. I'd been young. I hadn't fully understood what it meant to die. Johnny, on the other hand, was completely aware of what it was to be dead. He knew how it would happen to him, that it wouldn't be pleasant and that, unless they were right about all that god stuff (which I very much doubted), it was final. How could it not bother him?

Mrs. Shires' heart didn't seem to be in it when she got to her feet and pointed in the general direction of the shop where Cook had served his apprenticeship. Johnny sniffed and said to Patrick, "An apprentice *shopkeeper?* How ster-stupid is that? Not like he was learning carpentry or owt."

Mrs. Shires clearly heard Johnny, but she didn't say anything. She seemed glad, somehow, and took it as her cue to sit back down. "Basically," she said, "when you look at Staithes, you can see why our Mr. Cook didn't stick around too long, can't you?"

This was greeted with laughter and the odd "yes", Kelly making that hamster in a lawnmower noise again. Even Johnny perked up a bit, looking out of the window and muttering something to Peter about "mer-mer-mermaids".

"I take it you'd all rather we saddled up and headed straight for Whitby, without giving Staithes another thought, then?" Mrs. Shires said, and our response couldn't have been plainer. "Whitby it is, then, Mrs. Alexander. And don't spare the horses."

We parked up near the Abbey on the East Cliff, or Haggerlythe, as it was sometimes known—where the Synod of Whitby, or something, was held in 664 AD (Johnny insisted it was 666 AD, but had been "covered-up" by the Catholic Church to prevent claims that it was the work of Satan), although Mrs. Shires explained that this ruin wasn't actually a ruin of the original Abbey, but, rather, a ruin of the one that was built in its place after the original was destroyed by the Vikings. Apparently, the Synod of

Whitby was important because it gave the Catholic Church more power. I didn't understand it, really, because I wasn't all that interested, but Patrick reckoned that anything that gave the Catholics more power had to be bad. "Them nuns," he said. "Evil. Pure evil. Our mam said they made my aunty give her baby away."

"Can they do that?" I said.

"They did. Kind of proves they can, don't it?"

Johnny wasn't impressed. "Ner-nowt compared to what their priests do." Beyond that, however, he would say no more.

The rain was still coming down when we'd finished our lunch. We all stared out of the steaming windows, Patrick writing obscenities with his finger on his, wondering if this was it—if this was all our day out was going to amount to. Johnny was growing impatient, as most of us at the back of the bus were, and, unlike everyone else, he wasn't afraid to let it be known.

"Mer-mer-Miss?" he said.

"Yes, Johnny?"

"Are we going to ser-sit here all day, or are we ger-ger-going to *do* something?"

Mrs. Shires sighed and turned in her seat to look back at us. "I was hoping that the rain would ease off," she told us. "I wanted to show you around the Abbey and St. Mary's."

"St. Mary's?" Johnny said.

"The church near the Abbey," I told him, pointing. "It was in *Dracula*."

He nodded, as if to say he'd known that all the time, and said, "So why can't we still der-do that? Bit of rain never hurt no one."

Mrs. Shires considered this, looking at Mrs. Alexander in the driving seat beside her for support. "What do you think?" she said, quietly.

Mrs. Alexander said something about not all the kids wanting to go out in the rain. "Some might prefer to stay here," she said. "It is pretty nasty out there."

Mrs. Shires nodded and looked back at us again. "Okay," she said, "who'd like to go, and who'd like to stay?"

Johnny's hand went up immediately. I followed his example, not wanting Johnny to think I was a fairy. Patrick wiped away the obscenities he'd written in the steam on his window and had a right good look out before shrugging and putting his hand up, too. Kelly contorted her face in an effort to make it plain that she was staying right where she was, thank you very much, and Louisa, Andrew and the others were in agreement. It was just too wet and cold out there. Only someone who was incredibly brave or a complete idiot would want to go out in that—and I had no doubt which of the two we would be.

"Well?" Johnny was looking at Peter. He hadn't put up his hand and if the way he was gripping the edge of his seat was anything to go by, he wasn't going to. "Yer-you coming with us or not?"

"Not," he said, slow and deliberate as ever. "I'll... freeze... me... nuts... off... out... there."

"It's not that cold," Patrick told him. "And you've got a coat on. You'll be as snug as a bug in a rug."

"Staying put."

"Sure?" Mrs. Shires said.

"Positive."

"All right, then," she said. "So that's Carl, Johnny and Patrick. No one else?"

No one said a word. Except Johnny.

"Bunch of bleeding fairies," he said.

Within five minutes of us getting off the bus, the rain stopped and the sun came out. Johnny chuckled, telling us he'd known that that would happen. "Always the same at Whitby, innit, Miss?" he said. "The weather cher-changes like the..."

Mrs. Shires was pushing him around the graveyard at St. Mary's. We'd got a right kick out of the fact that there were *actual gravestones* in the path, and Patrick had spent whole minutes debating with Johnny whether there were bodies under the path, too. Quite typically, Johnny surprised us all by arguing that there weren't, because it would be wrong.

"Weather?" Mrs. Shires suggested, stopping to read one of the headstones.

"Aye, that'll ber-be it," Johnny agreed. "The weather changes like the weather.... Miss?"

"Yes, Johnny?"

"Is it true that at certain times of day, you can ser-see the ghost of that Abbess woman, Hild or whatever she wer-was called?"

Mrs. Shires looked impressed. She hadn't taught us any of this stuff and it was clear that Johnny, by whatever means, had been learning more about Whitby in his own time.

"Well," she said, "I have heard people say that." Patrick hung over the back of my wheelchair, his head next to mine, listening with us. I didn't mind it when Angela did that, but I wished he wouldn't.

"And der-do you think it's true?"

"Do I think there's really a ghost of the Abbess?"

"Yes."

She shook her head. "No," she told us. "I don't believe in ghosts. I go more for the optical illusion explanation."

"The light coming ther-through one of the Abbey windows ler-looking like her in her shroud and stuff at certain times of der-day, you mean?"

"Yes," she said. "You should always be wary of ghost stories set in a place like this, Johnny. You should always be wary of ghost stories set anywhere, for that matter. It's amazing how many people can conjure up ghosts when there's money to be made."

"So you don't ber-believe in them?" he said. "You don't believe in ghosts?"

Mrs. Shires shook her head a little sadly. "No, Johnny, I'm afraid I don't."

Resting for a while at a bench at the back of St. Mary's, looking down over the misty harbour—the rain threatening to return—Patrick said, "So what about vampires, Miss? Do you believe in *them*?"

Smiling patiently but nevertheless looking like she wished she'd stayed on the bus, she said, "Nope. Legend subjected to a centuries-long game of Chinese Whispers."

Me, Johnny and Patrick looked at each other, puzzled. I *thought* I knew what she meant, but I wasn't sure. She caught a whiff of our confusion, however, and explained.

"You've played Chinese Whispers, right?" We all nodded. "Then you must know what I mean. You start with one thing and end up with something totally different, because the mistakes made in the telling of the story just keep getting bigger and bigger."

Johnny curled his bottom lip over, thinking. "Ber-but it started off with something true, right?" he said.

"Possibly."

Johnny seemed content to leave it at that, settling back in his wheelchair to enjoy the view. Patrick, however, wasn't.

"Johnny reckons Captain Cook was a vampire," he said.

If looks could have killed, Patrick would have been a dead man. Or possibly an undead man. Johnny stared at him, jaw tightly clenched, as if this were the greatest betrayal he'd ever encountered. He shook his head at the hopelessness of it all. Nothing he could do would ever change a thing. Patrick had be born an idiot, he would live his life an idiot and die an idiot, and anything Johnny said or did, that shake of the head said, would be inconsequential.

"Captain Cook was a vampire, eh?" Mrs. Shires said. Her face was quite straight, but I could hear the smile in her voice. "Where did you hear that, then?"

"Didn't hear it nowhere."

"Anywhere."

"Didn't hear it nowhere," he insisted. "It's jer-just obvious, that's all."

"Well," Mrs. Shires said, "it's certainly a fascinating idea, but it doesn't seem all that obvious to me. Why don't you explain your theory?"

She wasn't being unkind, but she was teasing Johnny—and I wasn't entirely sure that that was a good idea. I'd seen people, other kids, try to tease Johnny before and it had always ended badly... for them. If he said the kind of thing I'd heard him say to others to Mrs. Shires, however, I had no doubt whatsoever that he would be the one in hot water.

"Don't feel ler-like it," he said, sullenly. "You're ner-not really interested anyway."

Mrs. Shires bit back a smile. "Well I'll admit it does sound a bit unlikely," she told him, "but I wouldn't say I'm not interested."

Johnny glanced at her out of the corner of his eye—but before he could decide what he was going to do, Patrick took the initiative. Starting at the very beginning, he outlined in great detail everything Johnny had told us, cleaning up the language but not diluting Johnny's message in the least. He even managed to create some of the atmosphere that Johnny had evoked, though this might have had more to do with the fact that the mist was now turning into a full-blown fog.

"There's no question in my mind," Mrs. Shires said, once Patrick had finished, "that Resolution wasn't the best choice of name for our school. Not be a long chalk. I would have much preferred Endeavour, after Cook's first ship. But the Resolution being a school of the undead? That's a bit far-fetched, don't you think, Johnny?"

He sniffed and shrugged, not looking at us—staring out into the fog as if he could see forever. "Believe what you want," he said. "But as fer-far as I'm concerned, Mr. Johnson is Cook on his ler-last voyage. If he ster-ster-starts kidnapping the ner-natives, I'm going ber-back to me old school."

Mrs. Shires laughed openly (something I found extremely encouraging—and a little unnerving) and was about to say more when we were quite unceremoniously interrupted by Mrs. Alexander running along the path towards us. She looked a little panic-stricken and Mrs. Shires immediately got to her feet.

"What's up?" she said.

Mrs. Alexander shook her head. She'd been running and was a little out of breath. "Nothing," she said. "Well, nothing like you're thinking. It's just this fog. It's getting thicker by the minute. We really need to be thinking about getting back.

Mrs. Shires looked down into the harbour. The boats and the amusements on the west side were now completely obscured.

"Okay," she said to us. "Back to the bus."

The journey home was tense. Mrs. Shires and Mrs. Alexander had decided to take the coast road home—not wanting to risk getting stranded out on the moors in the fog—but visibility was still poor and progress slow. Mrs. Shires encouraged us all to be as quiet as possible, so that Mrs. Alexander could concentrate, but this didn't stop Johnny from chuntering away at Patrick, condemning him for what he saw as the ultimate act of betrayal.

"How cer-could you even think of der-doing that?" he said. "Making mer-me look like a complete idiot when everyone knows that adults der-don't know the fer-fer-first thing about stuff like that."

"I thought she'd be interested," Patrick said, amused by Johnny's indignation. "She was dead impressed when you were going on about the ghost of that Abbess or whatever it was."

"That was der-different," Johnny said. "That was just something our dad told us. Ser-something he'd read in a book. Captain Cook being a vampire was my ster-story. If anyone told her, it should've been me."

I wasn't sure what Johnny was more annoyed about—Patrick robbing him of the opportunity to tell the story to Mrs. Shires himself or the fact that Patrick had told her at all. Truth be known, I didn't think Johnny was all that sure himself. He squinted out of the window at the fog—visibility now down to an approximate spitting distance—and again shook his head at the hopelessness of it all.

"You actually told her the story of Cook being a vampire?" Peter drawled in disbelief, and Patrick chuckled. I got the joke too. Or I thought I did; Peter was brain-damaged, but even he knew it had been a stupid idea.

As we passed through Guisborough, close to home, the tension started to ease a bit. Even Mrs. Shires and Mrs. Alexander were talking a bit more loudly and laughing occasionally, as if the relief of getting through the fog needed some kind of celebration, however understated.

Johnny elbowed me and I turned to him, half-expecting some glum assessment of the day. I needn't have worried, however. Johnny's mood was like the Whitby weather.

"Was that good?" he said. "Or wer-was that good?"

Chapter Six: New Horizons, Number One

Towards the end of my first year at Resolution School, it had been explained to me by Mrs. Shires that a mistake had been made. Taking me into the quiet room, that womb-like space that I'd already grown phenomenally bored with, she had parked me by the room's only window and sat herself down in front of me.

"It's ridiculous that it should have happened," she had told me. "And I'd like to tell you that heads will roll—because this is unforgivable, in my opinion—but I very much doubt that that will happen."

I had been anxious, imagining all kinds of crazy things as, very gradually, she had worked her way up to telling me, with much disgust (thankfully not directed at me), just what had happened.

There had been an administrative error, she had said. I hadn't fully known what that meant, but I got the gist of it all right—enough to know that it was probably Mr. Johnson's fault, anyway, or the fault of one of his cronies, possibly the very proper and serious Scotch secretary who got right on my nipple-ends. Hardly anyone I'd liked by this point, Mrs. Shires included, had any time for Mr. Johnson—he'd proved himself to be "all wer-wind and per-piss", as Johnny had been fond of saying—and if Mrs. Shires wanted to lay the blame at his usually closed door, that was just fine by me.

"It's a right cock-up," Mrs. Shires had told me, having a rare, unguarded moment. "Because your tenth birthday was in September, they just assumed that you should have been in my class. But, of course, your birthday's on the nineteenth. *After* the fifth. To really be eligible to be in my class, you should have been ten *before* the fifth." She had sat back, at this point, blowing out her cheeks and looking through the window at the tiny quadrangle outside. "Apparently, it's an easy enough mistake to make," she had said, more to herself than me. "If you know next to nothing about running a school."

"So what's going to happen?" I had asked her, a little anxious. "Won't I be going over to Almsby?"

Shaking her head, Mrs. Shires had said, "No, I'm afraid not. You're stuck with me for another year."

It didn't quite work out that way, however, and, in retrospect, I really should have known when I returned after the summer holidays that Mrs. Shires would do her level best to turn a negative into a positive.

She was waiting for me in her new classroom, and I could tell she had something up her sleeve the minute I set eyes on her. *Call me the suspicious type,* I thought, *but when a teacher grins at you like that, it either means something dead good is about to happen or something not so good that they* think *is dead good is about to happen.* Johnny would have had a name for that kind of grin, but I couldn't for the life of me think what it might be. And, of course, Johnny was nowhere to be seen, now; whilst he wasn't clever enough to go over into the Almsby Comp, he was at least old enough to go into the seniors in the Resolution.

More than could be said for me.

"Ah, here he is," Mrs. Shires said. "Just the man I was looking for." I glanced over my shoulder. Yup, she meant me. "Have I got some *brilliant* news for you, or have I got some *brilliant* news for you?"

"If I had to guess," I told her, "I'd say you've got some brilliant news for me." *Or you think you have,* I almost added.

"And you wouldn't be wrong."

She wheeled me over into the far corner of the room, where her desk was. I took a moment to look around, while she got herself sorted out. A few of the other kids had started to filter in, and I was dismayed to find that I hardly knew any of them—and that I liked them even less. They were young. The same age as me, most of them seemed *infantile* and, even though they weren't, more disabled than Johnny and the rest of us could ever be. I didn't like them, and I felt myself shrinking at the prospect of spending a year in their company.

"Right." Mrs. Shires pulled a sheet of paper from a pile on her desk and handed it to me. "There you go." She sat down, satisfied with herself. All I could conclude was that the summer holidays had made her considerably easier to please. "What do you make of that, then?"

"It looks like a letter."

"That's because it *is* a letter." She beamed at me. "Go ahead, read it." I'd got no further than the first sentence, however, when she took the letter from me (*ouch! fucking paper cut!*) and said, eagerly, "It's from my good friend and colleague Mr. Page. We worked together before I started here. In Swallowfields." She nodded and grinned at me, it has to be said, rather stupidly. From the look of her, I deduced that she believed that this was the only clue I should have needed.

Guess the poor cow can't get everything right.

"Oh come on, Carl," she said. "Stop being so dim. You can work it out."

"Can I?"

"You're too young to go into Almsby but..."

It didn't take a genius to see where she was going, but it was kind of fun letting her think I was none the wiser—so I dragged it out for as long as I could until she finally twigged that I was having her on.

"A word to the wise, Smarty-Pants," she told me, suddenly quite stern. "Don't get too big for your boots. The likes of Mr. Page won't put up with that kind of silliness."

God, I hated it when that happened.

Back in smiley mode before I even had time to apologise, Mrs. Shires started outlining "the plan" for me.

I was to be integrated into Swallowfields only during the mornings, to begin with. This would leave afternoons free for physiotherapy and the likes and allow Mrs. Shires and Mr. Page to properly assess how I was coping. Mrs. Shires, ever eager to push the "adventure" element, was quick to tell me that I was the first wheelchair user from the Resolution to go into Swallowfields and—even though the school wasn't as equipped as it could have been—everyone was very excited for me.

"When do I start?" I said—suddenly feeling quite apprehensive. It was another new school. My second in the space of a year, and with no real time for preparation. This had the obvious advantage of not having ruined my holiday, of course, but it also meant that I now found myself struggling all at once with the possibilities. How was this going to work? Would I manage in a normal school? What if they didn't like me?

"In about ten minutes' time," Mrs. Shires told me. "I've arranged for two of your new classmates to come over and collect you. They're lovely lads. You'll like them. I taught them in Swallowfields."

During that first year at the Resolution, I'd met a number of kids from Swallowfields—not only Angela, who I'd fallen out with long ago, and who was now in Almsby, anyway, but also a few others, some of whom hadn't been all that nice. Me, Johnny and the others had never had any problems with them, the four of us always quick to tell them to fuck off it we felt the need, which had usually done the trick for us but had never stopped them taking the Mickey out of the kids that couldn't stick up for themselves. Now I wondered just how easy it would (or wouldn't) be dealing with boys like that on my own. I didn't want to be in that situation.

I wasn't scared, and I had no doubt that my new teacher would keep a special eye on me—but such confrontation said things about me that, whilst I did my best not to think about it, forced me to see that, however clever and *with it* and handsome I might be, I would always be different, always be unable to merge into the background.

I made myself feel a little better by looking at the kids around me. Crutches, calipers, wheelchairs, and, in one case, a chin slick with spit. Some of them were like me, but most of them weren't. I couldn't have explained the differences at the time, but I thought it might have had something to do with the way the ones like me looked at the other kids, too. Maybe they don't like being here, either, I thought—and then pulled myself up short as I started to entertain the notion that they should be going into Swallowfields with me.

"Nervous?" Mrs. Shires asked me, a minute or two before my two new classmates were due to arrive.

"A bit, yes."

"Understandable," she said. "But there's really no need to be. This is just what you need, Carl." Her voice dropped to little more than a whisper. "You couldn't stay here for another year. You know that as well as me. Even with me teaching you. You'd be stifled."

I nodded. She was right, of course. She could probably see it in my eyes the way I could see it in the eyes of the other kids. "I know," I said. "It's just a bit sudden, that's all."

"Sometimes the best way." She was watching me carefully, appraising me, almost. I didn't want her thinking that she'd done the wrong thing. I wouldn't have minded betting that she'd stuck her neck out for me, and as tough as it might turn out to be, I wanted her to know I was going to give it my best shot.

"So what's this Mr. Page like, then?" I said.

Mrs. Shires looked over my head and smiled. "Why don't you ask them?" she said.

Sean Stevens spoke with an accent that I was already familiar with from my trips up to Newcastle General and from watching *When the Boat Comes In* on telly, but Graham Crag—the one with the twitchy cheek and the old-fashioned drainpipe trousers that made him look all ankles—was still quick to tell me that Sean was a Geordie.

"I know," I said.

"Do you?" Graham didn't look in the least bit impressed.

"Why aye, man," I said.

Sean smiled, but I couldn't really tell if he meant it. In a world of weird smiles, Sean had the weirdest of all. He smiled like a man who wanted to slit his wrists and had just found a razor blade.

We were heading out of the front doors of the Resolution, and taking our time about it. There was no connecting corridor between the Resolution and Swallowfields, like there was with Almsby, and it really did feel like I was going somewhere different, somewhere *apart*. This was nothing like starting Sunnyvale or the Resolution. This—as scary as it was—felt like the first real step in the right direction.

"So what's Mr. Page *really* like?" I said. I'd asked them, as she'd suggested, while Mrs. Shires had been around, but their answers had struck me as too polite and teacher-friendly.

"You don't want to know," Sean said.

"He's right," Graham added. "You *really* don't want to know."

"That bad?"

"Why it's worse, man," Sean told me. "He doesn't like anyone talking in lessons, and if he catches you, he goes mad, doesn't he, Craggy?"

"I once saw him pin a kid to the wall, just for asking his friend if he could borrow the rubber."

"And that's him on a good day. I've seen him much worse than that. He just about foams at the mouth."

They made him sound fiercer than any teacher I'd ever before encountered, but I wasn't entirely sure how much of what they were telling me I actually believed. I didn't know a lot about how the kids in Swallowfields operated—maybe they were a lot less sophisticated than I gave them credit for—but this had all the hallmarks of a wind-up. Had Johnny been with us, I was quite sure he would have seen right through it and put Sean and Graham firmly in their place (always assuming that Johnny hadn't been winding *them* up), but Johnny wasn't with us, and I had to rely completely on my own instinct.

"Has he got two heads, as well?" I said, my voice all serious and monotonic.

"What?" Graham said.

"It's just that you're making him sound like a complete monster," I said, "so I wondered, you know, if he had two heads. Or cloven hooves, like the devil?"

Sean had been pushing my wheelchair. Now he stopped and came round in front of me—standing beside Graham and staring at me. "God," Graham said, "you're weird."

"You don't *really* think he's got two heads, do you?" Sean wanted to know.

"What," I said, "you mean he's got *three?*" I couldn't help myself. The look on their faces was wonderful. They really didn't know what to make of me.

Sean glanced at Graham. The wrist-slitting smile was back and I was actually pleased to see it. "He's having us on," he said.

"You think so?"

"Of course he is. What did Mr. Page tell us before we left?"

"Close the door after you?"

"Before that."

Graham thought for a moment and then nodded. "That he's clever," he said.

No pressure, then.

"Exactly. Someone who's clever wouldn't really think that a teacher could have two or three heads, would they?"

Graham still didn't look too sure. "I don't suppose so."

"You had us going for a minute, there," Sean said to me. "Serves us right, I suppose, for trying to make you nervous."

"He's not as bad as you made out, then?"

"Not really," Sean said, heading round to the back of me and pushing again, Graham walking along beside us with a springy step that made me think of Tommy for the first time in ages. I told myself I would write him a letter that night and tell him all about how I was going to Swallowfields, now, but I knew I wouldn't.

"He *is* stricter than our last teacher," Graham contributed. "But he isn't horrible or anything. I feel sorry for him, sometimes."

"Do you?" I said.

"Why?" Sean seemed quite surprised. Obviously he'd never experienced the same sympathy for Mr. Page.

Shrugging, Graham said, "I don't know. It's just that sometimes when he thinks no one's looking at him he looks so sad. Like he's got all of the worries of the world on his shoulders. That's what our mam says."

I didn't ask when Graham's mam had seen Mr. Page. It didn't seem all that relevant—and, apart from that, Graham and Sean made it known that we had arrived. Apparently, we were going to be using the playground entrance to the classroom because the step wasn't too high, and as we came around the corner, the door opened and Mr. Page greeted us.

I'd never had a male teacher before, and even without Sean and Graham's assistance I could easily have found it an intimidating prospect. Women teachers, I supposed, were more *maternal* and somehow softer, and to not have that might well have prompted me to panic a bit, if I'd given it too much thought. As it was, Mr. Page couldn't have been nicer. Tall—all arms and legs, his head jutting forward on a slightly too long neck—he might only have been in his mid-forties, but he seemed much older to me, in a good way. I thought I smelt cigarette smoke on him, but if the Resolution staff room was anything to go by (when the door was open, you could smell it half way down the corridor) that didn't necessarily mean he was a smoker. He looked thin enough to be one, though, and I kind of hoped he was; I liked teachers who weren't too perfect—they, it seemed to me, were always the more accepting.

I knew right away what Graham and his mam meant about him looking sad. I spotted it immediately, even when he knew we were looking at him. There was a placidness in his eyes that was too profound—a tendency towards reflection, I would now be inclined to call it. When he looked down at me from his very great height (it could have been eight foot seven, for all I knew, but was probably more like six-two), there was no sense of power or strength. I was very much aware of his authority, but that seemed to come more from the feeling of vulnerability I got from him.

"Mr. Grantham, I take it," he said to me.

"Carl," I told him.

"Carl. Of course." We were still outside on the playground. I could hear the other kids whispering in the classroom behind Mr. Page—chair-legs making farting noises against the floor as they (the children, not the chair-legs) struggled to get a look at me. "Well, Carl—I'm Mr. Page and, as Mrs. Shires has no doubt told you, I'm going to be your teacher for the year ahead. Rumour has it you're a bright spark."

"Best not to believe all you hear," I said.

Mr. Page nodded indulgently. "I would say that that depends on the source, though, wouldn't you?" He had me, there. Mrs. Shires was reliable and, hey, who was I to argue with her or Mr. Page on this issue. If they thought I was a bright spark, that was all well and good by me.

"Now," Mr. Page added, "let's get you inside and introduce you to the rest of your classmates, shall we?"

The first thing that struck me was just how big the class was—not just the room itself (though that was on the large side, too), but the number of pupils in it. I was used to a maximum of around ten and, unless I was seriously mistaken, my new class had about three times that. Or that was at the very least how it seemed. Close on thirty kids, all eager to learn (yeah, right) and all staring at me like... well, the joke sort of came back to bite me; they stared at me as if I had two heads.

I didn't have a clue what I was supposed to do. I looked at Sean and Graham, but they were no help. They went to their places to stare with the rest of them, leaving me with Mr. Page.

Mr. Page had had a special table made for me—the inclined, easel-like affair that Patrick had suggested but which we'd never opted for. He seemed very pleased with it, telling me that the school caretaker had worked very hard at making it for me and that he hoped it would "do the trick". I didn't have the heart to tell him that I'd probably manage just as well at one of the ordinary desks (as difficult as that would be, writing on an incline meant that I had to reach *up*, and that was even more tricky), so I just nodded and said that it looked really good.

Mr. Page seemed satisfied with this. He rubbed his hands together and stood up straighter. I thought for a moment that he was going to hit his head on the ceiling, but I told myself not to be silly; he was at least an inch or two short.

"Well, everyone," he said. "I'd like to introduce you to our new class member—Carl Grantham. As I've already told you, Carl is joining us from Resolution School next door and he will be with us every morning for the foreseeable future. Hopefully, once we get this worked out, he might even join us some afternoons—go to the library with us, that kind of thing. You'd like that, right, Carl?"

My face felt hot. I nodded, wishing he would just get things moving and start teaching us something so that everyone would stop bloody looking at me.

"You like reading, Mrs. Shires tells me," he said, in a more conversational tone. "Ghost stories, at the moment, isn't it?"

"I don't mind," I said. "I like other stuff, too."

"What have you read recently that you enjoyed?"

I had a sudden urge to say, "*Five Go Bonking in Bournemouth*, sir," but I controlled myself and instead said, "*Treasure Island.* That was pretty good. I don't much like pirate stories, they're a bit childish, but this one was excellent. It wasn't just a pirate story, you know."

A few of the kids looked bored, but Mr. Page liked my answer. "Good, good," he said, turning back to the others. "Now, before we get down to business, does anyone have any questions for Carl?"

Well, I didn't expect that. About six hundred hands went up at once—and, coming from a class of just under thirty pupils, that was pretty impressive. Mr. Page was loving this. Everyone was doing just what he wanted them to do and I would have put money on him telling his friends about this for weeks to come.

"Wonderful," he said. "Now, let me see. Julie. Would you like to go first?"

Julie—a pretty girl with blonde hair and the reddest lips I'd ever seen— put her hand down and leant forward with her elbows on her desk. I recognised her right away as being one of the more clever pupils, like me, and I felt a momentary jolt of apprehension.

"What," she said, almost as precisely as Peter. "What's it like being in a wheelchair? If you don't mind me asking."

Mr. Page watched me carefully. I guessed he was new to this. He didn't know if this kind of direct question was advisable—if I could cope with it. It was nice that he was so concerned, but he really needn't have worried.

Shrugging, I said, "Not bad, I suppose. Not as bad as some people think it is, anyway. Sometimes getting in places can be hard but usually it's okay. I've never not been in one, sort of, so it's just ordinary to me."

"Why can't you walk?" another kid, a chubby boy with sunken eyes, asked. "Did you have an accident?"

"No," I told him. "I was born with this *condition*..." I'd already learned to avoid the inaccurate and socially lethal word "disease"... "I was born with this condition what stops the signals reaching my muscles properly so they don't work the way they should."

"What *signals*?" The poor sod was already lost.

"From my brain," I said. I didn't know how right this was, but I was sure it was close enough for a fat kid. "My brain sends the signals to tell my muscles what to do, but they don't all get there."

The chubby boy stared at me blankly. "Oh," he said.

"Do you sleep in the Resolution?" another girl said. Unlike Julie, she didn't look all that clever. In fact, she looked as thick as two short planks with her too-big eyes and her rubbery bottom lip.

A ripple of sniggers passed around the classroom and, as Mr. Page shushed them, I tried not to laugh.

I answered the question with all the patience of someone much older, explaining that the Resolution was a school much like Swallowfields and that I went home to my mam and dad every night, just like they did. I could tell Mr. Page was impressed with me. *Who wouldn't be?* I thought, remembering that long ago day with Tommy at Sunnyvale, when we had encountered the kids in the school next door. *I'm a bloody genesis.*

Break time wasn't all that new an experience. I'd mixed many a time with kids from both the adjacent schools and whilst the initial enthusiasm for the whole experience had quickly worn off, being surrounded by kids with no obvious disabilities was a far from new thing to me.

It was chilly for the time of year and Sean and Graham took me around to the far side of the school, where we would be more sheltered from the cold wind. Graham told me that him and Sean liked it best here because there was "a really great wall for playing football cards against." I didn't have a clue what he was on about, but as we rounded the corner I saw a couple of other kids flicking cards against the wall and I quickly worked it out.

"The one whose card lands closest to the wall wins both of the cards," Sean explained. "You don't have to throw it hard or anything. It's easy." He tilted his head a little to the left. "Wan' a go?"

Sean and Graham very generously gave me five each of their crappiest cards, just to get me going. I didn't have a clue who the players were, anyway—liking football about as much as I did going to the dentist. I had a few practice shots, just to get the hang of it—Graham insisting I was a natural—and then I was thrown in at the deep end, my first match against a kid called David Barrows.

"He's the best in the school," Sean warned. "And he's dead hard, too. He doesn't like being beat."

"That's his hard luck," I said, pretty sure I was going to like this game.

"No, I mean it," Sean said. "He *really* doesn't like being beat—and he won't like you to start with."

"Why?" I thought I knew.

"He doesn't like anyone," Graham said, impressively diplomatic.

"No," Sean agreed, "he doesn't. That's true. But he hates kids in wheelchairs more."

Perversely, that sounded like the best reason I could have had for beating him.

Word gets round quickly in any school when something worth seeing takes place, and Swallowfields was no exception. Before we'd even started, Barrows doing his best to stare me out—his crew-cut shimmering in the early autumn sunlight—a crowd had gathered around us, and even I wondered (for about a zillionth of a second) if beating him really was such a good idea. Total humiliation might be dangerous, but I sort of got the feeling that it was just what he deserved.

"I'm going first," he told me, his grey-blue eyes slitted to a knife-edge.

With a bored shrug (one of Johnny's most precious gifts), I said, "Fine by me. I prefer going second, actually."

"Oh do you, *actually*?" he said. "What are you, some kind of posh poof or summat?"

"*Actually*, no." I looked at all the kids crowded around us. He wouldn't dare try anything. Not with all them around. "*Actually*, I'm just some kid who's getting bored waiting to beat you at football cards."

He laughed like this was the best joke he'd ever heard—even better than the definition of agony one about the elephant sliding down a razor blade using its balls as breaks. Elbowing his mate, a runty little git who would have been one of David's victims, I suspected, had he not been such an arse-kisser, and said, "Did you hear that? The silly fucker thinks he's going to beat me. Shows what a loony he really is, eh?"

"Yeah," the soft-in-the-head sidekick said, laughing like he'd been told he'd die if he didn't. "A *right* loony. The looniest loony I've ever seen."

I looked at Sean and said, nice and loudly, "No mirrors in his house, then."

This went down really well with the kids that had gathered round to watch, but Sean was looking increasingly uncomfortable. He glanced over the heads of the others—to see if there was a teacher nearby, I suspected—and muttered something about how he didn't like this. It never occurred to me at the time that he and Graham had been given orders by Mr. Page to look after me, but even if it had, I doubted I would have behaved differently.

"Are you gonna throw then or what?" I said to Barrows, wanting to get this over with before everyone lost interest.

Barrows sneered and stepped up to the line chalked onto the paving and, with a nonchalant flick of the wrist, sent the card flying towards the wall. It glided elegantly, caught a gust of wind, wandered off course slightly but still managed to land a few millimetres short of the wall. Impressive. No doubt about that. But I was still convinced I could beat him.

My first card fell about three centimetres short, and I heard Sean breathe a huge sigh of relief. Our audience groaned and I felt a little annoyed with myself. I just hadn't given it enough welly, that's all there was too it. I hadn't *committed* to it, as I'd once heard someone say on *Grandstand.*

Barrows picked up the two cards, chuckling to himself. I had nine cards left and he had a huge fucking wad of the things. He was already convinced that he had me beat, but if he thought I was going down without a fight, he had another thing coming.

I lost with my next six cards, and the crowd started to drift away.

"I knew you'd see sense," Sean whispered, looking a little easier. "Not worth the grief, right?"

Wrong, I thought. So wrong I couldn't even explain how wrong it was. It was like... it was like... like laying down in front of a train, because we were all going to die eventually, anyway.

Sort of.

I won with my next card, and a cheer rang out, a few of the lost audience returning.

Sean groaned and it was the best sound I thought I'd ever heard in my entire life. For the first time in the game, I'd actually increased the number of cards I had. Okay, it was only by one card, so far, and I was still well down, but it was a start—and if Sean's groan was anything to go by, it was a very promising one, too.

The next seven tosses where mine and the crowd of kids was soon back up to full size, even the teachers who were on yard duty standing among them (much to Sean's relief—he was actually cheering for me, now.) I lost the eighth, and then won nine through to twenty, really knocking hell out of his stack of cards. David seemed to be taking it quite well—even, towards the end, picking up my winning cards for me—but I was under no illusion; it would take more than beating him at a game of football cards for me to get the better of him, I was sure.

By the time the bell rang for us to go in, I was thirty cards up and David Barrows still managed to smile at me. The teachers left and only a few of us older kids remained, sensing that this wasn't over, yet. David chuckled and ran his hand over his crew cut, bouncing his hand against the bristles before saying, "So you're good at cards. Thing I want to know is this."

"What?" I was ready for him. Whatever it was, this was it. Real Jets and Sharks face-off shit.

"What's it like being a fucking ugly spaz, then?"

If that was the best he could come up with (and I was fairly sure it was), then I was home and dry.

I took my time, letting the gasp from the other kids die away. I looked at the floor thoughtfully, I glanced up at the cold, azure sky, and finally I looked him right in the eye. "Fucked if I know," I said. "Why don't *you* tell me?"

During my year at Swallowfields, David Barrows never once spoke to me again. Seeing the grief he inflicted on some of the other kids, I was more than happy with the arrangement.

~

This was something I'd been wondering about for a while, now, and I was glad that Carl had finally provided me with the opportunity to broach the subject.

"There must have been a lot of that," I said. "Bullying, that kind of thing—what with the three schools being so close and everyone coming and going the way they did."

"Not as much as you might expect," he said. "Or not in the way you might expect. There's a perfectly understandable assumption that disabled kids will get bullied more, but in my experience, it didn't work that way. It's more complicated than that."

"In what way?"

It was a bright Saturday afternoon and Carl and I were sitting by the window in the day room. He was looking so much better, dressed and in his wheelchair, but he still wasn't well. I could tell by the shallowness of his breathing as his considered my question that he still had a way to go.

"That old thing about some people having a victim mentality and attracting trouble," he said. "I've never liked that. It puts the onus too much on the one suffering the attacks. But there is a grain of truth to it. As politically incorrect as that might be."

"I'm not sure I'd agree with that," I said, thinking, albeit reluctantly, of my own experiences at school.

"No," he said, "it's a difficult one. But you have to try and look at it dispassionately and see that it's about behaviour pattern reinforcement. The bully bullies and the reaction from the victim goes some way towards determining whether the pattern of behaviour continues. That's not to say that the victim is in any way to blame, merely that they haven't been fortunate enough to learn the right methods of dealing with such behaviour."

This seemed a little idealistic and, our friendship now being what it was, I was quick to tell him so. I liked him, but sometimes I got the feeling that he could be quite uncompromising in his views—and occasionally, though he was quite guarded about what he said, rather radical.

"You're probably right," he said.

"But you don't think so."

"Not really." He winked at me, and then continued. "You see, all I can really do is tell you how it was for me. I saw and experienced things and drew conclusions based on that. Whether that can be applied to integrated schooling in the Twenty-First Century, I don't know. I sort of feel it can, but with certain conditions and adaptations. But, like I say, that isn't my concern. I saw bullying, but it had very little, if anything, to do with disability."

"So you were never bullied." It was hard for me to conceal the fact that I didn't believe him. It just seemed so counter-intuitive to suggest, as I thought he was, that disabled kids aren't all that much more likely to be bullied than able-bodied kids.

"A few tried," he said, "but it never persisted."

"Because?"

"I was lucky?" he said. "I don't know. The most I can say, Marisa," he added, patiently, "is that I never sat back and accepted someone calling me names. I hit back and hit hard, figuratively speaking, even if it meant I risked getting a thumping—because I could do that. I had a mouth on me. But not all kids are the same and... well, this was thirty years ago."

"A very different climate," I said, relieved that he hadn't taken this in quite the extreme direction I'd half expected.

"Different, certainly, but not very. Some schools today... I wouldn't have played it the same way, there's no doubt about that—but, at heart, I think similar rules and patterns apply." He looked a little embarrassed. "But I'm no expert," he added. "Like I've said, I can only tell you how it was for me. Draw your own conclusions."

Chapter Seven: Suspicion

It was a tense time, in the run-up to Christmas 1977. The days grew shorter and life in the Resolution and Swallowfields should have been festive and light. But it wasn't. People, pupils and teachers alike, cast each other furtive, sideways glances and everyone huddled together in their little cabals, whispering and pointing, formulating their cockeyed theories from tenuous observation. For weeks, the word had been out—ever since the first incident. We were all under suspicion. We all had to take care to watch our backs and the backs of our friends.

There was a thief in our midst.

It had started off with paltry things—a handful of pencils from the art room, a Pyrex beaker from the science area, that kind of thing—but it had soon got a lot worse, with a tape recorder and, most recently, a toaster from the Home Economics room walking. The police hadn't been involved, yet, the teachers and staff wanting to avoid that if at all possible, but it made for an uneasy time and I for one wished that they *would* bring in the fuzz. At least then the innocent among us would be able to stop feeling so bloody guilty.

The main finger of suspicion, however, had, quite typically, been pointed out over. This wasn't a problem that could ever have originated in the Resolution, the consensus seemed to say. These were *disabled* kids. They wouldn't do something like that. It had to be someone from Almsby or Swallowfields. It was the only sensible conclusion.

From day one, Resolution School had had an open door policy. It was intended to break down the physical and social barriers between the three schools, foster a sense of "oneness" and inclusion, and from the point of view of a pupil it had been very successful. I liked the fact that you never quite knew who you were going to see around the next corner—a friend from Swallowfields, the Resolution or Almsby—and so I was especially saddened when it was announced that, because of the increasing number of thefts, the rules were to be tightened.

"Ber-best way," Johnny said to me, Sean and Graham one break time. "Ner-no one can keep an eye on all those people coming and going. It was ber-bound to happen."

"They're just giving up," I said, not in the least bit uncomfortable about disagreeing with Johnny. "That was the whole idea behind the school. That everyone would mingle together. And the first problem that comes along they start locking people out."

"That's ber-bollocks. No one's locking no one out. They just have to be with someone from the Resolution and have a rer-reason for being there."

That wouldn't last, I insisted. The thefts would continue and the rules would be tightened even more, and it would be worse than ever—because the ones who did have a proper reason for being in the Resolution would then be the main suspects, when it was probably someone from the Resolution doing it in the first place.

Johnny sniffed at this, but I could tell that he thought I had a point.

The following morning, Mrs. Shires took me to one side before Sean and Graham came to pick me up. She had been frowning a lot more than usual just lately, and this morning was no exception. Leading me into the quiet room (both Johnny and I had BEC electric wheelchairs, now, so I followed under my own steam), I was reminded of that day when she had told me that I would not be going over to Almsby. I had no idea what she was going to say to me today, but I got the distinct impression it was going to be much worse.

"Don't look so worried," she said. "You haven't done anything wrong. Or nothing that I know about, anyway." She winked at me, to prove she was kidding, I supposed, and then got straight to the point. "These thefts," she told me. "Keep it under your hat for the time being, but we've had another one."

I knew that would happen. *Wait until Johnny finds out,* I thought, a little smugly.

"Another one? When?"

"Yesterday, as far as we can tell. It wasn't anything big, but it was... it was almost as if whoever is doing it wanted to take just enough to let us know that he's still there."

I nodded knowingly. Criminals did that kind of thing all the time on the telly. They liked to show off—and it was always this that dropped them in it at the end.

Mrs. Shires was studying me. I knew what that look was all about. She was trying to decide whether she could trust me or not. She was going to ask me something and, however highly she thought of me, she knew she had no real way of knowing whether I would tell her the truth.

"You have friends in all three schools, don't you, Carl?" she said, and I nodded. "Have you heard anything?"

"About the thefts?"

"Yes."

"Not really," I told her. "There's lots of rumours flying about, but nothing that I believe. Just kids being stupid and trying to scare each other."

She nodded. She'd probably heard most of them herself.

"Where do you think the thief is from, Carl?" she asked me. "Swallowfields or Almsby?"

It was an interesting question, but far too limited in its scope, as far as I could see. When I thought about who the thief might be, I considered everyone I knew—from Swallowfields, Almsby *and* the Resolution—and it struck me as a bit odd that Mrs. Shires didn't think along the same lines. It wasn't like her at all and I wondered if the stupidity of Mr. Johnson and some of the other teachers had rubbed off on her.

The Resolution had changed since those first days a little over a year ago. A lot of the energy and enthusiasm had gone, and whilst I didn't understand all the ins and outs of what had gone on, I knew it hadn't been the easiest of times for Mrs. Shires. Her ideas, it had seemed, had encountered resistance from day one, from Mr. Johnson (who never liked to do anything that wasn't his own idea, if Johnny were to be believed) and from his arse-kissing cohorts, of which there were a considerable few, and it now occurred to me that maybe such unfailing opposition had finally taken its toll. Faced with such unyielding foes, had Mrs. Shires perhaps finally buckled and given in, buying into their lame opinions and prejudices for the sake of a quiet life?

I hoped not—but right then just about anything seemed possible.

"I think it's someone from the Resolution," I told her. "I know people still come in from Almsby and Swallowfields but someone's always with them. I think someone from the Resolution has more opportunity."

Mrs. Shires had clearly considered this possibility, and she seemed relieved to have me come out and say it. It was a really strange situation. I felt like a spy or something, someone who only knew part of the story and had to try to fill in the gaps himself. But the more I talked with her, the more satisfied with what I was saying she seemed to grow. The need for confirmation of her own beliefs from an eleven-year-old. She must have been in a really confused state of mind.

"So what about Sean and Graham?" she said.

"They wouldn't steal," I assured her. "And if they did, I'd know about it."

"So we're back with the Resolution."

"I'd put money on it."

Her frown softened and she came close to actually smiling. "How much?" she said.

"Any money you like," I told her.

Laughing, Mrs. Shires patted me on the leg. "You better get going," she said. "Sean and Graham will be looking for you."

In physiotherapy the following day, sprawled out beside him on the red mats doing our breathing exercises (it seemed utterly ludicrous that breathing could ever be considered *exercise*), Johnny told me the news—a little begrudgingly, since it proved my predictions correct.

"There's been another," he said. "Jer-just like you said."

"I know. Mrs. Shires told me."

"Bastards." He seemed angrier than I would have expected, and I rather uncharitably wondered if that had something to do with my being right. "They're locking them out, you ner-know," he continued. "Just like I told you they would. Can you ber-believe that?"

"You told me?" I said.

"Yup." He grinned. "Isn't that how you 'member it?"

"Not quite."

"Thought not." Apparently, that was the end of the subject. He did a couple of showy intakes of breath as Mrs. Redfern returned from her office, where she'd been making a phone call about sputum cups, and then said, "Far as I can see, it has ter-to be someone from the Resolution."

Mrs. Redfern knelt down on the mat between our legs. She looked a bit like Ester Rantzen off *That's Life*, only a bit more intimidating at times. Me and Johnny liked her, even though we'd try every trick in the book to get out of physio. She liked a good laugh, if she wasn't in one of her world famous bollock-crushing bad moods.

"What we talking about?" she said.

"*We*," Johnny very pointedly said, "were ter-talking about the thefts. You can jer-join in, if you like."

"Very kind of you," she said, slapping his leg. "So, who's the number one suspect, do you think?"

"It's an inside jer-job," Johnny quickly told her. "There's no way it could be someone fer-fer-from the other schools."

"Why not?"

"Because."

"Oh come on, Johnny," she said. "That's not an answer. You can do better than that."

"Someone from the Resolution would have more opportunity," I said, rehashing my conversation with Mrs. Shires.

"Zackly," Johnny said. "Per-pupils from the Resolution are here all of the ter-time. Stands to reason it has to be one of ther-ther-them."

Mrs. Redfern pursed her lips, ruminating. "Makes sense, I suppose," she said. "I know a lot of people who wouldn't agree with you, though."

Johnny couldn't have cared less, and he was quick to tell Mrs. Redfern as much. "Stupid per-people don't count," he said. "When they der-disagree, it doesn't matter ber-because no one who's really smart ter-takes any notice of them anyway."

"And in this case the stupid people would be...?"

"Anyone wher-what doesn't agree with me and Carl," he deadpanned—enjoying this almost as much Mrs. Redfern. "I reckon anyone wer-with even a bit of ser-sense will see we are right, though. It doesn't take a genius."

Shaking her head and chuckling, Mrs. Redfern rolled the two of us onto our stomachs to stretch our hips, smacked each of us on the arse and then told us she'd just be a minute. She had to make another phone call. My guess was you could never have too many sputum cups.

"Yer-you know what it was ther-that was taken this time, don't you?" Johnny said, whispering—though for the life of me I couldn't say why. "The fer-fucker only went and whipped Kelly's wer-wing-mirror. Isn't that just about the rottenest ther-thing you've ever heard?"

For a minute, I didn't know what he was talking about, and then it came back to me.

During our first few weeks at Resolution School, we had all learned many new things—teachers and pupils alike. Some of these things had been the usual classroom stuff of sums and spelling, the discovery that the Anaconda could grow up to thirty feet long and came from the Amazon jungle. Others, however, had been more discovery than lesson, and the observation that had led to Kelly getting her wing mirror had been one such case.

Mrs. Shires had always been on the lookout for ways to build on the positive back then. If she spotted that you were good at something, she would quickly focus on it and try to use it, if at all possible, to underpin any weaknesses you might have. She watched all her pupils just as she had watched me that day when she had realised that I had trouble writing and it had been during one of these periods of observation that she had spotted that Kelly had a particular talent that no one had given her credit for.

Kelly had very little control over her limbs. Her arms were all but useless—flying out and twitching as though under the stringy spell of some half-cut puppeteer—and she had to write with a huge IBM electric typewriter, picking out the letters with a stick that was attached to a helmet she wore on her head. Because of this, the very idea that she could somehow find a way of propelling herself around school seemed quite ludicrous, but that was just what Mrs. Shires saw she had the potential to do.

When she got excited, Kelly would push with her feel against the floor. If her brakes weren't on, this naturally resulted in her wheelchair moving. Okay, so it moved in the wrong direction—but move it she nevertheless did, and Mrs. Shires quickly pounced, doing a few experiments to see how useful this talent really was and (once she had seen that Kelly could actually control her wheelchair remarkably well like this) getting her husband to adapt a car wing mirror so that it could be fitted to Kelly's wheelchair and allow her to see where she was going.

It had been a massive success—Kelly zooming about energetically, happily bumping into anyone or anything she set her mind to bumping into—and I now found myself agreeing with Johnny. Nicking her wing mirror had indeed been the rottenest thing I'd ever heard of.

"They'll get her another one, though, won't they?" I said, and Johnny nodded (as best he could, given his current position).

"Sure," he told me. "Someone's already wer-working on it. Ber-ber-but that's not the per-point, is it? It shouldn't've been stolen in the first place."

"No, it shouldn't."

"It's bad. Rer-really bad. Someone should do something about it."

It wasn't what he said so much as the way he said it. Heavy and in a considered monotone, his voice sent a thrill up my spine—the anticipation momentarily all I could acknowledge—before settling with stodgy dread in the pit of my stomach. When Johnny said something like that, I knew from experience, it invariably meant that he was no longer prepared to sit back and do nothing. In a world where people sometimes told you really shitty things like "you're going to die", Johnny had learned that being proactive was the only way.

"What do you mean, 'someone'?" I said.

"What do you ther-think I mean?"

"I don't think I'm up to thinking right now."

"Yer-you mean you don't want to."

"You're right, I don't want to."

Johnny made a tutting noise and buried his face in his arm. He mumbled something I didn't quite catch and then said, much more clearly, "What you wer-wanna do? Just let her-him keep nicking stuff off people like Kelly?"

"No," I said, "of course I don't. I just don't see what we can do about it."

"We can do lots," he said, turning his head and grinning at me.

I wasn't paying as much attention as I should, and if I wasn't careful I knew that Mr. Page would notice and single me out for a particularly difficult question (that, I was learning, was one of his favourite tactics). But there wasn't a whole lot I could do about it. My conversation with Johnny from the previous day just kept coming back and nothing I tried would stop it. As Johnny had put it, it was a "very urgent and pressing matter".

"Walk before you climb," Mr. Page was saying, strolling back and forth. "That's the golden rule. If you only remember that, you won't go far wrong." He was teaching us map reading but I already knew how to do it from Mrs. Shires' class last year, so my mind had plenty of opportunity to wander, try as I might to keep focused. Everyone in class had their rulers out, using them to line up with and work out the coordinates, but I could do it just by looking and so didn't bother.

Terence Coleman.

See? There he was again. The focal point of my conversation with Johnny. Our *prime suspect*. There was nothing I could do, short of hit my head against my inclined desk, to keep the little shit away.

"Now," Mr. Page said. "Find me the coordinates for the church."

We've gotta go undercover, I heard Johnny telling me again. *Coleman is a rer-right little ter-tosser, poncing about like he owns the per-place. So we'll watch him closely and wait for him to mer-mer-make a mistake.*

I still didn't like the sound of this. Terence Coleman was a right hard case. He was diabetic, so it wasn't like he had a *real* disability or anything, and if he got mad I was sure he'd be really happy to blacken a few eyes. And apart from that, as I had been quick to tell Johnny, we had no evidence that it was him. Shouldn't we be looking for clues?

Ther-this isn't Scooby-fucking-Doo, Johnny had said. *This is rer-real life. Per-pick a likely suspect and ther-then pin it on 'em. That's how The Sweeney does it.*

I didn't know if that was the way it worked or not, but, as far as I could see, it was all academic, anyway; Johnny's mind was made up, and nothing I could do or say would conceivably change that. Terence Coleman was public enemy number one (or, as Johnny preferred it, "per-public *enema* number one") and we were now doomed to watch him like hawks, waiting for him to make the mistake he was destined to make.

"Mr. Grantham."

Bugger. I knew that would happen.

Mr. Page was looking at me, eyebrow slightly raised. "Would you care," he said, "to give us the grid reference for the Post Office in Normanby?"

Everyone was looking at me, the mouths of the thicker kids open slightly. I briefly speculated on just why it was thick kids always seemed to have wetter mouths than everyone else and then turned my attention to the Ordinance Survey map on the inclined desk before me. It took me a moment to find Normanby, the Post Office easy to spot once I was there.

"Two zero six five one nine," I said, working it out quickly, without the need of a ruler. Fast and accurate, just what the gawping faces demanded. An exceptional performance, if I did say so myself.

I was therefore very surprised when the rest of my classmates (even Sean and Graham—the bastards) started laughing at me. I glanced at them, my face hot, and then looked back at the map. "He's got it wrong!" some twit said, victoriously. "Carl actually got something *wrong!*" But I hadn't. I checked the grid reference again and I was right on the money. I was sure of it.

Mr. Page—though maybe I didn't deserve it—came to my rescue. "No," he said, quietly, everyone turning to look at him. "No, Carl hasn't got it wrong. He has simply given us the more accurate six-figure reference." Looking up at me, he added, "We are still doing four-figure references, Carl."

"Ah," I said. "Sorry, Sir. Force of habit. That'll be twenty fifty-one, then."

Mr. Page was silent for a moment or two, and then he nodded and smiled. "Very good," he said. "Class, make a note of how skilled Carl is at map-reading. He doesn't even need to use a ruler. That's how good he is and that's how good you should aspire to be."

If I could have found a hole, I would have crawled into it.

"Holding the ruler on the map is a little difficult for him," he continued, "so he's taught himself to do without it. That's what I want to see each and every one of you doing by the end of the week."

They hated me. I was sure of it. If I'd been them, I'd have hated me, too.

That's where being clever gets you.

In physio that lunch time, Mrs. Redfern on the telephone again, talking to someone called Marlene about a conference or something, saying how she'd like to attend and everything but she had her mother in hospital and she was run off her feet and it just wasn't possible, Johnny told me what he'd observed earlier that day.

"It's the ber-best evidence we've got so far," he told me. "He was down by the Home Economics rer-room, just sorta hanging about."

"Acting suspicious?"

"Yep. That about covers it. He wer-wer-was *acting suspicious.*"

"And what happened?" It seemed a reasonable enough question.

"What do you mean, *What happened?* Ner-nothing happened. He was jer-just stood around waiting for an opportunity that never came. That's the ber-biggest part of a criminal's job. Waiting and watching. Everyone knows that."

I told him I understood that, but as far as evidence went, it was nevertheless a bit on the flimsy side. If we were going to prove it was him, we'd need a bit more than that.

"Ter-true," Johnny conceded. "But it at least shows we are on the rer-rer-right track."

"Did he see you?"

Johnny, who was working on his ankle rotations, nodded. "Give me a right looking at, too."

"He probably thought you were acting suspicious."

Johnny rolled his eyes and looked at me, doing his best not to smile. I sometimes found it hard to know how seriously Johnny took all this stuff—his little stories and schemes. Was it for real, something he believed in in the same way he believed in fish fingers and chips with loads of salt and vinegar, or was it just his way of keeping himself entertained? I was already more than familiar with his wind-ups. Could this just be an extension of that? All this time I'd thought I'd been in on all of the jokes—but was I just deluding myself?

"Do you really think he did it?" I asked him, keeping my voice as low and neutral as possible. "Or is this just you having a laugh, again?"

That shrug. Try as I might to emulate it, I knew I could never perfect it the way he had.

"What's the der-difference?" he said. "If he's guilty, we'll ger-get him anyway. Ther-that's the important thing."

"I'd still like to know," I told him.

"Mer-me too."

"I'm serious."

"So am I."

"You don't know what you think?"

"Wish I der-did."

"That's stupid."

"Everything's ster-stupid, wer-when you get right down to it."

Johnny's back had started to curve severely over the past six months. I'd been wearing a Milwaukee spinal brace on and off for a number of years, now, to help prevent mine from going the same way. I hated it. It rubbed and made it difficult to get nice clothes to fit right. But looking at how Johnny was starting to shrink accordion-like into himself, I thought my brace might not be such a bad thing, after all.

Nevertheless, the smaller he got, the more enigmatic Johnny became.

For a while, at least.

Every two weeks, on Thursday afternoon's, Mr. Page would take us to the local library to change our books and generally have a bit of a lark about. The lark about bit wasn't exactly official, but as long as we kept the noise down and didn't raze the place to the ground our anything, it was generally accepted that libraries should be fun places and that we should be encouraged to talk about the books we were reading (which we understood to mean that we could talk about whatever we wanted as long as we *looked* as if we were talking about the books we were reading.)

This particular Thursday, however, I was in no mood for larking about—or even talking much. I was feeling a bit glum and I really didn't know why. I thought it might have had something to do with the whole Terence Coleman thing, but I couldn't be absolutely sure. I didn't like the fact that we weren't anywhere near being sure that he was guilty, whatever Johnny might believe to the contrary, but I wasn't actually convinced that that was enough of a concern to make me feel this down in the mouth.

Sean had been quick to spot that I wasn't my usual self. Misery loving company and all that, he seemed eager to sit with me in the library— casting me the odd glance as he tried to figure out if I was anywhere near as fed up as he was. I didn't mind, though. There was another bunch of kids in from another local primary school today, and the last thing I wanted was one of them annoying me, and so Sean suggested we read our books in a quiet corner towards the rear of the library, near the radiator where we could be warm.

"Good plan," I said—tucking my copy of Ray Bradbury's *Something Wicked This Way Comes* down the side of my wheelchair and joining him.

Sean had a book on model aircraft and he seemed uncharacteristically excited about its contents. He wanted to tell me all about the radio controlled aeroplane he was going to build, once he had enough money saved up, but he saw that I just wanted to sit quietly and read my book and so shut up.

I already knew that I was going to love this story about Will Halloway and Jim Nightshade. It was just my kind of book—a book about boys and life and all the weird crap it could throw at them—and within a few pages I was well and truly hooked. Will reminded me of me a bit, and I liked that. It made me feel like I was in the story, waiting for the lightnings to come and stomp the earth. *Shit*, I thought, *that's good. I've never thought of lightning stomping the earth, but it does. It* really *does.*

I didn't know if Johnny was Jim Nightshade, though. He was certainly the most likely candidate, but he didn't seem to fit in quite the way that first few pages of the novel suggested he should. Like Jim, Johnny would definitely want to leave the lightning rod off the house, just so he could watch what happened when the lightning hit the place—but I got the feeling that Johnny would change his mind at the last minute and put the rod up, whereas Jim wouldn't. Jim, without Will's influence, would watch it burn and cook potatoes in their jackets among the flames.

Another thought occurred to me. Maybe *I* was Jim. Maybe I'd been him all along and just hadn't realised it. It was true that I sometimes thought some really weird and terrible things—like the time I'd imagined myself beating up this kid down our road who didn't like me—and that I quite often really *enjoyed* thinking about those weird and terrible things, but was I really like Jim? It didn't seem possible. *Maybe*, I thought, *maybe me and Johnny are both a bit of each. Will and Jim. Maybe that's why we are such good mates, because together we make two whole people.*

I made a mental note to share that with him—he'd get a right kick out of it—and as Sean got up to go to the loo, Mr. Page came over to join me.

"Anything good?" he said, nodding at my book as he folded his lengthy frame into a chair. He had a copy of George Eliot's *Middlemarch* with him and he set it closed and dusty on the table before him. He looked exhausted.

"*Something Wicked This Way Comes*," I said.

"Bradbury." He smiled like he was thinking about a bike he'd got when he was five and I nodded. "One of my favourites." He closed his eyes and tilted his head back. "He has such a poetic ear has our Mr. Bradbury.

Remarkable writer. Simple, and yet not." He opened his eyes and looked at me. "Enjoying it?"

"It's the best book I've read in ages," I told him. "That bit at the beginning about lightnings stomping the earth? Gave me goosepimples."

"It'll do that."

"Thing is, though," I said, a little sullenly, "I can't take it home."

"You're parents wouldn't approve?"

"Oh, no—they like me reading books like this. It's just that it isn't from the children's library and..."

"Ah, yes." Mr. Page nodded. "Children's library. I've always thought that was an especially stupid idea, and now I can see why." He rubbed his hands on his trousers, looking suddenly ten years younger. "Not to worry, though," he told me. "I'm sure I can find a way for you to take it home."

I briefly entertained the notion that he was going to steal it for me, but the reality was a lot simpler than that (not to mention more legal).

Mr. Page got up and left me for a while, his gangly stride full of purpose and spring. He'd taken my book with him, after I had carefully marked my page, and I was faced with the choice of just sitting looking around (since Sean had obviously fallen down the bog or got lost on his way back) or reading of Mr. Page's *Middlemarch* book. I'd never heard of this George Eliot bloke, but I could tell from the front cover that he wouldn't be a patch on Ray Bradbury—and so I contented myself with a casual perusal of the kids from the other school.

There was a girl among them. Well, there was a few girls among them—as there usually is with a mixed class of primary school kids—but this one girl kept looking over at me and then glancing away the second she saw that I'd spotted her. I'd seen people do that before, of course. You couldn't be in a wheelchair and not have that happen now and then. (*Especially when you're as good-looking as I am,* I thought.) But this was different. Those other people who had looked at me like that in the past had always made me feel uncomfortable—so uncomfortable that I would stare back, especially if they didn't look away quickly enough—but the girl didn't. I liked her looking at me. I wanted her to look at me again and keep looking at me.

She was nothing special. Not really. Just a ten-year-old girl with mousy hair and a nice shaped face. She had a green Adidas tracksuit jacket on and a skirt that wasn't all that fashionable, and I sort of got the feeling that she didn't much care. The clothes did what they were supposed to do and that was that.

I thought about going over and talking to her. I could do that. I was good at talking to girls. I'd talked to just about every girl in Mr. Page's class, apart from the smelly ones, and four of them had even been my girlfriends for a while (not at the same time, though—I was a bit fond of breathing), so talking was not a problem. But I couldn't decide whether I did actually want to speak to her or not. She was nice. I could see that. But she wasn't like the other girls I'd liked, and it was a bit of a struggle to figure out whether this was a good thing or a bad thing.

By the time I'd decided that it was probably a good thing, Mr. Page had returned with my stamped book and the girl and her class had gone. I resigned myself to the fact that I would never see her again (*like someone in one of those crappy Saturday Matinees that always made Mam cry*) and looked up, up and up at Mr. Page.

Handing me the book, looking oddly pleased with himself, he said, "I've taken it out on my card. Look after it, or else."

It was a bitterly cold day a week before we were due to break up for Christmas, and I was out by the cage with Johnny, Sean and Graham— watching a few flakes of snow fall and wishing I was inside. The "cage" was a wire-meshed area set aside for ball games on the Resolution's playground and, a windy, barren spot, it had never seen a ball in its life, that I recalled. Johnny had taken to "her-hanging out" there over recent weeks because it provided a perfect vantage point for his surveillance operations (that's what he actually called them, leaning in conspiratorially every time he said it with a coded glint in his eye.) He liked the fact that the ground was slightly higher here and that, if we wished, we could go inside the cage, shut the gate, and still see everything whilst feeling a little more hidden and secure. I'd told him that it was all just an illusion—we were just as visible inside the cage as out—but he wasn't having any of it. Johnny's world was Johnny's world, and as incomprehensible as it might be to others, it made perfect sense to him...

... I sometimes allowed myself to believe.

"I really don't think we should have anything to do with this," Sean was saying of him and Graham. We'd been filling them in on the Terence Coleman case and Johnny had managed to make it sound a lot more exciting and dangerous than it actually was. "We could get into a lot of trouble cos it might look like we were picking on him or summat."

"Wer-won't be like that," Johnny assured them. "You won't even have to do owt 'cept ster-stand around looking mer-mean."

"You make it sound easy," Graham said, his cheek twitching more than usual.

"Ther-that's because it is," Johnny told him.

"You don't have to help us if you don't want to," I said, knowing *exactly* where they were coming from. Johnny fired me a whole fucking volley of warning glances and I quickly added, "But he's right. It's not like you'd actually have to *do* anything. It won't come to that."

"Well it might," Johnny said, grinning with one side of his face.

"No," I told him, "it won't."

Johnny seemed to accept this, and with a little more reassurance from me, Sean and Graham agreed to stick around. For a little while, at least.

"I know it's her-him," Johnny told us, peering out of the cage to where Terence Coleman stood with his best mate—a cockeyed drip with crutches and who wore nappies. "But we've got no evidence. Best wer-we can hope for is to ger-ger-get a confession out of him."

I wasn't sure I liked the sound of that. Whenever Starsky and Hutch or Kojak or someone said something like that on telly it invariably meant that they were about to get tough with the suspected "perp"—or, worse still, *rough*. I looked at Sean and he seemed to be having similar misgivings. He mouthed something at me that I didn't quite catch, but before I could ask him what he had said, Graham chirped up.

"So what we gonna do, then?" he said, his cheek twitching like someone was using it to communicate a message with Morse code—and I really could have thumped him one. "We going to just keep watching him or what?"

"Wer-won't get a confession out of him like that," Johnny mused. "He prob'ly doesn't even know we *are* wer-watching him. No. We've got ter-ter-to do something."

"That sounds dangerous," Sean said.

"Depends on wer-what we do," Johnny told him.

Christmas and the stereo-radio-cassette player I was wanting seemed suddenly a very long way away. The day grew even colder as dark, heavily burdened clouds rolled in from the north—their distended, pregnant bellies brushing the tops of the distant maisonettes. I looked up, the few snowflakes I'd seen earlier multiplying, making me shiver as I thought of words like "consequences", "punishment" and, the coldest by far, "retribution". I didn't feel well. Not in the usual sense. This was something new—or a new shape of something already familiar. The world, Nature Herself, struck me as suddenly quite hostile, the once-pretty snowflakes now sharp and jagged crystals designed to snag and penetrate the skin, sink into vein and artery alike, freezing the blood and numbing the senses. It wasn't enough to think of warm winter fires, the family parties ahead.

Christmas in all its fading magic still held a certain charm and attraction, but it couldn't steel me against the cold in quite the same way it once had. When Johnny said those words, *Depends on wer-what we do,* I heard cogs grinding together, a frozen mechanism screeching with complaint as it fought the predestined. There was nothing we could do. There was nothing anyone could do.

I felt like Will and Jim in *Something Wicked This Way Comes.* But maybe that was because I wanted to.

"The wer-way I see it," Johnny was saying, "it's no good jer-jer-just barging in. We've got to be subtle about it or there's no telling what might happen."

This was a good sign. Sean nodded quickly, his suicide-smile still suicidal, but notching up the scale a little way towards the good-smile end of its range. Graham studied Johnny, appearing bemused, and then a little light went on behind his eyes.

"We're going to befriend him, aren't we?" he said, eagerly. "We're going to befriend him and wait for him to tell us about how it's him what's been doing all the thefts. Right?"

"That's a good plan," Johnny said. "Wer-we could do that."

Graham beamed. "A good plan," he told Sean.

"Wer-we could," Johnny added. "But we're not going to."

"Ner-now then, you thieving fucker."

Johnny's definition of "subtle" seemed to be rather different to everyone else's. Not that that should have surprised me. He grinned up cockily at Terence Coleman, squaring his crooked, hunched shoulders as best he could, and moved his wheelchair a further couple of inches forward—invading Terence Coleman's space, as Johnny would no doubt have had it, *subtly.*

"So what's ther-this I hear, then?"

Coleman stared down his spotty, blackheaded nose at Johnny—taking his hands out of his trouser pockets and folding his arms across his chest. "About what?" he said.

"About how you're a thieving little fer-fuck."

"That's what you've heard, is it?"

"That's what I've heard."

"Who from?"

I had a terrifying moment when I was utterly convinced that Johnny was going to point at me and say "him". Thankfully, he didn't. He pointed at Sean and said, "Him."

I thought poor Sean was going to faint dead away. His knees almost buckled and I moved closer to him so that he could rest against my wheelchair.

"Him," Coleman said, studying Sean—his, Coleman's, mouth small and tight, like it was the opening of a plimsoll bag and someone had just cinched it closed with the cord.

"Don't matter who told mer-me, though," Johnny said. "Fact is, he overheard it and when he told mer-me, I thought maybe wer-wer-we can do you a favour."

"How?" Coleman's best mate was shuffling his feet like he needed the toilet. I watched him, wondering if he was actually shitting in his nappy right at that minute.

"You ger-give Kelly her wing-mirror back," Johnny said, "and ster-stop nicking stuff, and we make sure ner-ner-no one finds out it was you."

"There won't find out it was me anyway," Coleman told him. "Because it wasn't me in the first place."

I was sure that Johnny wasn't stupid enough to believe it would be that simple, but the slightest shadow of disappointment and resentment passed across his face—and as I watched, it seemed that he was momentarily at a loss. He played with his joystick, moving his wheelchair back before returning to his former position. And I thought that was it. This was over before it had even begun. Johnny had tried. Johnny had failed.

"What if I der-don't believe you?" he said—and the game was on again.

"Believe what you like," Coleman told him. "You can't prove owt cos there's nothing to prove—so what fucking difference does it make what you do or don't believe?"

"Lots." *Unconvincing, Johnny, mate.*

"Lots?"

"Yes."

"How?"

"With a rer-reputation like yours," Johnny said. "Sher-sher-sher-shit like this sticks. Der-don't matter whether it's true or not."

"It der-der-don't, der-der-do it?" Coleman mocked. It was a cheap shot and we all knew it. Coleman was worried.

Johnny smiled and said, "Give Kelly her wing-mirror back and ster-stop doing it. Ther-that simple."

Completely reasonable. No one could argue with that. Johnny nodded reassuringly. Who could say fairer?

Coleman grabbed Johnny's arm and twisted it so violently it could really only do one thing.

With a rasping crunch, it broke.

And as Johnny screamed, Sean threw up on Graham's shoes.

With Johnny away at the hospital, it was left to me to explain just what had been going on.

Mrs. Shires sat on the edge of her desk, mildly assessing me, and I felt the weight of the world on my shoulders. No eleven-year-old should have to feel like this. The responsibility of explaining the events in a way that would make her understand that what had happened hadn't been deserved, that we'd only been trying to get to the bottom of the thefts, should have been someone else's. I watched her as she watched me, and heard again the noise Johnny's arm had made when Coleman had twisted it mercilessly.

"What happened?" Mrs. Shires asked me—and, as if a stopper had been removed, it all came gushing out.

I told her of the conversations Johnny and I had had in physiotherapy, how incensed he had been when he had discovered that Kelly's wing-mirror had been the latest item to be stolen. Looking at my shoes, I explained that I'd had concerns that something like this might happen— but added that Johnny had been convinced that Terence Coleman was responsible and, after him breaking Johnny's arm and everything, I was inclined to agree with him.

"Coleman's a right bad un," I told her. "The teachers think they know that, but they don't, not really. You have to be a kid to know just how bad Terence flipping Coleman is."

I was a little choked, thinking of Johnny and his arm again—wondering also if Sean was all right—and Mrs. Shires (her frown oddly sympathetic today) gave me a moment to compose myself.

"You really think Terence is the thief?" she said, finally.

I nodded.

"But you have no way of proving it?"

I shook my head.

Mrs. Shires sighed and stood up, walking around her desk and staring out of the window—her back to me. "You know," she said. "If you and Johnny had come to me with your suspicions—which, let's face it, would have been the sensible thing for you both to do. If you had come to me with your suspicions, we probably wouldn't be any further on. We wouldn't have found anything. We would have had no proof. And we would have still been stuck with Terence Coleman in our school making life miserable for everyone." She looked over her shoulder at me. "Maybe we should be thanking you and Johnny," she added.

"You mean…"

"Yes. Terence has been expelled. Whether he was behind the thefts or not—and I tend to agree with you and Johnny—breaking Johnny's arm was the last straw."

Time would prove us right. Christmas would come and go with its fairy-lights and its heart-warming smells of turkey, stuffing and wrapping paper, New Year would arrive, Johnny revelling in his "wer-wer-war wounds", and by the time half term arrived without any further thefts, we would have all the proof that was necessary. But right then, sitting there in Mrs. Shires' classroom, I had all the vindication I needed.

And I very much doubted that Johnny, busted humerus or no busted humerus, would have argued with that.

Chapter Eight: New Horizons, Number Two

Neither of us had spoken for a while. I sat there with my pen and note-book in my lap, watching Carl as he in turn, sitting in his wheelchair by the dayroom window, watched the rain falling outside. His story was growing increasingly fascinating—the layers and subtlety of his recollections almost hypnotic. Even had I not been working on my dissertation, I would have wanted to hear more, and because of this I again warned myself to be careful. His possible bias would not help me.

Looking down at my notes, however, I read, *His story isn't an idealised story of childhood. It has none of the freak show monsters of the Ray Bradbury novel he so loves, but it has its horror lurking beneath the surface. I keep reminding myself that this is only his interpretation and that I mustn't allow him to think for me... but isn't bias, or something close to it, what this is all about? Isn't that the truly important thing here? The fact that he has a very precise and unwavering opinion on this very singular moment in time?*

Can a purely academic, sterile analysis of the period and its revolutions ever give us the full, working picture we need in order to learn?

Under this, in block capitals, I had added, *HUMANITY*, and as I underlined this for extra emphasis, I saw that maybe I was approaching my dissertation from the wrong angle. All this time, I'd been trying to make Carl's history fit my dissertation when, in fact, what I needed to do was reverse that, make my dissertation fit with what Carl was telling me. Admit the bias. Acknowledge and embrace it. See it for what it is, the actual, revealing truth of personal experience and interpretation.

"You look tired." Carl's eyes were shadowed, the barely sufficient light behind him. "Or bored."

"Never bored," I assured him, "but, yes, I am a little tired."

"I'll be here tomorrow."

"You better be."

I paused by the door and looked back at him. He was staring out at the rain again, his hands in his lap. *Where are you, Carl Grantham?* I wondered.

104

Are you still back there with Johnny, righting wrongs and breaking bones?
Are you still back there?
Will you always be back there?

~

And so it began again—another morning of new beginnings, of fresh faces and landscapes that demanded explanation. The experience was already growing old. I was bored with what I had once heard a teacher describe as "our ground-breaking efforts". School was just that to me, now. Yes, there was a mild excitement at entering the Almsby Comp., but, by and large, I now saw it for what it was; yet another building where I would have to work hard, stick rigidly to ridiculous homework schedules and show respect to people I probably wouldn't much care for. That hadn't been my experience in Swallowfields, of course, but, on the latter point especially, that was how it was quickly becoming with the Resolution. Teachers weren't perfect. In fact, some of them were downright incompetent. And, fast closing in on my twelfth birthday, I was all too quickly beginning to see the multitudinous forms such incompetence could take.

Apparently, I wasn't yet ready to be fully integrated into Almsby. None of us was. That was the ultimate goal—for academically able pupils from the Resolution to gradually filter over into the fairly run-of-the-mill comprehensive and become a part of it—but for the time being we were still registered in the Resolution, our form room the room where Mrs. Alexander had brought me that first day to show me the glass corridor that led to Almsby.

I was feeling well after the summer holidays—tanned and alert in my new school uniform—but, sitting in that room, waiting for our form teacher, Mrs. Hoffman, to arrive, I noticed that I was the only one wearing the Almsby school tie, white shirt and grey jumper. We'd been specifically told at the end of the last school year that we would be required to wear it and, yet, there I was, sticking out like a sore thumb but nevertheless relieved that I at least wouldn't be getting a good bollocking.

Mrs. Hoffman was the Resolution's P.E. teacher and when she eventually arrived, stinking of cigarette smoke and dressed in her habitual track suit trousers and T-shirt, the first thing I noticed about her was just how much bigger her tits seemed to have grown over the holidays. The T-shirt didn't help. It was tight and clingy and I made sure not to get too close; her nipples could have taken an eye out (*though maybe it would be worth it,* I remember thinking.)

"Morning, class," she said, rather too breezily for my liking—slapping her register down on a table with the mug of foul-smelling coffee she'd brought with her. "Everyone have a nice holiday?"

As a girl called Anna Hart—who I remembered from Sunnyvale—told Mrs. Hoffman all about her trip to Dorset or somewhere, I waited for the uniform issue to come up. I was feeling pretty bloody conspicuous, and I really resented this. If I thought about it too much (which I was growing inclined to do), it was almost as if I didn't belong here with Anna and Mrs. Hoffman and the others. I'd been singled out... I'd singled *myself* out and as a consequence appeared too eager to get away from the Resolution—and being made to feel this way was my punishment.

But Mrs. Hoffman didn't mention their lack of uniforms. She didn't even comment on how smart I was looking (which, admittedly, came as something of a relief). She merely took the register before handing out our timetables and filling us in on the six-day system we would now be using.

"It's a way to avoid having those Monday morning, Friday afternoon feelings affect the same lesson every week," she explained. "And it's really quite simple. Today, Monday, is Day One." She held up a timetable to show us and Anna yawned. "We work our way through the week until we get to Friday. Which will be?"

I didn't even bother. It was beneath me.

"That's right," she said, sarcastically, when no one answered. "Day Five. My Lord, we are a bunch of brain-dead buffoons today, aren't we?" Pausing for the titters (*Jesus, those nipples...*) to die down, she then added, "So what do we do with the day we have left over? Day Six."

"I could tell her," I whispered to Anna, "but I really don't think it would be very polite, do you?"

Anna had Spina Bifida. Thin, underdeveloped legs and shoulders like an Olympic swimmer from pushing her wheelchair. She also had one of the loudest laughs I'd ever heard—and when she let it rip, everyone looked around.

Mrs. Hoffman sipped her coffee and waited for Anna to calm down. An eyebrow raised, actually looking genuinely amused (which might have had something to do with how clearly shocked I was by the enthusiastic response to my comment), she said, "Something tickle you, Anna? Maybe you'd be kind enough to share the joke with us, Carl?"

Thinking on my feet, so to speak, I said, "I... I was just saying how I don't much fancy having to come in on Saturdays. I'll miss *The Multi-Coloured Swap Shop.*"

Anna chuckled again, and if she hadn't had those impressive shoulders on her I would have probably elbowed her in the face—*accidentally on purpose.*

"Of course you were," Mrs. Hoffman said. "But, joking aside, that is the obvious conclusion that a lot of people jump to. A six-day timetable requires a six-day week. But, you will be pleased to know, Carl, it doesn't quite work that way. All that happens is that the following Monday becomes Day Six. See? And then we start back at Day One on the Tuesday."

"So the Monday after that will be Day Five?" a kid I didn't know with blue lips said.

The conversation continued like this for some time, working through the good and bad points of a six-day timetable, some of the kids— especially the one with the blue lips—worried that they might not be able to remember what day they were on. Mrs. Hoffman assured them that that wasn't going to be a problem; they would soon get the hang of it but, until they did, she was going to have a sign on the wall of our form room telling us which day it was. "I'll change it every day until we get into the swing of things," she said.

I just wanted to get on with this. It was already ten a.m. and I hadn't yet set a wheel in Almsby. Mrs. Hoffman waffled on some more about how we might find it all a little overwhelming to begin with and I tuned her out, saying to Anna in a whisper, "Have they told you what class you're in, yet?"

She wrinkled her nose. I wasn't completely sure what that meant but it seemed to imply a certain indifference to my question. "1B, I think they said," she told me. "I probably should have paid more attention but I couldn't be bothered."

"1B?"

"That's what they said. I think."

"Are you sure?"

"No. That's why I said I *think*."

This wasn't what I'd been expecting at all. Unlike Anna, I *had* been paying complete attention, and I was one hundred percent sure that 1B was *my* class. This, as far as I could see, meant one of two things. Either Anna had got it wrong and she wasn't in 1B at all... or...

... I didn't want to be in the same class as her. My year in Swallowfields had revealed very nicely just how much of a benefit it could be to be the only disabled kid in the class, and the thought of having to share the distinction spoilt it somewhat. I was the only one who'd gone to the effort of getting and wearing the proper school uniform (although, admittedly, Mam had had a lot to do with that), so why should they be allowed to cramp my style by coming over to Almsby with me—by *being in the same class?* It seemed unfair, and the thought of going through my first year—maybe, even, all five of them!—in the same class as Anna filled me with a sense of loss that I found difficult to express. I felt like I was taking a very real step backwards. Sort of. I liked Anna. From the little I'd seen of her over recent years, I knew she could be a right moody cow—but on the whole she was probably a good laugh. Nonetheless, being in the same class as her... it just wasn't *right*.

Sure enough, when Mrs. Hoffman handed us our timetables, Anna and I compared and found that we were indeed in the same class. 1B. The B no doubt standing for "bugger", "bummer" or "bollocks".

"First lesson, English," Anna said. "In the library. I hope you know where that is," she added. "Cos I bloody well don't."

"Books," our English teacher, Mr. Lance was saying. "Oh, I know what you all think. Books are for brainy, boring people. You'd rather be watching telly, right?" Most of the kids nodded. I didn't. "Well," he shrugged, "I can understand that. I like telly, too. Don't laugh, but I'm a huge fan of *The Man from Atlantis*." Everyone, naturally, laughed. The very idea of an English teacher watching crap like that (crap that I, incidentally, loved) was beyond ridiculous. "Yeah, well, maybe I shouldn't have admitted that—but I wanted you to know that I'm familiar with the competition. When I tell you that books can be just as exciting as—quite often more exciting than—telly, I want you all to understand that I know what I'm talking about. I've watched telly and I've read books. And, whilst I like both, I much prefer books."

He was preaching to the converted as far as I was concerned, so I felt perfectly justified in not paying too much attention. The room was packed with kids, sports bags, coats and books. It already had that damp dog smell about it that I had associated with school for a very long time now and only ever really noticed on the first day of term. I looked around at the row upon row of books, some clearly very new, others seemingly older than the school, and I thought once again what a bloody huge coincidence it was that I should see her again in this of all places. Another library.

We'd spotted each other the minute I'd entered the room. She'd been sitting at a table with another girl, arranging her pencil case before her—a new track suit jacket hung over the back of her chair—and it only took me a moment to recognise her. She smiled softly and I felt my face get hot. The girl from the library all those months ago. The girl I'd discovered around the time I'd discovered Ray Bradbury. The girl I'd been sure I'd never see again.

Mr. Lance—shirt-sleeves rolled up, flashy tie loose around his open collar—had shown us with a flourish to our places and, sure enough, Anna and I had ended up on the same table as the girl from that other library, that girl who would later tell me her name was Carrie Dunn. I hadn't much fancied the idea of sitting with three girls, but there were no more free places that I could get to in my wheelchair—and the prospect of sitting facing Carrie sweetened it a bit (not that I would have admitted it)—so I made up my mind to make the best of it.

"I've seen you before," Carrie whispered while Mr. Lance prattled on about how good books were. "At the local library."

I nodded. "I was there with my primary school."

Anna made an odd little disgusted sound at the back of her throat and I looked at her. I didn't need to ask. I knew from the slight sneer and the far-from-impressed look in her eye that she thought I was getting a little above my station. The Resolution was my school, that look told me. Not Swallowfields. And all the wishing and pretending in the world wasn't going to change that.

"I was there with my primary school," I repeated, "and I saw you looking at me."

"You were looking at me, you mean," Carrie said. There was a playful smile on her soft-pink lips. I imagined that that smile could spell trouble under certain circumstances, but today I liked it. "I looked round and you were staring at me. You couldn't take your eyes off me."

"Yeah, right," I scoffed. "More like you couldn't take your eyes off me."

Our voices were gradually growing louder and she cast Mr. Lance a sideways glance before, laughing quietly, telling me to keep it down. "You looked right fed up," she whispered. "I remember that. I looked at you and I thought, 'There's someone who looks right fed up.'"

"That's because I *was* right fed up," I told her. "I had a lot on my mind."

Anna and the other girl on our table, Dawn Ross, were fascinated by our conversation. So fascinated they looked about ready to nod off. Mr. Lance prattled on about how he liked to think he could get a good idea of what people were like from the books they read, Dawn sat staring at the wall with her elbow on the table, head resting on her hand, Carrie asked me just what it was I'd had on my mind, Anna bit the nail varnish off her fingernails (leaving ridiculous cerise flecks around her lips) and me... well, I wondered if talking to Carrie Dunn like this was such a good idea. Apart from the obvious risk of Mr. Lance overhearing and giving us a bloody good telling off, I wondered if I was setting myself up for trouble later on. It was bad enough that I'd been forced to sit with three girls, but to also be seen to be getting on with one of them? If I wanted to get on with the boys in the class, wasn't that just about the worst thing I could do?

Not wishing to be rude to Carrie (she was nice, when all was said and done), I said I'd tell her later and turned my attention to the ebullient Mr. Lance and his equally ebullient tie. And just in time, too.

"Mr. Grantham," he said.

"Sir?"

"I was just wondering."

"Good for you, sir. What were you wondering?"

Anna was giggling. She was beginning to get on my bloody nerves. A year of this and I just might have to slap her one. (I looked at her power-lifter shoulders.) A year of this, I amended, and I just might have to pay someone *else* to slap her one for me. She thought I was in trouble for talking to Mr. Lance like that but I thought she was wrong. This wasn't the Resolution and, even with the crap tie, Mr. Lance struck me as pretty cool. He even looked like he blow-dried his hair, just like me, so he couldn't be *too* bad.

Thankfully, this was one of those very rare occasions when my judgment was right on target.

"Well," he said, putting his hands in his trouser pockets and walking around our table—Anna craning her neck to follow him. "What I was wondering was... well, you look like a bit of a book-lover, if I'm not mistaken. Am I correct?"

Well I've never shagged one, I thought, *but I like them, yes.*

"You are, sir," I answered.

"Excellent. At least I have one kindred spirit." He stopped pacing, spun and pointed at me. "Favourite author."

He caught me on the hop a bit. I liked loads of authors, but mostly I liked *books*. I could remember stories, but on the whole I didn't tend to bother too much about who'd written them. Nonetheless, Mr. Lance wanted an answer, and I knew we'd both end up looking like a right pair of pillocks if I didn't supply one. Me looking like a pillock wasn't such a bad thing. I was about to have my twelfth birthday, so I was already fairly used to it. But if I made Mr. Lance look like a pillock... well, that was another matter entirely. He would make my five years at Almsby hell. I was sure of it.

I looked at him.

He looked at me.

I looked at Carrie, remembered again that day in that other library and said, "Ray Bradbury, sir."

He clicked his fingers and pointed some more, waggling his index finger at me and chuckling. "Thought as much," he said. "I just had to look at you once to see that you're a dreamer—a futurist and a fantasist. The classic Ray Bradbury reader. A daydream believer, in the immortal words of *The Monkees*, ladies and gentlemen," he said to the rest of the class. "A poet and lover of circuses, our friend here looks at a cloud and sees a unicorn where we see a splodge. Am I right, Carl?"

Five years, I thought. *Five years and every minute of them a potential hell.*

"Dead right, sir," I told him. "You couldn't be more right if you tried."

Nodding with evident satisfaction, he again rolled up his right sleeve—which had worked its way down while he'd been pointing at me—and turned his attention back to the rest of the class.

We were going to get on just fine, I thought. *Putty in my hands.*

Mr. Lance sat down in one of the comfortable chairs near the fiction section—where I and just about everyone else in 1B was trying to find something worth reading. He waved a book at me and beckoned me over. His new best buddy. God, I hated that.

"Got something for you," he said. "You like science fiction, right?"

Truth be known, I wasn't much of a science fiction fan at all. I watched *Doctor Who* and *Star Trek* once in a while, but for the most part I steered clear of it. But what could I say? The poor bloke looked so eager to please, so intent on being my literary soul mate, that I didn't have the heart to give him a flat "no".

"*Some* science fiction," I said. "It depends how good it is. I don't like anything where it's just spaceships shooting at each other."

"I think you'll like this," he said, handing me the book. I looked at the cover. It had a clumsy-looking, miserable robot picking flowers from a regimented garden. The title was something about clouds and tin, something really dumb, and the author's name today escapes me. I was, suffice to say, suitably unmoved—but I tried my best not to show it.

"Looks good," I lied.

"It is. Really makes you think about what it would be like to be a robot. To be that different." *Oh*, I thought, *I get it.* "The author has a particularly impressive insight. I was captivated." Nice word. I made a note to use it when I gave him my opinion of the book. He'd like that.

Leaning forward, he clasped his hands between his knees. "Have you read Bradbury's *The Martian Chronicles?*" he said, studying my face like I was some kind of wise man or something.

"Yes," I answered.

"And what did you make of it?"

I thought for a bit—just so he'd know that I wasn't the type to draw rash conclusions—and then said, "It was all right, but I didn't know what it wanted to be. It was like it was a bunch of short stories trying to be a novel. It was good, but I didn't feel as if I got to know any of the people in it."

He seemed to approve of this. He clapped me on the shoulder and got to his feet, pointing to the book and saying, "Give it a go. I think you'll get a kick out of it."

Once Mr. Lance was out of the way—off helping Anna find something good to read (which delighted me no end)—Carrie came over and sat beside me, a book on Olympic heroes in her hand.

"What he give you?" she said, and I flashed the cover at her. "Looks... interesting. You like science fiction, then, do you?"

"I prefer horror."

She pulled a disgusted face. "Can't stand that stuff. You have to be pretty sick to like that kind of thing, if you want my opinion."

"I don't." Johnny would have told her to "fer-fuck off" and left her to her book, but I couldn't quite bring myself to do that. As I saw it, if I left Carrie, I'd probably only end up being lumbered with Anna. I couldn't be doing with Anna *and* a poxy book about robots. That was just too much to expect of anyone.

Carrie was grinning at me. She was a wind-up merchant, just like Johnny. I could see that. Just like Johnny and yet so very much *not* like Johnny. "I watched *The Devil Rides Out*, once," she told me. "I really enjoyed it, if I'm 'onest, but it gave me dead bad nightmares for weeks after. Our mam banned me from ever watching any more. Kept waking everyone up."

It was hard to imagine Carrie in bed having nightmares, but I gave it my best shot.

"They don't bother me, much," I said. "But I've been watching them for years. I'm used to them. *The Devil Rides Out* is one of my favourites. I love all that black magic stuff."

Grinning at me again, she said, "You're weird."

"In a good way, though, right?" *Way to go, idiot.*

Carrie Dunn pursed her lips and made a contemplative sucking sound. "Maybe," she said, and went to put her book back.

***

I found Johnny on the Resolution's playground, hanging about with a new friend called Owen Alderman beside the cage. He looked as pleased to see me as I was to see him. Owen on the other hand looked as if he had toothache or a throbbing bollock. His miserable, pained expression made me feel unwelcome, but I was soon to learn not to take it too personally. That was just the way Owen's face was hung.

"He's got what I've ger-got," Johnny would tell me later, even though I'd already put two and two together myself. "He got it ler-later, though, so he's not as fer-fucked as me. Yet."

The day was quite warm and Johnny and Owen were both in T-shirts. I was sweating like hell but I didn't want to loosen my tie, as Johnny suggested, for fear of messing up my Windsor knot. I'd have taken my jumper off, but that would have meant asking someone to help me and I just couldn't be bothered.

"What's it like, ther-then?" Johnny said, nodding in the general direction of Almsby. "You ler-like it or what?"

"Or what."

"You don't like it?" Mild disbelief.

I shrugged. "Not sure," I said. "It's okay. Everyone's nice and everything. It's just that it all seems... I don't know. I feel like I should be there and... well, that I shouldn't, as well. Does that make sense?"

Owen sniggered. "No."

"Cheers." I liked him, I decided. He was straight up.

"So where sher-should you be?" Johnny said. "The Resolution?"

I shrugged and Johnny gave me a filthy look. "That's what you want," he said, "you can her-have it. I'll swap with you any der-day of the week. This per-per-place is the shits, mark my words."

It wasn't difficult to see what he meant. I hadn't been around it as much as he had, but only a blind man could have failed to see that the Resolution was not heading in the direction that had originally been intended. Already, there was talk of Mrs. Shires leaving—the best teacher in the school and the only one, in my opinion, who really understood the Resolution's possibilities—and there was a definite, growing sense that something wasn't quite right with the place. There was an air of neglect, the fixtures and fittings looking shabby and somehow forgotten, and when I looked at the teachers employed to teach the likes of Johnny and Owen I sort of felt that I could do a better job. A condescending, ill-qualified bunch, they were, in my unforgiving opinion.

"I don't want to swap," I told Johnny. "Of the two, I'd rather be in Almsby. But that doesn't mean it feels right. It doesn't mean that it feels the way I thought it would."

"It's your fer-first day," Johnny insisted. "You're ber-ber-bound to feel weird. It's all new and everything."

I looked at him—sitting there all hunched and bear-like, hair in his eyes and his chin pulled down into his neck. He was weaker now, was Johnny. When we'd first met, he'd been marginally stronger than me, but now, here he was, my weak and failing friend—trying to reassure me like only a true friend would.

And maybe he was right, I thought. Maybe Mr. Lance and his point-making robot book wasn't the shape of things to come. Maybe all that was needed was for me to settle in, find or even make a place for myself—the small, badly formed little fish in the big pond.

I didn't know what it wanted to be, I heard myself saying again—talking to Mr. Lance about *The Martian Chronicles*—and now it took on a wholly different meaning. Now it was about me. I thought of that book and thought that I saw myself in its confusing form. Neither one thing nor the other.

A foot in both schools, I thought. *My head and heart—in spite of my growing friendship with Carrie—truly in neither.*

Johnny was studying me. I thought he understood but I might have been wrong. With a long prelude of a sniff, he said, "Ser-so—any her-hot girls, or wer-what?"

Chapter Nine: Divided Loyalties

Those first couple of months might not have been as difficult as I had been expecting that first day—but they were difficult nonetheless. I felt adrift for a while, surrounded by people who threatened to overwhelm, confused by my own feelings of disparity and isolation. I worked hard at fitting in, my intelligence and wit a godsend, and on the whole succeeded admirably. But all that was essentially surface, and whilst I would never have admitted it, for a while I felt as alone and hesitant as I ever had.

During this period, I was called—along with Anna—back over to the Resolution. Apparently, we had an appointment with someone called George, who wished to talk with us about our experiences in Almsby. It was the last thing I wanted or needed, truth be known; if I was going to successfully fit in and *feel* like I was fitting in, I certainly didn't need some up-himself tosser asking me *probing* questions.

George was nice, though. He spoke to Anna and me together in the Resolution's library—something I didn't mind, since Anna was actually a really good laugh and it made it all feel more casual and relaxed. One of those student types who never seem to know how or when to sever the academic umbilical cord, he was already greying at the temples, the flesh a little saggy and wrinkled around his eyes. When he spoke, his voice was soft with an only occasionally perceptible lisp—and I immediately felt sorry for him. I couldn't have said why, but I did.

"Now," he said. "This is all very informal—we none of us need stand on parade, so to speak—but before we start I would like you both to know that what you tell me may ultimately be used in a book I'm working on, but you will both remain anonymous. I won't publish anything that will get either of you in trouble. Yes?"

Anna nodded.

"You're a writer?" I said.

George squinted his right eye, considering my question before holding his hand out before him and wiggling it to express his lack of a definite answer. "Sort of," he told me. "I write academic books, mainly. More a research and interpretation skill than a writing skill, if you know what I mean. It's not like I'm Tolstoy or Dickens. Just an academian with too much time on his hands."

"You should get out more," Anna told him. She was trying to be genuinely helpful. I thought. "Too much thinking's bad for you."

I groaned and she squinted at me banefully. "You serious?" I said, risking, I knew, life and limb.

"Deadly." *Ouch*. "It's common knowledge," she added, a little more reasonably. "People go mad from thinking too much. If you don't know that, you've been reading the wrong books."

George was proving to be an avid spectator. He sat there in his chair across the table from us, leaning back a little and *observing*. I could almost hear some of the words he'd use in his book to describe this interaction—and I was quite sure that neither Anna nor myself would recognise ourselves in them.

"How do you know?" I asked her, quite suddenly—seeing a possible route to victory.

"How do I know what?"

"How do you know *you* haven't been reading the wrong books?" I said. "Maybe my books have got it right and yours are full of shit."

Anna's jaw dropped open. I didn't know why, at first, and thought that maybe she'd seen something unusual out of the window. And then it dawned on me. It hit me with all the force of a speeding, runaway articulated lorry.

I'd said "shit" in front of George.

I turned my head slowly to look at him—sure that he would be staring at me censoriously, his podgy lips tightly pursed. How could he not? It was the cardinal sin, as far as I was concerned—to be caught swearing by a teacher, or any adult, for that matter. The crime was grave and I dreaded to think what the punishment would be.

But George only smiled at me. He didn't care what language I used. In fact, I got the distinct impression that, from his point of view, the more colourful it was, the better. I didn't know what point it proved, but it certainly seemed to in some way flatter whatever pet theory he had.

"Okay," he said, as if I hadn't said anything bad at all—sitting forward and lacing his fingers together on the tabletop. "I'd like to start, if I may, by asking you both for your general impressions regarding Almsby. What was the first thing you noticed when you went over there?"

I thought of telling him about Carrie Dunn—how I had first seen her in another library many months before and how funny it had been, her being there in the Almsby library like that, waiting for me—but that would have been bloody stupid and, anyway, Anna was already speaking.

"How big it was," she was telling George. "That was the first thing that struck me. How big it was and how many people there were in the corridors between lessons. I felt... small."

Well you are *small,* I thought. *We all are.*

"And you, Carl?" George said.

Aware of Anna staring at me, I briefly considered telling George how I hadn't felt like I belonged in Almsby *or* the Resolution. I wanted him to understand, because it was his job to understand and we were meant to be helping him. I wanted him to see that it wasn't as simple as some people might think—that sometimes two options just created a third, more powerful way of not belonging—but all I could do, ultimately, was agree with Anna. Almsby had seemed big. Big and *imposing.*

"I wasn't worried about getting lost or anything," I added, "because there was always someone to ask. But it was a lot to take in all at once."

Anna was nodding. "Made my head spin."

George scribbled something in his notebook and made sympathetic noises. "So," he said, "it was all a little overwhelming."

"Yes."

"Yes."

"But you soon settled in, right?"

I nodded, thinking that this was something of an exaggeration, and Anna said "yes", not quite as confidently as I would have imagined.

"And what about friends?"

"What about them?" Anna said. She could be a right belligerent cow, sometimes. And I didn't think she even realised it. Or maybe she did, I told myself. Maybe she knew exactly what she was doing. Maybe... just maybe it was the only way she had. The only way of coping with her *own* sense of not belonging in either school.

It came as something of a surprise to me to think that she might be finding it difficult, too—and so, as George explained how he'd like to know how easy we were finding it making friends, I stopped listening, wondering if this, talking to George, was the wrong thing altogether. Shouldn't we be talking to each other? I thought. Without some nice but intrusive bloke from the poly listening. That would make more sense. We had so much in common. We had to contend with so many similar things. It made sense that we should make proper allies of one another—that we should each support the other.

It would never happen, of course, but it should have. I was convinced of that.

"And what about you, Carl?" George was saying. "How are you finding it—making friends and everything?"

I was growing bored with this—with knowing what I should say but never saying it. I wanted it to be over and therefore gave the easiest answers I could find, the ones I knew he would be hoping to hear. When Anna answered first, I followed her lead because it would have seemed churlish and disloyal to do otherwise—when I answered first, I kept to the middle ground.

The only place I believed I would ever truly belong.

Mr. Roberson, my maths teacher, was a fragile looking gent with a blue-black beard that always seemed to contribute to his emaciated look. In class, he was a right bastard. He demanded the kind of silence that Mr. Page in Swallowfields could only have dreamed of, and made us work our socks off—doing equations until we ached from the effort. Out of lessons, though, he was actually quite a good laugh, and all in all, I liked him.

He caught me outside the gym, looking in through the window at Carrie in her leotard—bouncing up and down with expert ease on the trampoline. It looked like the kind of thing she'd been doing all her life and I couldn't help wondering what her leotard smelt like when she'd finished.

"Mr. Grantham." I recognised his voice right away and looked a little to the left, seeing his reflection in the window. I felt guilty, even though there were no rules against my being here during lunch break.

Turning my wheelchair so that I could get a better look at him, I said, in my most relaxed, cheery voice, "All right, sir?"

"Never better, thank you, Carl." He nodded at the window and the bouncing girls beyond. "I never had you down as a gymnastics fan."

"I'm not," I quickly said. "Not really. I was just passing and I spotted Carrie bouncing on the trampoline. I just had to stop and watch."

"I'm sure you did." He was smirking. The cheeky git was actually *smirking*. "Still, as... *impressive* as I'm sure you find her, it's not exactly the best use of your lunch break, now, is it?"

Oh, I don't know about that.

"I wasn't planning on staying here forever," I told him. "Just until she finishes bouncing."

Mr. Roberson made a thoughtful breathing sound through his nose, clasping his hands behind his back and lowering his chin. "Well, it kind of looks to me as if she might be bouncing for quite a while, yet," he said. "And, as I see it, however good she is at it, watching could get a little monotonous."

I didn't have a clue what he was leading up to—but from where I was sitting, whatever he might believe to the contrary, it would have to be fairly impressive to entice me away from my place at that window. Watching Carrie bounce was somehow relaxing. When I watched her, I stopped thinking about all that other stuff about not belonging in either school. It took me away from myself and made me think of altogether more entertaining scenarios involving me, Carrie and the girls' changing room. Whatever Mr. Roberson had in mind (and I was in no doubt whatsoever that he had *something* in mind), it would need to promise untold riches and Christ alone knew what else if it was ever going to stand any kind of chance of getting me away from that window and Carrie's leotard-clad, bouncing body.

"When it does get monotonous," I told him, "I'll just go and find something better to do."

"Anything in particular in mind?" he said.

It was a trick question. It had to be. Mr. Roberson was famous for his trick questions.

I shrugged. Under the circumstances, it was the safest bet.

He nodded and grinned at me—or, at least, I think he did. It was hard to tell with the beard. "Chess," he said, and I could have told him right then and there that he was going to have his work cut out for him. "The game of thinking men. Do you play, Mr. Grantham?" I was getting a bit sick of him calling me Mr. Grantham. Technically, I wasn't even a mister, yet, and it made me feel weird—like our dad was going to pop up at any moment. But I nonetheless nodded a reply, noticing that Carrie had finished her bouncing, anyway, and was already heading out of the gym. "I thought as much," he said. "I was speaking to Mr. Lance about you, and he reckoned you had the kind of brain that would enjoy a solid game of chess."

Good old Mr. Lance. I already had so much to thank him for. Shitty books on robots, and now this.

Mr. Roberson grew more business-like. I turned my wheelchair to face him fully, now that Carrie was no longer in sight. "It's like this, Carl." *That's more like it.* "I run this little chess club during lunch breaks. I'm on my way there now, actually. And, the fact of the matter is, we're a little short on good players. We could do with a few more members..." He stared at me earnestly, as if I would be doing him the biggest favour in the world. "Fancy giving it a go? They're a good bunch of lads. I'm sure you'll like them."

It was ages since I'd played last and I certainly wasn't sure that I could ever be described as a good player, but, with Carrie gone to shower and change (now *there* was food for thought), he actually succeeded in making it sound rather appealing.

"We were hoping to get a team together to go in for the county's school competition," he continued, "but that's looking a bit shaky right now."

"I have physio two lunch times a week," I told him. "I wouldn't be able to come every day."

"No problem with that," he said. "We make a point of all trying to be there on a Friday—Fridays are okay for you, aren't they?"

"Yes. I do physio Tuesdays and Thursdays."

"Excellent," he said. "As I was going to say, we all make a point of trying to be there on Fridays, but the rest of the week is fairly casual. There's always someone around to have a game with, but Friday's the day when we work on game analysis and strategy, that kind of thing."

Mr. Roberson seemed extremely eager to have me join, and it occurred to me that there was maybe more going on here than met the eye. This wasn't about membership size or anything like that, I was sure. It was Mr. Roberson's way of trying to make me feel a part of Almsby.

In that moment of realisation, I felt uncharacteristically moved. Mr. Roberson was working a little hard at it, I thought, but at least he was trying. If the teachers in the Resolution had forgotten what this was all about, he, at least, hadn't.

Even if Carrie had still been bouncing, I think I would have agreed to join chess club and gone along with him. That was how much I appreciated his gesture.

Allen Barnaby was my first opponent. A nervous kid who giggled too quickly and had trouble making eye contact, I'd seen him around and knew that he was already having problems with our year's numero uno bully, Alfie Limb. I felt sorry for Allen, because Alfie was such an unrelenting little tosser, but I could also sort of understand where Limby was coming from, too; as much as I liked Allen, there was just something about him that made you want to give him a right good slapping.

"Check," he said.

And that really didn't help.

"Where?"

"There." He pointed to the bishop he'd revealed by moving his rook. "I was hoping you'd move your knight there. It's opened up the game for me. You really need to look at the whole board before you make a move. You're playing well, but then you miss something silly and it all turns to rot."

"Thanks for the advice," I said, with just a hint of bile.

"You're welcome." *Whoosh*.

"Now are we playing, or what?"

"It's your move."

Lovely. I really did need to look at the whole board.

"I knew that," I said, grinning. "Just testing."

Allen giggled in that silly way of his and, however irritating I found him at that moment, I tried to follow his advice—concentrating on the game and actually managing to get myself back into it. I forced an exchange of queens and in the process took one of his pawns whilst establishing a passed pawn of my own. He fought back by attacking the rank my passed pawn was on with his rook. A fatal mistake on his part.

"You need to watch the whole board," I told him, taking his rook with my lying-in-wait bishop. "You were doing so well, too—and now it's all turned to... what was the word you used? Rot?"

Allen took it well, I had to say that for him. He grinned and shrugged, as happy to be beaten as he was to win, it seemed, and then placed his elbows on either side of the board, set his face against his fists and frowned intently.

I knew pretty much right away that it was game over. Allen came back with a force and determination that I just couldn't equal—ultimately mating me easily with his remaining rook and two bishops.

"You need to look at the whole board," a boy with long hair and rough complexion said. He'd been watching our game and introduced himself to me as Matt Stokes.

"Is that all anyone round here ever says?" I asked, and Allen and Matt nodded, smirking.

"It's Mr. Roberson's favourite piece of advice," Matt explained in a whisper. "He's always saying it to us. He reckons it's the one rule that should never be forgotten. Without it, we're stuffed."

Mr. Roberson was over in the far corner of the room watching two greasy, ugly girls play. He seemed engrossed, and I found myself wondering how good *he* actually was at the game.

"Does he ever play?" I said to Matt.

Both Matt and Allen shook their heads. "I've never seen him," Matt said. "Never thought about it until now, but it's a bit odd, isn't it? Maybe he's crap and doesn't want us to know."

"Or maybe he's a secret Grand Master who's defected from the Soviet Union," Allen contributed, rather unhelpfully.

Matt looked at him as if he'd just stepped in the mother of all dog turds. "Shut up, Allen," he said.

Allen took this amiably enough. "Okay," he said, and dutifully shut up.

"Maybe someone should challenge him," I said.

Matt sat down on the edge of a desk and folded his arms. He was a big lad, was Matt. Not fat and not really muscled, he nevertheless possessed an imposing bulk that, as a friend, could only ever be reassuring to have around. I doubted even Limby would have a go at Matt. He was that kind of lad.

"It's sort of understood that we don't do that," he told me. "Like I say, I've never thought about it, really, but it's something we just don't do."

This seemed a bit odd to me. I couldn't see what harm it would do to ask Mr. Roberson if he wanted a game. Heavens, it only seemed polite, if you looked at it from the right direction.

"Sir?" I called over to him—and Matt rolled his eyes at Allen.

"Yes, Carl," he said, getting to his feet and striding over to us. "What's the problem?"

"No problem, sir," I said. "I was just wondering if you fancied a game."

Mr. Roberson raised an inquisitive eyebrow. "Oh," he said, "you were, were you?"

Allen sniggered and Matt kicked him.

I should have realised, but I didn't.

"I was. Allen's rubbish and I could do with a tougher opponent."

"I thrashed him to within an inch of his life," Allen told Mr. Roberson.

"That was only because I let you," I said. "Because we've only just met."

"Oh. That explains it, then."

"And you think I might be more of a match for you?" Mr. Roberson said. I listened very carefully for a Russian accent when he spoke, just in case Allen was right.

"Well," I said, "you never know."

I'd believed that he wouldn't actually be too keen on the idea. The last thing in the world he would want to do, I'd assumed, would be to play a kid and risk being humiliated or looking like a heartless show-off, depending on his ability. But Mr. Roberson was quite happy to sit down across the table from me and prepare for battle. Lacing his fingers together, he cracked his knuckles over the board, and then picked up a white and a black pawn—one in each hand. After first juggling them beneath the desk where I couldn't see, he brought out his closed hands for me to choose.

I nodded to his left hand and he revealed a white pawn.

I opted for a Queen's Pawn opening, hoping he might be impressed. He wasn't. He responded with an Indian defence and I followed with the standard moves until I lost track and started to improvise. I tried to dominate the centre of the board, he refused to let me—using knight and bishop combinations to really keep me in line—and by the time we were halfway into the middle game I was well and truly besieged. Three more moves and I saw that the end was in sight. Mate in four. With anyone else, I would have played it out to the inevitable (or possibly not) conclusion, just in case they'd missed it; with Mr. Roberson, I didn't bother. He knew exactly where this game was heading. He had from the very first move.

I resigned.

Matt and Allen were grinning stupidly, Allen all but wetting himself with glee. I'd been stitched up. I think I'd realised that even before we were through with the opening. They'd played me like a violin, and all I could do about it was... well, smile.

"You do this to every new member, don't you?" I said.

"Yes," Matt answered, beaming victoriously.

Allen nodded eagerly.

"Welcome to the club," Mr. Roberson said, and shook my hand.

Belonging can encompass the simplest of acts. With their gesture, the mildest of initiations, I felt myself shift ever so slightly away from the Resolution. A foot still in each school, I now found one foot planted far more solidly than the other.

"You need to look at the whole board," Mr. Roberson told me, and winked.

The following day, feeling a little more content with my place in the world—winter steadily creeping in, but nonetheless conciliatory in its shade and tone—I finished my lunch (which I still took in the Resolution at this time) and headed off to the physiotherapy room at the front of the school, knowing that, since they had already clearly finished lunch when I'd arrived in the dining hall, Johnny and Owen would be waiting there for me.

There'd been a great film on telly the night before about a woman who turned into a black-widow spider, and I was expecting to have a very long discussion with Johnny about it—possibly with a fair few interjections from Mrs. Redfern, who wasn't averse to a good horror or science fiction movie herself.

But the moment I arrived I knew something was wrong. Mrs. Redfern was still finishing her lunch—she'd called to me that she wouldn't be two minutes as I'd been leaving the hall—and Johnny and Owen were seated by the red mats in their wheelchairs, faces set and ungiving. I greeted them cheerfully, driving over to them, but stopped dead when I got no response.

"What's wrong?" I said.

Nothing.

Johnny stared into space, his lips as tightly pursed as his jaw was clenched. I'd seen him like this before, but I'd never had his unbending disapproval directed so wholly in my direction. It was a novelty, and under different circumstances it could even have been amusing—but this was Johnny. He was my mate, and if I'd done something to piss him off, I wanted to know what it was, so that I could either apologise or tell him not to be such a bloody prick.

"Johnny," I said, trying to sound all calm and reasonable. "What up, mate?"

God, he was stubborn.

A little exasperated, I tried once more. "For Christ's sake—Owen, will you tell him to say something to me? If I've done something wrong, the least he can do is tell me what it is."

Owen wasn't going to deviate from his brief, that much was obvious. He smirked and looked away, somewhat uncomfortable—but not to such a degree that it would prompt him to betray Johnny.

He didn't have to, though. Johnny had apparently had enough of giving me the silent treatment.

"What's wrong?" he spat. "Yer-you wer-want to know what's wrong? I'll ter-tell you what's wrong—yer-you're a sly, that's what's wrong."

A *sly?* I'd been called lots of things in my time, but this was the most surprising to date—especially coming from Johnny.

"A sly?" I said, quietly. "I'm a sly?"

"That's wer-what I said."

"And how did you work that one out?"

"I'd have ther-ther-thought that was obvious."

"Well it isn't." I was getting angry, now. So angry my eyes felt like they were going to pop out. "It isn't at all, so why don't you just tell me—*how did you work that one out?*"

I'd moved my wheelchair in close to his. I knew he wouldn't like this.

Johnny hated having his "sper-space invaded". He moved back a few inches, and I thought about closing the gap again—deciding it probably best if I left it for now. It was always a good idea to keep something in reserve.

"You want me to ter-tell you?"

"Yes. I want you to fucking tell me."

Johnny suddenly looked uncertain of himself. Normally so cock-sure, I didn't like to see him looking like that. It wasn't him. It wasn't the *real* him—the one that spat in the eye of God and death, and anything else that got in his way. When he blinked rapidly and fought hard to stare me out, even though it looked as if this was the last thing he wanted to do, I felt something pull coldly inside me, a cruel realisation that Johnny was nothing like it said on the cover. He wasn't the tough nut daring you to try to crack him. His shell was paper-thin, and only a mixture of grim denial and usually resilient bravado stopped it from tearing apart altogether.

I'd always known this, I suppose, but in that moment, it really hit home—it really hit home and I found myself faltering. Johnny was *dying*. I could see it, now. Everyone could. His torso was sinking into itself like a concertina pipe and just moving his arm onto the armrest so that he could steer his wheelchair using its joystick took far more effort and concentration than it once had. He was slipping away a cell at a time, a slow and highly visible passing, and I shouldn't be doing this to him. He was my mate. Probably the best mate I'd ever had. And he wouldn't be around forever. Sooner or later, he was going to pop his clogs, and then I'd be sorry for all the times I'd been a little shit to him.

"All rer-right," he said, "I'll tell you. You're a fake twat what der-drops his old mates when ner-new ones come along, and I wer-wer-want fuck all to do with you."

I knew what he was referring to immediately, of course. The past few days, even before I'd started chess club, had been fairly hectic during break times. I'd been hanging around Carrie a fair bit, ostensibly double-checking homework with her and helping her get her head around Pythagoras and his hypotenuse. I *had* seen Johnny, but they had been fleeting visits compared to our usual times together and I could certainly see how he might be pissed off.

Nevertheless, I wasn't prepared to let him talk to me like that. So what if he was dying? We were all dying and—who could say?—maybe I would die before him anyway. Stuff like that happened all the time. One minute here, the next minute discussing football scores with the worms. That was the way life worked, and if Johnny thought I was going to make concessions because he'd inherited the wrong faulty gene then he had another bloody thing coming.

"You want nothing to do with me?" I said.

"No."

"Good. Well that's just fine by me. If you can say shit like that about me without finding out what's been going on first then I want nowt to do with you either."

"I don't need to fer-find out," he told me. "I know."

"What do you know?"

Johnny knew nothing, but he wasn't about to admit it.

"I know per-plenty."

"Good for you. Like what?"

"Like you've been hanging around wer-with a *girl* when you could have ber-been seeing your mates."

Okay, so he knew more than I gave him credit for.

I took a deep breath and looked at Owen. He was staring at me quite sympathetically. He knew what Johnny was like. He'd probably discovered already just how much loyalty he demanded from his friends. Smiling tightly, making sure that Johnny didn't see, he gave a that's-the-way-it-goes twitch of the eyebrows.

"And it didn't occur to you to ask why I've been hanging around with a girl?" I said, trying to keep the moral high ground.

"I'm ner-not interested."

"No, you wouldn't be."

"What does that mer-mean?"

"Just that you don't care about the truth. You're only bothered about your version, not the real one—just like you've always been. But real-life isn't Captain Cook and Dracula, Johnny. Real-life does things differently to the way you pretend it is."

"Yer-you think I don't know that?" he said, solemnly.

Now I felt like a proper shit. The lowest of the low. I looked at him sitting there like that, all slumped and sullen, and I knew I should back off. Either I stopped now, or there was no telling where this would end.

"I don't know what you know," I said, my anger getting the better of me. "All I can see is someone who bends the truth to make himself feel better—and that's all right sometimes. We all do it. But it's not all right when you do it to make out that your mate's a sly."

"Yer-you weren't with a girl, ther-then?" I could see that bit about bending the truth had got to him. I was saying more and he knew it. Johnny might have been slow academically, but he sure as shit wasn't thick. He could read between the lines when he had to. But still he persisted. Still he had to push it.

"Yes," I said, "I was. Her name's Carrie and we're in the same class. I was helping her with her homework."

Owen sniggered, but I ignored him. It was all down to Johnny, now. However this turned out, I had no further say in it. We would be friends, or we wouldn't be friends—but nothing I could say or do would significantly alter the outcome. I looked at him and he looked at me. And finally he spoke.

"I her-hope you'll both be very happy together," he said.

It didn't help my introspective mood that in R.E. that afternoon we did Judas's betrayal of Jesus. I sat there at my desk, scratching my name onto its surface with the point of my compass, Matt beside me, as I listened to our teacher, Mr. Dawkins, go on about cocks crowing and Judas kissing the big J.C. on the cheek in the Garden of Gethsemane, and I couldn't help substitute myself and Johnny in the roles. Johnny was going to die to expunge the sins of all Humankind and I'd somehow helped facilitate that by betraying him. In such a light, it could almost be viewed as noble (even Judas had been specifically chosen; he was as blameless as Jesus himself, as far as I could see.) So why didn't it feel that way? Why did I feel like the biggest turd in the ocean, bobbing about merrily among all the far inferior pollution?

"What we need to ask ourselves," Mr. Dawkins was saying, "is why Jesus was so kindly towards Judas? Why was he so understanding and forgiving?"

"Because he was Jesus and that's what Jesus does," Alfie Limb said.

"Well, yes," Mr. Dawkins said. "But isn't there more to it than that?"

"The whole plan wouldn't have worked without Judas," I said. "No arrest, no crucifixion, no resurrection—nothing.

"Exactly," Mr. Dawkins said, enthusiastically. "Which brings us to the question of blame..."

Got there before you, I thought, putting the finishing touches to my carved name. *Who's to blame? Me for not going over the Resolution to see him often enough? Carrie for distracting me? Pythagoras, who never really had a lot to do with it, anyway? Or was it Johnny? Is this all about him wanting things to be a certain way, again, and doing everything in his power to see that it works out?*

I didn't know, and when Matt elbowed me and asked me what was wrong, I quietly told him that I'd had a fight with my best mate in the Resolution, and that I didn't know what to do about it.

"What was it over, this fight?" he said.

I didn't want to tell him. Telling felt like a further act of betrayal. Sitting there beside Matt, listening to Mr. Dawkins go on about Judas and Jesus, I thought of Johnny and how small he had seemed, sitting there in the physiotherapy room. It would have been the easiest thing in the world for me to have resented him for the demands he made of me but I couldn't—not then, and probably not ever, because the bottom line was that he was right. I had neglected him the minute new friends had come on the scene. It had been too easy for me to forget all about him over there in the Resolution, too easy for me to file him away with Tommy and all the other people I'd left behind and forgotten. I wasn't blameless. I'd made a friend who quite possibly already felt bad about his place in the world, about being left behind in the Resolution while kids like me moved on, feel even worse, and from my perspective that was just unforgivable.

I reluctantly told all this to Matt, and he listened kindly—agreeing that it was a horrible situation for Johnny, but also being quick to point out that it was difficult for me, too.

"I can't be in both schools at once," I said, and Matt nodded. "There are things I like doing over here, like chess club and stuff." I didn't mention watching Carrie on the trampoline. That didn't strike me as such a good idea. "I see him in physio, and at other times, too, but I can't be with him all the time. And it's not like he hasn't got other friends."

Matt had had an idea. I'd seen it as I'd been talking, lighting up his face with this bloody big grin that made me think of solar flares and summer days.

"What?" I said.

"Dead simple," he said. "I don't know why I didn't think of it sooner."

"What?" I repeated. I was a little alarmed. It felt odd seeing Matt looking all enthusiastic like this. In the short time I'd known him, it had never once occurred to me that he could be enthusiastic.

"You don't want to give up chess club, right?" he said.

"Right."

"Then don't. There's no need."

"There is if I don't want to lose Johnny as a mate."

"You're not looking at the whole board," Matt told me, grinning. "Think about it." I'd thought I had. Apparently my efforts weren't good enough, though. Matt rolled his eyes and added, "Bring him along to chess club. Mr. Roberson won't mind. In fact, he'll probably be glad of another member."

I wasn't sure. It sounded like a good idea on the surface—but I didn't even know if Johnny could play chess. "It could make matters worse," I explained. "If I ask him and he can't play, it might make him feel even more left behind."

"You're ashamed of him," Matt said, matter-of-factly. "You don't want to be seen with him over here in case it makes you look bad."

He couldn't have been further from the truth and I was quick to tell him so. Johnny was cool. He wasn't like the other kids in the Resolution. However many times I argued with him, nothing would ever change my opinion of him.

"He's a right laugh," I told Matt. "He's as good as anyone in Almsby. He knows it and I know it."

"Then invite him over, then."

~

It was a beautiful, unexpectedly warm day and Carl and I had decided to go down into the gardens to continue our talk, the two of us tired of the dayroom and its rather worrying smells.

Carl was dressed in a light hoodie and jogging pants. Expensive labels, I noticed as I parked his wheelchair beside a bench and applied the brakes, but definitely not the latest season. He cared, but somehow he didn't, I concluded. He wanted to be seen as just like you or me, but he wasn't about to put any more effort into it than was absolutely necessary.

Sitting down on the bench beside his wheelchair, I let out a breath, closing my eyes and tilting my face up to the sun. I knew he was looking at me. I could feel his eyes on me. So I stayed like that for a few moments longer than I otherwise would have, happy to be there with him like that, knowing there was no real rush.

"It shook me up when Matt said that to me," Carl told me, continuing where we had left off back on the ward, with Andrea dropping by every few minutes to see that we were "all right". "I mean, if he could think it, it wasn't that big a leap to imagine Johnny thinking it."

"And you weren't ashamed of him?" I said. I didn't want to push it, but I felt I had to; sometimes Carl seemed rather too good to be true. "It would be understandable in many ways. You were a kid and the pressures were new and many. Anyone might have felt that way."

Carl didn't dismiss the question out of hand, which was something of a relief. He thought about it, picking fluff off his joggers, and then said, "Don't think I haven't cross-examined myself on this one time and time again. I have. I know just how easy it is to fall into that trap of revising the past, and where my friendship with Johnny is concerned, I don't want to do that. Johnny was a special guy—oh, don't get me wrong, he was no saint—"

"Or no Jesus to your Judas?"

Carl laughed. "Quite right. He was a kid who didn't always understand things the way he liked to make out—but he was tough and he was real, and I can honestly say, hand on heart, that I was at no time, under any circumstances, ashamed to count him among my friends. Quite the opposite, in fact."

I liked listening to him talk about Johnny. When he spoke of his old friend I got a distinct sense of who Carl the boy had really been. Yes, it was still sometimes all too easy to doubt him—to see his responses as too perfect, too manufactured—but I was beginning to feel that that might actually have more to do with my own experience of the world than his. I listened to him and, perhaps quite naturally, I substituted my own feelings, my own slant on how the world and the people in it worked. It was my way of understanding his story, my way of empathising, but I supposed it was logical that I should get it wrong on occasion. I was still getting to know him. In many respects he was still a stranger to me. I couldn't know him completely. It was too much to ask of myself that I take everything he told me at face value. Our friendship was new and there were still hidden rooms to explore... and I suspected there always would be.

"How are you feeling, now?" I asked him, filling a lull in the conversation.

He nodded, an act of assessment rather than a positive expression. "Not too bad," he said. "I'm feeling stronger, my chest is loads better and..." he smiled wistfully... "my spirits are much improved."

"You aren't still in here just for the pneumonia, are you?" I said, on a bit of an impulse, which I immediately regretted. "I'm sorry," I quickly added. "Tell me to mind my own business. It's nothing to do with me."

Carl laughed and told me to shut up. "You want to know and I'm happy to tell you," he said, "so quit with the 'tell me to mind my own business' nonsense."

"Yes, sir." I saluted playfully and he shook his head, looking out over the gardens and smiling.

"I got myself in a bit of a state," he told me quietly. "Don't get me wrong. My life is and was pretty good. I could see that, but getting ill the way I did obscured it, somehow. I had things I wanted to do, but I just couldn't see a way of pulling myself together and getting on with it."

"Things you wanted to do?" I asked.

"I write. Novels. I'm quite close to securing a deal with an American publisher and there's a new project I have in development. So it was—*is*—

all looking quite promising. But the pneumonia... it just drained the ambition and purpose from me. I didn't see the point in any of it. Everything seemed fairly futile."

"Not good."

"No. Apparently it's reactive."

"So all you have to do is not get ill anymore," I said with a smile.

"Or learn to react more positively."

I folded my hands in my lap, wishing I'd brought my notebook with me. "Easier said than done." I shouldn't have said this. I saw that right away. He'd given something extra of himself and my inclination had been to do the same. But now I hoped he wouldn't follow through and question my statement. Now I hoped he would prove to be more self-absorbed than I'd given him credit for.

I really should have known better.

"The voice of experience?" he said, and I knew there was no going back now.

"Sort of," I said. "I had a pretty bad time at school and... it kind of persisted. Stayed with me, you know. It's only in the past five years or so that I've really learned to manage the insecurity."

"Depression?"

"Some of the time. Mostly it just manifested itself in an overwhelming sense of lack of worth. That's why this degree is so important to me, I suppose. It's helped me understand... well, let's just say it's helped me understand many things."

"A lot like me and my writing," he said. "So what kind of trouble did you have at school? Bullying?"

"Yes. It was relentless. For just about the whole five years of secondary school."

Carl made a sound, a sad little sigh that didn't seem quite right coming from him. It implied depletion and confusion, complete loss where solutions and wisdom should have been. "You think we'd have got it all worked out by now," he said. "Wouldn't you? All the experience we've had. And yet it all just keeps rolling along, more or less as it always has."

"You don't see much improvement, do you?" I said, glad to be able to steer the conversation away from me.

"Do you? Truthfully."

"I think things have got better in certain areas," I said.

"Example."

"I think..." I was already struggling, and his teasing grin told me he knew it... "I think there are more opportunities for kids today and I think, as a general rule, individual needs *are* catered for more than they once were."

"But still kids—far too many—slip through the net. Why is that still allowed to happen?"

"I haven't got all the answers, Carl," I said. "No one has."

"That's true. The problem I have with it all, however, is that in many cases the non-existent answers aren't the issue; there seems to be, from my point of view, a general unwillingness to ask the right questions."

It wasn't a new subject, we'd covered it peripherally a number of times over the past couple of weeks. Carl seemed to remember this and applied the brakes before he slipped into full rant-mode (an entertaining but time-consuming prospect.) Winking at me, he massaged his left knee and said, "Anyway, if I'd have gone to the same school as you, I'd have watched out for you."

"I'm sure you would have," I said. He would have been right there by my side, I knew, making sure everything was all right, just as he would have for Carrie.

Just as I suspected he would have for anyone.

~

I found him out on the cold playground by the cage—blowing his nose on a tartan handkerchief and looking reflective and arresting. Owen was nowhere to be seen, and I wondered if the two of them had had words. It wasn't totally inconceivable that Johnny wasn't only being temperamental with me, and I took it as a further sign to proceed with caution.

It felt odd being out there by the cage—and I didn't initially realise why. It took me a moment to see how much of a rarity this now actually was. Not only being out there by the dilapidated cage, but actually being on the playground at all. When I wasn't over Almsby, now, I was either in physio, or hanging about in the corridors—and I saw just how right Johnny was, how much I had inadvertently let slip away.

Approaching him tentatively, the other kids from the Resolution—poor, broken kids who hadn't yet realised it, I thought, and probably never would—shouting and laughing in the cold-edge distance, I wondered again if I was doing the right thing, if, perhaps, I wouldn't be better just leaving well alone. Johnny was entrenched, and just maybe the best thing I could do was write our friendship off altogether, let it go. It had been good while it had lasted, but now it could well be time for us to move on. We'd outgrown one another, I thought, and no amount of effort on my part was ever going to change that.

Johnny finally spotted me. First giving his nose one last wipe with the handkerchief, he then pushed it safely between his legs, tucked carefully under his balls in fairly typical Johnny fashion, and turned to face me.

"Ner-now then, stranger," he said—and I felt the grey winter morning brighten just a little. It was all going to be good. Unless I said something really bloody stupid, we were going to be mates again.

I parked my wheelchair beside his and we sat looking out over the school field together. We'd been to the bottom of that field, I remembered, even though it was strictly forbidden. All the way down to the beck and the trees that overhung it. A rare period of what had seemed absolute freedom, we had laughed along with Peter and Patrick, eating the packets of cheese and onion crisps we had brought with us and generally feeling like we'd just reached the summit of Everest without oxygen.

"Remember when we went down to the beck?" I said to him.

"I ger-got dog shit all over mer-mer-my wheels."

I grinned. "I forgot about that. We had to bring water out and wash them down cos Mrs. Shires wouldn't let you back in the school."

"Jer-just as well, really," he said. "It whiffed pretty bad."

"Would anyone have really noticed?" I said. "Since you smell like shit anyway."

It was a risky tactic, but if I knew Johnny as well as I believed, I thought it would pay off.

He glanced at me before turning his attention back to the field. "Bastard," he said, a mist of a smile playing on his lips—and I knew we were home and dry, right back where we belonged.

"I'm sorry about... you know," I said. "Not coming over enough to hang out and everything. It's just all been dead weird. Like I've been trying to fit in and... well, it's just been weird."

"Forget it. I wer-was a prat."

"It was wrong of me. You're my best mate."

"You've ster-ster-still gotta have other mates," he insisted—and though neither of us said as much, we both knew why.

"I was talking to Mr. Roberson," I said. "He's the teacher that takes chess club over Almsby. He sorta pushed me into joining. Anyway, he said you can join, too, if you want."

Johnny raised an eyebrow, and a chunk of heavy fringe shifted slightly in the wind. "Chess?" he said.

"There's no need to say it like that," I said, smiling nonetheless.

"Aye, I know, but cher-chess. That er-is what you said, right?"

"Yes. Don't you play?"

"Oh I play all right, ber-but I can't ser-say it's her-her-how I'd want to spend me free lunchtimes."

He had a point, I supposed. Truth be known, I was beginning to find it all a bit inhibiting and tedious. I liked Mr. Roberson and his obvious attempts at making me feel included, but there was only so much chess you could play before you started having peculiar dreams about queens and pawns. Plus Allen's simpering laugh was really beginning to get on my tits.

"So you don't want to join?" I said.

"Nah," he told me. "Apart from owt else, I'd only humiliate them with my mer-mating skills."

Chapter Ten: Sweet Rock Musical

We were listening to Elvis singing about Old Shep growing old and, truth be known, it was starting to wear on me just a little. Consequently, I reached for the switch of the Johnny's radio and turned it off, much to Johnny's annoyance.

"Hey," he said. "Wer-what you think you're doing? It was just getting to the good ber-bit."

"What good bit? It's *Old Shep*. As much as I like Elvis, there *is* no good bit."

"What about where he aims his ger-gun at Shep's head and ber-blows his brains out?"

"He doesn't do it. The wimp bottles it."

"Yer-you sure?"

"Positive."

Johnny, looking extremely disappointed, turned the radio back on and started to tune it to another station. "No one ler-listens to *Elvis* anymore, anyway," he said. "What we ner-need is some Gary Numan. That *Cars* is bloody brill."

We were in the corridor between schools. It was a glaringly bright day in February, spring still too far off for me to be deceived, and I was well into my third year in Almsby. The problems I had experienced in that first year had largely disappeared and I now found it all too easy to move between the schools without any sense of contradiction or betrayal—even though I was by this time, officially, fully integrated into Almsby, with my name on the register to prove it. By and large, however, break times found me in this in-between place, hanging out with Johnny and, quite often, Matt and Owen, listening to music and just being who we were. We shared no great spoken insights, our views were largely concerned with girls and what we'd like to do to them, but in our eyes no one could compete with us. We were not invincible, but we were right. Sitting there in that corridor, Carrie at the far end with Anna and her cronies, we had no doubt that the world around us was an off-kilter place of stupidity and Puritanism—a screwed-up realm that held no place for us that we actually wanted. Disaffected youth didn't come into it. We had lived through the whole anticlimactic punk scene and hadn't yet felt the need to be quite so pretentious. It was merely that we had found a relatively cool place on the fringes, and we were happy with it.

I put my hand up to my left earlobe, fingering the new gold stud that now adorned it. It felt good. A gentle two-fingers up at those who didn't see me the way I did—a distraction that worked remarkably well. Strictly speaking, it wasn't forbidden. Almsby was quite liberal in that respect. But I could tell that a few of the older teachers didn't much care for it. Which, of course, only added to the thrill.

"Wer-wer-we ought to be getting along," Johnny said, giving up on trying to find some Gary Numan and turning the radio back off.

"Eh?" I hadn't been listening. As well as thinking about my earring and the message it sent, I'd been looking down the corridor at Carrie. I'd known her about two and a half years, now, and the problem she caused me still hadn't got any easier. I wanted to, but I didn't want to. She made me, but so did others. I could, but there was no way I ever imagined that I would. I liked her, but I couldn't let her know how much. She had great tits, but I didn't care about that.

"I said," Johnny repeated, "we rer-really should be getting along. Ter-to physio... Jesus, Carl—why don't you just ask her?"

I heard that all right.

"Ask who what?"

"You know."

"I don't."

"Ther-that Carrie lass," he said. "You've fer-fer-fancied her for years."

"I—"

"And don't say yer-you haven't, cos I've seen you looking at her."

I very deliberately turned my back on Carrie. She still wasn't the best looking girl in the school, not by a long chalk—but as much as I fancied her in *that* way, it wasn't just about looks and what she had in her knickers (though the latter was pretty high up on the list.) I *liked* her. I enjoyed talking to her, just being quiet with her, even. She was a good mate, apart from anything else, and however much she might pull my leg on occasion, I always got the feeling that she'd help me out if I let her.

I thought about explaining all this to Johnny. He was a man of the world, after all—he would understand and sympathise. But, quite typically, I didn't. I instead bumped the side of my wheelchair against his and drove past him, saying, "Come on. Redfern'll give us all kinds of shit if we're late."

Behind me, I heard Johnny mutter something.

Neither Mrs. Redfern nor the new student physiotherapist (who me, Johnny and Owen had nicknamed Miss Hard-On, due to the extremely therapeutic effect she had on us) were there when we arrived. Owen was sitting glumly by the parallel bars sucking his teeth, but apart from him, the place was empty.

"You're eager," Johnny said to Owen. "Ther-thought we'd see you in the corridor."

"Weren't worth bothering by the time I got out of lunch," he said. "Did you see the queue? Bloody ridiculous, if you ask me. 'Bout time they did something about it. It's not like they have thousands to feed."

Everyone got the initial impression that Owen was a bit of a miserable, moany old bugger, but he wasn't—not really. He had this really cool, dry sense of humour that you sometimes had to really think about. It was cutting and precise, but I couldn't help wish he'd let it show a bit more.

Johnny listened to his gripe, going along with him—agreeing and sympathising, happy to have further proof that this world wasn't our equal. I, meanwhile, parked myself before the red mats (which hadn't been replaced since the Resolution had opened and, like everything else about the school, were starting to look a little the worse for wear) and thought about the Carrie problem.

It was all so simple, really, but for some reason I couldn't see it that way. I'd never had any trouble getting girlfriends in Swallowfields, so I really couldn't see why it would be any different now. Carrie liked me, I knew that. It might have taken a pair of thumbscrews and the threat of a dunking to get her to admit it in front of Anna and the other cackling witches, but there was no mistaking the smile that sometimes escaped when she was trying to be annoyed with me. She fancied me as much as I fancied her (*well, who wouldn't?*), so why didn't I just do what Johnny said? Bite the bullet and ask her.

"Now that *is* cool." I looked round, not quite able to place the voice. "Is it real gold?"

Mrs. Green was an old school hippy. The Resolution's music teacher, it had not been unusual in the early days to see her sitting cross-legged on the floor in the school hall, playing the sitar like a Sergeant Pepper reject or strumming away on an acoustic guitar singing *Kumbaya*. Montessori trained, she was a big believer in nurturing creativity in the individual, and every time I spoke with her (a very rare occurrence these days, sadly) I came away smiling, convinced that there was at least one teacher remaining in the Resolution (Mrs. Shires having left at Christmas) who understood that we were all unique individuals. With her long hair halfway down her back and her flowing print skirts, the bangles and beads that so often provided perambulatory musical accompaniment, she was an antidote to the more uptight teachers the Resolution now seemed to be attracting, and when she delicately touched my earlobe, admiring the earring, I grinned a little stupidly—happy to be the focus of her unique attention, however temporarily.

I told her that, yes, it was indeed gold—nothing but the best for me—and she nodded approvingly. "I've always marvelled at just how creative Nature can be when left to Her own devices," she said, sitting back on her haunches. "So much beauty for us to see, and yet we still need more. Don't you think that says something about the way we are?"

"Ner-never satisfied," Johnny contributed. He and Owen had joined us whilst Mrs. Green had been talking. "Always wer-wanting more, more, mer-more."

Mrs. Green chuckled at this, but I could tell Johnny's cynicism had unnerved her a bit. Hers was not a world where boys Johnny's age had such unforgiving perceptions of humanity. "Well," she said, "that wasn't quite where I was going with it. I was thinking more of our need to constantly add to the beauty we see around us, our appreciation driving us to enhance it further—always striving for the ultimate spiritual beauty... bringing the beauty from within out, so to speak."

Three blank faces stared back at her. I got what she was on about, but it was so nineteen sixty-nine that there was no way I was ever going to admit it. Owen's mouth hung open slightly, Johnny fiddled around with his balls—finally pulling out his tartan hanky and blowing his nose—and me... well, I tried a slight nod on for size, hoping it would make Mrs. Green feel a bit better without giving Johnny any ammunition. I actually found myself wishing Mrs. Redfern would arrive, just so this awkward moment might be over—that's how bad it was. But Mrs. Redfern was nowhere to be seen (I was, in fact, beginning to think that physio might have been cancelled and someone must have forgotten to tell us.)

"I'm glad I've seen the three of you, though," Mrs. Green said, changing the subject as quickly as possible. "I've been meaning to have a word."

"Wer-what about, Miss?" Johnny sounded relieved. He hadn't enjoyed the awkward silence as much as he once might have.

"Well..." she sat forward eagerly with her hands on her knees, "... I'm arranging a bit of a night out for some of the senior kids and I wondered if the three of you would be at all interested in coming along."

"A night out?" I said.

"The three of us?" Owen added.

"Where ter-to?" Johnny asked.

"Ah, well," Mrs. Green told us. "There's the thing, you see. My brother is a budding Andrew Lloyd Webber and he's written this sweet rock musical for the school where he works. It's a retelling of Solomon and Sheba."

"Wer-what's it called, Miss?"

"Solomon and Sheba."

"Oh."

"Anyway," she continued, "it's the final night a week on Friday and I have eight tickets. You'll need parental permission, of course, because the school's up Durham way and we won't be back until around midnight. But if your parents are okay with it and you want to come along—"

"Midnight?" Johnny said.

"Well, it's a long drive, you see, and the show doesn't finish till late."

Johnny looked first at me and then at Owen, grinning. "Wer-what do you reckon, lads?" he said.

"Sounds like a good night out," I said. "I like rock musicals."

"Me too," Mrs. Green said, patting my leg and looking loads more comfortable.

"It might be a laugh, I suppose," Owen said sullenly.

"Then you're interested?" Mrs. Green said, enthused but also rather amazed.

"Ah-absolutely," Johnny said. "Count us in."

I felt invigorated after our conversation with Mrs. Green—especially when, just as I'd suspected, Miss Hard-On came along to tell us that there would be no physiotherapy today because Mrs. Redfern had a migraine— and so broke away from Johnny and Owen at the earliest opportunity and went in search of Carrie.

She wasn't difficult to find. She never was. I always seemed to have an in-built instinct for where she would be. I'd tried a number of times to work out the logic behind it (were her moods dictated by the weather or was it something more prosaic?) so I could perhaps more easily understand that connection between us, but so far I'd never managed it. Nevertheless, I was once again anything but surprised when I went out onto the

Resolution's main playground and found her sitting, alone, on the low brick wall at its centre.

I stopped for a moment to think this through. She was alone. She was hardly ever alone. Was that intended to mean something, to *communicate* a finer truth—give me the *message*, should I only take the time to stop and think? I didn't believe in God even then, unless I wanted something really badly, but very briefly I entertained the notion that maybe this was His way of nudging me in the right direction. He'd provided me with the opportunity, but it was now up to me to help myself.

Shit or bust time. The moment that would separate the man from the boy, the wheat from the chaff, the... shit from the sugar.

Taking a deep breath, squaring my lopsided shoulders as best I could (I wasn't wearing my spinal brace... there was talk of me having an operation, but now was not the time to be thinking about *that*), I started over to her—knowing that she was already aware of me, but also knowing that she wouldn't turn and smile until the very last minute.

The whine of my wheelchair's motors was unmistakable, but when she did finally turn to look at me she still tried to look surprised. "I thought you were in physio," she said, rummaging about in her bag for something.

She was working on the English Lit homework we'd been set, I noticed. Steinbeck's *Of Mice and Men. How does Steinbeck present loneliness and isolation in the novel?*

"It's been cancelled," I said, nodding at the novel. "You're not doing that now, are you?"

"As good a time as any." She studied me for a moment, frowning, and then added. "I wanted an excuse to get away from Anna and those other friends of hers. They were being pains."

"Not like them," I said.

"You don't know."

"I was joking. I don't know how you put up with them. They're like the Weird Sisters in Macbeth—only there are more of them and they aren't as much fun."

"You're cruel." She let out a little laugh nevertheless and opened her notes on Steinbeck. "What do you make of this homework we've been set? I think it's way too difficult. Mr. Lance would never have set us anything this hard."

"Mr. Lance was a long time ago," I reminded her. "We wouldn't stand a chance if we were still being set the kind of homework he used to set us."

"True," she said. "It's still difficult, though, don't you think?"

140

"Not sure. I haven't really thought about it. I suppose it'll be easy enough when you've had a good read of your notes. That's what I always find."

I didn't want to be talking about Steinbeck and Lennie and those bloody rabbits. I had a job to do and I intended on seeing it through even if it killed me (which I sometimes thought it might). Carrie would waffle on about nothing all day if I let her, and it would be all too easy just to let her and go with the flow—but I couldn't afford to do that. If I did, lunch break would be over before I knew it. And it didn't take a genius to work that if I didn't get it done today, I probably never would.

"Good point," she said. "But your notes are probably better than mine. I always end up writing about the unimportant bits."

"There's something I want to ask you," I quickly said.

She stopped dead in mid-flow—which, given her track record, came as something of a surprise. The tone of my voice must have communicated the gravity of the situation. Either that or she was merely fed up of talking about Steinbeck, too.

"Sounds important," she said.

"It is," I told her—suddenly wishing physio hadn't been cancelled after all.

"Should I be sitting down?"

She was taking the piss, now, grinning mischievously, but I let it pass. "You are sitting down," I said.

"So I am. Silly me. So, you were saying you wanted to ask me something important."

"Yes."

"I'm listening."

And as far as I was concerned, she could just keep listening. She could listen for as long as she wanted, but she still wouldn't hear anything because my mouth had dried up and I was suddenly quite sure that I was utterly incapable of speaking. She could wait and listen and continue to look at me expectantly and do whatever the hell she wanted, but right at that moment I had no doubt that she was going to be disappointed.

Carrie's eyes softened ever so slightly. She could see I was struggling— and whilst a part of her seemed to find my predicament amusing, it was also apparent that she didn't want me to suffer too much. This and the way in which she quietly told me to take my time gave me the courage to proceed.

"I was wondering," I said, trying to work up some spit. "I was wondering... you and... well, we've been mates for... it's been a few..." I stopped and took a deep breath. If I kept on like this, she'd think I was a right sodding idiot. "Will you go out with me?" I suddenly blurted. "Will you be my girlfriend?"

There. It was done. Now all I had to do was sit back and wait for her to say no. I thought that even I could manage that.

A fine drizzle was starting to fall. Lunch break was almost over and in ten minutes' time I would be sitting next to Matt in double maths—the Herculean labour behind me, finally able to get on with the rest of my life knowing the rejection was in the past. The rain would fall more heavily, the afternoon would darken preternaturally, and all would be well with the world.

"Okay," Carrie said—and started putting her books away.

"What?" I hadn't heard her correctly. She hadn't said "okay" at all, she'd said "no way".

She looked up at me. I'd never noticed before what lovely dark eyes she had. They were more alive than anything I'd ever seen—and right then I was sure that Carrie Dunn would never grow old. That aliveness would remain in her eyes forever, while the rest of us grew jaded and forlorn.

"I said 'okay'," she repeated. "I'd like that."

"You sure?" It was a stupid thing to say, I knew—but it was at least two hours since the last stupid thing I'd said, so I figured I wasn't doing too badly.

"Of course I'm sure. Why? You having second thoughts already?"

"No. Not at all. I just thought you'd say no."

"You wanted me to say no, you mean?"

I shook my head and smiled. "No. I wanted you to say yes."

Standing up, she flung her bag over her shoulder and said, "Which I did. So stop fussing."

As we headed off to double maths together, I briefly wondered if I should hold her hand or something. It struck me as the right thing to do. But that would mean that people would see, and I wasn't sure she'd like that. I could have asked her, of course, but I wasn't actually convinced that I would like them seeing, either, so I didn't.

Instead, I did the only thing that occurred to me. I told her I needed a quick word with Johnny before maths, and went off to find him.

With little of the anticipated excitement, the night of the sweet rock musical arrived—and, staying back after school, eating there, Johnny, Owen and me started to question the wisdom of participating in this "night out". Sitting in the room where Mrs. Hoffman had once introduced me to the wonders of the six day timetable (something which had now finally been abolished), it dawned on us as we ate our sandwiches that we'd made one fundamental mistake when we'd so blithely accepted Mrs. Green's apparently kind invitation; we'd neglected to ask her who else would be going.

"Too ber-bloody late now," Johnny said, nibbling at a bit of crust with little appetite. "We'll just have to make the best of a bad job."

"I never thought she'd ask *them*," Owen mumbled. "They're the stupidest bunch in the school."

I couldn't help feeling that we were acting like right snobs—but Owen was dead right. At least two of the other three kids that Mrs. Green had invited were definitely candidates for the loony bin. From the little that I knew of them, it wasn't so much that they were thick or anything, it was more that they were *extraordinarily* silly. About the same age as Johnny and Owen, they behaved like daft seven year-olds.

"Kelly's okay," Johnny said. "She can't her-her-help the way she is." Owen and I quickly agreed. Kelly was still the same Kelly from way back in Mrs. Shires' day. No one could really dislike Kelly (though I still secretly wished she hadn't been coming with us.) "It's jer-just those other two. Pinky and fer-fucking Perky." Owen and I cracked up at this—Owen nearly choking on a bit of ham sandwich. "They just do me head in."

"With any luck we won't be sat with them," I said, a bit too optimistically.

"Like right," Johnny said. "Wer-when was the last time you went somewhere with a group of disabled kids and ger-got to sit wherever you wer-wanted?" He had a point. "We'll be penned in together jer-just like we always are. Like black people used to be in America—wer-with their own places on ber-ber-buses and stuff."

I wasn't sure that it was quite that bad, but I knew enough to know that it wasn't all that wise to argue with Johnny when he was being "political".

"Ask me," he said, pointing at some imaginary foe with his cheese and pickle butty, "there sher-should be a law against it. Same when yer-you go to the footy. They per-put all the fucking cripples together."

"On the field, judging by recent performance," Owen said—but Johnny ignored him.

"That's to do with safety and fire regulations and stuff," I pointed out.

"Bollocks. They're just too tight to sper-sper-spend money on finding a better way. It's ler-like, 'Oh, we'll just stick 'em there, that'll do.' Criminal."

"It's not like we could go in the Stands, though," Owen pointed out dryly. "They'd have to rename them the Sit and Stands, or something.

Don't got the same ring to it, do it?"

"Now you're just ber-being daft." Johnny chewed another mouthful of sandwich, slowly and methodically (looking as if he wished food had never been invented), and then added, "And wer-what's this Solomon and Sher-Sheba all about anyway? Is it some shit from the Bible or what?"

I shrugged. "There was a film on telly about them," I said, "but I never watched it. I think it was one of those with loads of sand in it, though, so it might have been out of the Bible."

"It's a love story, I think," Owen told him.

"Any sex?"

"I doubt it."

"A good stoning? Ser-someone always gets stoned in those Bible-type stories, rer-right?"

"Couldn't tell you."

"At least the music should be good," I said, trying to pick our spirits up before the evening was totally ruined. "A rock musical can't be all bad."

"A *sweet* rer-rock musical," Johnny reminded me. "Ner-now I don't know what that means exactly, ber-but I'm betting it's more Peters and Lee with electric guitars ther-than Ozzy Osbourne."

That was possibly the most disturbing image I'd encountered since Johnny had told me about this bloke who'd had such severe diarrhoea that he'd shat his lungs out—and I knew that if I didn't change the subject pretty quickly it would haunt me for the rest of the night.

"I might have to go into hospital soon," I said. (It was the first thing that came into my head; not exactly the most uplifting of subjects, for me, especially, it was nevertheless far better than thinking of Peters and Lee with rock guitar accompaniment.)

Johnny stopped eating. Not that he needed much of an excuse. "What fer-for?" I was surprised to hear genuine concern in his voice. I shouldn't have been, but I was.

"I might be having an operation on me back. To straighten it. I have to have tests and everything first, to see if I'm up to it, but I sort of think I will be."

"Scared?"

"A bit."

"You'll be fer-fine," Johnny assured me. "You're tough ler-like me. Der-don't make 'em like us no more."

Owen snorted. "Thank fuck," he said.

Johnny stuck two fingers up at him (I noticed that, however hard he might try to conceal it, even this was now a struggle for him) and just as I was about to tell them the details of the operation I was probably going to be having—Johnny was fascinated by details of that kind—Mrs. Green popped her head round the corner. It seemed it was time for us to be going.

"If you want to be there for curtain up," she said, "we better get our skates on."

Dutifully, we disposed of what was left of our sandwiches and their wrapping and followed her along the corridor. I didn't know how Johnny and Owen were feeling (though I suspected their hearts were no longer in this), but I didn't want to be there anymore. I could have been at home, eating a proper tea and then going out somewhere with Mam and Dad—maybe to play on the Space Invader machines at Redcar or just for a drive around in the dark, which I always enjoyed. Even if we'd just stayed in and watched telly, I got the distinct impression that it would be better than this, especially if there was a good film on. Mrs. Green talked enthusiastically and as we got onto the school bus, the whining, straining wheelchair lift at the rear not exactly filling me with confidence, I realised that she wasn't all that convinced that this evening was going to be as good as she'd hoped herself. She told us how hard her brother had worked, how talented he was and how proud she was of him—and, as Mrs. Alexander (driving the bus again, just like all those years ago on our memorable trip to Whitby) pulled out of the school gates, she sat down near me, Johnny and Owen with a sigh like a tooth ache and said, "He's a lovely boy. Life hasn't always been good to him. He deserves this success."

A school play, I thought. *If that's her idea of success she really needs to open her eyes a bit more.* But I didn't say anything. It didn't seem right somehow.

It was just a comprehensive school—much like Almsby, much like any other. The school hall packed with kids and adults, Mrs. Green herded us, like the injured sheep we were no doubt imagined to be, to our places over to one side of the hall. Pinky and Perky giggled and whispered and Kelly made her by now world famous hamster in a lawnmower noise—and as I watched, Johnny seemed to grow even smaller. I knew how he felt. It was as if we were on show, stuck over to one side of the hall like that, and Pinky and Perky (it was hard to also blame Kelly, but, in truth, we managed okay) weren't making it any easier. However good this sweet rock musical was going to be—however talented Mrs. Green's brother—there was no doubt in my mind that it was going to have to be a pretty special production to take our minds off our discomfort. It would have to be nothing short of Royal Variety Performance standard, in my opinion.

"Remind mer-me not to come to anything like this again," Johnny whispered to me.

"Me too," Owen said, frowning at Pinky and Perky, who were talking animatedly about how exciting this was. "Anyone'd think they'd never been nowhere before."

"Maybe they haven't," I said. "Let's face it, if they were *your* daughters, would *you* want to be seen out with them?"

Johnny seemed to enjoy this. Chuckling, he, much more discretely than usual, removed his hanky from beneath his balls and dabbed at his nose and eyes, nodding a little. Owen gave me his biggest smile (which, admittedly, wasn't *all* that big) and said that he reckoned I had a point.

"If they were mine," he said with a noticeable shudder, "I'd keep them chained up in the cellar."

"Her-have you got a cellar, then?" Johnny said.

"I'd have one dug especially."

From the front of the hall, behind the stage curtain, there came the sound of an electric guitar fanfare and the main lights went out. I felt a tingle of expectation up and down my arms. Maybe this wasn't going to be so bad after all. Now that the lights were out I didn't feel as if I was quite so on display, sitting there with the suddenly silent Pinky and Perky—and that apart, those bloody guitars sounded amazing. It was nothing like Mrs. Green's acoustic guitar playing, as good as that was, and it didn't take a genius to see that this evening had musical potential, at least. However shitty the acting might be (they were school kids, so I wasn't expecting too much), the music was looking like it was going to be pretty cool.

I wasn't disappointed. The music, whilst lyrically a little lame ("Solomon / oh what a man", for example), was a blood-pumping delight and the acting, whilst patchy, was adequate. Today, the plot is difficult to recall. If memory serves me well, I don't think there was actually that much of it. But that didn't matter because Johnny, Owen and I were caught up in the music and captivated by the rare beauty that was Sheba.

She was simply stunning—and when she came on stage, set in a soft-amber light, I thought of Carrie for the first time that night. Carrie my girlfriend. Carrie, the girl I should have wanted here with me tonight, but, I realised, didn't. Carrie, a world apart from the girl playing Sheba.

Johnny and Owen were as enraptured as me. One look at them with their mouths open whenever she was on stage was more than enough to see that. She had a real presence (an acting ability that was as skilled and refined as any of the Hollywood greats) and legs that went... well, all the way up. Without my really wishing it, Carrie was revealed for the very ordinary girl that she was whilst the girl playing Sheba was everything a boy my age could have wished for, with a side order of something I couldn't quite put my finger on but which I suspected might have had something to do with the sensitivity she showed when she sang—a look I imagined I saw in her eyes when she mellifluously uttered the words "my heart is torn". I wanted to ask Johnny or Owen if they'd seen it, too, but I got the very real impression that they wouldn't hear a word I said until the show was over, and even then I suspected I would have to shout *really* loud.

Towards the end of the show, Kelly, for some unknown reason, started to get even more excited and had to be taken out, squealing and twitching, by Mrs. Alexander. I watched her go, wondering if she was having some kind of fit but nonetheless glad to see the back of her. She was really distracting. Even Pinky and Perky had shut up, now, and Kelly's hamster-in-a-lawnmower squeaks had seemed all the louder because of this. Once she was gone, however, I settled into my wheelchair more completely, sitting back and really enjoying the third and final act—applauding loudly along with everyone else when the final curtain fell.

"Wow," Johnny said, "ther-that was bloody good."

"That Sheba was a bit of all right," Owen added.

"The music was the best part," I insisted, and they looked at me as if I'd just said that I'd like to shag Maggie Thatcher. "All right," I conceded, with a grin, "the second-best part."

"That's mer-more like it. You her-had me worried for a minute there."

"I liked the part where she did that dance," Owen whispered. "The outfit she wore looked like it was going to fall off at any minute."

I'd stopped listening to them. I was thinking about Carrie again. Now that the lights were up, I could see loads of pretty girls—girls who could never have matched the beauty of Sheba, of course, but who were nonetheless very attractive. I smiled at a few of them when they looked at me. I'd never really smiled all that much at girls I didn't know, and it struck me as a bit of an interesting experiment—the result pleasantly surprising. Most smiled back at me and one or two even blushed as well. Very promising, I thought, their responses prompting me to think that my Carrie doubts—the wavering that had resulted in my taking over two years to ask her to go out with me—actually might have a very good and solid foundation.

"I'm too young to get tied down," I said, very gravely, to myself, and Johnny turned and looked at me.

"What?"

"Nothing."

"You said ser-something."

"I was talking to myself."

"They lock you up for that," Owen said.

"What were yer-you talking to yourself about?"

"Nothing."

"Didn't sound like nothing."

"Well it was."

"Ser-sounded to me like you were ser-saying you're too young to get tied down."

"You misheard me."

"If you say so," he said. "Don't think I did, though. Ask mer-me, you're having second thoughts about ther-that Carrie lass."

"And what if I am?"

Johnny shrugged. "Jer-just that, in my opinion, it's about ber-bloody time. She's nice enough, ber-ber-but I reckon you can do better."

Dropping the defensiveness, I said, "Do you think so?"

"Absolutely. What do you think, Owen?"

"About what?"

"Carl and ther-that Carrie lass. Can he der-do better or what?"

Owen couldn't have cared less. "I suppose so," he said. "I'd give her one," he added, obviously feeling something more was required of him, "but I wouldn't much fancy going out with her."

Johnny seemed satisfied with this. He turned back to me and said, "See? Wer-what more is there to say? Your two best mates ther-think you're too good for her."

"I wouldn't want to hurt her feelings, though."

"Sher-shoulda thought of that before you asked her out."

He was right, of course, and if I'd allowed myself to dwell on it for too long it might have spoiled the evening. As it was, I turned my attention back to thoughts of Sheba and how stunning she had looked, and by the time Mrs. Green came over to introduce me to her denim and AC/DC T-shirt clad brother, all but the last, lingering remnant of Carrie-thought had been well and truly expelled.

"This is Toby, my brother," Mrs. Green told me, and I smiled and offered my hand to be shaken, just like Dad had shown me. "Toby, this is Carl. I was telling you about him, remember?"

"Our prospective Pip," he said, flicking his long hair out of his eyes. "I see *exactly* what you mean, sis. The perfect look."

"I thought you'd agree."

"The earring will have to go, of course."

I didn't have a clue what they were going on about, but this really caught my attention. I didn't care how cool he was, the earring was staying and if he thought I was going to take it out for him or anyone else, *for whatever reason*, he had another bloody thing coming.

The horror at such an unreasonable prospect must have shown on my face because Toby started laughing. Gently slapping my shoulder while Mrs. Green grinned at him, he said, "Only kidding, mate. I like it. It rocks. Been meaning to get one myself but I've never got round to it."

"What did you mean, 'prospective Pip'?" I said.

Mrs. Green and Toby exchanged a knowing glance that troubled me right away. I had no idea what they were up to but the fact that it so clearly concerned me—that they'd been *talking* about me, for heaven's sake—caused an ominous stirring deep down in my bowels. Either there was danger ahead, I thought, or I was about to drop one.

"Ah, that," Toby said. "Yes." He looked at his sister, cueing her in.

"I was going to discuss it with you on the journey home," she told me. "It's really very exciting… there's really nothing for you to look so worried about, Carl."

I was, naturally, going to take some convincing.

"Toby," she explained, glancing proudly at her brother, "has another masterpiece in the pipeline. Bet you can't guess what it is."

"A sweet rer-rock musical," Johnny ventured—never one to be left out of the conversation.

"Well, yes," Mrs. Green said. "That goes very much without saying. But I was thinking more of the story. Can you guess what the story's going to be?"

The other people in the school hall were milling out around us, some lingering by the stage—talking in whispered clusters to members of the cast, sons and daughters one and all. Pip, I thought. That really wasn't too difficult. There were only two fictional Pips that I'd ever heard of. One was from Bradbury's *The Halloween Tree*. The elusive Pipkin that Tom and the rest of the boys have to save. And the other—the far more likely of the two, in my opinion—had to be from—

"Dickens' *Great Expectations*," I said, and Toby and Mrs. Green did that looking-at-each-other thing again, all congratulatory smiles and informed nods.

"If that was a nail," Toby informed me, "you'd have just hit it square on the head."

"And you want me to be Pip?"

"There he goes again, sis! Nail head *wallop!*"

"Not *quite*," Mrs. Green said, "but almost. We'd like you to audition for the part, along with everyone else. That's the fair way of doing it, you see, and... well, we won't be sure if you're right for the part until we've seen you, you know?"

"That's if you're interested, of course," Toby added, and Mrs. Green fired him a look that could have burned a hole through six inches of steel.

"Of course he's interested," she said, before turning to me and saying, "aren't you?"

I liked books. Everyone who knew me was aware of that. I liked books and I liked film and telly. Sitting and reading, watching an old Hammer horror movie, this was my idea of a pretty perfect night—and, yes, sometimes I imagined myself in an active role, Van Helsing slaying Dracula (again) or some hithertofore unknown (even to Dickens himself) hero, striding into *The Old Curiosity Shop* and whisking Little Nell away from it all before she had chance to pop her clogs. But, really, I'd always thought of myself as more of a watcher than a performer. Even when I was being creative, I liked to do it in a way that allowed me to hide—writing stories about people I would never be... people I would never truly *want* to be. Acting was something different. Yes, it involved pretending to be someone else, much like writing—hiding behind character and costume—but you still had to put yourself right out there on stage, in front of everyone. I knew I could do that, if I really had to, but I wasn't entirely sure that I wanted to.

"Some of the actors from tonight are going to be in it," Toby cleverly added. "Myfanwy, the girl who played the Queen of Sheba, she'll be taking on the role of Estella, and—"

"I'm interested," I said. "It sounds like a great play, I'd love to try out for it."

"Me, too," Johnny said.

"And me," Owen added.

Estella. *I mean*, I thought to myself. Estella. *She's a right bitch, but doesn't Pip get to kiss her? Or did I imagine that? Either way, I'll be, like, dead close to her. We'll get to know each other. We'll become friends. She'll teach me Welsh (because with a name like Myfanwy she just has to be Welsh) and I'll teach her to... well, I'll think of something, and...*

Mrs. Green was speaking to me. She'd taken me to one side whilst Toby talked to Johnny and Owen about their favourite music. I'd been that busy thinking about the Myfanwy possibilities, however, that I'd completely missed what it was she was saying.

"Sorry, Miss?"

"I've got a script on the bus," she repeated. "If you want, I'll let you borrow it over the weekend, see what you think."

I smiled and nodded. She really wanted me to have a crack at this. How good was that?

"Pip is a very multi-dimensional character," she told me. "We need someone who can play him when he's young and when he's old. You've read the book, right?"

Again, I nodded... and then shook my head, just managing to push the lie aside before it got right in my face and convinced me it was true. "I've seen the film, though," I told her. "The black and white one with John Mills."

"Good enough," she said. "In fact the film probably shows better than the book the huge task the person playing Pip will have before them."

"Can't we have different people playing him at different ages?" I suggested. "Like in the film?"

"We could, but Toby doesn't want that. He believes that it's different when you're producing something for the stage. You need to work really hard at keeping a connection with the audience—and he says that's nigh on impossible if you switch your leading actor halfway through."

Mrs. Green didn't sound completely convinced, and I thought I sort of agreed with her. She looked around at the almost empty hall and then seemed to rouse herself, remembering her primary role in all of this.

"Okay," she said. "We better find Kelly and Mrs. Alexander and be getting ourselves home."

~

"I spent the weekend learning every part, word perfect," he told me. "The more I thought about it, the more I wanted to do this—and not just because of Myfanwy, either, although I would have never admitted that to Johnny and Owen. I suppose, deep down, it was something I'd always secretly wanted to do."

"A closet drama queen?" I said, having a sudden image of him backstage, slamming doors and throwing vases of flowers at members of the supporting cast.

"Not quite," he said. "On stage or off." The sun was somewhat stronger today and he turned his face away from it to look at me, a little flushed. "It was the singing that appealed to me more than anything. I'd always enjoyed it, since I was a toddler—singing along with the Beatles, Elvis, Little Jimmy Osmond, you name 'em—but I never really knew if I had a good voice. This was the perfect opportunity for me to find out, and

I was determined that I wasn't going to balls the audition up."

As I sat listening to him, I thought about the story he had just shared with me, how he had got the girl (an able-bodied, non-disabled girl, I noted) only to notice, as if he hadn't before, that there were lots more girls out there, some of them far prettier than Carrie, who I was already feeling sorry for (this couldn't end other than badly for her). He hadn't been a bad boy, I thought, but I was beginning to amend my too-good-to-be-true assessment of him. His attitude to the disabled girls watching the show with them, for example. That kind of cock-eyed snobbery bothered me, and, judging by the way his voice faltered, it bothered him, too. Pinky and Perky, and Kelly, had just been girls enjoying themselves, excited at the prospect of a fun night out. Something that was no doubt a rare event for them. Carl, Johnny and Owen had judged the girls and found them wanting, and when I put that together with Carl asking Carrie out, I couldn't help feeling that there was something more complicated going on here.

"You didn't think much of disabled girls, did you?" I said, rather more bluntly than I'd intended.

Carl studied me. I thought for a moment he was going to respond angrily. The little muscles twitched in his jaw and his eyes narrowed. And then the moment passed.

"I was never attracted to them, if that's what you mean," he said. "Or, rather, I'd never met one at that point that I'd found attractive." He paused, mulling over how best to say what he next had to say. "It isn't about the disability," he insisted. "It's about the girls. Pinky and Perky are a bad example. The girls in the Resolution were nice enough, but you could have counted the ones that were my age on one hand. Almsby was different. And Swallowfields. Swallowfields, especially. There were more girls, and, yes, there was a statistically much higher proportion of pretty girls than there was in the Resolution—but that doesn't mean that if there'd been a pretty girl in a wheelchair that I'd liked that I'd have had nothing to do with her."

"Really?"

He almost let his annoyance show. "Really," he said, before adding, "You aren't all that good at believing me sometimes, are you?"

He said it in such a way, softly and with the merest hint of regret, that I felt immediately guilty.

"It just doesn't look all that good from where I'm sitting," I said, determined to be straight with him. "I mean, I know you were just a boy, but your attitude to those three girls was—"

"Honest," he told me. "But I think you've inadvertently hit the nail on the head. Our attitude was directed at the *girls*, at the way they *acted*, not their disabilities. Kelly was different. We tried not to get annoyed with her because we knew she couldn't help it. The other two, though, they *could* help it. They were silly and they drew attention to themselves and to us. That was the problem we had with them. It had nothing to do with their disabilities—except, maybe, insofar as we didn't want people thinking that all kids with disabilities were silly."

"I see," I said, glad that I'd asked but also annoyed with myself for not guessing that Carl's explanation would show me up for the silly girl I no doubt was. "I'm sorry if—"

He silenced me with a shake of the head and a smile. "It was a good question," he said.

I thought he was being rather too generous, but I wasn't about to argue with him. I felt foolish. Not quite as foolish as I might have had he not been the man he was, but foolish nonetheless. I continued returning to the notion that "disability" was central to his story, the Resolution sitting between the two mainstream schools his own personal metaphor, but it wasn't, and it struck me as a little ridiculous that I still had to be reminded of that.

After all this time, I really should have known better.

~

It had been a weekend of ease and fun, of last-minute homework and long evenings reading the script of *Great Expectations*. Saturday afternoon had been a typical adventure spent with my cousin and his friends, hanging around the flats and maisonettes near where he lived—and when I returned to school on Monday morning, I did so with a whole treasure trove of things to talk about, even without the show of Friday night. I felt filled with expectation (appropriately), and even thoughts of the operation I probably had ahead of me couldn't dampen my spirits.

The first person I went in search of at break time was Carrie. I didn't rightly know why, since I was having very definite second thoughts about "us", but I did anyway—maybe as a way of testing my doubts, but more than likely because I knew she'd be excited about the play.

I found her in the corridor with Anna and the Weird Sisters, looking bored and somewhat distracted. When she saw me, she jumped down from her seat on the wooden, chest-height "bar" that spanned the windowed side of the corridor and followed me outside.

It was cold and she shivered. I thought of offering her my coat since I wasn't wearing it and it seemed the gentlemanly thing to do, but I couldn't really be bothered. It would only mean that I'd have to remember to get it back from her, and right now I had a lot on my mind. I was likely to forget.

"How was it?" We were by the cage. It creaked as she leaned back against it. "The play," she said, when I stared back blankly at her.

"Good," I told her, feeling on show again and unexpectedly uncomfortable. "It was... it was better than I thought."

"What was it about?"

"Solomon and Sheba."

"Well, yes," she rolled her eyes, "you told me that much. But what was it *about*? What *happened*?"

Matt, Johnny and Owen were over by one of the doors into the Resolution and as I glanced in their direction, I couldn't help but wish that I were with them. Remembering Johnny and Owen's conclusions regarding my "relationship" with Carrie, it struck me again that they were right and that by attempting to talk to her like this I was merely putting off the moment when I would have to end it, when I would have to hurt her. It didn't seem fair. None of it. But what option did I have? As far as I could see, the least I could do was let the poor girl down easily.

"It was kind of a love story," I told her, wishing that it hadn't been. "More or less. There wasn't a lot of story, to tell you the truth. It was more singing and dancing than anything else."

"Sounds okay, I suppose." She was as bored with me as she had been with Anna and the Weird Sister.

"That wasn't the best bit though," I told her, trying to make it sound a lot more exciting than I supposed it was (why did I still feel the need to impress her?) "You know Mrs. Green?"

She shook her head.

"She's the music teacher in the Resolution," I said. "It was her brother who wrote the Solomon and Sheba play thing."

"She the hippy?"

"Yes."

Nodding, she said, "I know who you mean, then. What about her?"

"Her brother's doing a musical version of *Great Expectations* and they've asked me to audition for the part of Pip. They sounded really keen to have me do it but, you know, they have to be seen to be doing it properly and everything."

"That's cool." She didn't sound all that impressed—but, then, she very rarely did. "And you're going to do it?"

I shrugged, suddenly not as enthusiastic about it as I had been. She was like one of Johnny's bloody vampires, sucking all the good thoughts the right fuck out of me.

"Be silly not to, really," I said. "It sounds like too good of an opportunity to miss." I thought again of Myfanwy, of the amber glow that had surrounded her on stage, how I would get to kiss her and, after the show, celebrate our success in ways I didn't even dare imagine. "Plus I think it'll be fun," I added. "These things always are."

She didn't look all that convinced, and, frankly, I couldn't really have cared less. Making my excuses (I told her I had to help Johnny with "something"), I said goodbye to her and joined my three friends—sighing deeply to let them know what hard work this whole boyfriend/girlfriend thing could be.

"Ber-bad?" Johnny said.

"Not good."

"She pissed off wer-with you about summat?"

"No," I said. "It's worse than that."

"How?" Matt said.

Shrugging, I said, "I dunno. We just can't talk to each other the way we used to. She's not as much of a laugh as she used to be."

"Cher-chuck her," Johnny advised. "You can't be der-doing with that. Life's too short. I bet she hasn't even let yer-you finger her, right?"

I didn't say anything. It was none of his business. Talking about her like that wasn't right and I wasn't going to join in with it. Maybe she *was* a crap girlfriend, but she was still a good mate, and Johnny really should have known better.

He was right, though. She hadn't.

When the bell went for the end of break, Matt and I left Johnny and Owen and headed off to English.

"It's nowt to do with them," he reminded me. "If you want to keep going out with her, you should."

"That's just it, though," I told him. "I don't think I do. I *really* don't think I do."

"Then do something about it."

That afternoon, as I was passing through the Resolution—looking forward to getting on the bus and getting home, where life always seemed far less complicated and, well, *safer*—Mrs. Green caught me and asked if she could have a word.

Taking me into an empty classroom, I realised she wasn't her usual self. She looked glum and constipated—in need of a good physic, as my gran would have said. I knew something was wrong right away. It was probably something to do with her letting me see the script. I was guessing it wasn't the final draft and, I presumed, Toby had found out that she'd given me a copy and gone stark raving bonkers, the way artistic types were apt to do.

But that wasn't it.

That wasn't it *at all*.

"I've been speaking to Mr. Johnson," Mrs. Green said. Her voice seemed especially toneless today. Far from its usual musical self. Even her bangles and beads didn't seem in the mood to tinkle and jangle. "It's not good news I'm afraid."

"The play's been cancelled?"

She shook her head.

What Mrs. Green was about to tell me would change the way I viewed things for a long time to come—perhaps even forever. As I sat there and listened to what she had to say, I couldn't quite believe what I was hearing. It was initially confusing. It was unfair. It was ridiculous. No one in his right mind could have actually *said* that to her, surely.

"I'm afraid you can't be in the play," she said—with genuine regret. "You can't even audition for it." She took a breath and, sitting down on the edge of a table, looked at me gravely. "Mr. Johnson caught me in the staff room. Apparently he'd heard me mention that you were really looking forward to auditioning. He pointed out that you're fully integrated, now, that you're, as he put it, 'no longer a member of this school' and said it was simply out of the question that you should have any involvement in this production. And, as much as I regret it, I'm afraid I have to abide by that."

I was speechless. Mrs. Green continued to look at me with a mix of sympathy and apprehension for a few moments longer, and then she got to her feet. "Try not to take it to heart, Carl," she told me. "You're a clever and talented lad. You'll have plenty of opportunities to prove what you can do in the years to come. Just don't let this put you off trying. Silly stuff like this happens all the time but we can't give up. We really can't."

Once she'd left, it occurred to me that maybe Mrs. Green needed to take some of her own advice. Whatever I imagined she would say in her own defence, it struck me that she had given up—that she had just accepted what Mr. Johnson had said without any thought of fighting for what was good and right. Then it occurred to me that I was maybe being a little ungenerous. What was she, after all, but a music teacher without one single aggressive bone in her body? How could I expect her to argue my case—to fight for me—especially when I probably didn't even have one? She had been placed in a horrible position. A decision all but made, she had been forced to reverse it and lose face with one of her (former) pupils. Mr. Johnson—the rigid, self-righteous little prick that he was—had spoken, and anyone who knew him would have quickly agreed that arguing with him would be futile. He knew he was right, even when he was wrong (which was most of the time), and any attempt to sway him would be met with pig-headedness and a reminder of who they were talking to. No, I couldn't be angry with Mrs. Green.

I couldn't be angry with her at all.

But I could be angry with Mr. Johnson.

On the bus home, sitting at the front, near the driver and the escort, I thought of all the gossip I'd heard about him over the years—all the stuff that possibly wasn't true, but just might be. Could I use any of it to work this in my favour, I wondered, or would it all blow up in my face and make me look like the silly, naïve child I no doubt was?

It wasn't worth it, I thought, suddenly more tired than I'd ever been in my life. He was a fool and all I could really do was make sure that everyone knew it. The decision was petty and too inflexible—and I would tell everyone I knew all the pathetic details. That was revenge enough...

... in this case, at least.

~

"That *was* ridiculous," I said, angered by the injustice of it.

"Integration was just another form of exclusion," Carl said, the sardonic smile with which I was already very familiar playing across his full lips again. "The funny thing is, I'd have put money—still would—on him believing it was the right thing to do. A 'can't have his cake and eat it' lesson."

"Well he'd have been wrong."

"Indeed. I could never have participated in anything like that in Almsby. Rehearsals for plays and concerts were always after school affairs over there, and I always had to catch the bus. So without the chance of taking part in the Resolution's productions, it was an avenue that was pretty much completely closed to me."

"You should have argued your case," I said. "Had a word with your form teacher and told him that."

Carl shrugged. "I should have done a lot of things, I suppose," he said. "But I was a kid. A kid with, perhaps, a slightly above average intelligence, but a kid nonetheless. On the whole, I just wanted to keep my head down and get through the whole school thing without drawing too much attention to myself one way or the other."

"Hence your wanting to be in the production of *Great Expectations.*"

"If you remember," he chuckled, "that had more to do with Myfanwy than any real wish to participate."

"Did you ever get to kiss her?" I knew I was jumping ahead, but it suddenly seemed important. I wanted Carl to get his kiss from Myfanwy. I wanted that chapter of his life properly closed so that he could get on with the rest of it without having to think about all the what-ifs. I knew about what-ifs. I'd had a whole circus of what-ifs, in my time, and they'd done nothing but hold me back until I'd succeeded in shaking them. I didn't want that for Carl. He deserved better.

Smiling a sweet, sad smile, Carl tilted his head back and watched the clouds coming in from the north. "No," he said, "I never got to kiss her."

Chapter Eleven: The Show Must Go On

I hadn't been paying attention. Preoccupied with thoughts of what I had done to Carrie, how cruel and cowardly it had been of me to finish with her by sending her a message via Anna, Matt's words had just gone in one ear and out of the other. Our teacher, Mr. Marks, had rambled on about Brownian motion or something equally mundane, and I had drifted, lulled by his soporific rhythm, wondering how Carrie was feeling and if she would ever speak to me again, and when Matt had spoken in a whisper, his head low to the desk, pretending to make notes, his words had barely registered. I looked at him, face blank and at a complete loss, and when he repeated what he had said, I tried to pay more attention.

"I said," he said, "are you coming to chess club after lunch?"

I was tired of chess club. I had been for a very long time. There were only so many ways you could lose graciously before it became a bit tedious. But even if it had still been my favourite pastime in the whole world, I doubted very much that I'd be able to attend today.

"Why?"

"It's Johnny," I told him.

"He being a little shit again?"

"No. He's dying."

Matt thought I was joking. He started to tell me, chuckling quietly, that I was "one right sick fuck", and then stopped—studying my set face before saying, "You're not joking, are you?"

I shook my head. "He mightn't be about to die right now," I told him. "But he's definitely getting a lot worse. The past couple of months, since that play we went to... well, you can just see it. He's ill more and... you only have to look at him."

"Isn't there owt they can do for him?"

"No. It's incurable. They can treat his chest infections with antibiotics and stuff, but sooner or later his heart'll just pack up under the strain, I expect."

"Shit." Matt looked at me out of the corner of his eye, trying to figure something out. I thought I knew what he was going to say. In many ways, it was only natural. "But don't you and him have...?"

I shook my head before he could say anymore. "He has Muscular Dystrophy. I have Spinal Muscular Atrophy."

"And yours isn't as bad as what he's got?"

"It can be worse. It can kill you when you're a baby, if it's bad enough. But if it doesn't get you then and it hasn't done too much damage... no, it's not as bad as what he's got. Not for me."

"So you're not...?"

"No. I can live as long as you, they reckon."

"That's lucky."

"Aye. Unless you get hit by a bus tomorrow."

"I'll make sure to stop, look and listen."

"I'd appreciate it."

Mr. Marks wasn't talking about Brownian motion after all. He was talking about cell division. I thought. As decent and gentle a bloke as Mr. Marks was, he was possibly the most long-winded and uninspiring teacher I'd ever encountered. I wouldn't have minded betting that there were coma patients out there somewhere with more get up and go. As my dad would have said, he could have talked a glass eye to sleep.

"So this is it?" Matt said. "With Johnny? He's, like, *nearing the end?*"

He made it sound like a marathon race—a marathon race or something just as heroic.

"I don't know," I said, honestly. "He's bad, though. Worse than I've ever seen him."

"So you won't be going to chess club?"

"No."

"Me neither, then. I'll come and see him with you." He thought about this for a moment and then added, "If that's all right with you, I mean."

Johnny was the best mate I'd ever had. We understood each other in ways that, even now, are difficult to describe. He watched my back and I watched his. But now it was, at times, difficult being around him. To see him like that wasn't good. Even though the fight was still there, just, it was plain to see that the final battle of the long war was close to being lost—and to witness it was to almost live it.

"That's fine," I said.

Johnny was at the far end of the corridor with Owen. I could see him from the vestibule near the lift where I now paused. Matt, about to open the door into the corridor, stopped and looked back at me when he heard my electric wheelchair stop.

"What's up?" he said.

I nodded and he followed its direction; Carrie, Anna and the Weird Sisters were huddled together in their cosy little coven about a third of the way down the corridor. We had to pass them and their cackling to get to Johnny and Owen.

Matt glanced back at me, smirking. "It has to happen sooner or later," he said. "You can't go on avoiding her forever."

"I can try."

"Bite the bullet, you poof. What are you, a man or a mouse?"

"A rat, according to Carrie."

"She said that?"

"No. But I bet she thinks it."

Matt was bored with my hovering. Shaking his head, he decisively pushed open the door, and stepped aside to let me through.

I hesitated and then saw Carrie look up. Whatever else she might think of me, I didn't want her believing that I was afraid of her—even if I was. I was better than that. I wasn't a man, that was true, but I certainly wasn't a mouse, either. Or a rat. I was a boy. A well-meaning boy who sometimes got it wrong, that was all. I had nothing to be ashamed of.

As I passed her by, Anna growing suddenly silent and threatening, I risked a quick glance in Carrie's direction. She met my eye openly—level and unruffled, kind and understanding. And when she smiled, I smiled back, glad to have such a weight off my shoulders, glad to have things back to how they should always have been.

Johnny watched us approach, knowing all about what had happened between Carrie and me, and no doubt realising how difficult this had therefore been. He moved his wheelchair to make room for me to enter his little cabal with Owen, almost seeming to use his whole body to shift the joystick, and I thought I could hear his chest rattling louder and louder the closer I got to him. Certain phrases sprung to mind. A shadow of his former self. A husk of a man. One foot in the... I wouldn't let myself finish that one. I couldn't *allow* myself to finish that one. Johnny was still there, still with us—still staring at me as if he were perfectly aware of every thought that was going through my mind. He knew his predicament but, more to the point, he knew that *I* knew his predicament. I couldn't afford to let the pity and discomfort show. I had to at least try to conceal it.

"How you doing, mate?" Matt said, patting Johnny on the shoulder. The tone of his voice was all wrong. I should have warned him about that.

He sounded like a cracked bell, hollow with solemn uncertainty.

"Jer-just fine and fer-fucking dandy," Johnny snarled sarcastically. "You?"

Matt looked at me helplessly. I smiled my encouragement and he said, "I'm okay, ta."

"What were you whispering about?" I asked Johnny, once the pleasantries were out of the way.

"When?" Johnny said. I got the feeling it was going to be one of *those* conversations.

"When me and Matt were coming along the corridor. You and Owen were whispering about something."

"I der-don't recall no whispering," he said. "Do you, Owen?"

"I'm not sure. Do I?"

"No, you don't."

"Oh, well, in that case—"

"Why wer-would we be whispering?" Johnny said, the corners of his mouth twitching. "What have we got to wer-whisper about?"

"Where do you want me to start?"

"Wherever you like."

Matt was watching us closely. However much time he spent around Johnny and me, he never seemed to *get* these exchanges. He thought there was real aggression and animosity behind them. He couldn't quite grasp that it was just our way.

"Okay," I said. "How about I start with your losing fifty house points and being sent to Coventry. I'd bet good money that your whispering had something to do with that. Am I warm?"

"Frigging boiling," Owen mumbled.

Johnny gave a long, liquid sniff and winked at me. "Can't ger-get nowt past you, can we?"

"Fifty house points *and* sent to Coventry," Matt said. "Fucking hell. What did you do, rape the school secretary?"

I shook my head, smiling at the memory. "It was better than that," I said. "Can I tell him, Johnny, mate?"

"Might as well. Everyone er-else knows about it."

"Physio had been cancelled again," I told Matt. "Mrs. Redfern had another of her migraines. This was during lessons so I had to stay over the Resolution for fire regulation purposes. I had to be in the school my timetable said I was in, which meant I had to sit in on one of the lessons. So I chose Johnny's Environmental Studies class, and that's when the fun really began..."

***

... It was one of the most pointless and badly planned lessons I could recall. Sitting next to Johnny in the small classroom, about seven other kids, including Owen, shuffling and whispering around us, I was struck instantly by how different it was to lessons in Almsby. It was a good while since I'd had an actual *lesson* in the Resolution, and I was amazed by (if this was a fair example) just how far the standard had slipped.

"So," the teacher said. She was a god-loving woman called Miss Mathers, whose thick waist started just under chin and went all the way down to her ankles. I hadn't liked her since she'd taken exception to my earring, telling me that if God had meant us to have holes in our earlobes, we'd have been born with them. I'd wanted to tell her that I didn't believe in God but if He really was "up there" He was, as far as I was concerned, a bit of a wanker and I didn't really care what He did or didn't want, but I'd bottled it—remembering that I was now considered a guest in the Resolution and as such was representing Almsby. "So," she now said, "why is rubbish a bad thing?"

"Ber-because it stinks," Johnny said. There was a subtext. There had to be. With Johnny, there always was. Miss Mathers didn't get it, though. She was a bit dim like that.

"Well, yes," she said, "it can smell. That's a good one." As she chalked Johnny's point on the board, I wondered why she pitched her voice the way she did. She sounded like she was talking to a room full of five-year-olds. *Severely retarded five-year-olds*, at that.

"What else?" she said, turning back to us. "Carl. What about you and your earring. Any ideas?"

Oh, I had plenty of ideas, all right—but few that I thought she'd want to hear. I gave her my most winning, butter-wouldn't-melt smile, faked a suitably thoughtful look and finally said, "It poses dangers for wildlife and the planet's whole ecological system." I was pretty proud of that. It was something I'd heard someone say on television and it had just suddenly popped to the front of my mind. *And they say*, I thought, *that telly isn't educational!*

Miss Mathers thrust her lips up under her nose and nodded. "Very good," she said. "So who came up with that? You or the earring?"

She wasn't going to let it drop, was she? The argument had been made and, yet, she still had to continue trying to score points like the insecure no-hoper she really was. Johnny mumbled something. I thought he was telling me she wasn't worth it, but he really needn't have bothered. I'd already drawn the same conclusion.

"The earring, I expect," I said.

My tone was neutral and accepting. Not in the least bit challenging. As accidental as it was, it was probably the best thing I could have done. She was (for whatever bizarre reason) looking to bring me down a peg or two. By reacting the way I did, I robbed her of the opportunity.

As she continued with her sorry excuse for a lesson, Johnny nudged me.

"What?" I whispered.

"Yer-you got her," he told me. "She thought you'd be mer-more cocky. Nice one."

"Just wish I knew what I'd done to her. She fucking hates me."

"You know sher-she's a fake," he said, keeping an eye on her in case her attention turned back to us. "And she ner-*knows* you know. Ther-that's what it is."

I wasn't about to argue with Johnny—he was generally pretty astute on such matters, after all—but that didn't seem to be it from where I was sitting. There was more going on. There had to be. I suspected I would never quite put my finger on it, but I felt as if she resented me, somehow. That didn't make a whole lot of sense, but that was how it felt.

About halfway through the lesson, one of the auxiliary nursing staff—a busybody called Mrs. Cullum—came into the small classroom. Mrs. Cullum and I had a relationship quite similar to the one I shared with Miss Mathers, and I had to struggle not to groan out loud. I never had these problems in Almsby. Yes, I occasionally got a bit of a bollocking for not handing my maths homework in on time, but I never—*never*—felt as if I had to watch my back like this. It was like I couldn't be myself. I had to pretend to be some forelock-tugging parody of a cripple.

"Just checking to see if anyone needs the loo," Mrs. Cullum explained to Miss Mathers. "That all right?"

"That's fine," Miss Mathers said—after all, it wasn't as if she was actually *teaching* us anything.

"I like to ask regularly," Mrs. Cullum explained, "just so's there are no, you know, little accidents."

Did she really say that? I looked around me. There wasn't one kid there that, as far as I knew, was ever likely to have an "accident", little or otherwise—and if there was, that just made it even more tactless. The insensitive little woman had surpassed herself, I thought... but her visit was not yet over.

Mrs. Cullum asked a few of the kids in wheelchairs if they needed the loo, skipping me altogether, thankfully, and finally arriving at Johnny.

"Need to go, Johnny, pet?" she said, and I could feel Johnny's sigh rattle through me, all liquid and resigned. *Why,* I imagined him thinking, *can't she just get it into her thick skull that I can piss in a bottle myself, and if I need owt else, I'll ask?*

"Ner-no, ta," he said, keeping it remarkably polite. "I'm fine."

"Ah, yes," Mrs. Cullum said, with an informed glance in Miss Mathers' direction. "I thought not. He wouldn't want to miss any of his lesson and, well, it can be a bit of a long job, sometimes."

Johnny's head snapped up. The room was totally silent but for the know-it-all sound of Mrs. Cullum's voice.

"It isn't always easy for him," Mrs. Cullum said.

I thought Miss Mathers might stop her. Everyone could hear. *Surely* Miss Mathers would stop her. But she didn't. She just let her continue like it was a perfectly acceptable way of behaving.

"He suffers from terrible constipation," she clarified.

I turned to Johnny; red with rage and embarrassment, I could feel the heat coming off him. It was like he had a fever. Any minute now, his head would explode, I thought—wondering if I should say something calming to him as he had me, but knowing it would be futile.

"He has to sit and strain for hours, sometimes," Mrs. Cullum told Miss Mathers—not to mention the entire class. "Sometimes—"

Bang! The valve blew.

"Will you," Johnny said, enunciating very carefully, without the slightest trace of his usual stammer. "Will you *shut the fuck up?*"

It had the desired effect. Mrs. Cullum, growing very pale (*pass out, you cow,* I thought), did indeed shut the fuck up. She, in fact, shut the fuck up faster than anyone I'd ever seen shut the fuck up before. If they gave prizes for shutting the fuck up, Mrs. Cullum would certainly have won one—that was how quickly she shut the fuck up.

But the silence that followed... oh, that was the thing. It was intense, seeming to drag on forever—all the while promising a fate for Johnny that I was sure none of us wanted to contemplate. I counted to ten, and then counted to ten again, and then Miss Mathers finally spoke.

"What did you say," she asked.

She really was quite stupid.

"I said," Johnny told her, "'Will you—'"

"I *heard* what you said." The anger made her neck-waist swell even more. "Get out! Go on. Down to Mr. Johnson's office right this minute."

As Johnny pulled out from the desk and started leaving, a mingled look of disgust and resignation on his face, I whispered "nice one, mate" to him, wanting him to know that I was completely with him on this—even if I hadn't spoken up. What she had done had been appalling, and I hoped that this would show that I hated her as much as he did. Now, today, I can't help wishing I'd done more. I wish that I'd had the maturity to say how wrong Mrs. Cullum had been—to head down to Mr. Johnson's office and tell him that Johnny had been provoked and that his outburst had been justified—but I didn't, I couldn't, and as Johnny left, giving Mrs. Cullum a right good looking at as he went, I decided that I wanted to be just like him. Oh, not the dying bit. That I could well do without. No, I wanted to be like him in his attitude—in that fuck-you approach to life he had, when circumstance occasioned it. I didn't want to back down when the likes of Miss Mathers went on about my earring. I wanted to give her hell, just like Johnny would.

Alone in the classroom with the other kids, I felt the space where Johnny had been begin to dominate.

What the hell was going to happen to him?

"Mr. Johnson made an example of him," I told Matt, back in the corridor. "He took the house points off him in assembly and then ordered everyone in Johnny's house not to speak to him for the week. He also suggested that everyone else could voluntarily ignore him if they wished."

"Bastard."

Johnny shrugged. "Doesn't ber-bother me," he said. "Means only the per-people I want to talk to me talk to me. All the arseholes turn away ler-like they're punishing me, but really, they're doing me a favour."

He was actually quite convincing. I could almost have believed that he meant it.

"Still a shitty thing for Johnson to do," I said.

"True," Johnny agreed. "Ner-nowt I can do about it, though."

"Isn't there?"

"No."

"So what were you whispering about?"

He'd thought I'd forgotten about that. "Nothing," he said—the corners of his mouth twitching ever so slightly again.

"You're planning something. I know you."

The grin finally broke free. "Wouldn't ber-be no fun if I didn't try to get my own back, now, would it?" he said.

"You're going to get in such *deep* shit," I told him. "You do realise that, don't you?"

"I'm cleverer than ther-that."

"How?"

"I'm ner-not going to get caught."

Johnny was the kind of kid who nearly always got caught. In fact, I sometimes believed that he actually went out of his way *to* get caught.

"I've heard that before." Owen was smiling. He knew exactly what I was talking about. He'd seen it, too. Many times. "So what've you got planned?" I said. "Something really complicated, I bet, knowing you."

"We haven't managed to come up with anything, yet," Owen said, smirking. He didn't hold out much hope, I could tell. As far as he was concerned, this was just another of Johnny's convoluted schemes that would be abandoned the minute something more interesting came along. But Owen hadn't known him as long as I had. He clearly didn't know about the Terence Coleman incident. Johnny was prepared to have bones broken for something he believed in.

"We ther-thought you might be able to help," Johnny said.

"*He* thought you might be able to help," Owen corrected. "I said you'd be too busy playing chess and chasing girls."

"Cheers, mate."

"You're welcome."

"Nice to know I'm so well thought of."

"So wer-what do you think?" Johnny said. "Yer-you gonna help us, or wer-what?"

I'd seen firsthand a number of times the kind of trouble he could get himself into and, however much I wanted to be like him, I wasn't sure that this was something to which I again wanted to subject myself. If he was planning on taking on Mr. Johnson, the ultimate opponent, there was no telling where this one might end. Nonetheless, he was my friend. He was my friend and I'd seen him humiliated. In my mind, what they had done to him had been unforgivable.

"Get the bastard ber-back for ner-not letting you audition for the play," Johnny said quietly.

He knew he had me. I'd been going on about it almost non-stop for the past couple of months, calling Mr. Johnson all the names under the sun and wishing every conceivable terminal illness on the pontificating little prick. Johnny had his reasons for getting his own back on Mr. Johnson and, obviously, I had mine. If Johnny could use that as a little leverage to get me to do what he wanted me to do, he would. That was just another interesting facet of our friendship—what made it real. He had no qualms when it came to doing a bit of arm-twisting, even where his best mate was concerned.

Matt was watching me carefully. He'd already made it clear a couple of times that he thought I took too much notice of Johnny. He still thought that I'd chucked Carrie because of what Johnny had said about her—which wasn't true, even though I had valued Johnny's opinion on the matter.

"I'll help with the planning," I told Johnny. "But I don't want to take part in whatever it is we decide to do."

Johnny shrugged but didn't say anything.

"Something like this," I said. "It could get me suspended or expelled. I have to be careful."

"We'll mer-make sure no one knows you were involved," Johnny promised. "Won't wer-we, Owen?"

"Scout's honour."

The summer holidays closed in on us—a sweet promise and, yet, because we were no further along with "the plan", also a bitter threat. Johnny still wasn't well, his breathing rattling like a load of marbles in a Tupperware tub and his colour reminiscent of some goat's cheese I'd once seen on a cookery programme on telly. Everything seemed even more of an effort to him, and as we filed into the Almsby hall for a performance of *Great Expectations*, I could tell he wasn't really taking a lot of notice of what I was saying.

Owen was nodding along with my little invective, however, so I continued, angry as hell and three times as hot under the collar.

"I couldn't audition," I said, as if Owen and Johnny were unaware of this. "That bastard Johnson wouldn't let me because I'm an Almsby pupil. There's the Resolution and there's Almsby—and the two can't... you know, *overlap*, even though that's what we do all the fucking time. But, like, okay, so I can't be in the play. I could just about accept that. It's life, right?"

"That's what they tell me," Owen agreed.

"But where do they decide to put the play on? After telling me that I can't try out for the part of Pip?"

"On the Almsby stage," Owen said.

"On the Almsby stage." I was *livid*, as our mam would say. It was such a... a thingy... what did they call it? A *double standard*. First Johnson tries to teach me a lesson and then what do they do? They use the Almsby stage because they haven't got one of their own. The spirit of cooperation and all that rubbish. Two schools acting as one. Strength through unity.

"What a load of bloody crap."

"I der-dunno what you're getting yer-your knickers in such a twist about," Johnny rattled. "It's ner-not like we didn't expect something like this to happen. Ther-that's the kind of bloke Johnson is. He'll do whatever he wants, and fuck everybody else."

He was right, of course. We all knew what he was like and this really shouldn't have come as all that much of a surprise. But that didn't make it any easier for me. I wanted to stand (figuratively speaking) at the front of the hall and tell everyone what a bloody liberty it was—what an *injustice*. They all had a right to know. The staff of Almsby, especially. They were being used. They were being used and Johnson wouldn't hesitate in dropping them like a hot potato should the circumstances demand it. But I could do none of that. I was a kid. I probably couldn't even have articulated all of what I thought and felt. *It isn't fair*, I thought. *It just isn't bloody fair.*

Finding somewhere to sit over to the left side of the hall and to the rear, Johnny, Owen and I settled down as the rest of the schools (the Resolution seniors and all of Almsby) filed in. At least it wasn't like the night we went to see Solomon and Sheba, I thought to myself. At least we didn't stick out like sore bloody thumbs.

"We need to get that plan sorted out," I said. "And quick." Since hearing that the play was going to be staged in Almsby—in *my school*—I'd grown rather more enthusiastic about the idea, even going so far as to say that I'd participate fully, do whatever had to be done. At the same time, Johnny, quite typically, had seemed to grow tired of the project, telling me and Owen that he couldn't come up with anything "really good" and that if we didn't think of something soon we'd just have to call the whole thing off. Johnny could be contrary. That was a vital part of his make-up. But this... this brand of defeatism just wasn't like him at all, and I was determined to rally him.

"Soon be the summer holidays," Owen agreed. I didn't think he especially enjoyed seeing Johnny quit like this, either. "Won't be able to do owt then."

"Ger-got any ideas?" Johnny said, rather begrudgingly, it seemed—sounding exhausted and fed up.

"I had one," Owen said, looking over his shoulder to make sure no one was listening. This came as something of a surprise to me. Owen was not exactly what I would have described as our *ideas man*. He leant in close and added in a whisper, "I think you'll like it."

"That good?" Johnny said, with just the faintest hint of scepticism.

"I'm not sure," he told us. "I think so, though."

He was already having doubts. I tried to encourage him, especially since I'd had no ideas of my own.

"We need to plant something incriminating in his office," Owen whispered.

"Ler-like what?"

"I haven't figured that bit out, yet."

"But wer-when you have, we per-per-plant it in his office?"

"That's what I said."

"How?"

"What?"

"How do we get into his office?" I said, noticing that Johnny was looking more exhausted by the minute. "We can't just wander in there when he's not in, stick it in his desk drawer and wander back out."

"I'm still working on that bit, too, Owen conceded. "I was thinking we could use some kind of distraction, though. Maybe set off a fire alarm or something like that."

"Wer-we'd be sent outside before we could get anywhere near... anywhere near her-his office."

Johnny was not looking good. Gem-like speckles of perspiration nestled among the bum-fluff on his top lip and his head nodded slightly, rhythmically, as if to the beat of his no doubt pounding heart.

"One of us could hide," Owen said. He was getting carried away. Under different circumstances, this could have been fun. Now I just wished he'd shut up.

"They check all the rooms," I pointed out. "There's no way that we'd be able to get past them. We'd be found right away."

Johnny nodded and, ever so slowly, the lights dimmed and the audience in the hall fell quiet. Owen knew he was beaten. Continuing trying to persuade us that his scheme would work was like, as he would no doubt have put it, pissing against the wind. The play had started, Johnny wasn't really all that interested in what he had to say and me... well, I wanted to get Johnson back for what he'd done to me *and* Johnny, but I certainly didn't want to waste time talking about something as doomed to failure as planting "something" in his office. That was the kind of pie-in-the-sky plan we would have come up with when we were ten. Now we required something with a higher degree of sophistication. What we needed was something that would totally outfox Johnson and reveal him to be the inadequate fake that he really was. We had to be subtle and clever. We had to think like he thought, get inside his head so that we could really figure out how to play him.

"It's like a game of chess," I whispered, and Johnny looked at me quizzically—breathing through his mouth, dark shadows under his eyes. "It's like a game of chess. We have to think about reactions as well as actions. If we do one thing, what will he do in reply? Tactics and strategy. The whole board."

"That's a big help," Johnny said, turning his attention back to the rather boring events on the stage.

"Makes my idea sound like the work of a genius," Owen mumbled.

But I thought I was really onto something. It was no good rushing. There was no way we were going to get this done before the summer holidays. Not if it was going to be successful. (Of course, the reality was— and I think I secretly knew it at the time—that we were never going to get a working plan up and running. Circumstances would conspire against us and in time we would forget all about it.)

By the time that Pip (that should have been *me*) met Estella for the very first time, Myfanwy not looking as impressive as I'd imagined she would, I was bored and a little concerned by Johnny's breathing. He sounded like he was sucking up the last dregs of soup through a straw and I was sure he could be heard five rows back. Leaning in close to ask him if he was okay, I caught a whiff of his sickly-sweet odour and pulled back quickly, not wanting to smell it any more, thinking of rotting apples and death, bodies degrading and failing.

"I'm fer-fine," he said. He could barely manage a whisper and I thought (though it was difficult to tell in the poor light) that his lips had turned a worrying shade of blue. I wanted to tell someone. Mrs. Redfern was a few rows back, but when I looked round at her Johnny fired me a warning glance and said, "I ter-*told* you, I'm fine. I want to see the end of the play."

He was going to be lucky to see the end of the second act, the way he was going, I thought—but there was no way I would be able to shift him. If Johnny wanted to sit between Owen and me and die watching a crappy sweet rock musical version of *Great Expectations*, that was just what he would do.

Owen looked over Johnny's head at me. He was getting worried, too— and if *Owen* was getting worried then there really *was* something to be concerned about.

Very softly, knowing that I had to at least *try* to do something to help him, I said, "I think you need to lay down or something, mate. Go to the nurse. You don't look well."

"Stop fer-fer-fer-fer-fer-fer-fussing." Wow. That had to be the longest stammer yet. "I'm... I'm all right. Jer-just... just let me watch... I want to watch..."

He struggled to get the words out but, finally—with an impressive jet of vomit that showered the jumper of the girl in front, Johnny's trousers and baseball boots, and Owen's shoes—he finished, "... watch the show..." and passed out.

I shouted to Mrs. Redfern and she came running, the girl in front of us screaming. All action on the stage stopped, Myfanwy and the less-than-impressive Pip frozen mid-song. The hall started to buzz as people craned their necks to get a look at what was going on—and I thought to myself that this wasn't how it should be. If Johnny was going to die, it should be with more dignity, with more purpose. He shouldn't have to go to meet his maker with sick on his pants and everyone staring at him like this.

Mrs. Redfern gently patted his cheek and said his name, and his eyes opened. He didn't seem to be focusing very well, but Mrs. Redfern nevertheless looked relieved. He wasn't dead yet. There was hope. A chance, however slim, that he might get through this.

"Come on," she said, quietly. "Let's get you out of here."

I sat with Owen at the entrance of the Almsby Comp., Johnny's sick drying on Owen's shoes, and watched Johnny being taken away in the ambulance. I was sure I would never see him again. The journey to the hospital would be the last he would take with beating heart and the likes of Owen and I would have to find a way of filling the considerable void he would leave behind. The summer would become autumn would become winter, and would we forget about him? Would we reinvent him as a myth of mayhem or just... what? Remember him when the light fell a certain way?

Mrs. Redfern came over to us, looking about as exhausted as I felt. The ambulance had long since passed from view, but still she seemed to be following it with her eyes. "He'll be all right," she said.

And the three of us nodded, watching the ambulance we couldn't see.

But I didn't for a minute believe it.

Chapter Twelve: Entropy

Carl looked tired again, but this wasn't the tiredness I'd grown accustomed to during my earlier visits. This was something different. Sitting outside with him once more, the two of us wearing our coats against the slight chill breeze, it occurred to me that he actually looked better than I'd ever seen him look. Mouth relaxed and with the merest hint of a smile, he surveyed the gardens and actually seemed to be *seeing* them this time. Yes, he looked tired around the eyes. There was no question of that. But it was a more natural tiredness. One that I associated with a job well done rather than the possible threat of a relapse.

"It wasn't a good summer for me," he was saying, and I didn't see any pain in the recollection for him. His face remained soft and frown-free, and I felt a little relieved at this; however bad his story was set to get, he was still here and, perhaps remarkably, perhaps not, glad about it. "I finally had my operation. A spinal fusion with stainless steel bars called Harrington rods attached to my spine for additional strength. Not a good experience."

"A big op.?"

Carl nodded. "For me, especially. They didn't know if my lungs were going to be up to it. As it turned out, they were, extremely, but it was still a horrible experience. Almost as bad as what came afterwards."

"Which was?"

"The infamous Stryker bed." I frowned at him, puzzled, and he smiled. "I had to lay completely flat for about nine weeks after the operation," he said. "No sitting up or turning over myself. At all. In such situations, they then used a Stryker bed, which allowed the patient to be flipped over onto his stomach, to prevent bed sores."

"Flipped?" I didn't quite get it. Without any experience of such a thing, it was impossible for me to see how it would work.

"Imagine you're laying on your back on an ironing board," he explained. "Someone then lays another ironing board on top of you and straps the two together, with you sandwiched in the middle. Now, these two boards—they aren't really boards, but, rather, metal frames with a canvas base and foam rubber mattress, but we'll stick with the ironing board analogy... these two boards are attached to the main body of the bed by a pivoting mechanism at each end, and in another way too complicated for me to explain. The upshot is, this allows the ironing boards to flip through one hundred and eighty degrees so that the bottom becomes the top and the patient is on his stomach."

"Sounds like a bad fairground ride."

"It wasn't pleasant," he admitted. "Not initially, anyway. With time, I suppose I got used to it. At least I didn't have to go on one the second time I was in."

"You were in a second time?"

"Just after Christmas. The beginning of eighty-two. I rejected the bars," he told me. "My back had never healed and one night Mam was changing my dressings and, well, there it was. The definite glint of stainless steel in amongst all the gore."

"Must have been a shock for her." I was smiling and thought that maybe I shouldn't. And then I realised that the reason I *was* smiling was because Carl himself was also smiling. It had once been a painful time for him. Now it was just a good story to tell.

"She practically shat herself," he said, grinning massively. "We both did. She phoned my dad at work, so that he could get himself home, and then called the hospital. That calmed us both down a bit. They'd seen it loads of times, of course. They told her to re-dress it, put my brace back on—I still had to wear the spinal brace at this point—and bring me in the following morning. There was no danger."

"That was good, then."

"Put my mind at ease. I was actually pratting about on my new ZX81 computer an hour later, not really giving a damn. The bars were going to have to come out and I was glad. I'd never felt right since they'd put the bloody things in."

"How?"

Carl shrugged. He wasn't grinning quite so broadly, now. "It's hard to explain," he said. "I felt ill a lot of the time, of course, but that wasn't it. My body had changed a hell of a lot. I'd lost a huge amount of weight and I couldn't move the way I once had because of the spinal fusion. That would take some getting used to, even after the bars came out. But with the bars in..." he shook his head, "... with the bars in it was as if I wasn't me anymore. My whole personality changed, believe it or not, and whilst it took me a long time—years, in fact—to get the real me completely back, the post-bars Carl was a definite improvement."

We were silent for a minute or two, me thinking how far we had come, how he would never have talked to me quite like this during our early encounters, Carl no doubt reliving some of the finer details of those long-gone but still difficult times. My dissertation was now, I had to admit, all but forgotten. I was still ostensibly working on it, dutifully taking notes, but now more than ever that was no longer what this was about. I didn't know what I had with Carl, and, truth be known, I was a little afraid to look at it too closely, but it was definitely more than just a research relationship. I liked him and I think he liked me. I doubted, somehow, that he would ever let me get as close as I possibly might like, but we were friends, now, and I didn't think either of us would argue with that.

"You'll be going home soon," I said.

"Yes."

"When all this is done, will I still be able to come and see you?"

Pulling his chin down into the collar of his jacket, he looked at me and said, "I'd like that."

~

I felt cold. I always seemed to feel cold, these days.

Sitting in P1, the physics lab which was also my tutor room, I listened to Mr. Dixon talk to us about the importance of "doing things right" and wished I had the energy to believe that this was something I would ever be able to really care about. He was a good teacher, was Mr. Dixon. He'd put himself out while I'd been in hospital, bringing Matt all the way up to Newcastle to see me and generally showing real concern. Mam and Dad liked him, and I liked him, too. He was a no-nonsense ex-copper with real heart and commitment, but right now I just wished we didn't have to have a lesson on how to behave every morning.

"Meeting people for the first time," he told us, "it's important to make a good first impression because, contrary to what some people might tell you, first impressions *really do count.*"

I didn't think this was going to be all that much of an issue for a fair few of my fellow pupils. The only new people some of them would be meeting would be their cellmates and probation officers.

"In interviews, I suppose it goes without saying—"

So why on earth was he saying it?

"—making a good first impression is especially important. That first handshake, believe you me, can be the difference between success and failure."

"Don't revise," Matt mumbled. "Just practice your handshake. Sounds good to me."

"I heard that, Matt," Mr. Dixon said, without looking at him. "And that's not what I'm saying at all. And you know it. Life isn't about doing this thing or that thing. It's about doing all that you can do as well as you can. All I'm doing is supplying you with a few... a few *tricks*, if you will. I'm trying to give you a slight advantage in a world where every little counts. Whether you choose to take my advice is up to you. But please don't deliberately misinterpret it. That's something I really don't appreciate."

"Sorry, sir."

I couldn't find it in my heart to enjoy seeing Matt taken down a peg or two like that. He probably deserved it—for Mr. Dixon was, after all, only trying to help us—but I was sure he had only said what we had all been thinking. I tried a reassuring smile on for size, but dropped it when it didn't feel right.

"Did you get that Computer Studies stuff copied up?" Matt asked me a few minutes later.

Ever since getting out of hospital again, I'd been pulling out all the stops, trying to get caught up with my course work. As well as keeping up with current homework assignments, I'd also been copying up notes that I'd missed and generally trying to make sense of it all. It hadn't been easy, but, as lousy as I felt most of the time, I thought I was finally getting there.

"I just have to finish the stuff on the Difference Engine and all of the notes you gave me on Lady Lovelace and then I'm done."

"Who'd you get to do it for you?"

"Hmm?"

"The notes. You didn't really copy them all up yourself, did you? You got Allen to do it, right?"

Shit. That hadn't even occurred to me. The right tone of voice and the promise of something I would probably never deliver and Allen, the unpopular sucker he was fast becoming, would have done it like a shot. Anything to feel like he had friends again.

"No," I said, the biggest idiot on the planet. "I did them myself."

"Really?"

"Really."

"Fuck. No wonder you look like shit. Don't think even *I* could keep up with what you're doing."

I looked like shit? That was news to me. I certainly *felt* like shit, but I hadn't realised that it was quite so obvious to everyone else. Since getting out of hospital the second time, it was true that I was feeling a little bit better—but everything was still more of an effort than it had once been. I felt bony and sore, cold a lot of the time, and my boyish good looks? Well, they were still there but I was sure they'd taken a bit of a battering.

At the end of registration, as I was about to start filing out with everyone else, Mr. Dixon called me back. I got the pang of guilt I always got when a teacher asked to speak to me, quickly working through everything I'd done recently, just in case there was something that might require a good story, but I was sure there was nothing for me to worry about. I hadn't been up to anything, and Mr. Dixon had already more than proved that he was one of the good guys; he wouldn't give me any crap unless I gave him a reason to, and I was quite sure I hadn't.

"How's it going, Carl?" he said, sitting on one of the high stools by his desk.

"Not bad, thanks, sir."

"I've been hearing good things about you since you returned," he told me. "Everyone's very impressed with how hard you're working to get yourself back up to speed. Very impressed."

I shrugged. I didn't really know what to say. It was difficult to know where he was going with this.

"And a one hundred percent attendance rate since you got back," he said, glancing at his records. Turning back to me, his voice dropping a register, he asked me, very deliberately, "So how's it *really* going, Carl?"

The question was almost too much for me. I swallowed hard, trying to ignore the tiredness and the way in which the room seemed to grow larger, the open spaces icy and ruthless.

"It's going good, sir," I insisted. "Really."

Mr. Dixon was no fool. He'd dealt with hardened criminals in his time, and I was sure he knew a lie when he saw one. He leant back on the stool and stared down his nose at me. I could hear his breath purring at the back of his throat as if he were a contented cat, and for a moment I thought he might stay like that forever—regarding me from the longest of distances whilst actually quite close, working me over in his mind as he delved ever deeper for the truth. The first physics lesson of the morning would begin around us, and he would remain sitting there like that, toying with me, waiting for me to confess, knowing that it was just a matter of time before I would crack.

"And you're not... you're not overdoing things, at all?" he finally said to me—apparently deciding that the good-cop approach was what was called for.

"Overdoing it?"

He sighed. "Carl," he said, patiently. "You've had two fairly serious operations in the space of—what?—eight, nine months? And now you're back here, pushing yourself harder than ever. From where I'm standing... well, it just looks as if you might be pushing yourself a little too hard."

"Mam and Dad wouldn't let me," I told him.

"Oh, I'm sure they wouldn't," he said. "If they were apprised of all the facts. It's just that after the conversations I had with them at the hospital, I'm not completely convinced that you'd tell them if you were struggling."

"They'd know even if I didn't tell them," I insisted.

He nodded thoughtfully and leant forward, clasping his hands between his knees. "Yes," he said. "I realise that. But tell them anyway, Carl. If things are too much, let them know. Don't hide how hard it is for you from them."

"I won't, sir," I said, and I thought he knew I was lying because he sighed that sigh again and shook his head.

As I was leaving, he put a hand on my shoulder and looked down at me gravely. "Just remember, lad," he told me. "There's more than one way to crack an egg. There are always other options."

I didn't really have a clue what he was on about—I was late for English Lit. and the delights of *The Ragman's Daughter*—but I gave him a look that, I hoped, suggested I did.

Mr. Dixon was indeed one of the good guys. He was up there with Mrs. Shires, as far as I was concerned. But, Christ, he could be a well-meaning pain in the arse sometimes.

Johnny hadn't died that long ago day of the *Great Expectations* sweet rock musical, and he hadn't died the day after. Or the week after. In fact, Johnny hadn't died at all, and every time I saw him now, his frail, broken appearance, the grief and worn discomfort on his face, it seemed to hammer home the miracle of this.

I arrived at physio that lunchtime feeling typically cold and empty. I hadn't eaten, simply not having the appetite for it. Mr. Dixon's little speech had been niggling away at the back of my mind all morning, and it just wasn't helping. Was it really that obvious that I was finding things hard? First Matt and then Mr. Dixon had commented on it, so who else could see? Everyone? No one? Only those who chose to look closely enough? And what *did* they see when they looked? Someone like Johnny—on his last legs, running hard in an attempt to stay where he was, and still failing, still losing ground?

I tried not to think about it. I was doing all right. Compared to

Johnny—compared to *lots* of people—I was more than getting by. I was *achieving*. What was it they said? There was no gain without pain? Well, yes. That was all that this was about. Life was struggle, and however much I might have wanted to crawl into a hole and pull a blanket over my head, I knew that whatever people like Mr. Dixon might think, that was the *only* way. I wasn't about to crack under the pressure. I was better than that.

Something was wrong with Johnny. Something was always wrong with Johnny, these days, but this was a new kind of something—something that seemed to be puzzling Mrs. Redfern and the new physio, Mrs. Malvern.

I parked my electric wheelchair close to the red vinyl mat where they were and looked down at them—my brace pinching against my hip as I leant forward.

Johnny was on his back, his head about five inches from my footrests. He swivelled his eyes up to look at me while Mrs. Redfern and Mrs. Malvern pulled up his jumper and T-shirt to examine the side of his abdomen. *Help me out, here*, his look said. *They're fucking clueless.*

"What are they doing to you, mate?" I said. "I know you like older women but two at the same time?"

"Thank you, Carl," Mrs. Redfern said. "A little less of the 'old', if you don't mind."

"Can't ber-bleeding breathe per-properly," Johnny said. "It's... it's like there's summat er-inside mer-me locking up."

"What do you mean, 'locking up'?" I said.

Mrs. Redfern gave me a sad, troubled look. I tried to ignore her.

"It's ler-ler-like summat's catching." His voice was pitched higher than usual. Weak and afraid, he was uncharacteristically close to tears.

"Whereabouts, mate?" I said, my own discomfort and fatigue forgotten.

"Around here," Mrs. Malvern said, Mrs. Redfern lifting Johnny's jumper and T-shirt to show me his ribs and waist on the right side. "Nothing's visible, but—"

"Does it feel like two pieces of bone hooking together," I asked him, and he nodded, too upset to speak.

I'd known what it was the moment I'd seen just how curved he was down there. It had simply been a matter of remembering some of the admittedly less severe problems I'd had before my operation.

"His pelvis is catching against his ribs," I told Mrs. Redfern. "It started to happen to me when I got thinner." I looked down at Johnny. "You need fattening up," I told him.

Johnny almost managed a smile. It was awful seeing him like this.

Everything was such a soul-destroying effort for him. When I looked at him, it was difficult to see the boy I remembered from only a few years back, however closely related they might be. Now I saw only a carapace with a shabby moustache and the fading remnants of a ballsy attitude, a Johnny that I suspected even he had trouble recognising. I tried to help what was left of the friend I had once known, but I knew in my heart of hearts that in my own troubled state I just wasn't up to the task.

Mrs. Redfern gave Mrs. Malvern a thoughtful look and they then studied Johnny's waist and pelvic region a little more closely, gently feeling about with their hands—Johnny wincing occasionally, but saying nothing.

"It looks like you might be right," Mrs. Redfern said. I may well have been pleased with myself under different circumstances. As it was, I couldn't see that I'd helped all that much. Johnny was still uncomfortable, his breathing restricted, and Mrs. Redfern and Mrs. Malvern still seemed unsure about what they could do to improve things for him. "You say it got worse for you when you lost weight," she asked.

I nodded. "It definitely got more noticeable," I said. "I don't think mine was ever as bad as Johnny's, but it could certainly get uncomfortable sometimes. Especially when I was thinner."

"I wonder if some foam might do the trick?" Mrs. Malvern said to Mrs. Redfern.

She was a bit of an old-fashioned-looking woman in her forties, was Mrs. Malvern—all demi-waves and old-lady lipstick—but she was nice enough. Johnny, however, wasn't all that keen on her. He preferred Mrs. Redfern's no-nonsense, granite-crunching approach.

I therefore jumped in quickly before he could sneer something disparaging at her. "It might help," I said, "but it would have to be quite thin. Thick enough to stop the rubbing and catching, but not so thick that it pops out of place."

"What do you think?" Mrs. Redfern said to Johnny.

"Wer-worth a try."

"Good." She patted his leg, getting to her feet and gesturing for Mrs. Malvern to follow her to the office. "Back in a sec."

Left alone with Johnny, there was an oddly uncomfortable—not to mention uncharacteristic—moment of silence. I didn't know what to say to him. The truth hung between us like a thick, dusty curtain, suffocating and allergenic, and no amount of mental effort could shift it. Johnny looked up at me, and I looked down at his upside-down face, both of us fully aware, lost in the pain and awkwardness of that knowledge, and when Johnny did finally break the silence, it took me a little too long to form a reply.

"Yer-you okay?" he said.

I paused. Johnny shouldn't be concerned about my health. He had other, more pressing matters to focus on.

"I'm fine," I said.

"You der-don't look it."

"I've just been working too hard," I said, dismissively. "How about you? Apart from the thing with your side, how are you doing?"

"Fer-feel like crap," he said, his voice low and weak. "They der-don't make it any better, either," he added, nodding as best he could in the direction of the office where our two favourite physiotherapists were now whispering.

"They're doing their best, mate," I told him. "It's just not easy for them to get their heads round what's wrong with you when they haven't experienced it themselves."

Johnny was shaking his head. I wished he wouldn't. He looked so frail I thought his neck was going to snap.

"Ther-that's not what I mean," he said, a little impatiently. "They keep *pretending* all the ter-time. I jer-just can't stand that."

"Pretending what?"

"Don't yer-you fucking start. You know what I mean."

This was probably the closest we had come to talking about it in a long time. I became aware, once again, of just how cold the room was, making a real effort not to shiver, and as I looked down at my dying friend I tried not to think about what it must be like for him. It was too easy for me to empathise. Too easy for me in my own difficult place to put myself in his baseball boots and imagine that he was fine—that he was fine and I, in fact, was the one that was dying. There was so much left to do. So many things I hadn't seen or experienced. I simply couldn't, as exhausted as I was, even begin to know how I would handle such loss of possibility, the cruel withdrawal of hope and dream, expectation and promise. With as much honesty as I could muster, like Johnny? Or with denial and fantasy—the constant, unfounded faith of the miracle cure? I didn't know. I didn't want to know.

But still I asked.

"What's it like, mate?"

He seemed relieved. I thought I could understand why.

"Ser-sometimes I want it," he told me. "I jer-jer-just want to go to ser-sleep and not wake up. But most of the ter-time, I hate it. I der-don't want it, Carl. Even when I do."

181

I nodded, thinking—*hoping*—he was finished. But he wasn't.

"Mer-make sure they know," he told me, but before I had chance to ask who or what, Mrs. Redfern and Mrs. Malvern returned with the foam.

Prior to kneeling down on the mat beside Johnny with Mrs. Malvern, Mrs. Redfern stopped and looked around. Something was bothering her but she couldn't quite put her finger on it. Handing the foam she'd brought with her to Mrs. Malvern, she rubbed her bare arm. I could see the goosepimples, even from where I was sitting.

Spotting the open window, she shook her head and mumbled something about it being "bloomin' freezing", before going over to close it. The window had other ideas, however. It resisted her effort to slide it shut, and within a few short moments Mrs. Redfern was cursing under her breath and banging the casing with the heel of her hand in an attempt to unstick it.

"Giving you bother?" Mrs. Malvern said, a little unhelpfully.

"You could say that. I tell you, I've reported this I don't know how many times—but does anybody give a damn?"

My guess would have been *no*.

"No," Mrs. Redfern said. "They couldn't give a flying fig. They lumber us with lousy nineteen-seventies design and expect us to put up with its failings until... when? Forever?"

As she retreated into her office to find "something heavy to hit it with", I looked around me at the physio room. She was right, of course. The room and the school in general had indeed seen better days, just like me and Johnny. The gloss had long since gone. It had vanished within the first year, that initial sense of promise quickly going with it. But now the decay (for that was the only word for it) seemed to go deeper than that. It was, I can now see, systemic—all-pervading and reflective of entrenched attitudes and changing policy. People just didn't care anymore, or if they did, they simply didn't care *enough*. There was talk of building a new, specialised unit within Almsby, now, for *all* of the Resolution's senior pupils, the first move towards the two schools finally and irreversibly becoming one. I wasn't sure how I felt about this. I didn't know the details, how it would be for pupils like me. Would I, for example, be expected to have all my lessons in this new unit or would I be integrated in the same way I was now? It was all academic, of course, since I'd be in sixth form college before the unit was built—but it was clear to me that this newly proposed development was in some way contributing to the sense of abandonment I could see in the Resolution. The era was crumbling to a close, and I couldn't help feeling that Johnny was somehow being taken along with it. The window stuck, Johnny's ribs caught on his pelvis. The paint faded, Johnny grew pale. A light failed, Johnny's eyes lost some of their sparkle.

The Resolution closed, Johnny...

Mrs. Redfern, having finally clobbered the window into submission with a hardback book, returned to Johnny and Mrs. Malvern—kneeling down beside them and taking the foam and a pair of scissors from Mrs. Malvern (who hadn't progressed very far in her efforts to get Johnny suitably padded). As I watched them—realising that I probably wasn't going to get any physio done myself today—I again thought of what Johnny had said. *Mer-make sure they know,* he had told me, and I made a mental note (one that would inevitably be overwritten by something "more important" and be forgotten) to ask him about it later. It was such a typically Johnny-type thing to say, but I couldn't help feeling that this went deeper than anything he'd said to me before. There was more to it than revenge or the simple setting straight of the record. I believed he wanted them, everyone, to know *everything*, the good and the bad, the hope and the futility... the automatic doors and the sticky windows.

"How does that feel?" Mrs. Redfern said. She'd inserted a thin piece of foam between his rib and pelvis, securing it with some tape.

Johnny—who would be leaving at the end of the school year (assuming he survived that long), making me the last remaining member of Mrs. Shires' first class—pulled a face that made me think that he at least *wanted* to say something positive. He shrugged as best he could and tried to take a deep breath, before saying, weakly and with regret, "About the ser-same only... a ber-bit worse, I think."

"Maybe we should try hitting it with a hardback book," I said, and, in spite of everything, Johnny smiled.

Chapter Thirteen: Revolutions that Never Happened

June week was a time that every fourth year student in Almsby looked forward to. The fifth year pupils finished with their exams and no longer a part of the school, we were finally the oldest year, the top of the food chain, and June week was intended to give us a clearer sense of that. Words like "independence" and "personal responsibility" were carelessly tossed about and, our normal timetable of lessons cancelled, we found ourselves listening to career-related talks given by everyone from Child Care Specialists to Army Sergeants. There was a definite focus on decision making, however, and whilst I was initially rather sceptical, I soon found that I was enjoying myself.

Sitting with Matt and Allen (who we had begrudgingly let "back in"), I listened as the Head of Upper School, Mr. Oswald, outlined the next couple of days for us.

"Wednesday afternoon," he was saying, "is yours to do with what you will. That doesn't, however, mean that you can go home early or head into town for a burger. No. You must remain in school and *organise* something, in groups. A debate or some kind of event. It doesn't even have to be especially educational, as long as you set it all up yourselves and keep it running smoothly—without too much disruption to the rest of the school."

Hands went up. Carrie's was one of them.

"Yes, Carrie."

"Can we use the gym equipment, sir?" she said.

"I couldn't tell you," he said, with an amusingly smug smile. "You'll have to make enquiries and see what you can *arrange*, won't you?"

Matt and I were already formulating a plan—heads together, excluding Allen as was the usual way of things. While Mr. Oswald went on to tell us about an orienteering exercise that was going to be held out Barnard Castle way later in the week, we quietly worked through our options. The obvious choice was to organise a video screening, something that could be easily set up and which wouldn't require a lot of work. This was Matt's idea and as much as I liked the thought of an afternoon spent watching *I Spit on Your Grave* or *Cannibal Holocaust*, I still believed it was a wasted opportunity.

"What do we always need more time using?" I said and he gave me a look that heavily implied that he didn't really give a fuck. He wanted to watch a video, and nothing I could say was ever going to change that. He thought. "The computers," I told him. "We're always fighting for computer time, right? Well this is a sure-fire way of having a computer each for a full afternoon. We could do some work on our projects and then play some games. We get ahead of everyone else and have a bit of a laugh at the same time. That's got to be better than watching some shitty video nasty."

Matt didn't need any persuading. He saw the sense in it right away, and the appeal. Truth be known, we probably wouldn't actually do all that much work on our projects (we weren't complete fucking swots, after all), but our teacher, Mr. Xavier, would nevertheless applaud our enthusiasm and might actually be a little more inclined to be generous with his marking over the coming months. Matt got this—and got it big time.

"Sounds like an excellent idea to me," he said. "I can't believe I didn't think of it."

"You haven't got the necessary," I told him, tapping the side of my head with a finger. "Takes years of study and practice to get where I am. I wouldn't even bother trying to keep up if I were you."

"A losing battle?"

"Indubitably, old chap."

He grinned. "Fucking prick."

"That's me," I said, "the fucking prick who thought of using the computers on Wednesday afternoon when you wanted to watch *The Texas Chainsaw Massacre*."

"It *is* a good idea," he admitted. "But do you think Mr. Xavier'll be okay about it?"

Mr. Oswald was finishing up and everyone was filing away for the morning of Communication and Relationship-Building Activities. We had a few minutes before they were due to start, however, and I now nodded in the direction of the stage, where Mr. Dixon was standing and talking to the very man we wanted to see, Mr. Xavier. "We'll soon find out," I said. "Come on."

Mr. Dixon saw us coming and must have understood that we had something to discuss with Mr. Xavier for he quickly walked away as we approached, giving me a puzzling wink.

"Something I can do for you, gentlemen?" Mr. Xavier said, smiling a friendly smile. A tall chap, I always remained a little distance away from him, so that I didn't have to crane my neck too much. It quite possibly made me seem somewhat aloof, at times, but, frankly, I had enough aches and pains as it was, without adding another to the list—so I did whatever had to be done.

"Carl has something he wants to ask you," Matt said.

I glanced at him and sneered, before looking at Mr. Xavier and turning on my charm. "Wednesday afternoon, sir," I said.

"What about it?" he asked, his mouth twitching his amusement.

"Well, I was wondering—*we* were wondering—if it might be possible for us to borrow a couple of computers?"

"The purpose being?"

He was determined to be a twat, but it was clear he was just teasing us, so I wasn't too concerned.

"Matt wants to play Space Invaders and I want to work on my temperature conversion project."

Mr. Xavier was chuckling to himself now, whilst Matt looked daggers at me. Maybe he'd think twice about dropping me in it like that next time, I thought.

"Mr. Dixon said you'd be coming over to ask me something like that," Mr. Xavier told me. "I'm impressed, Carl. Such dedication. Unlike some we could mention," he added, looking at Matt from beneath furrowed brows.

"I want to work on my project, too," Matt insisted, rather lamely, it had to be said.

"Of course you do. And what's your project, again? How to achieve a high score on Space Invaders without getting seven shades of space dust zapped out of you?"

"That was nearly funny, sir," Matt said.

"Glad you think so, Matthew. Now, the computers..."

Mr. Xavier was happy to let us use them. In fact, he thought—jokes aside—that it was a splendid use of our time. There was one slight problem, however.

"The computer room itself is in use that afternoon," he said. "I could take the class elsewhere, of course, but I have all my materials up there, so that might be rather inconvenient."

"What if we arrange to move the computers to an empty classroom?" I suggested.

"And bring them back when you're finished?"

"Naturally," Matt said.

Mr. Xavier didn't see a problem with that, and so we told him that we'd sort it and get back to him later that day to confirm everything.

"Well," said Matt, as we headed over to the far end of the hall—where the facilitator was gathering everyone together, "I think I dealt with that pretty good, if I do say so myself."

"Like putty in your hand," I said.

As we joined the others, I couldn't help feeling that this was going to be a long morning. My communication and relationship skills were probably as good as I needed them to be and, fatigue already making my limbs heavy, even this early in the day, I was not looking forward to the morning of corporate America-inspired team exercises—as good as I would probably be at them.

The school year was fast drawing to a close and this break from our usual routine couldn't disguise that. There was a definite sense among the rest of my year, Matt included, that it was, for all intents and purposes, already over—books ready to be packed away, doors waiting to be locked, uniforms ready to be sloughed off like dead skin—and whilst a significant part of me shared their keenness, it was also a time I wasn't looking forward to all that much. The holiday, yes. That was something I could only ever favourably anticipate. Days of doing just whatever I wanted to do, answerable only to Mam and Dad and the whims of the occasional summer storm. But the breaking up part itself—the thought of saying goodbye to Johnny (the best mate I'd ever had) on what would be his final day at school, of knowing that I'd have to return in September to a school that, even if Johnny were still alive, would itself be a little closer to death— that was something I just wasn't looking forward to. Whilst the facilitator introduced herself (she was a Pippa—I would have put money on her being a Pippa), finishing just about every sentence with a Sloane Ranger "okay?" but thankfully stopping short of the "yah?", I looked around me at the people with whom I'd spent the past four years. I hardly knew any of them, that was the thing. They knew me, because I kind of stuck out a bit, but by and large, all but a handful of them were relative strangers to me—even those like Matt, who knew me well, nowhere near being the kind of friend that Johnny had been... that Johnny *was*. What would the following year be like without him? We'd never actually been the type to see each other outside of school (Johnny also liking to keep school and home separate), so, if he lived, would I ever see him again? We would make promises and exchange phone numbers, I thought. People always did. But pretty soon he would be just another of the people who would be left behind, like Tommy, like all the other kids whose names I had long since forgotten.

"The young man with the rather stylish dangly earring." I almost didn't hear her, but Matt gave me a nudge at just the right time.

"Yes, Miss?"

"Pippa, okay?"

"Sorry. Yes, *Pippa?*"

"Your name is?"

"Carl."

"Okay, Carl." That was novel. This time she'd put "okay" at the beginning of the sentence. A slippery character, if I wasn't mistaken. "What do you think the most important ability we need to have as an individual working in a group is?"

Better sentence structure sprang to mind, but instead I said, "The... ability to listen to other people's ideas... or to cooperate in general. Yes. The second one. Cooperation. We're stuffed without it."

"Well said!" She surveyed the rest of the year, beaming. "Stuffed without it, ladies and gents. The thing that underpins the very fabric of the society we live in, okay? Fundamental. So fundamental, in fact, that even our *genes* cooperate. Without it, we have nothing. Species die, cultures crumble, whole societies go tits up."

Did she really say that? I glanced at Matt. Yup, she said it.

"And so that's what our first exercise is going to be all about, okay? Cooperation and, because it's so vital to how successful we work together, *communication.*"

Minefield. I might have known. Didn't any set up like this—whether in drama or games—always begin with Minefield or one of its variants? Matt, who, oddly, hadn't played it before, seemed quite intrigued, and whilst I feigned indifference, telling him not to get too excited ("It's as dull as dishwater"), I was also actually quite looking forward to it. This was something I was really pretty good at. Clear instruction came naturally to me, and I was sure I could more than manage to talk a blindfolded Matt through the "minefield" of upturned chairs Pippa was setting out.

"Gary," she said to me when she'd finally finished.

"It's Carl, Pippa."

"Sorry?"

"My name's Carl, not Gary."

"Well, you look more like a Gary to me," she said. "But, all right. *Carl,* you can wear the blindfold and... you. What's your name?"

"Carrie."

"Gary?"

"Carrie," I interjected. "Like the Stephen King novel."

"Ah. Carrie, okay? You'll be giving *Carl* his instructions. Think you can manage that?"

Carrie and I appraised each other. We'd had very little to do with one another since we'd broken up—speaking, occasionally, but generally only exchanging the odd smile now and then. I had no wish to go back to how it had been between us, even though *things* still stirred a bit when I looked at her, and I now supposed I'd gone a little too far out of my way to make that obvious. She was a nice lass, when all was said and done, and if I was honest I'd done bugger all to keep what might have been a good friendship going. Just the opposite in fact—and I now wondered if this might be a good way of breaking the ice between us. *Again.*

"Well?" Pippa said. "What do you think?"

With a shrug, Carrie said, "I can give it a go—but it might all go horribly wrong. He only ever hears what he wants to hear."

I didn't know what she meant by this—and, if she were truthful, I doubted that she did. It was just something to say, I thought. A way of getting a dig in that fit with the conversation, and I wasn't too concerned by it. This was fairly typical Carrie stuff, really. Much the way she had been before we had "gone out" together, and I think I welcomed it. Sort of.

The exercise went better than I might have expected. Carrie called out her instructions succinctly and clearly, remembering, as I had pointed out before we had began, that my wheelchair was a front-wheel drive—the rear swinging out whenever I turned. I wouldn't say that we completed the course in record time, but we definitely worked well together, and after everyone else had taken his or her turn, we found that we weren't actually *that* far from the top of the list.

"Not bad," Carrie said to me. "Better than Anna and that other lass, anyway."

"With instructions like that," I told her, "I couldn't go wrong."

"You're too kind." She performed a mock-curtsy and we both laughed. "Seriously, though, this has to be the biggest waste of time ever. That Pippa woman. She's nice enough but she's like... I don't know, a second-rate Princess Diana. The hair!"

Carrie wasn't really in a position to talk about hair, but I knew what she meant. "Everyone's wearing it like that, now, though."

"Yeah, but some people actually *suit* it. On her it just looks like a wig."

Pippa didn't look that bad from where I was sitting. I certainly wouldn't have said "no"—but, then, I couldn't exactly afford to be choosy. It wasn't as if I was inundated with offers. Okay, so a few girls *might* have been interested. Girls like Carrie. But the ones that piqued my interest were always inaccessible these days, since my operations and the weight loss. It wasn't at all like it had been when I had been in Swallowfields—and whilst I regretted that, I also found that it was far simpler this way. I had enough on my plate, without the perpetual uncertainty of a teenage *relationship*.

The rest of the morning was spent working in small groups on a NASA Survival Exercise—Survival on the Moon. Our group consisted of me, Matt, Allen and Carrie, and the object of the exercise was to arrange a list of items in order of importance. We did okay to begin with, all agreeing that the oxygen should be top of the list, but quickly ran into trouble when we came to the rope and food concentrate. Matt insisted that the rope was of greater importance, and even though Carrie was very patient in explaining to him just why it was vital that we placed the food concentrate higher up the list than the rope, he dug his heels in and refused to budge.

"What if we run out of water?" he said. "What if we run out of water and have to go looking for more."

"We're not going to run out of water," Carrie said, sighing.

"We might," Allen said, sucking up to Matt—who barely tolerated him, these days.

"That's stupid," Carrie said, close to losing it. "We have five gallons of the stuff. It's stupid. It's stupid and you bloody know it."

"Don't call me stupid." Matt was turning a little pink in the face. This was going to get out of hand, I thought. If someone didn't do something soon, this was going to degenerate into a slanging match and if that happened we couldn't hope to pass the exercise.

"We haven't eaten," I said calmly, and all three of them looked at me. "We're running short of water and we have to go looking for more. A futile effort because this is, like, the moon, right? But for the sake of argument, we go looking for water and we come to a large hill we have to scale. Using our rope, we start climbing—but before we get even halfway, we're all exhausted. Why?"

"Because we haven't eaten," Matt said begrudgingly.

I became aware of someone standing behind me. Turning my head as best I could in my spinal brace, I saw Pippa watching us. She put a hand on my shoulder and nodded, before walking away.

Once the session was over, however, she caught up with me just as I was heading out of the hall.

"Gary," she said.

"Carl."

"Yes. Sorry. Carl. I'll get that right one of these days." Her smile was tinged with uncertainty and I realised that this didn't come easily to her. She had to work at it as well, and this only served to make her even cuter and more shaggable.

"What can I do for you, Pippa?" I said. *My name's Bond, James Bond.*

"Well, nothing, really," she said. Her jeans were nice and tight at the crotch. I had to force myself to look her in the eye. "I just wanted to congratulate you on a job well done. I was very impressed with your communication and mediation skills and... well, I was wondering if you'd ever considered a career in counselling."

"Not really."

She nodded thoughtfully. "Well I know it might not appeal to you now," she told me. "But don't rule it out, okay?"

I watched her as she walked away. *Nice arse*, I thought. *I wouldn't mind counselling that.*

I found Johnny by the cage that lunchtime—alone and thoughtful, as tired and battered as the cage itself. I made a point of not asking him how he was—he liked it better that way—and instead merely parked myself beside him, silently looking back at the school, pulled into his hunger and loss... that sense that I often got these days of something fallen by the wayside suddenly amplified.

It had been a long six years. A six years during which we'd seen fads come and go—slime and rider boots, glam rock and, most strikingly, punk, the promised revolution that never came. The world had changed so much in that short time. All the promise had gone, or that was how it seemed as I sat there with Johnny. The newness... the freshness of the Resolution in those first days, with its poppies (so poignant now, dripping with meaning) and all those girls, had long since faded, as I had observed many times over recent years, but more than that it now seemed to me, with Johnny by my side, that it had somehow lost its meaning, its reason for being. Yes, it was still needed. Yes, there was still a role for it to play in the lives of so many. But the school and the people in it... they didn't seem to care like they used to. The revolution had, like so many others, fizzled away before it had even begun—a wasted opportunity, an ideal that, with work, could have become the envisaged reality. Instead, more walls were being built. A special "unit" within Almsby, the two schools destined to be one and, yet, possibly always doomed to remain separate on some level. A step forward, perhaps, but still somehow not quite what I would have hoped for.

It was a warm afternoon. I felt more comfortable in my shirtsleeves than I had in a good while but Johnny... Johnny must have been sweating his balls off in his favourite blue polo neck jumper. I considered asking him if he wanted me to ask Carrie, who I could see in the corridor, if she would help him take it off—but as I listened to his sharp, shallow breathing it seemed to me that being a little hot was probably the last thing on his mind.

"I ther-think it's going to be good," he said to me, quite suddenly—sounding unexpectedly cheerful. For one bizarre moment, I thought he meant being dead. He was having a bad day. Everything was dark and depressing, but somehow he had reconciled himself and found hope in the promise of an afterlife. Then he continued, and everything became, thankfully, much clearer. "At ther-this college I'm ger-going ter-to after I finish here," he told me. "I think it's going to be good."

I knew the place he was talking about. Barrowdales, it was called—and to think of it as a "college" was a bit of an exaggeration. At best, it was a training facility, at worst... a day centre.

"You been to see it, yet?" I said, holding my face up to the sun.

"Went last ner-night. They've got this der-dead good woodwork department. Lathes and everything."

"Cool."

"I think so. And if fer-fits in wer-with what I want to do."

"Which is?"

"Yer-you know how I'm good at carving animals from wood and ster-stuff?"

Oddly, I didn't. This was completely new to me and I couldn't help thinking that this might be some elaborate trick or joke—a bright, brief flash of the old Johnny through the long, dark night of his passing soul. So it was with much caution that I said, "Yes..."

"Well, that's what I'm going to do," he told me, far more willingly than I would have expected. "They rer-reckon... they reckon I mer-might even be able to make a good living at it, if I ger-get really good."

"That's what they said?"

"Well, not in so mer-many words. But I could ter-tell that that was what they meant."

"Have you found God or something?" I had to ask. This just wasn't like him.

"Wer-what do you mean?"

I shrugged. "I don't know. You just don't seem yourself. It's like you've suddenly been hit with a happy stick—and I'm not sure I like it. You've turned into a fucking Stepford Johnny. It's scary."

Johnny chuckled. There was actually a little colour to his cheeks and I found myself entertaining the notion that they'd got it wrong. Johnny was not dying. He was just going through a bit of a rough patch and once he came out the other side, all would be well. He would be his old eat-shit-and-die self, and the doctors and esteemed professors would have to hold up their baby-soft hands and admit that for all they knew an impressive amount about Duchenne Muscular Dystrophy, they knew sweet sod all about *Johnny*. All the study in the world could never prepare them for the variety of spanner that my mate Johnny was capable of throwing into their prognostic works.

"A Stepford Johnny?" he said, grinning. "I like ther-that." Growing more serious, he moved his wheelchair closer to mine—like he didn't want anyone else to overhear (not that there was anyone about *to* overhear.) "You ther-think I've ger-got all... what's the wer-word? Where you see the world ther-through rose-coloured specs and stuff?"

"Optimistic?"

"Yeah. That. You think that's how I am, ner-now? Everything's per-perfect and we're all going to ler-live happily ever ah-after?"

"I don't know. Are you?"

He sighed as though he had just stopped crying—the hitching gasp at the end, just before he breathed in again, filling me with the kind of dread I'd only previously experienced in the dead of night, lying on my back on a Stryker bed with no one to talk to.

"I'm... I don't know," he said. "I'm mer-making the best of things, Carl. I know what that college rer-really is but... I'll go ner-nuts if I think about it too much."

Again, I found it difficult not to put myself in Johnny's baseball boots—impossible not to immerse myself in his thoughts and feelings. It wasn't too long ago that dying had been a real possibility for me, too, under the knife with all kinds of doubts and uncertainty surrounding me. Remnants of that still persisted, and as I thought of him being shown around that college that wasn't a college, I found myself sinking deeper and deeper into the reality of his predicament. Johnny knew what he was. He was fully aware of all that he would never be. Also, however, he understood all that he could have been, had the dice fallen rather more fortuitously. Even looking at me, as tired and bony as I was, must have been difficult for him, at times. Seeing me—in so many ways like him and, yet, different in that one, vitally important way—must have seemed to him the cruellest of mockeries, but still he had never let it show—still he had never once turned round to me and told me how lucky I was, how grateful I should be for all that I had and all that I would be. He had tolerated his condition. But not only that, he had tolerated the intense light the lives of others shone on him. In sharp contrast, Johnny moved with a kind of grace and forbearance that I couldn't have then expressed but which I nevertheless felt in that mystical place that some might have thought of as the soul, but which I, with my years of experience and intellectual superiority, preferred to call my heart.

"Will you mer-miss me?" he said to me, quite suddenly—smiling as he sank ever further into himself.

I knew what he was saying. There was no misunderstanding this time. Johnny wasn't talking about death. Johnny wasn't talking about *his* death. I could never have taken it to mean that. He was simply referring to his leaving the Resolution. Would I miss him when he left the Resolution? The answer to both questions would always have been the same, however; I would miss him. I would miss him in a way that I had never missed the others I had left behind.

Because this time, as I think I had already realised, Johnny was leaving *me* behind. And occasionally—*very* occasionally—I almost resented him for that.

Chapter Fourteen: The Duffel Coat He Never Got

Sitting alone by Carl's bed, I thought about all that he had most recently told me, trying to ignore the man in the next bed, who kept looking over at me with what I could only think of as a lecherous glint in his eye. That summer had been a fairly good one for him, he had told me. The relative ease of not having to go to school and the long warm days all conspired to improve his appetite, and before long, whilst he was still a long way from being his old self, he was feeling greatly improved. He thought of Johnny only occasionally during that time, he'd told me, sounding ashamed and sadly reflective, but on the countless visits with his parents and family friends to Whitby, it was hard not to remember him on that long ago school trip, giving his theories on how Captain Cook had been a vampire and how they were his undead crew, sailing along in the doomed ship Resolution. He couldn't look up at the Abbey without thinking of how fitting that now seemed, he had explained to me. "I couldn't be in that place," he had said, "without attributing to Johnny the most indescribable wisdom. He had understood. He had grasped it in a way that no one else had—and I couldn't for the life of me put that down to blind chance." Carl struggled at times, he had gone on to tell me, struggled to keep Johnny real in his memory, to not turn him into some idealised, late-Twentieth Century soothsayer. "But he did have an uncanny knack for seeing things for what they were—and down in the harbour, looking up at the East Cliff... well, it made me shudder a little, I can tell you, thinking how bang on the button he could be at times."

More than ever, as he had talked about that summer, telling me how optimistic his parents had been that he would do well in his final year and pass his exams (something Carl felt increasingly unlikely, though he managed to keep this from them), I was aware of just how much of a refuge his home life was for him. In many ways, it seemed to me that everything else was artifice. The Carl we had been discussing for the past

195

weeks was merely the Carl he allowed the world to see, and as he talked about his parents, Bob and Sonia, I started to see a more vulnerable Carl, a Carl who needed stability and freedom from change. To move on and to *continue* to move on, Carl needed to remain still. To reach for the future, he had to maintain a strong foothold not in the present, but in the past. His parents were that foothold, that refuge, and seeing how Carl had turned out (thoughtful, deep, compassionate, flawed but in ways he understood) I couldn't help but envy him just a little.

That was why I was now still on the ward. Once Carl had finished his final consultation with his specialist, Bob and Sonia were due to pick him up and take him home. I wanted to be there when they did. I wanted to meet them.

Going to the window and looking down at the car park, as much to get away from the bloke in the bed next to Carl's as anything else, I found that I was actually quite nervous. I liked Carl and I wanted his parents to like me, but more than that, I didn't want Carl being annoyed with me. I hadn't mentioned to him that I was planning on sticking around to meet them, and now wondered if this was actually a good idea. I was robbing him of control, of the opportunity to have a choice, and knowing him as I did, that suddenly didn't strike me as such a wise move. My meeting his parents... it should have been at his instigation. I saw that now.

Turning from the window, having every intention of leaving, I found myself looking directly into the faces of Andrea and Carl. Too late. His consultation over, she had brought him back to wait for his parents.

"You still here?" Carl said, amiably enough.

I nodded, my mouth dry. Andrea was smirking to herself. We had got drunk together the previous weekend, round at her flat, and I couldn't help feeling that I'd maybe told her too much. She could be an interfering cow when she wanted to be, and even though I wasn't yet all that sure how I felt, *exactly*, about Carl, or even if he would let it amount to anything if I wanted it to, I hoped to God she hadn't been doing a number on him, dropping hints and nosing around for truffle-like clues in the replies to her probing questions. She could ruin this altogether, if she set her mind to it. Of that I was sure. Just one wrong word from her and that would be it. The friendship that had developed between Carl and me would be over. Whatever else I did or didn't want, that in itself would have been enough of a loss.

"Something you forgot to ask me?" Carl said, frowning.

"No," I answered, sitting down on the edge of his bed and trying to look more comfortable than I actually was. "I just... I just thought I'd hang around for a bit. Finally meet those parents of yours."

Andrea parked Carl beside the bed and put on his brakes. She gave me a hopeful look and, the aberrant height of discretion, backed slowly away.

Carl looked at me, trying, it seemed, to work something out. I had to force myself to breathe. I was sure I was making too much of it. How could he really object? Why would he?... But this was Carl. He was a lot more complex and multi-layered than he first appeared. I knew that, now, and I understood it because I had listened to his story. So much had been beyond his control during those early years. The world had revealed itself to be a harsh and random place, and how he had ultimately got beyond that (if, indeed, he had), I didn't yet know. But what I did know, what I really should have given more consideration, was that he was not someone who liked to feel he was being manipulated, and whilst that was not (I told myself) what I was trying to do, I at least saw that there was a chance that it might be viewed that way. Especially if Andrea had been dropping her hints.

Looking around at the slightly whiffy ward, however, he only said, "Christ, I'll be glad to be out of this place. Remind me never to get ill again, okay?"

Relieved, I nodded and grinned, rather inanely, I believed. "I'll do that," I promised.

We were talking about the end of June Week when Bob and Sonia arrived, how it had all been fairly anticlimactic and how the following year had started off with a heightened sense of barrenness and futility. He had just told me how he had merely been going through the motions, doing the bare minimum and still feeling that it was more than he could manage, when the two of them came through the door, all smiles and open warmth.

I liked them right away, I think, primarily because they were immediately nice to me, chatty and interested, genuinely pleased to finally get the chance to meet me. It was evident from what Bob said that Carl had, in fact, told them rather a lot about me, and while Sonia packed Carl's things for him, he, Bob, sat with me on the edge of the bed and asked me about my dissertation.

"So he's been helpful, then?" he said, nodding in Carl's direction.

"Very. I would never have found information like this anywhere else. He's provided an insight that... well, it's unique and analytical. Carl isn't just concerned with providing the facts. He has opinions, too."

Bob chuckled and nodded. "Oh, he has those, all right," he said. He nudged me. "Get him onto the subject of God and religion, sometime, and just sit back and watch him take the subject to pieces. More entertaining than... well, something very entertaining." He paused for a moment, watching mother and son chat quietly while she packed for him. "I am surprised, though," Bob said to me, his voice dropping in volume.

"Surprised about what?" I said.

"That he's shared so much with you." When I frowned at him, Bob added, "He likes to play his cards close to his chest does our Carl. He doesn't tell just anyone stuff like that. Not as a rule."

"I did get that impression."

"It's not that he isn't trusting," he went on. "Just the opposite, in fact. Sometimes he can be too trusting, though he knows that now and, you know, compensates. No, it's more that... well, he doesn't like everyone knowing how vulnerable he is, I suppose."

I didn't think that was it at all, but if I'd disagreed with Bob I would have felt presumptuous, presumptuous and unable to support my argument. I therefore simply nodded in agreement, and waited for Sonia to finish Carl's packing.

When she was finally done, Carl looked at me. There was a tenderness in his eyes that seemed a reflection of his parent's general demeanour, but wasn't. He smiled and looked at the ward with something like satisfaction, ready to say his goodbyes. Before so doing, however, he met my gaze evenly as I experienced yet another moment of doubt and said, "Can we give you a lift, Marisa?"

"You're not going my way," I told him.

"Yes we are," he said.

~

The snow was falling outside and the day was about the greyest of the winter so far—canvas-like and overawing, bringing me and everyone around me down, it seemed. With Christmas a good month behind us, any last remnant of those warm-fire festive days was gone, and I now found myself battling against the burden of tedium in a sub-zero world.

I was struggling. More than ever the obscurity of those chill days during my final, Johnny-less year in Almsby was influencing my mood, dragging me under with it—each school-day morning a painful, soul-wrenching threat, each evening a blessed if temporary release. I tried to fight it. I made myself think of all the good things in my life, how bad it had been not so long ago and how, in comparison, life was now nothing less than a bowl of fucking cherries. But that wasn't true. It wasn't true at all. Life was about as bad as it had ever been... or, rather, my *school life* was about as bad as it had ever been. My home-life was... well, something dependable, secure and familiar... *warm.*

I could almost have smiled, had I not been so physically and emotionally drained. Warmth. The one thing I now relished more than ever—just like my old friend Tommy Blackbird and the duffel coat he never got. A simple need and, yet, one that was always so elusive when I wasn't at home. It was almost as if the school were not heated. The cold got into my bones and there was just no budging it.

Mr. Mann, our T.D. teacher and acting headmaster, was watching me. I was meant to be working on an elevation of a mortise lock but, sitting before my specially adapted draughtsman's desk, I just couldn't get my fingers to work. I picked up my pencil and set square, but my hands were so cold that I couldn't grip them well enough to get anything down on paper. It was frustrating and embarrassing, and the more I tried, the more desperate I felt myself becoming.

I could have cried, had I not been so close to losing my temper.

Mr. Mann had always reminded me of the comedian, Jim Bowen—the one that did that completely annoying Sunday afternoon darts game show. I looked at him as a rule and was always sure he was going to say "smashing, marvellous, super" and then show me what I could have won. But today was different. Today he looked at me from his desk with a slight frown, chewing the inside of his cheek.

I'd been here before, so I wasn't in the least bit surprised when he got up from his chair and came over to me—looking concerned and extraordinarily gentle.

"Having problems, Carl?" he said—quietly, so that the rest of the class didn't hear.

Reluctantly, I nodded and held up my fingers. "Can't seem to get them warm, sir," I said. "I'm having a hard time gripping the pencil."

"Ah," he said. "I see. Have you... have you tried blowing on them?"

"Till I'm blue in the face." He was doing his best, the poor old sod, but I really could have done without suggestions like that.

"No improvement?"

"Not so's you'd notice."

He nodded thoughtfully and then said, springing into action, "Only one thing for it, then. Matt. You're a strong lad. How do you feel about helping me move Carl's desk nearer to the radiator?"

Matt looked a bit fed up, but he knew better than to place unnecessary obstacles in Mr. Mann's way and, so, dutifully got to his feet, giving me a look that heavily implied that I would be held personally responsible if he didn't pass his T.D. exam with top marks.

"See how that goes," Mr. Mann said, trying to look encouraging. "But don't worry about it, Carl. We'll work something out."

I warmed up quite quickly near the radiator, but I felt more conspicuous than ever—working my fingers to get the blood flowing, trying to grip the pencil and finding that, yes, it was much improved but still not reliable enough to draw the careful, precise lines I needed to draw. I looked around and found a few of my classmates stealing the occasional glance at me, but there was nothing I could do about that. Staring back at them would achieve nothing. They knew me. They were not on the whole malicious. Some of them may have even been concerned for me. Nevertheless, I wished they would stop looking. I really didn't need it.

Out of the window, I could see a tree in the distance—little more than a sapling, really, stunted and fragile, its slender, brittle branches burdened by a precarious layer of snow. It was not healthy; I only had to look at it to understand that. Subjected to years of pollution, of growing in an environment to which it was not wholly suited, it seemed to me only a matter of time before it must either be transplanted to more sympathetic surroundings or simply cease to grow entirely, withering, curling back in on itself in a vain attempt at self-preservation. It seemed absurd that something so potentially wonderful had to suffer in that way—all for the sake of propriety, of making an effort to "do the right thing" and at least attempt to give the people on the estate the one thing they probably needed least. A political decision. A showy act of window dressing. And for that a tree had to die.

By the time break came around, my fingers had warmed up enough for me to be able, still with some effort, to get a little work done. When the bell rang, I thought about staying back for a while—but my conscientious days were by this point well and truly over. Even though it meant leaving the warmth of the radiator, I couldn't quite bring myself to put in the extra, required effort.

It wasn't worth it. However I tried to dress it up and validate it, it just wasn't worth it.

At first, I thought I was seeing a ghost. I paused in the corridor and looked out through the reinforced glass at the grey, snow-spangled landscape and I just couldn't absorb or make sense of what it was I was seeing. I looked away, briefly, and then looked back again, my heart thudding in my chest as I told myself that I needed to eat more—I needed to eat more and keep warm. Something was wrong with me. That could be the only explanation. He had left, for Christ's sake. He had left a good seven months before and what I was seeing... it could only mean that he was dead... dead and come back to haunt me for not keeping in touch as I had promised.

Slowly heading outside, I approached the figure sitting slumped in his wheelchair by the edge of the school field, holding my breath—thinking that I really had lost it this time. The strain had finally taken its toll and I was regressing. Yes, that was it. I was becoming what I had been—returning to the times, the places, the people that had made me feel most at ease. It couldn't be real. We'd said goodbye. It had to be a ghost or a hallucination. It was the only possible explanation I thought I could cope with.

"Johnny?"

It was as if we were the only two people out there. The clamour of laughter and excited yelling fell away and I sat staring at him—wearing the familiar coat that now looked as if it belonged to someone three times his size, pale and irrevocably lost, my friend the human cave-in.

Looking round at me, half-heartedly, he smiled, his eyes too tired, it seemed, to hold my questioning gaze. I felt a hole inside, one I hadn't previously even known I'd had, grow suddenly larger. *So this is what it's like,* I thought. *This is what it's really like.* All those other times when I thought he had been close to death. They were nothing. Not even a rehearsal. No, this was it. This was the real thing. This was how it had to be for Johnny. This was how it would have to be for me and for everyone I knew. Friends, loved ones—enemies, even—this was what they were all coming to. The falling away, sudden or slow, of meaning.

"What the fuck are you doing here?" I said, wondering if he would be able to answer me. "Shouldn't you be at college?" I was aware of just how easy it would have been to keep on asking him questions. If he couldn't answer me, if he was too far gone to be capable of holding anything even remotely resembling a conversation, that was a sure-fire way for me to forestall ever having to know it. Nonetheless, I forced myself to hold my tongue. Knowing now that I was not dealing with a ghost or hallucination, I gave him an opportunity to speak.

"Couldn't mer-manage there," he told me, and I had to lean in close to hear what he said. "It wer-wer-was... it was ter-too much for me so... they ber-brought me back here wer-while they fer-figure out what they're going to der-do with me."

"I have a few ideas," I joked, and he smiled. I almost wished he hadn't, though. It was like watching a lakebed dry up—heart breaking and destined to fruitless attempts at recovery. "So what really happened," I said. "You got expelled, right? Got caught with your cock in some girl's mouth and they threw you out on your ear, am I correct?"

Johnny sniggered and bit back a cough. "Ner-not quite," he said. "I didn't ger-get caught." He turned his chair round and, before I could work out whether he was joking, asked, "It's ger-got even wer-worse, hasn't it? Or did I 'magine it?"

During his final weeks at the Resolution, it's decay and the evident neglect surrounding it had become our main topic of interest. We had held onto it like a piece of flotsam in a stormy sea, seeing its observation as our last remaining reason for being there—its reality the motivating force behind our getting away from it as quickly as we could. We'd taken the place to pieces, brick by brick, talking about how incapable some of the teachers really were and, on one sweltering day a week before Johnny had said goodbye, had recalled that day up near Whitby Abbey when Johnny had, with peculiar authority, sealed our fate with his predictions as surely as anyone could have. He'd remembered that day only reluctantly, I now recalled, dismissing much of what he had said as childish nonsense, but as we both once more sat there looking back at the Resolution, I couldn't help but think that the ghost at my side at least partially authenticated what that other, more corpulent Johnny had said.

"You didn't imagine it," I told him. "It's worse than ever."

"Yer-you're leaving soon, though, right?"

"After my exams. Back end of May, middle of June—somewhere around there."

"And wer-what you doing after?"

"College."

"Proper college?"

I nodded. "Sixth form college."

He seemed satisfied with this. "Jer-just promise me something," he nevertheless said.

"What?"

"Der-don't ever come back here. Not ever."

"I promise," I said.

It was like that day in the Almsby school hall all over again—Myfanwy up on the stage, so distant, so oddly disappointing, Johnny beside me, struggling to breathe, coughing and generally looking like three-day-old shit. I watched him, my promise freshly made satisfying him only briefly before he slipped into that other Johnny once more—the Johnny that would never again be satisfied, the one I doubted ever really had been.

"You're not going to throw up again, are you?" I said.

Shaking his head (a slight, barely perceptible gesture), he answered between gagging, racking coughs. "No," he told me. "I... I der-don't think so." Another spasm caught hold of him. Spittle formed at the corners of his mouth and the colour seemed sucked from his face. His right hand gripped his joystick, unmoving but clenched and claw-like, and he leant forward against the belt that now held him in his wheelchair, drawing in air through the densest of materials, struggling and fighting in a way that I'd imagined he no longer could. "I ner-need... I need to ger-go in," he said, and I nodded, thinking that now might be a good time for me to make my excuses and leave. This had to be it. This had to be the end for Johnny. This time he was going to die—*really* die—and when he did, I didn't want to be there to see it.

Nevertheless, feeling the bond of friendship between us stronger than I ever had before, I said, "I'll come with you."

The nurse, Mrs. Emmett, was outside the M.I. room, talking to Mrs. Redfern. She took one look at Johnny and ended the conversation right away—Mrs. Redfern coming over to stand beside me (she looked as though she wanted to put a hand on my shoulder; blessedly, she resisted.) "I think we need to get you home, my lad," Mrs. Emmett said, leading Johnny into her tiny, antiseptic room. "That cough is definitely getting worse."

The door closed, leaving Mrs. Redfern and me staring yet again after a Johnny we could no longer see... a Johnny I suspected we hadn't seen for a very long time.

"I wish I had something reassuring to say to you, Carl," Mrs. Redfern said.

"I know."

"You do understand that—"

"Yes," I said, with just the slightest trace of irritation. "Yes," I said again, my tone softer this time. "Yes, I understand, Mrs. Redfern. I understand perfectly."

"Did he say anything to you?"

It seemed an odd thing to ask. "What do you mean?"

"Did he say goodbye? Did the two of you say goodbye?"

"In a way," I said. "He made me promise that whatever happened, when I leave here I won't come back."

Mrs. Redfern smiled her toothy, Esther Rantzen smile. "That sounds like Johnny," she said. "Still pretending he hates the place."

"I don't think he's pretending," I told her. "Far from it. He hasn't liked it from day one. Not really."

"Nonsense." She laughed, nervously.

Shrugging, I said, "Please yourself. That's how it's always seemed to me, though."

I thought Mrs. Redfern was going to argue with me, but she didn't. Instead, she merely smiled and shook her head. "I suppose it makes sense," she said. "A contrary, obstinate chap is our Johnny. I suppose he hates me, too, right?"

Laughing gently, I said, "No. He hates physio, but he likes you. If you like *Star Trek* and *Blake's 7*, you can't be all bad as far as Johnny's concerned."

"Well that's all right, then."

Our awkward silence was punctuated by the sound of Johnny coughing on the other side of the M.I. room door. Seal-like and dry, painful to hear. I no longer wanted to be there.

"I'd better be going," I said. "Wouldn't want to be late for double maths."

"Heaven forbid."

Driving my wheelchair away, little did I know that that coughing would be the last sound I would hear Johnny make. It would stay with me for a long time—waking me in the night, warning me when I started to take my relative good health for granted, taunting me when I entertained the notion that I was capable of anything. *Stop and think,* that coughing said, *but don't stop and think for too long.*

A couple of weeks before our exams were due to start, I saw Carrie in the corridor on a grey, overcast day—sitting on the floor revising trig. She wasn't in uniform, that was the first thing I noticed about her. She had on this white and red spotted ra ra skirt and an uncharacteristically stylish white blouse, and had it not been for her well-developed calf muscles, I could almost have failed to recognise her.

"Just when I thought I was going to get a bit of peace and quiet," she said. I parked opposite her, where I had I nice view up her skirt. "I suppose I can forget all about revision now that you're here, right?"

"I'm not stopping," I told her. "Just passing through, as they say. On my way to physio." I didn't relish the prospect. Johnny hadn't returned after taking ill earlier in the year and physiotherapy was now almost intolerable without him. So much had changed. *Remarkable, really,* I thought, *that such a little guy could leave such a huge fucking hole.*

"You say that with such enthusiasm I almost want to join you."

"You'd make a good physiotherapist," I told her. "Always so quick to pull my... leg."

"You had me worried for a minute there."

"I had myself worried."

She smiled. There was none of the tension there had once been. It was nice. "Funny you should say that, though," she said.

"About you pulling my..."

"About me being a physiotherapist." She closed her legs, blushing, when she noticed I was getting a good look at her knickers. "I've been working at a children's respite centre on Saturdays and helping out a bit in the Resolution and... well, I'm thinking of going into nursing."

"You want to be a nurse?"

"That's what 'I'm thinking of going into nursing' generally means," she told me. "Why? Don't you think it's a good idea?"

It was a slightly disturbing notion, truth be known. The thought of Carrie tending to frail, ailing folk with what I thought of as her *gymnastic enthusiasm* could have grave consequences, I was sure. It wasn't that she wouldn't care enough. Far from it. It was more, I thought, that she would have to struggle against her natural tendency, which had become increasingly evident the older she got, to go at things like a bull in china shop. Giving a bed bath (of which I'd had a fair few in my time), she would grab at *things* carelessly, and whilst I could certainly envisage some interesting scenarios developing, I also knew that it could be a painful prospect.

"I think it's a great idea," I lied, measuring my words and their tone with care, not wanting to hurt her feelings.

"I'm not so sure," she said—and through the chink in her impressive armour, I saw the insecurity I'd always known was there.

I'd could have asked her, then. At that moment, I would have happily taken a shot at trying again—older and possibly wiser, less likely to fail. I thought about how cold I sometimes felt, a coldness that was as much inside me as out, and realised in those fleeting seconds that Carrie could change that—would want to, even. Maybe she would say "no" this time. That was possible. Likely, even. But eventually she would say "yes". If I kept asking, she would say "yes" and I wouldn't feel cold again.

"Why not?" I said, and the moment passed—just like that.

"I just don't think I'm up to it." She waved her maths book at me. "You know, academically."

I laughed and she squinted up at me, letting her legs fall apart—by way of a thank-you, I liked to think.

"What?" she said.

"I've never heard anything so ridiculous in all my life," I told her.

"You haven't?"

"No," I said. "Christ, Carrie, over the last few years I've met more than my fair share of nurses and, believe you me, some of them were as thick as pig-shit. Take my word for it, you'll make a great nurse." I thought about what I'd said, and then added. "That was a compliment, by the way."

She smiled. "I did wonder."

"I meant that you're far superior to the competition. I wasn't saying that you're like them."

"I know that."

"Because you're not thick as pig-shit," I insisted. "And even if you were, I'd probably be too scared to tell you."

She was laughing, now. And so was I. "Carl?" she said.

"What?"

"Why don't you just quit while you still can?"

"You think that'd be a good idea?"

"I think that'd be an excellent idea."

I smiled and then, on a whim, pointed to her open legs and said, "You want to watch that, incidentally. If a train comes along you could be in bother."

Carrie was on her feet before I could say "ungentlemanly-like conduct", wresting my joystick from me and, trying her best to look affronted, pushing me and my wheelchair back against the wall. Our faces mere inches apart, my hands gripping her wrists, Carrie biting back laughter as I smiled my well-practiced winning smile, I was sure she was going to kiss me. There was an eerie calm between the two of us. A moment when the sails sagged and all was silent. I felt her breath on my face and inhaled, wanting to own a part of her even as I held fast to the conviction that I still didn't want this—that it was just physical and could never work.

"What am I going to do with you?" she said.

"Walk me down to physio?" I quickly suggested, more as a way of stopping myself from saying something far more dangerous.

She nodded slowly, thoughtfully. "Beats revising, I suppose," she said, pulling away from me and collecting up her things.

I thought I'd hurt her feelings, but when she turned to look at me again, she was smiling. "Come on, then," she said—so I did.

Passing through the Resolution with Carrie at my side felt right, somehow. If anything was an appropriate measure of the success of the whole integration programme, I supposed that this was it. Two people, both very different, whose friendship had grown and developed over a number of seasons, finding a level, testing, accepting, never once truly questioning that, in this, at least, progress had been made. It set me apart in those environs, being seen with the moderately pretty girl in the ra ra skirt, but that wasn't such a bad thing—because, as it had been made more than clear to me, this wasn't my school anymore. Indeed, it hadn't been since the days of Mrs. Shires.

"It smells," Carrie whispered. "It never used to smell."

I think she'd caught it on a bad day, but it was difficult to be sure.

"The respite place I work on Saturdays doesn't smell like this," she went on, "and they, you know, have some *really* bad cases there."

I didn't want to talk about it. This was the kind of thing I normally only talked about with Johnny. I didn't want Carrie to be touched by it. Our conversation should be about her nursing ability and... well... trains.

"They're starting on the new unit next week," I said, hoping that by this I might lead her away from the subject of how smelly and neglected the Resolution was becoming. "In Almsby."

"Let's hope they take better care of it than they have this," she said. "It used to be such a bright, warm place. What happened, Carl?"

Resistance was futile. I shrugged. "People stopped trying," I said. "If they ever truly started."

"That sounds unfair."

"The truth usually does."

Even as I said it, I found myself questioning what I had told her. Was it really as simple as that? There were some good people, some of genuine ability, working in the Resolution—people like Mrs. Redfern and... well, people like Mrs. Redfern—and maybe I was being harsh when I attributed the Resolution's decline to their inaction. There had to be more to it than that. A whole system had broken down almost before it had started. Something on that scale required more than just the incompetence of the few.

But then I thought about my latest computer studies project. A simple invoicing program I'd been working on for weeks. All had been going well. The dry runs had suggested that I was on to a winner. Mr. Xavier walked behind me repeatedly, glancing over my shoulder and nodding approvingly. And then, the program running nicely on the Commodore Pet, everything stopped—everything ground to a halt, the program unable to complete its task because of... what? A major programming oversight? A hardware malfunction? No, the program failed because of one little syntax error. Half of one line of BASIC couldn't be made sense of and there had been no other option than for it to pull down the blinds, fold its arms and say, "That's me done. Wake me up when you've fixed it."

For want of a nail...

Mrs. Redfern was in her office when we arrived. She stuck out her head when she heard my wheelchair and told us to join her. She sounded tired and preoccupied, and when we, a little reluctantly, entered, we saw that she was finishing up writing something in what looked like a journal. That made a kind of sense. Mrs. Redfern could be a great storyteller when she wanted to be. She'd worked at one time in Borneo or some place like that, helping rehabilitate a kid who had lived in the wild and been brought up by wolves. She'd told me, Johnny and Owen all about it, once, and the detail to the story, the smells and emotional textures, had certainly implied that Mrs. Redfern had a methodical side to her—and that she would make sense of her experiences by writing in a journal.

She smiled rather feebly when she saw Carrie and said, "Hello, love. Long time no see." Mrs. Redfern knew Carrie from a few years earlier. She'd always been around the Resolution with Anna, then. "How you keeping?"

"I'm good, ta."

"Carrie's thinking of becoming a nurse," I said. I felt awkward, but didn't quite know why.

"Really?" She looked at Carrie, an eyebrow raised. "That is good news. We're always in need of good, conscientious nurses."

"I need to get my exams, first," Carrie said—the implication being that she wasn't planning on holding her breath.

"You'll sail through them," Mrs. Redfern said. "Bright girl like you."

Carrie looked as uncomfortable as I felt. She rubbed her arm and shrugged, and try as I might, I just couldn't figure out what was going on here. Mrs. Redfern liked Carrie. She always had. And, as ever, she seemed genuinely pleased to see her. Looking from one to the other, there was nothing obvious to separate them—but still it seemed to me that... I couldn't be sure, but it was almost as if Mrs. Redfern didn't want her there.

Carrie got this, too. Smiling uncertainly, blushing, she said her goodbyes and quickly went on her way, giving me a puzzled look.

When she was out of earshot, Mrs. Redfern sat back in her chair and dropped her pen onto the open journal. "She likes you," she told me. "Have you asked her out, yet?"

"We're friends," I said. I didn't want to talk about this. Not with Mrs.

Redfern. Come to think of it, there wasn't a whole lot I wanted to talk about with *anyone*. I just didn't see how it helped.

"Of course you are. That's why she looks at you the way she does." She sighed. Was this really such hard work? I wondered. "Don't tell me you can't see it, Carl? You get on really well together. It's obvious."

"We get on well together because we're friends. We tried it the other way and we like it this way best."

"When?"

"When what?"

"When did you try the other way?"

"A few years back. We went out with each other for about a week and it was horrible. We hardly spoke."

Mrs. Redfern rolled her eyes. "Fair enough," she said. "You know best."

She studied me for a moment and then put the top on her fountain pen and closed the journal.

"What's wrong?" I said. The suspense was overwhelming. I looked at her sitting there like that, her posture curiously bad today, and found myself wishing that I'd left with Carrie. I could have still been staring up her skirt but, no, here I was having to endure this tense, foreboding silence.

"I had a phone call a couple of hours ago." She was looking me directly in the eye. I had a bad feeling. "I wanted to be the first to tell you. I didn't want you hearing it from anyone else. It's Johnny, Carl. He died the early hours of this morning."

Johnny couldn't die, I thought—knowing how ridiculous this was, but nevertheless holding onto it for all it was worth. It just wasn't possible. He'd been close so many times before and survived—why should it be any different now? It was a joke, a pretty sick one, but nonetheless one that was right up Johnny's street. He was sitting quietly somewhere, chuckling away to himself while people cried and shook their heads at the injustice of it all. "And there's yobs out there," someone would say (because someone always did.) "Walking around as healthy as you like. God, indeed." As alive as me or Mrs. Redfern. Alive and revelling in the attention that his corpse-that-wasn't-a-corpse was receiving.

Calmly—perhaps a little *too* calmly—I said, "What happened?"

It was pretty much as I had expected. The strain of his condition had finally become too much for him. "He just fell asleep and didn't wake up," Mrs. Redfern told me. She sighed and looked me very deliberately in the eye. She was waiting for some kind of reaction—something that would reflect the friendship I had shared with Johnny and possibly express the loss I felt now that he had finally gone. But I couldn't deliver. Not then. Not ever.

The loss I felt for Johnny was real enough. As I sat there, looking at Mrs. Redfern and as she in turn looked at me, I felt all the emotions you might expect; sorrow, shock, anger at the years that he would miss out on. But expressing all that seemed... well, somehow pointless. Johnny had died a good while ago, if the truth be known—or, at least, the most significant parts of him had, the fight, the need for justice, the humour that had won through every time. However shocked I might be that the *ultimate* end had finally been reached, nothing had really changed much since Carrie had been standing by my side. Johnny was gone, but Johnny had not been there to start with. Not today, not last week, not even the month before. All his death really did was further define a space with which I was already very familiar.

"Do you remember the time he broke his arm?" she said, and I nodded.

"He accused that Terrence lad of being a thief."

She shook her head. "No," she said with a quiet smile. "Not that time. The other time. When he went down the ramp at the front of the school in a manual wheelchair."

I didn't—but then I recalled returning after my first operation to find Johnny in a foam sling and with faded cuts and bruises on his face, and nodded with a peculiar enthusiasm. "I missed the event itself," I said. "I think I was in hospital. But he was still a bit of a mess when I got back."

Mrs. Redfern grinned a toothy, utterly infectious grin. "His electric wheelchair had broken," she told me. "And, well, I suppose he just saw the opportunity for a little daredevilry and went for it."

"Spitting in the eye of God and death," I said, thoughtfully.

"What?"

"It was what he did. Especially in the early days. It was like he wanted to prove he could cheat death. You know the pool?"

"What about it?" Mrs. Redfern had an excited, expectant look on her face. She knew this was going to be good.

"One day he decided to drive his electric wheelchair along the entire width of it, getting his wheels as close to the edge as possible. We both had colds, so we hadn't been in. Everyone else was getting changed and we were all alone. I thought he was going to go in at any moment. You remember what the electric wheelchairs were like back then, right?"

She nodded, her eyes wide with disbelief.

"The microswitches used to stick when they got old." She was nodding more frantically, now. "They'd stick and the chair would start spinning out of control until you managed to turn the power off—which usually took Johnny between five and ten seconds."

"He wouldn't have stood a chance."

"I told him that, but he wouldn't listen," I said. "He just had this classic Johnny look on his face—a slight smile that was... I don't know. It was like he knew. He understood that nothing bad was going to happen. He was certain of it. But he knew I could never know that. And that was the joke."

Mrs. Redfern shook her head, and sat back in her chair again, letting her hands hang between her legs. "Christ, there'd have been hell on," she said. "If something had happened..."

"The scariest part was," I told her. "We were trying to think up ways to get our own back on Mr. Johnson and when I saw Johnny driving along the pool edge I just thought, 'Oh, God, no, he's going to do it. He's going to go in on purpose'"

"Get your own back?"

"Mr. Johnson wouldn't let me audition for *Great Expectations* and Johnny... he'd just lost all those house-points for telling Mrs. Cullum to shut the you-know-what up."

Mrs. Redfern was laughing, now. "Bless him," she said. "He really overstepped the mark that day."

"I wouldn't say that." I paused, something occurring to me. "Do you know the full story?"

"Only that she asked him if he wanted to go to the loo and the told her where to go and what to do when she got there."

I looked at the floor. "I thought as much," I said.

"What?"

"There was more to it than that. A lot more."

And I told her.

She was quiet and still when I'd finished, chewing on the side of her mouth as if trying to figure out whether it was too late for her to do something about this. Her breath hitched and her eyes remained locked on the journal on her desk. "That woman," she finally said. "That woman ought to be ashamed of herself."

"She was just... it was horrible, really. Johnny... his anger and the way he dealt with it made it all right. It was like he grabbed what she'd taken from him—"

"His dignity."

"Yeah, that's it. He grabbed his dignity back when he said what he did to her, but before that... I could feel him getting angry but... I don't know—it was almost as if he was getting smaller, too."

We didn't say anything else for a long time, just sat there together—both thinking our private Johnny thoughts. I remembered Johnny telling me, in the physio room outside this very office, that sometimes he wanted it—sometimes he wanted to die—and I wondered if that had been how he had felt earlier that morning. Had it been fate, or had dying been Johnny's final wilful act?

"I suppose it was for the best," Mrs. Redfern said—but we neither of us really believed that.

With the disaster that had been my exams behind me—an exhausting experience that had left me with an overwhelming sense of what I didn't know... or, more to the point, what I couldn't be *bothered* to know—I felt myself finally begin to settle. An odd calmness came over me as I realised that this was it. My final day. All that was required of me now was that I get my release form signed by my teachers in Almsby and have one final conversation with the headmaster, and then I was free. No longer a pupil in the Resolution (rejected by the self-serving Mr. Johnson long ago) and, now, no longer a pupil in the Almsby Comprehensive. It was comforting. Whatever else had happened with regard my exams, getting this far was in itself an accomplishment.

It seemed only fitting that, before leaving, I should visit old haunts—a phrase that now seemed more appropriate than ever. Braving the stares of teachers and injured-looking children (*were we that small once?*), I stopped outside what had once been Mrs. Shires's first classroom, the classroom in which I had found myself all those years ago. I remembered the excitement, the sense of adventure. I remembered a feeling of being somehow removed from all that I had previously known, of being glad about this even as it had scared me. Nothing much had really changed, not with the layout of the classrooms, at least, but as I sat there remembering I was again struck by how different it now felt. Even with the children there—as untainted and accepting as we had been—I couldn't find and revive that lost feeling of promise. I thought it might merely have been a matter of *perspective*. Maybe it was still there for these children. Maybe all the conversations I'd shared with Johnny had merely robbed me of any ability I'd had to see it and it was, in fact, as real and alive in these kids today as it had ever been with us. I hoped that that were the case, but I doubted it somehow.

"Can I help you?" A teacher I didn't know was standing before me. She didn't seem that much older than I was. Possibly in her mid-twenties, if that.

I shook my head and smiled. "Just saying goodbye," I told her, and she moved to my side—folding her arms and looking back at the classroom with me.

"This used to be your classroom?" she said.

"Yes."

She glanced down at me, doing the maths. "You must have been one of the first," she said. "When the school opened, I mean."

"That's right. The first of the guinea pigs."

"That's how you felt?"

Shaking my head, I smiled and said, "Not really. But, looking back, that's what we were."

"Someone always has to be first, I suppose."

I liked this teacher whose name I would never know. She reminded me a little of Mrs. Shires, but that may have simply been a side effect of my mood and the surroundings.

"One small step for a man," I said. "One giant leap for a kid in a wheelchair."

She chuckled. "You must have seen a few changes in your time here," she said.

"A few," I agreed—neglecting to add that just about all of them had been, in my opinion, for the worse.

"Maybe you'd like to come back some time," she said. "Give the kids a talk about what it was like back then—what makes the Resolution so special and everything?"

Remembering the promise I had made to Johnny, I shook my head. "That's a nice thought," I told her. "But I don't think I'm cut out for the job."

Studying me, she said, "That's a shame. I have a feeling you'd have a lot to say that'd be worth hearing."

"Perhaps. But I wouldn't want to inflict it on a bunch of kids just starting out."

"Jaded?" She was smiling at me. It was a comfortable smile. This woman really knew where she was. It was good to see.

"It's a phase I'm going through."

As she said her goodbyes, leaving me to my own, she touched my shoulder and said, "Come back and see us, okay? When you're feeling a little less jaded."

I smiled reassuringly and said that I wouldn't rule it out.

And, of course, I never would—because, when all was said and done, for good or bad, Johnny had already ruled it out for me.

Mr. Dixon perched on the edge a stool and looked at Matt and me, his arms folded as he appraised us. Our release forms were already signed and there was only the headmaster left to see. We knew, however, that this wouldn't be over until Mr. Dixon had given the two of us one final speech.

"So, this is it," he said.

"Looks like it," Matt replied.

"The end of an era."

I'd known he was going to say that. Mr. Dixon might have had heart and genuine commitment, but he could be terribly clichéd, at times.

"The end of one chapter, the beginning of another." Matt was taking the piss—and however gentle he was being about it, I still didn't find it appropriate.

"Couldn't have put it better myself, Matthew." He was onto him. He only ever called him "Matthew" by way of a warning, in my experience. "Yes, the beginning of another. I think that's the important thing to focus on, here. New beginnings. The chance to make your mark on the world." He sighed wistfully and rolled his eyes in my direction. "Sixth form college, right, Carl?"

"Yes, Sir. East Park."

"I went there when it was a grammar school. Haven't been back there since, I'm sad to say, but I have heard good things about it from former pupils." He winked at me. "The social life is especially good, I hear."

Mr. Dixon became a little misty-eyed—no doubt recalling what it had been like to be mine and Matt's age, heading out into the world without a care, without even an inkling of the self-imposed responsibilities that would lay ahead. I thought about what he had said about the social life, and felt only the slightest spark of excitement. I didn't want to go to sixth form college—not really. I'd had enough of education, but... well, I just couldn't see any other option. The few jobs that were available to me in those mass-unemployment Thatcher days were ones that I would not have touched with a ten-foot barge pole, and sitting around at home, watching the second-hand slowly glide its apparently eternal way around the clock face, simply had no prospect, no hope or direction. Opting for that would be to opt for a grim conclusion, I sure. The kind of defeat that Johnny had experienced—a defeat that, in his way, he had made me promise I would avoid. I could only go to sixth form college. That was how I saw it. Anything else would be to give up the illusion, withdraw from everything that I thought I believed in.

"We will never be far away," Mr. Dixon was telling us. "I know it feels as if the curtain is falling on this part of your life—something you probably think you welcome, at the moment. But we'll always be here. If you need references or just a good-old chinwag, don't hesitate. I *will* be expecting progress reports."

Matt gave him his word that he would send him a telegram the minute he got his first service medal (Matt had opted for a career in the Army). Mr. Dixon seemed to catch a whiff of Matt's irony, but he let it pass—showing us to the door as he waffled on about new phases and continuing "friendship".

At the door, holding it open for me, Matt already out in the corridor, Mr. Dixon paused and looked down at me. "Remember that egg," he told me. "There are always other ways, Carl."

Chapter Fifteen: Acceptance and Its Not-So-Thinly-Veiled Counterpart

A chilly autumn day, the light brittle and heartless. Somewhere in the distance, I heard a wood pigeon—solemn and solitary, lost in a world and time it couldn't comprehend, as baffled as his call suggested. Watching the bus that had dropped me off drive away, I felt as alone as that pigeon sounded. Cast adrift from the security I had once had, the Resolution always an unimpressive but reliable safety net in the background, I felt suddenly quite sure that I wouldn't last a single day. As promising as the orientation day had been during the summer holidays, this was now the hard-edged reality, and it could only prove to be a trial for which I would never be a match.

Other students were filing past me—heading inside to the relative comfort of the common room. So far, I hadn't spotted a single familiar face. It worried me, even though I received a lot of friendly smiles. The whole prospect of having to start over again, make new friends and forge new alliances... I wondered if I had the energy... I wondered if I had the inclination.

Going with the herd, I finally went inside—feeling a little buoyed by the sheer volume of attractive girls but nevertheless wishing I could find someone I actually knew, however distantly. Wishes didn't help in the least, however, so I reluctantly tried a silent prayer (desperate times calling for desperate measures, and all that) .

And as it turned out, there was a god, after all—and he was a right sick fuck.

"Carl!" a squeaky voice said. "Thank fuck for that. I thought there was going to be no one here from Almsby."

Allen Barnaby. Possibly the last person I would have expected to see here. Possibly the last person I would have *wanted* to see here.

He looked even taller than I remembered—taller and broader at the shoulders—and it occurred to me that maybe he'd passed through his loser phase, come out the other side ready to impose himself in a more authoritative and admirable fashion. One look, however, at the way in which he dropped his chin and glanced around sheepishly quickly disabused me of that notion.

"Allen," I said—suddenly quite depressed at the prospect of possibly having to spend my time at East Park paired up with him. "What are you doing here? I thought your dad had got you a job on the bins."

"Aye, well, he did," he told me, his eyes following a girl with bright orange hair and jeans so tight it looked as though she'd simply had her lower half painted indigo. "He did, but... I reckoned I could do a bit better than that."

"Only a bit?" I said.

He laughed that fucking irritating laugh of his. I wasn't going to be able to take much of this. If I didn't get away from him soon, I'd either start chewing on the furniture or—worse still—become intractably associated with him, destined to never make the cool friends I deserved. "He wasn't too pleased, I can tell you," he said. "Apparently, I'm a let-down. He gets me all set-up so I can earn some real money and pay my way, and what do I do? I throw it back in his face. If it wasn't for our mam, he would have gladly chucked me the fuck out."

I nodded noncommittally, surveying the concourse and wondering just what the hell I was supposed to do next. I didn't want to ask Allen, because he might take that as an offer of friendship, but I was at a complete loss. Something had been mentioned during the orientation day about how the first day would work and so on, but for the moment, somewhat overwhelmed, the detail escaped me.

Just when I thought there was no other option than for me to stoop low and do the very thing I didn't want to do, I noticed a figure approaching.

Large and impressive, though not actually fat, she strode towards me with a pleasant smile on her face and an A4 folder under her arm, fashionably dressed and coiffed. Aged thirty to thirty-five, I took her to be a teacher—though I couldn't recall having met her on the orientation day.

"Carl?" she said, offering me a hand, which I took.

"That's right."

"My name's Gail." Her hand was almost as cold as mine. Two warm hearts together. "I'm your... well, I'm a nursing auxiliary, but you might be best thinking of me as your assistant."

"Assistant?" I hadn't been expecting this at all.

"Yes—if there's anything you need help with, it's my job to see that you get it."

Allen sniggered and I threw him a suitably unimpressed snarl. Blushing and staring down at his shuffling feet, he excused himself—telling me he'd see me in the common room.

"Not if I see you first," I mumbled as he walked away.

"Friend of yours?" Gail had a mischievous smile that I immediately warmed to. She was like none of the nursing auxiliaries I had previously known. We were equals. That was how she saw it. She was not in a position of authority, she was a friend, a colleague—a concept that, in this context, was very new to me, not to mention refreshing.

"Not quite," I said, smiling. "Let's just say you did me a favour turning up when you did."

She gave a little bow, being careful not to drop the A4 folder. "Happy to be of service."

~

Our surroundings were so much more comfortable than I'd been accustomed to. Sitting in his parents modern, sparsely furnished living room, drinking tea and eating biscuits (from Marks and Spencer, if I wasn't mistaken), it was far removed from our time spent talking at the hospital—and I couldn't help feeling that, as in his story, we had also reached a new stage in our friendship, a place, perhaps, that was fittingly casual. When we talked, now, I no longer bothered with my notebook; it sat on the settee beside me, a forgotten pretext.

"So you weren't totally cast adrift, then?" I said to him.

Carl sat in the corner of the room in his wheelchair, an affixed tray holding his mug of tea (with orange plastic straw) and his smartphone. He again appeared radically different to the man I had encountered that first day in the hospital, more relaxed and less concerned with appearing in control. I suspected that this was yet another aspect of his "layering", a reflection of the gradual peeling away I'd observed before, and wondered how much further the process would go. What would be left at the end? Someone I didn't recognise at all, or someone who was a more solid, unequivocal version of the man I thought I already knew?

"No," he said. "Not totally—though Gail did only work mornings for the most part."

"Someone else taking her place when she wasn't around?" I already knew the answer, of course. I merely needed a little clarification.

Carl shook his head. "That was as good as it got when it came to accommodating my needs," he told me. "Smacked of tokenism."

I sat forward, putting my mug of tea down on the small table. "Let me get this straight," I said. "They acknowledge that you need additional help by giving you a nursing auxiliary, and then limit the hours she can work?"

"That's about the long and short of it," Carl said. "As it turned out, it wasn't such a big deal, really. There wasn't a whole lot that Gail had to do for me, other than open a few doors and generally be there if I needed a little support. But, to me, it was a very definite underscoring of the half-hearted attempt at making East Park work for me. To be honest, I think I saw from day one that I was fighting a losing battle."

"How?"

"Little things like the classrooms and the common room being on different levels."

"I don't follow."

"There was a flight of stairs between the two," he told me. "And no ramp. To get from one part of the college to the other I had to go outside and go through the car park, which was on a gradual incline. Not so bad when the weather was okay, but during the winter it was hell. It'd be pissing down, and there I'd be, trundling along in my far-too-fucking-slow electric wheelchair, getting soaked to the skin and freezing my nuts off. And, of course, when I got to my class my fingers were often too cold for me to write."

"Couldn't Gail have taken notes for you?"

"Possibly," he conceded. "But I really didn't like the idea of having her sit in lessons with me. It wouldn't have addressed the underlying problem and..." he smiled, "... and, well, it wouldn't have been cool."

"And being cool was important to you?"

"I was seventeen and had already fashioned a reputation for being the trendiest cripple in town. My hair—yes, I had lots of hair back then—was usually a nice shade of burgundy, I had a dangly silver earring—it was like a stud with a thin rod hanging down with another stud-like bit on the end, very classy—jeans that were too tight for sitting in all day but which I nevertheless wore constantly... oh, and white shoes! Yes, being cool was important to me."

"Burgundy hair?"

Carl shrugged, smiling. "Looking back, it's regrettable," he said. "A tragic state of affairs, as all fashion statements usually are when viewed retrospectively. It looked good enough, I suppose, by the standards of the day, but I can't help feeling now that maybe I was trying a bit too hard."

"Don't we all at seventeen?"

Again, that shrug. "Maybe. I'd come through the really difficult fashion phase—where I was trying really hard and still getting it largely wrong—but the white shoes...." He laughed. "Can they ever be a good thing?"

"Maybe not," I said, intending to pull his leg, "but I still want to see photos."

"Don't hold your breath."

"Not planning on showing me any? I could always have a word with your mam... "

"That's not what I meant," he said, shaking his head. "There are none in existence. That I know of, at least. I used to... well, I avoided cameras like the plague. I didn't like the bloody things at all."

"Why ever not?"

"Because, in spite of my efforts at looking trendy, I was still a mess."

"In what way?"

"Physically. I wasn't eating properly, I was pushing myself too hard, again. Plus there was the added strain, now, of being popular. I'd somehow managed to propagate this image of myself as... I don't know, all bravado and bullshit, that's how I look to me, now, but I suppose that that wasn't what everyone else saw." He smiled again. "I was fashionably tragic," he added with a chuckle.

"But at least you were popular."

Matching my smile, he said. "Yes. At least I was popular.

~

It had taken only a couple of months for us to establish ourselves as the bad boys and girls of the common room. Taking over one corner by the Klix drinks machine, ensconced in what had once been a small serving area—complete with sink and counter—we crammed in an old settee and couple of armchairs and looked out on the main common room concourse with its pool table and its Pac-Man and Zaxxon games, firing evil glances at anyone who came too close. The girls had a reputation (sadly undeserved, in my experience) of being slags, and the guys... well, we weren't outcasts or anything. We fit in wherever we *wanted* to fit in, but we were generally considered to be a little weird—which was fine from where I was sitting, since by late 1983 weird was highly acceptable. Some of the people I liked most were considered weird by the majority. It was as much a status symbol and affirmation as the earring I wore.

The end of November, snug in our little corner of Paradise, found us planning—or, initially, for the most part resisting it. With my wheelchair, the settee and the two armchairs, there wasn't a whole lot of room—so there were limbs and bodies everywhere. Carrie (who had opted to try East Park at the eleventh hour), sat on the side of my wheelchair, her hip rubbing nicely against my arm, my footrests were being shared with an elfin girl I'd have shagged at the first opportunity, given half a chance, called Marie Wales, five people were crammed on the settee, with Jack "Eddie" Masters and Nazrul Sahadev sitting up on the worktop near the sink. It was lunchtime on a Wednesday, with a long afternoon of general studies ahead of us (if we decided to turn up for whichever activity we'd elected to take—which I for one seldom did), and the mood was oddly like that of a Friday afternoon. Marie was sharing her hot chocolate with me, Carrie was tapping the heels of her trainers gently against the box that housed the two car batteries beneath my wheelchair and Eddie... well, Eddie was calling us all a bunch of boring, short-sighted fuckers.

Jack "Eddie" Masters was what can only be described as a most individual individual. Waxing and waning through various fashion trends, he had recently metamorphosed from a fringe-flicking New Romantic into a fringe-flicking, parka-wearing Mod, strolling around the common room in his typically high-chinned way like he was the new Roger Daltrey. He had an elevated opinion of himself, did our Eddie, and we all got a kick out of calling him a wanker behind his back—but I got the feeling he was all bluff and bluster. I recognised the signs.

"Why does everyone call him Eddie if his name's really Jack?" Carrie whispered to me. "I still haven't worked that one out."

"You ever seen that TV programme, *The Munsters?*" She nodded. "Someone thought he looked like that kid that's in it and the name stuck."

"And he likes it?"

"Seems to."

"It's just around the corner," Eddie was saying. "It's just a few fucking weeks away and you're sitting here like a bunch of unwashed dildos giving me all this 'oh, there's plenty of time yet'-crap. Bloody amazing. And you call yourselves *students?* You're a fucking disgrace."

"I think that's a bit strong, mate," I said. "Especially the bit about unwashed dildos. I don't think any of us are unwashed. Right, Marie?"

"I had a shower just this morning." She stuck her arm under my nose. "Smell."

Happy to oblige, I said, "Scent of the forest, unless I'm mistaken."

"Pears soap, actually, but close."

"You're just not going to take this seriously, are you?" Eddie said, sighing exasperatedly.

"Of course we are," Carrie said. "Just not yet. It's way too early."

Marie seemed uncomfortable. She wriggled about on the edge of her armchair, switching her drinking chocolate from her right hand to her left as she turned to get a better look at Eddie.

"What you getting your knickers in such a twist for, anyway?" she said.

Looking embarrassed, Eddie said, "I like Christmas, that's all."

That was about the biggest heap of bullshit I'd ever heard. The way he said it, he made it sound like he was looking forward to opening his Advent Calendar and hanging his stockings when, in reality, what he really meant was that he was looking forward to having the mother of all piss-ups.

"I just want us to have a nice, festive time," he added.

"Defined as waking up in your own vomit with your duds around your ankles," Naz interjected. "Preferably with some fat lass sat on your face, if I know you."

"I keep telling you," Eddie said, clearly annoyed that Naz had chosen this particular moment to wake up. "She isn't fat. She's *Rubenesque*."

"Which is nothing less than a fucking pretentious way of saying she's got an arse on her like the back of a bus. Christ, man, you are so up yourself, at times."

"And that *has* to be frustrating," I added, "when what you really want is to be up the fat lass."

"How many fucking times do I have to tell you?" he said, pushing his foot against Marie's armchair in order to readjust his position. "*She isn't—*"

"Oh you bloody clumsy idiot!" I said. "What the fuck?"

"I couldn't help it," Marie said, thinking I was angry with her. "It was—"

"I know," I said, quickly. "Jesus, Eddie, look what you and your fat lass did. Go on, look, mate. Look what you did to my fucking shoes."

Eddie looked. Naz looked. Carrie and Marie, trying not to snigger, looked. Everyone looked.

Eddie pushing his foot against Marie's chair had had a rather unfortunate consequence—for me, at least. Jiggling an already fidgety Marie, who had been in the process of switching her hot chocolate back from her left hand to her right, she had almost slipped from the edge of her seat and had reflexively put out a hand to steady herself. This in itself would not have been a problem, had the hand she had used in this manner not been the very same hand into which she had also been transferring her hot chocolate. The plastic cup slipped, tilted and almost dropped, but she saved it at the very last minute—not before, however, she had sloshed copious amounts of the stuff over my lovely white shoes.

"They're not white anymore," Carrie said. Bless her (the bitch).

"Carl and His Chocolate-Coloured Dream Shoes," Naz added,

suggesting we should write a musical.

"You can't blame me for that," Eddie insisted. "Slopping shit on your shoes wasn't my intention when I did what I did."

"Lack of intent doesn't absolve you of blame." *When did I start talking like that?* "You dumb fuck," I added, so as not to sound too flash.

"Of course it does," he insisted.

"Oh don't be so ridiculous," Marie said. "It can't. If you kill someone, you're still responsible—whether you meant to kill 'em or not."

"Jesus. Now I'm a killer." He rolled his eyes. "I'll buy you a new pair. Happy?"

"They're Italian. Fifty quid should cover it."

"They're Ravel," he told me. "I'll give you fifteen and you can lump it."

"Ravel *are* Italian," Carrie pointed out.

"So's pasta," Eddie told her, "but you won't catch me paying fifty quid for that, either."

They were all grinning and, in spite of the fact that the drinking chocolate had got my socks, too—my *white* socks—I couldn't help but see the funny side of it. "Will you look at them?" I laughed. "Will you just fucking *look* at them?"

"We'll sort him out, won't we, Carrie?" Marie said. "What this calls for is a woman's touch."

As they disappeared from the common room, I said to Naz, nice and loudly, "I never say no to a woman's touch."

"Depends on where she's touching," he pointed out.

"I'll make a list in order of priority."

"And what they're touching it with, of course," Eddie insisted on adding.

"I'd keep quiet, if I were you," I told him. "I've had quite enough of your nonsense today."

When Carrie and Marie returned, it didn't surprise me to see that they came armed with dozens of paper towels. They made as much room for themselves as they could by pushing the armchair aside a little and knelt down on the floor before me—after first mopping up any residual spillage thereon. Eddie raised an eyebrow at me, and I winked at him, sitting back and making myself comfortable.

"Ready when you are, ladies," I said. "Help yourselves."

Marie frowned up at me. I could see right down her top. Not that I was looking or anything. "Do you *want* your shoes cleaning?" she said.

"Please."

"Well button it, then."

Who was I to argue? Doubting that they would be able to save my shoes (which I didn't like much anyway, to be honest—though I would never have told them that), I was nevertheless happy to let them get on with it—especially amused by the imagery a few minutes later when Gail came in.

"You just can't help yourself, can you?" she said, her eyes flickering in that mischievous way of hers. "I leave you alone for two minutes and the next thing I know you've got two more girls kowtowing before you... they are kowtowing, aren't they?" she added, sounding a little worried.

"They're just mopping up a little accidental spillage," Eddie told her. "That's what you get for wearing low-cut blouses, I guess."

"You should know," Marie told him. Then to me and Naz, "That's why he goes out with the fat lass—so her clothes'll fit him. Right, Eddie?"

I didn't catch what Eddie said for Gail, knowing from experience that this could go on for a very long time, was talking to me.

I listened to the noise around me and tried to pick out what it she was saying. It seemed perfectly harmless—nothing to really concern me. But for some reason, I just didn't want to listen to her. Everything was how I wanted it to be in that moment. I didn't want any additional complications. She smiled at me, shrugged her shoulders, and said, "The third of December. You have an appointment with the guidance counsellor."

This, in itself, was not something I was overly concerned about. I'd had plenty of meetings with the guidance counsellor over the years, and there was no reason for me to have any qualms about seeing her again. If anything, it was a formality. I would attend the meeting, be asked a few questions about what I did or didn't want to do in the future, and, if past experience was anything to go by, be handed a few perfectly useless leaflets about occupations I would never consider in a month of Sundays. I certainly didn't believe it would inconvenience me in any way. None-theless, I had a bad feeling. This was different now. This wasn't school. Now we were getting to the serious part of my educational career. Decisions would soon have to be made about the future, about what I would do after sixth form college.

"What time?" I said.

"Just after lunch," she told me.

I took a pen from my pocket and made a note of it, giving Gail my word that I wouldn't forget; she, like most people around me at that time, knew just how wilfully forgetful I could be.

Once she was satisfied and had left, the conversation turned back to the question of what we were going to do for Christmas. Eddie was still insisting that we had to start planning for it now. As far as he was concerned, this was the event of the year—even more important than New Year's Eve. Listening to him talk, it was easy to believe that he saw this as, quite possibly, the last Christmas we would all ever have together. He was that enthusiastic and driven.

"So," he said. "I'll arrange the booze—if you're all prepared to chip in, that is—and Naz can take care of the Christmas tree. Carl, you can—"

"Wait a minute," Naz said. "I'm afraid I can't have anything to do with a bloody Christmas tree."

Marie stared at him. "What are you talking about?"

"I just can't have anything to do with a Christmas tree. It isn't that I don't want to," he explained. "It's just that I can't. It goes against my religion."

"And just what religion would that happen to be today?" I said.

"What's that got to do with it?" he said.

I suddenly felt very tired. A few moments ago, talking to Gail, I'd believed that this was all I'd wanted. The camaraderie, the banter, the simple sense of belonging—all of this I had seen as the perfect way of living. Uncomplicated, it had struck me that this was the answer. Sitting in a room full of friends talking nonsense had, however briefly, been the way I had wanted to spend the rest of my life. But now—as Naz and Eddie started to go at it hammer and tongs—all I could think of was how I wanted to get away from them. As the conversation became ever more ridiculous, I wished I was somewhere else entirely—sitting in my room at home, listening to music, reading a book or, even, simply staring at the wall, following my own circuitous train of thought. Anything would be better than this.

As the silliness became rank stupidity, I felt it chafing and tried to think of a fitting excuse to get away.

"You're a licentious atheist like the rest of us," Eddie was telling Naz. "I don't know anyone less religious than you—unless we're talking about getting religiously drunk every Friday and Saturday night."

Naz stared at him evenly. He chewed the side of his mouth, nodded thoughtfully, and then said, "Good point. That never occurred to me. I'll take care of the Christmas tree, then, shall I?"

And with that the bell rang for the first lesson of the afternoon and we all went on our way—me with my ruined socks and shoes, Eddie with his thoughts of Christmas and Naz with no doubt detailed plans on how he was going to get a Christmas tree as cheaply as possible.

***

I was getting a cold. No, strictly speaking, that wasn't true. I already had a cold. I had a cold and, unless I was seriously mistaken, it was getting worse by the minute—my head throbbing, my throat sore and my chest itchy and rattly. Sitting in English beside Carrie, I thought how ridiculously excessive the preparations for Christmas were becoming (and how I really didn't want to miss out on any of it) and promised myself that I would take a couple of days off before the festive period arrived just to make sure I would be fit enough for the fun.

"It's getting crazy," I was telling Carrie. "Have you heard how much booze Eddie's planning on getting? There's absolutely no way we'll be able to smuggle it all into college."

"I'm not even sure we should smuggle *any* of it in," Carrie said. "I mean, if we get caught... well, it just doesn't bear thinking about. It's not like we haven't been warned about it numerous times."

I knew what she meant. Apparently, the year before, whilst we were still at school, the previous Lower Sixth had trademarked their own inimitable brand of Christmas celebration involving a few gallons of vodka, self-raising flour, eggs, naked girls and, most bizarrely, a pony that someone had found in a nearby field. Consequently, the powers that be were determined that nothing similar would happen this year. Form tutors had repeatedly warned that any inappropriate behaviour would be punished severely and leaflets had been passed round detailing just what, exactly, qualified as "inappropriate behaviour". If we got caught, the consequences would indeed be grave.

Returning to the essay I was working on, I tried not to think about just how unwell I was beginning to feel. I concentrated on building a cohesive structure, as we had been taught, introducing the topic, examining both sides of the argument and, if my plan worked out the way I wanted it to, finishing with a conclusion that was both insightful and original. My hand shook a little as I wrote and, try as I might, I couldn't get it to stop. I was exhausted.

And then it happened. The one thing I always dreaded most in a classroom situation. I felt the itch start at the back of my throat. It tickled, vying for attention as I did my best to focus on the essay. Holding my breath, I tried to swallow my way through it. I wrote another sentence, hand shaking all the more, but it was too insistent to be ignored. I started coughing. I started coughing and I just couldn't stop. The tickle became almost painful and as I hacked against it, I felt my chest start to rattle.

Briefly, as I heard the marbles rolling around in my chest, I flashed back to a long ago day and thought of Johnny. This was how it had been for him. However hard I tried to ignore the fact, he had been where I was now—struggling, afraid, feeling ill and yet terrified of what the consequences would be should he admit this to himself. I could tell myself I was different until I was blue in the face, replaying all the times that one person or another had told me my condition was nothing like Johnny's, but it didn't help. Not really. Whatever the prognosis might be, how I felt spoke volumes. Perhaps it *was* just a cold. But that wasn't how it felt. In my already weakened condition, I knew how dangerous such a simple thing could be, and as I glanced at Carrie beside me—Carrie who was throwing me concerned glances—the bout of coughing growing worse, I felt as if I were somehow slipping, sliding down into something I didn't understand, didn't want to understand, something dark and oppressive and all-encompassing. The lights didn't go out. I didn't grow dizzy and faint. I merely continued coughing... and coughing... and coughing until, no doubt unable to take any more, my teacher, Mrs. Moore, asked me if I needed to leave the classroom for a while.

"Go get a drink of water," she said, opening the door for me. "Carrie, you go with him—make sure he's all right."

The last thing I needed was a glass of water, but I was nevertheless thankful to be out of the classroom—thankful to be away from all the sympathetic stares. Heading straight outside for some fresh air, Carrie walking beside me, not speaking, simply waiting for the coughing fit to subside, the sense of relief was immense. Yes, I still felt rotten. Yes, my chest was now beginning to tighten up. Also, I'd somehow managed to hyperventilate and my fingers were tingling. But I was outside—I was away from that classroom and its cloying atmosphere. I didn't have to pretend any more. I could cough until my heart's content. My essay forgotten, I could admit to myself, however briefly, that I wasn't well. However much I enjoyed the social aspect of East Park, it was taking its toll. Pushing myself to compete, to remain popular and maintain the facade, was, bit by bit, wearing me down.

As I started to finally get it under control, Carrie put a hand on my arm and said, "Are you okay?"

She knew the minute she said it that it was a stupid thing to say. You only had to look at me to see that I was far from okay. I shook my head and, in spite of how lousy I was feeling, smiled at her. "Not really," I said.

"You should go home," she told me.

"I know—but I can't. Not yet. I have an appointment this afternoon with the careers officer... the *guidance counsellor*, I should say. I really need to get that out of the way."

"I'm sure you can reschedule the appointment," she insisted.

I didn't want that, and I was quick to tell her—perhaps a little too sharply. Maybe a little unreasonably, I had admittedly built up my appointment with the guidance counsellor into something that was possibly quite disproportionate. Having asked around, I had quickly discovered that I was the only student he was due to see—today or any time in the foreseeable future. He was coming to East Park very specifically to see me, and whilst that could just have been the way things were, it still seemed odd.

"And you don't think you're making too much of it?" Carrie said— once I'd finished outlining my misgivings.

"I don't know," I told her. "Possibly. It just doesn't feel right."

Watching me compassionately, she sat on a low wall beside me. "Maybe that's because you aren't well," she said. "Hasn't that occurred to you?"

It had, of course—everything that *could* be thought of had *been* thought of over the past few days. In great detail. I'd brooded silently, jotted down thoughts in a diary that I'd decided to keep, listened for clues in the backing tracks of favourite records—Christ, I'd even discussed it with Gail. And still I couldn't get away from the nagging suspicion that the guidance counsellor had something very specific to say to me... something that I most assuredly would not want to hear.

"What like?"

"That's just it," I told her. "I haven't got a clue. One thing I do know, though," I added, my breath short as my chest continued to tighten, "I don't want it hanging over me. I want to get it out of the way today, whatever *it* is."

I'd never met the guy before, but he introduced himself as Robert Warmington—a tall, scruffy gentleman who looked as if he just had to be the owner of the poxy yellow Citroen 2CV I'd seen in the car park. His jacket had patches on the elbows and his corduroy trousers were threadbare. But that was by no means the worst of it. His greasy hair stuck to his forehead as if it hadn't been washed in a month. This, together with the shifty way he kept looking at me—unable to meet my eyes for more than a few seconds at a time—only served to strengthen my misgivings.

"As you are probably aware," he was saying to me, shuffling paper so that he didn't have to look at me, "Miss London, your previous guidance counsellor, has been promoted—she is now working in our Newcastle office... we are all very envious," he added, smiling, trying to make a joke of it but still unable to look me in the eye. "And, as you can see, I've been assigned as her replacement."

What did he want? A fucking fanfare?

Robert Warmington possibly had the best of intentions. I really wasn't in a position to say. All I had to go on was what he said to me and how he behaved. Judging by these two factors alone, however, it seemed fairly clear to me that he was not feeling entirely comfortable. Continuing to shuffle his papers, as if looking for something important—something that would save him from his apparent misery—he said something about an "unusual set of circumstances" and how it was difficult for him to know "where to begin". I might almost have felt sorry for him had I not been so uncomfortable myself. Briefly, I considered offering him a lifeline—providing him with some easy way out, if only by agreeing with him—but I couldn't do that. Under the present circumstances, it appeared it just wasn't in my nature.

"You see where my difficulty lies, I'm sure," he said—appearing, in fact far from sure. "It's actually a very new area for me. I have no real experience working in this field. So, naturally, I've been pondering how best to approach the problem."

"Area?" I said. "Problem? I don't think I quite follow."

Again, he focused his attention on his papers, finally seeming to find something that gave him if not outright comfort then something close to a kind of consolation. He nodded thoughtfully but still didn't answer me. In that moment, I wanted to be out of that room. To say that he was ignoring me would be to overstate it—but he certainly didn't seem prepared to have an actual *conversation* with me.

"I have, however, arrived at a solution," he continued. "And, unless I am gravely mistaken, I think you'll be pleased with it."

"I can't wait," I mumbled under my breath.

"As I have already explained," he told me, "this is a very new area for me. So new, in fact, that I really don't think I have the expertise to offer you the guidance you need and deserve."

"You keep talking about this 'area'," I interrupted. "Before you say anything else, could you please explain just what you mean by that, exactly?"

Robert Warmington didn't like being interrupted. That was evident from the way in which he breathed out noisily through his nose, tightly clenching his jaw and, with mock patience, setting his papers back on the desk. Once again, I understood that he was not prepared to have anything like a real conversation with me. Either I wasn't worthy or, with his lack of expertise in this "area", he was under the misguided impression that—and I believed this was the more likely of the two explanations—I wasn't in fact capable of participating in a proper dialogue.

"As I was saying," he once more continued, "there are others who are more qualified to deal with your particular needs—which is why—"

"You mean disability, don't you?" I said. "When you talk about this 'area', you mean my disability, right?"

"—which is *why* I'm going to arrange for you to have a meeting with our specialist in this area."

"One minute," I said. He continued talking. But I wasn't having any of that. More forcefully, I sat forward in my wheelchair and said to him, "Now just one minute. If you're going to palm me off on someone—a specialist in this so-called *area*—someone I'm fairly sure I neither want nor need to see, the least you can do is have the common courtesy to be clear about what it is, *exactly*, you're telling me. You're saying that you can't supply the careers information I need, am I correct?"

Somewhat taken aback, Robert Warmington nodded. "That's right, yes."

"Because I need different things to someone who is able-bodied, yes?"

"That's correct."

I sat back in my wheelchair, resting my hands in my lap. Suddenly quite exhausted again, my lungs itching, a cough threatening once more, I sighed and wondered if it was worth it. I could argue with him, but what, really, was the point? His mind was already made up. His own apparent inadequacy and my supposed "specialist needs" had long ago—long before he had even met me—driven him to the conclusion that he needed someone else to do his job for him. Nothing I could say would alter that, but I had to at least try. That much I understood. As futile as it might be.

"All I need from you is advice—*information*—on what qualifications I need for the particular career I hope to pursue," I told him. "That's your job, and that's all I ask of you. Anything to do with the practicalities of doing a given job with my disability is my problem. Questions of access etc... that's for me to sort out."

"That isn't quite how we see it."

"How you see it isn't the point," I argued. "This is about me. About the choices available to *me*. I don't need a specialist adviser—whatever that might be. All I need is someone to answer my questions... not even that, really. All I need is someone to at least *listen* to them. You're capable of that, right?"

He was refusing to look at me again. Not that he'd ever looked at me in any real sense of the word. "I'm afraid the decision has already been made," he told me. "This is policy, now, and I'm sure you'll find it to your advantage if you just give it the chance it deserves."

I was being unreasonable. That was what he was essentially saying. By wanting a level playing field, by insisting that I required only a decent quality of information—the kind of information my peers took for granted—I was being an awkward, obstructive git. And I was happy to play the part, if that was what was required.

Not that it would get me anywhere.

"So what's the problem?" Naz asked.

Eddie was sprawled across the settee, Naz sitting on an armchair beside him. There were only the three of us in the common room—or, at least, in our part of the common room—this afternoon. We were meant to be in liberal studies, debating the decriminalisation of cannabis, but none of us was in the mood. I, especially, was feeling rather out of sorts. My cold was definitely getting worse, but that wasn't the half of it. My meeting with Robert Warmington was, a good hour later, still preying on my mind.

"The problem is," I said, as patiently as I could manage, given that I'd explained this to him twice already. "The problem is, this isn't the way it's been done in the past. The whole point is that for the last half of my education I've been integrated into the mainstream system. The choices I have had were the same choices that you've had. No restrictions and no special dispensations. Yes, I have additional support when I need it—to a point—but with something like this, all I need is good careers advice. Advice about how to get the job I want."

"I understand that," Naz said. "But if she knows more about—"

"More about what? That's what I'm saying. This isn't a disability issue. Okay, there are considerations. There always will be. But in this instance, specialist advice just isn't necessary—and I'd even go so far as to bet that any advice I get from this woman will in fact be inferior, at least as far as my particular requirements are concerned."

Eddie didn't seem all that interested. Making himself more comfortable, he glanced at the two of us and admitted that, as far as he was concerned, and as reluctant as he was to say it, he thought Naz had a point. He said it, it has to be said, in such a way that heavily implied that he just wanted to shut the two of us up—that he wanted a bit of peace and quiet. "I understand what you're saying," he told me—which made it clear to me that he didn't. "But I really don't see what the big deal is. Chances are, this'll be advantageous to you. She'll probably be able to offer you things, opportunities, that this guy couldn't. You're just surmising that the information she's going to give you will be inferior. You have no way of knowing that yet, so, as far as I can see, your best bet is to just give it a go and see what happens. If it turns out like you believe it will, then you'll have cause for complaint."

They didn't have a fucking clue what they were talking about. They had no experience of places like the Resolution, of the whole "special school" education system. Naz and Eddie simply had no idea where something like this could lead. They couldn't read the signs the way I could and nothing I could say would ever make them understand that.

Reluctantly, I fell silent. Nothing remained the same forever. Moods changed, circumstances were forced upon us that we would never choose. The hand of the clock moved ever forward but nothing—*absolutely nothing*—could guarantee that with its movement would come positive progress. Systems found their own ways of breaking down. What worked perfectly at one minute, fell completely apart the next; what worked less than perfectly at one minute, in my experience, fell completely apart even more quickly than that.

I had Christmas to look forward to, at least, I told myself—but as it would turn out, perhaps predictably, I would miss the East Park festivities altogether. My cold would develop into a full-blown chest infection and I would spend the fortnight up to Christmas dutifully taking my antibiotics in front of the telly. In many ways, it was a relief. Yes, a part of me was desperate to see if Eddie's dreams of debauchery would come to fruition without everyone being expelled—but the comfort and security I experienced in its place far outweighed that.

At home, I didn't have to think about "specialist" guidance counsellors who understood my particular "area". At home, reading the books I chose to read, listening to the music I chose to listen to, writing games for my Commodore 64 computer, I could look forward to Christmas with my parents and family without feeling set apart—without feeling that I had to keep up a facade that others wished to tear down for me.

At home, I could be who I wanted to be.

I could be the person I truly was.

Chapter Sixteen: Wicker Baskets and Stuff

It was true that as my exams approached I became increasingly disillusioned. My motivation went out of the window and everything became an effort. Even as the weather warmed and the days lengthened, my sense of purpose dwindled away and, bizarrely, I found myself wishing for the dark days of winter again—the days when the curtains could be drawn against the night and the world, when everything was somehow external and removed. I was depressed, I suppose, but I nevertheless managed to hide it from everyone around me and, somehow, continue with the day-to-day tasks set before me.

Naz and I were working on our computer projects, using an old Z80a-based computer. Even for the time, it was positively prehistoric, but for some reason—with what was fast becoming a quite typical perversity—I preferred using it to the newer, faster BBC machines. It felt and looked like a computer—a big metal box, with metal handles to carry it, it was that hefty, and an equally metallic keyboard and monitor. We joked often, the two of us, about what would happen if it shorted whilst we were merrily typing away on it. Would we be electrocuted, or would it just tingle a bit?

As I typed a line of BASIC into the computer, Naz watched me—quite patiently. He was well ahead with his project (they had to be handed in in a few weeks time) but still there were finishing touches he needed to put to it. Nevertheless, he sat and quietly watched as I worked away, trying in vain to make up for the time I'd missed during my latest bout of illness.

"And people will be able to type with this using only two keys or switches, right?" he said, sounding uncharacteristically—not to mention unjustifiably—impressed.

"That's the idea, yes." My arms and fingers were aching so I took this opportunity to rest for a moment while I explained to him just what I wanted the program to achieve. "It's for people—kids, too, I suppose—with really limited movement and who can't speak. Some of them, you know, can't even hold a pencil, and some of the electronic aids they have to help them communicate are just abysmal. They all seem..." I shrugged my shoulders. "It's like they're fucking half-hearted attempts, you know? If I can't do it properly then, frankly, I don't want to do it at all."

"Fucking right," Naz said. "Completely with you there, mate." He paused, staring at the computer screen—the VDU, as we used to call them—before asking, "And you used to know kids like this, right?"

I thought of Johnny. Not exactly the most extreme case where movement and speech were concerned. Nevertheless, he and many others would have benefited from something like this. Simply not having to hold a pencil would, in and of itself, have made life so much easier for him. To see the words growing on a screen before him as he clicked away... to him it would have seemed a kind of magic.

"Yes," I said. "I used to know kids like that."

Naz shook his head and sighed meaningfully. "Makes you think, doesn't it?" he said. "Got to thank your lucky stars. Don't know about you," he added, "but sometimes I just look around me and think, 'God? You're seriously telling me that there's a God? I don't fucking think so.'"

I nodded and continued with my work—not feeling up to a protracted conversation about theology. Naz, however, did not need any encouragement. He continued talking as I typed away and as he did so, something occurred to me. He ranted on about the severity of the various physical conditions he saw around him, the terminal illnesses and the sheer scale of the suffering, and I realised that as far as he was concerned, and in spite of the conversation we had had before Christmas regarding the "specialist" guidance counsellor, he did not see me in any of the categories he mentioned. When he spoke of just how bad some disabilities could be, even touching on Duchenne muscular dystrophy, he said it almost as if I were able-bodied. It was a peculiar moment—a peculiar *insight*—and one that I didn't quite know how to accommodate. This was a good thing, surely, I told myself. The fact that he saw me and *only* me justified everything I had been trying to achieve all these years. The wheelchair was real for Naz, I was certain, but he could now see beyond it in such a way as to, for all intents and purposes, completely negate it. I felt oddly moved by this—but it would also be true to say that I also felt confused by the doubt I heard muttering away at the back of my mind. Was this really such a good thing? Was he actually seeing the real me or merely the me I wanted to project? Had I simply fooled him? Had I simply fooled them *all?*... It was a frightening proposition. I wanted them to know who I was. Yes, I wanted them to understand that I wasn't all that different from them—but not seeing my disability, the thing that contributed so strongly, if some were to be believed, to my determined, pigheaded personality... that just made me feel uncomfortable.

"What was it like?" Naz suddenly asked me.

"What was what like?"

"The Resolution. The school you used to go to."

"I went to the Almsby Comprehensive," I told him.

"Yeah, but before that. You knew kids like the ones we were talking about, didn't you? In this school, the Resolution, yes?"

"Yes."

"So what was it like?"

All I wanted to do was get on with my project. I liked Naz. Yes, he could be a bit of a bullshitter at times, but by and large he was a decent bloke. He was dependable, in his way, and always good for a laugh—but the way I was feeling, this conversation was just too much for me. I didn't want to go back there. I'd promised Johnny that I wouldn't and whilst, in the literal sense, I didn't believe I ever would, even in the more abstract, figurative sense, it felt like a betrayal.

"Probably not as bad as you're imagining," I told him. "The kids weren't dying left, right and centre, if that's what you're thinking."

"But kids did die there?"

"Yes."

"What was that like?"

He was watching me carefully. Too carefully. I continued typing as I spoke, trying to keep this casual—trying to not let him see just how difficult I found it.

"It was hard, sometimes," I said. "If it was someone you knew. It was hard because it seemed so unfair—but it was also hard because sometimes you wondered who was going to be next... if it was going to be you, you know?"

This seemed to surprise him. "You thought you were going to die?"

Nodding, I said, "That kind of thing, it gets into your head after a while. You see it happening to younger kids, to kids the same age as you, and you realise far earlier than most people that it can happen to anyone at any time. Then... well, there was a point when I had to have a couple of operations. I wasn't that well and... I don't know. I don't suppose I was ever really about to die, but that didn't stop me thinking that I might."

"Scary."

"Yes—but that wasn't what it was like all the time. Sometimes, in the first year especially, it was actually a lot of fun. Things deteriorated fairly quickly, though. It was never going to work."

"The school?"

I nodded. "The whole idea was badly thought through," I told him. "It was meant to be the beginning of a bright new era."

"But it wasn't?"

"No. Not by a long chalk. Oh, don't get me wrong, everything had no doubt been planned and applied with the best of intentions—but the goals they set themselves were unrealistic... especially when you consider that the captain of the ship, so to speak, was—and I'm being generous—borderline inadequate."

Naz didn't really know what I was getting at. He couldn't have. He sat beside me staring at the VDU, nodding thoughtfully. "So did any of your friends die?" he finally said. "If you don't mind me asking."

"One," I told him. "Not long before I left Almsby."

"Sudden?"

"No—it took Johnny about six years, possibly longer, to die. All the time I knew him, he was steadily deteriorating." I met Naz's eye. "Duchenne muscular dystrophy," I told him.

"Nasty," he said. "Our mam's friend's son has that and he's in a pretty bad way at the moment."

"How old is he?"

"Nineteen or twenty—somewhere around there."

"A ripe old age for someone with Duchenne," I said, and Naz nodded.

We fell silent and I once again concentrated on my work. My heart wasn't in much, these days, but if there was one thing I wanted to get right, it was this project. Maybe it would never be used by anyone. It was, after all, fairly unsophisticated. But if I did it correctly it might at least prompt someone with greater ability than I to think about the problem again and apply themselves to producing something better—something that would truly help people like Johnny, people, frankly, who were far worse off than Johnny (at least as far as their abilities to communicate were concerned.)

"Let's hope it makes a difference," Naz said, nodding at the computer screen. "Every little helps—that's what they say, right?"

He hadn't been there. "Right," I said.

I waited outside the M.I. room with Gail, thinking how appropriate it was that my interview with the guidance counsellor—the *careers officer*, as I now insisted on calling her, for old time's sake—was being held here, given that I was ill most of the time these days and, in fact, wasn't feeling all that hot today. I closed my eyes briefly, trying to prepare myself for whatever it was I had ahead of me, and when I opened them again Gail was looking at me—a slight frown pulling her eyebrows together.

"You look tired," she told me. "I'm sure we can cancel if you aren't feeling up to this."

I shook my head. "No," I said. "I'm fine. Really. I've just been staring at a computer screen for too long. Not good for the old eyes."

"You sure?"

"Yes." I thought for a moment and then added, "I'll feel a lot better once this is out of the way."

"Not looking forward to it, are you?"

"I have a bad feeling."

Gail smiled patiently. She knew all about me and my bad feelings. I'd had enough of them during the time she'd known me—bad feelings about test results, bad feelings about why a particular teacher wanted to see me, bad feelings about the clouds rolling in from the North. In my depressed mood, it was true, I saw portents everywhere.

"I'm sure it'll be just fine," she told me. "I met her earlier and she seems nice enough."

"Define 'nice enough'."

Laughing, Gail said, "Okay, she struck me as a bit matronly. That I must admit. But she certainly isn't the harridan you like to imagine. If anything, she seemed quite gentle."

Gail was working a bit too hard at convincing me. I sat and listened to all she had to say about the woman—whose name was Christine Northam. In her mid-50s or so, Gail insisted that she was sure the Christine Northam didn't have an offensive bone in her body. Her job was to see to it that my career needs were accommodated and Gail had no doubt that she, Christine Northam, would see to it that that was just what she did. She told me how friendly she had been, how firm her handshake, and I considered telling Gail to stop. She was convincing no one. I didn't have the heart to do that, however. Gail was just trying to make it easier for me and I couldn't resent her for that.

"This isn't about her providing you with something that no one else has access to," she told me. "Her job is simply to see to it that your goals are realistic ones and that you are aware of every option that's available to you. That's all."

She was probably right, though I doubted it, somehow. If that were indeed the case, I really didn't see the reason why I needed a "specialist" in this "area". Maybe I was being dim—or simply obstinate—I don't know. But nothing Gail had said had reassured me. I wanted the interview over and behind me. I wanted to be proved wrong but I also wanted to prove

Gail wrong. Christine Northam was not here to benefit me. She was here because it was policy. Her job was to be seen to be *doing* her job, and, as far as I was concerned, I was already convinced that that was her only priority. I would have been happy to be proved wrong, but it would have been equally satisfying to come out of the M.I. room in the safe and sure knowledge that I'd been right all along and that the woman was, indeed, someone I could well do without.

When Christine Northam came out to show me into the M.I. room, Gail gave me a sympathetic smile and walked away. It was up to me, now. Whatever Christine Northam thought she could get away with, it was up to me to see that she didn't. I was determined not to be obstructive, however. I would put, for the time being, my numerous prejudices aside and make sure any reaction from me that might be required was justified. The last thing I wanted was to be seen as unnecessarily difficult. *Necessarily* difficult, I found perfectly acceptable, however.

When she smiled at me, Christine Northam did it with an odd sideways tilt to her head—as if she were trying to look at me, trying to *appraise* me, without my actually noticing. It was a sly little gesture and it really didn't do her any favours, especially given my already well-established suspicions. She sat down in her twinset and pearls at the same desk that Robert Warmington had used, smiling and slapping her hands down on her thighs as if she was about to play patty cake. She smiled again, not so much a Cheshire cat smile, more, it seemed to me, the smile of the cat that knows it's got the mouse cornered.

"Well," she said. "As I'm sure you already know, my name's Christine Northam and I'm here to help you make the right career choices. I'd therefore like to start by, well, just listening to what you'd like to do—what your thoughts already are on the subject."

Promising, I thought.

I returned her smile. It seemed appropriate, given that this might not actually turn out as badly as I'd predicted.

"Ideally," I said. "I'd like to work with computers. Preferably programming and development—maybe in the specialist area off adaptive technology."

Christine Northam made a thoughtful sound. It may have been somewhat premature of me, but I didn't see this as a good sign. I didn't think she had a bloody clue what I was talking about.

"Very good," she said. "It's always encouraging when a client has very definite ideas about what he wants to do." So why was I getting another of my bad feelings? "*However,* I always feel that it's very important to keep one's options open, don't you?"

"Within reason, yes."

Her eyebrows twitched slightly and she folded her hands together in her lap. Something about her posture, the way her shoulders stiffened somewhat, told me that she hadn't been expecting this. The qualification unnerved her.

"With this in mind," she continued, back on script, "I'd just like to run a few more possibilities by you—options that may not have occurred to you—and then, well, we can take it from there. What do you say?"

"I'm always open to reasonable suggestions." I had to admit, I was handling this far better than I ever thought I would. I was not about to be steamrollered and she knew it.

"Good. Good." She took a sheet of paper from the folder on her desk and quickly glanced at it before setting it back in its place. "Now," she continued. "I don't think we can ever set our sights too high. I'm all for achievement and excellence. I do, however, think it's sometimes important to understand that jobs we might consider to be... how shall I put it?... *mundane* can actually sometimes be quite rewarding and lucrative."

"What did you have in mind?" I said—trying not to sound too confrontational.

Christine Northam sat back in her chair and laced her fingers together in her lap, smiling at me with an air of complacency that suggested she believed she had me right where she wanted me. Her feet, she folded together beneath her chair, and when she started speaking, it was as one who was perfectly composed and in control.

"Well," she said. "There are a number of avenues open to us."

That "us" was, unless I was seriously mistaken, another *bad sign*.

"All of them quite appealing, in their own way," she continued. "But what I'd like to focus on first are the job opportunities that are available to you now. You see, equal opportunity employers have quotas that they like to meet. We are *very* big on equal opportunities—rightly so, in my opinion. This means that at a time like this, a time of high unemployment figures, someone such as yourself can actually be at an advantage. If you were finding, for example, that college was, say, a bit too academically challenging for you, I could quite possibly get you a job tomorrow."

"What kind of job?" I said.

"What kind of job would you like?" Her smile had become positively unnerving.

I shrugged my shoulders and said, reluctantly, "Something that fits in with my particular interests?"

"Okay, then," she said, picking a sheet of paper from the desk and studying it for a moment. "Ah, yes, here we are. How about this? I believe your communication skills are considered to be very good so how about something where that would put you at a definite advantage?"

"For example?"

"A station announcer for British Rail," she said with a premature air of victory.

I thought at first that she must have been joking. I smiled, waiting for her to start laughing. The very idea of me sitting in a stuffy room somewhere, talking into a microphone that would make me sound as if I had adenoid problems, telling people day after day that their trains were delayed—it was preposterous. So preposterous, in fact, that it was virtually impossible for me to believe that she was serious. I couldn't do a job like that. No, that wasn't true. I *could* do a job like that. All too easily, I supposed, as long as my health held out. What I really meant was, I would never *consider* doing a job like that. It wasn't beneath me, I told myself (though I didn't really believe that), but it would be a shocking waste of my ability.

When she didn't start laughing and realisation started to dawn, I said, "You're not pulling my leg, are you?"

Christine Northam shook her head, smiling. Momentarily bewildered, she asked, "Why on earth would I do a thing like that?"

"I'm studying physics and computer studies," I pointed out. "What makes you think a station announcer's something I'd even consider?"

"Your communication skills..."

"Yes, I know," I said, impatiently. "I can communicate. Big deal. That isn't what I want to *do*, though. I mentioned to you earlier, I'd like to do something with computers."

"British Rail has computers," she insisted.

"To tell their station announcers of the latest delay?"

"I would imagine so."

It was as bad as I'd thought it would be. Christine Northam really had no idea of who I was and what I wanted to do. She looked at me, she saw a wheelchair. Not all that unusual in general terms but utterly unforgivable given her profession.

I settled back and prepared myself to be *necessarily difficult*.

"It's out of the question," I told her. "What else do you have for me?"

I'd taken the wind out of her sails, but she was by no means sunk—not yet.

"Very well," she said, trying her best to sound all reasonable and compliant—once again picking up her piece of paper and making a show of studying it. "I thought, somehow, that that might not appeal to you. Understandable, really, an intelligent young man like you."

Patronising bitch.

"So how about this? Let me just run it by you." She took a breath, holding the piece of paper in her lap. "We have a place available on a wonderful residential course in Dorset—a rehabilitation—"

"Sorry?"

"It really is quite wonderful," she continued, determined to finish her spiel. "It focuses on broadening one's horizons—creating a sense of independence and focusing on the numerous possibilities available."

"Rehabilitation?" I said. "How is that of any value to me? I've been disabled all my life. Don't you think it's a little late in the day to start throwing rehabilitation into the pot?"

"We can all benefit from—"

"Listen," I said quietly, my voice tired and almost giving out under the stress of the situation. "I don't need to be taught a sense of independence and as for the numerous possibilities that you talk about, tell me about them. That's what you're here for."

This wasn't going quite how was she'd imagined. Finally beginning to appear a little flustered, she looked down at the floor, briefly studied her sheet of paper, looked up at me and, her voice dreary and emotionless—no longer trying to convince me with her tone that this was the best thing for me—said, "There is one other possibility."

"Yes?" I was pleased with myself. Whatever else I did or didn't achieve at East Park, I understood that this refusal to buckle and simply accept what this woman told me as a given would stay with me for a very long time. The absurdity of her suggestions and my refusal to accept them would mark in my mind a turning point—the point where I became a man, the point where, perhaps, I first started to realise that whatever they said, these people were not here to help me. They couldn't. I was the only one who could do that, either by accepting what they told me or, preferably, as I had, for all intents and purposes telling them to shove it. Basking in my momentary glory, but still appalled by the suggestions she had made to me, I waited to hear what this other possibility would be—a little amused (I could be a smug little shit when I wanted to be) to hear that the numerous possibilities had suddenly come down to just one. Odd, that.

"Do you know Colleen Berkshire?" she said.

"Should I?"

"She was also a pupil at the Resolution."

"I was integrated full-time into Almsby. I didn't know a lot of the Resolution pupils."

"You probably know her by sight," she insisted. "But, anyway, that isn't important. Colleen now works at a local employment centre. A very impressive place it is, too. They have a range of facilities within the centre but their primary focus is on producing high-quality craft products—very specialised stuff."

"Like wicker baskets, perhaps?"

She paused a moment before speaking—assessing me, letting the moment drag out for effect. "You're not very receptive, are you, Carl?" she finally said. "I mean, I've come to you today with all these wonderful possibilities and... well, to be brutally frank, there are only so many doors open to you and if you keep insisting on slamming them in our faces... well, there's only so much we can do."

I thought about asking her what was so "wonderful" about the possibilities she had offered me. There had been no mention of university or the other options for extending my education and improving my qualifications, the jobs, what they were, were limited and of no interest to me—so how could she claim that they were wonderful? But I realised that I would simply be wasting my breath.

"What doors there are, Carl," she said with what she would no doubt have liked to think of as "infinite patience". "What doors there are, need to be kept open."

"I'd like to leave now."

Christine Northam studied me very carefully—her eyes moving from the tips of my shoes to the top of my elegantly coiffed head of burgundy hair. I felt her scrutiny like a very physical discomfort, a sharp spring in a mattress upon which I was laying or, perhaps, a trapped pubic hair. I waited for her to make the decision with which she was obviously struggling, wondering if I'd pushed it too far (it was quite possible that she could issue some kind of complaint with the principal). I had quite clearly been obstructive. No one could argue with that. Granted, I had had good reason; the choices that Christine Northam had made available to me had been utterly ridiculous. Nothing she had suggested even came close to my desires or expectations. Anyone in his or her right mind would be able to see that. But the fact remained; I had not exactly been polite. I hadn't gone out of my way to be rude, this was true, but I had made up my mind to be *necessarily* difficult. I had a feeling that no matter how justified my position, that would be frowned upon.

With a sharp exhalation, Christine Northam picked up her pen and turned to the desk—her back almost to me.

"Of course," she said. "You may leave wherever you wish. Before you do, however, would you mind if I had your telephone number?"

"What for?" The implication being we had nothing left to talk about.

"I don't feel that I can just leave this the way it is," she said, turning to me again. "I feel that I must discuss this with your parents—see what they have to say on the matter."

"They'll ask you what *I* said on the matter," I told her. "They believe in letting me make my own decisions where such things are concerned."

"And making your own mistakes?"

"If that's how it turns out, yes, to a point."

"Be that as it may, I'd still like your telephone number."

I'm sure you would, I thought to myself. *But there's no fucking way you're getting it.*

"We're in the process of moving house," I lied. "We're changing our number and I'm not sure what the new one is, yet. If you give me yours, I'll make sure you get it as soon as I do."

Staring at me with a sceptical tilt to her head, Christine Northam narrowed her eyes and nodded. She knew I was lying. She knew, and she knew *I* knew she knew. And I didn't care. In fact, I would even have gone so far as to say that I *wanted* her to know that I knew that she knew I was lying. It was important to me that we both knew where we stood in this matter.

As I left the M.I. room, Gail was waiting for me—leaning against some lockers on the far side of the corridor, her arms folded. Pushing herself away, she started walking towards me, asking immediately how it had gone.

"Bloody wonderful," I said ironically. "A complete and utter waste of fucking time. Seven years of integrated education and what's the best they can come up with? Wicker fucking baskets, that's what."

Gail was ushering me through some double doors a little way along the corridor, pulling faces at me and hissing something between her teeth that, still expressing my frustration in no uncertain terms, I didn't quite catch.

"It was exactly as I knew it would be," I said. "I went in there determined to be... what's the word? Receptive. I went in there determined to be *receptive*. I thought, *I won't let my prejudices get in the way.* Because, you know what I'm like, I could have, right? But I didn't. I was determined—I know I'm using that word too much, but I was—I was *determined* to be positive and open until it was proved to me that I'd been right all along. You know something, Gail? I don't think I've ever heard such a complete load of fucking bollocks in all my life."

Gail was laughing openly now and when I frowned up at her, perplexed, she shook her head and patted me on the back. "Well done, Carl," she said. "You really played a blinder there, didn't you?"

I didn't know what she was talking about.

"Christine Northam," she said, grinning. "When you launched into your little tirade back there, she was right behind you—following you out the M.I. room."

"She was?"

"She was."

"So she heard the bit about it being a complete and utter waste of fucking time?" I said.

"Absolutely."

"And the bit about integrated education and wicker baskets?"

"Without a shadow of a doubt."

"Good," I said. "She deserved to hear it. Every bloody word."

"So it really was as bad as you envisaged?" she asked me.

"Worse, if anything."

On the way back to the common room, I filled her in on all of the details—leaving nothing out. I didn't dress it up or exaggerate. I simply covered the points one after the other, keeping, as much as possible, emotion out of it. I wanted Gail to understand that I'd tried. I hadn't gone in there expecting the worst, in spite of what I'd said to her beforehand. I'd given Christine Northam a fair chance, and if Gail was ever to understand my frustration and anger, she needed to know that.

When I'd finished, she stopped and looked at me. "I don't think," she said, "I've ever heard anything quite so ridiculous in all my life. She really said all that to you?"

"Every word."

"The bloody woman wants shooting," she said. "You do know that you'd be well within your rights to make an official complaint, don't you? I'll go with you now to the principal, if that's what you want."

"I'll need to think about that," I said. "I'm not sure it'll be worth the effort."

"You owe it to yourself, Carl. And to others."

I was beginning to believe that I'd already fought all my battles. I'd done all I could do and only history could now decide who the ultimate victor should be. I'd stood my ground and whilst I didn't see that I'd actually achieved anything, I also hadn't allowed myself to be debased or devalued. As for others, well, they would have to manage their own conflicts themselves. It was not something I could do for them, no matter what Gail believed to the contrary.

"I'll think about it," I said, and headed into the common room.

"You should have told the old bint to go fuck herself," Eddie was saying.

Today, it was just me, Eddie, Naz and Carrie in our little corner of the common room—the four of us on a free period. I'd returned from my meeting with the guidance counsellor with a face on me like a well-smacked arse and the three of them had immediately deduced that things hadn't gone quite how I would have liked. After only a little prompting, I had told them the selfsame story I'd shared with Gail (though I did, admittedly, spice it up just a little this time).

"It's like," Carrie said, "they've spent seven years showing you what it can be like, only to take it away from you."

"Did she really say 'wicker baskets'?" Naz asked me.

"Not in so many words," I admitted. "But that was the gist of it. She wanted me to go to some poxy centre and sit with a bunch of drooling imbeciles making craft items."

Naz shook his head indignantly. "Where do they get these people?"

I appreciated their support, I really did—but a part of me couldn't help wondering if, perhaps, Christine Northam had a point. It wasn't as if I was finding college life easy. Academically, I was struggling, not because I was not academically gifted, but, rather, due to the fact that I was taking a great deal of time off due to illness and... well, when I was actually at college, I was spending most of my time in the common room, too exhausted and uninspired to attend lessons. It was Johnny all over again, if I were truthful. Johnny at his college—unable to cope, slowly going under, resigned to the rejection heap that was a return to the Resolution. That wouldn't happen to me. Of this I was confident. Such an action would have been highly inappropriate and, frankly, I would never have stood for it. But what of the other alternatives? Had her suggestions really been so bad? Had she in fact looked at me, seeing that I was quite clearly struggling when no one else could, and provided me with options that were realistically within my capabilities?

I didn't want to accept that. I couldn't afford to. In my heart of hearts, I believed then—and I believe now—that even if I had gone in there looking physically strong and with an impressive academic and attendance record she would have made the same suggestions. Yes, it was true, my time at East Park was beginning to look fairly untenable, but that didn't mean that her behaviour, the sickening level of prejudice she had shown, could be excused. I deserved better. I was trying. I was determined to make something of my life and, at that time, this was the only way I saw of doing that. Holding such a position of responsibility, she should have been able to recognize that. However I had looked, she should have been determined to work with me, not against me. If I'd said I wanted to be the first disabled astronaut, should have gone about finding what qualifications I would need for the job—working with me until it became obvious in a very natural way that this was not the occupation for me. Instead, she presented me with pat proposals that she probably used for everyone she met.

Naz was mumbling something about incontinent stroke victims when Gail came in. She stood for a moment listening to him, and then shook her head as if to clear it of the image and said to me, "I've just been speaking to your new friend."

"You have my heartfelt sympathy," I said, with a slight bow of the head.

"She expressed a few concerns." The right side of her mouth twitched playfully.

"I somehow imagined she might."

"She said she was worried about your unreasonable obstructiveness," Gail told me—Naz, Eddie and Carrie expressing their disgust with expulsions of air and well chosen expletives. "I told her that, judging by what she had told me and what you had said, I considered your obstructiveness perfectly reasonable."

"You did?" I'd known that Gail was on my side, of course, but I'd never realised that she would stick her neck out quite so far. I was moved. Almost.

"I most certainly did, Stanley." Her best Oliver Hardy impersonation. It wasn't very good, but forgiving her was easy. "I also told her that if it had anything to do with me, you'd be making an official complaint."

Eddie reached across and patted her on the back. "Nice one, love," he said.

"I bet that went down well," I wagered.

"Like water off a duck's back. It was almost as if she heard stuff like that every day of the week."

"Now *that* wouldn't surprise me," Carrie said.

"She also wanted to know if you were really moving house," Gail told me. "I said you were."

Smiling, happy to have Gail on my side, I said, "Thanks. I appreciate that."

Looking somewhat bewildered, Naz glanced from me to Gail and then back again. He scratched his head, looked down at the floor, stared at me for a few moments again and finally said, "I didn't know you were moving house."

~

"So she didn't have a point?" I asked Carl.

We were sitting alone in his parents back garden. It was a glorious summer day—one of the few—and we neither of us really seemed to feel the need to talk all that much. I listened to the trickle, light and brittle, of the water feature over by the garage wall, and waited for him to reply, happy to let him take his time.

"With the benefit of hindsight, absolutely not," he said. "She was there to work with me, not against me. Her whole attitude was, at best, patronising. Supposedly, she was a specialist in disability employment issues—but she approached my interview like something out of the disability dark ages. How can there ever be a sense of equality in education and employment with people like that holding positions that, in that form at least, should probably never exist?"

"But you were finding it difficult?"

"Oh, yes, there's no arguing with that. I was in extremely early every morning—not long after eight o'clock—because the bus that picked me up had to drop me off before it did its school run, and I sometimes wasn't home until after five. It was a long day that I suffered not necessarily under the best of conditions. But none of that could ever have justified the way that that woman behaved towards me. It was as if... she was like an educational throwback. By that point, I was so unaccustomed to dealing with people like that... well, it could have gone very badly."

Carl fell silent, again. I realised that this could not be it, now. His story was drawing to a close and any excuse I might have to visit him would go with it—but I could never reconcile myself to not seeing him. I was slowly beginning to realise that nothing might ever come of it. Carl was so private at times as to be almost unreachable, except when we were talking about his past. He locked his thoughts and feelings away behind a wry smile that said that he knew exactly what he was doing, and I supposed I had to accept that. But I could not be without his friendship. To not see him— for him to finish his story and my accept it as an end to our friendship—it was just unimaginable. If I had to, I realised I would fight for that—fight him or anyone else who proved an obstacle. I owed it to him but, more to the point, I owed it to myself.

My hand was on the arm of my chair, not far from his. It would have been the simplest of gestures, the easiest thing in the world. Just to reach out and take hold of it. But I couldn't do it. Even now it seemed too much of a presumption.

Sitting there, listening to the water feature struggle to soothe away my growing regrets—regrets that had been, regrets that were and regrets that possibly would be—I waited for Carl Grantham to speak again, hoping and praying, even as I knew it to be a futile wish, that he would say what I wanted him to.

Chapter Seventeen: The Art of Falling Apart

I remember the winter of 1984 as frigid and hopeless. Having returned after the summer to resit the exams I had failed (all of them, just like most of my friends), I found myself once again in a familiar downward spiral, this time worse than ever, the endlessness of it all, the interminable cold and disillusionment, filling me with a heavy, icy feeling in the pit of my stomach. I felt removed from everything about me. But that was the way I wanted it, I told myself. I was not a part of it, it was not a part of me. I steered my electric wheelchair through those corridors not so much in a dream, but in a daze. I went through the required motions, nodding, smiling—greeting people in my usual, friendly manner—but inside I felt isolated and lost, desperate for a solution, for an alternative I couldn't see. When the weather turned bad, it was almost a relief to see on the outside what I felt on the in. Short days, long nights, an overriding sense of dislocation and reduction. The Incredible Melting Man. Soon I would be little more than a puddle on the floor. And I would be grateful for the fact.

A Monday morning towards the end of November saw me sitting beside Naz in computer studies. We were working on logic networks, *again*, utterly appalled by the degree of complexity we were now finding in the coursework. It was clear to both of us just why we had failed the summer before. We had not been taught in this kind of detail. As we had suspected, the standard of the exam had been increased but what we had been taught had not been in accordance with that.

"It's bloody disgusting," Naz was saying. "If we'd been taught the proper stuff—"

"We wouldn't be here now," I said, drearily.

"Exactly. We should complain, you know. This kind of thing—it just can't be allowed to happen."

I shrugged. "What difference would it really make, though?"

"It'd let them know that we know."

"And that's important?"

"I think it is, yes."

"Then complain," I said—the implication being, *You complain but leave me the fuck out of it.*

Naz studied me out of the corner of his eye. He could see—surely, he could see. On the rare occasions when I caught my reflection in the windows or in the glass in the doors, *I* could see, so it seemed perfectly logical to me that it must be obvious to the likes of Naz that all was not well with me, that I was ill and vainly fighting it, unwilling to give in even as the consequences became more and more apparent.

"You okay?" he said.

"I'm fine," I lied.

"You don't look it. What's up, mate?"

I shook my head, suddenly unable to speak. If I answered him, I thought I might cry. I felt weighed down, my limbs heavy and weak— weaker than they had been during the summer holidays and, I knew from experience, weaker than they would be during the forthcoming Christmas holiday. Mrs. Portnoy, our computer studies teacher—a big, fat, black American with an arse the size of a barrage balloon—stood with her back to us at the board, filling it with logic gates and scrawled instructions on what we should do with them. I didn't need them. They served no purpose for me and it suddenly occurred to me that this was what I should be telling Naz. I wasn't meant to be here. The "and" gates, the "not" gates, the "or" gates—all of them, they filled no void for me, they served no purpose and didn't offer the possibilities I wanted or needed. It was a waste of time. A waste of energy. A waste of a life I only just had.

"Do you need me to go get Gail?" he said.

Again, I shook my head. "No," I finally managed to say. "I'm all right. Honest. I'm just a bit... I'm tired, that's all."

Mrs. Portnoy hadn't liked me from very early on in our teacher-student relationship. Her sarcasm had pissed me off from day one—a crude blend, as it was, of what passed for American wit and British irony—and I had made it plain by my reactions that I hadn't found her in the least bit amusing. It also hadn't helped that she'd heard me discussing her name with Naz, me observing that maybe she was related to the Portnoy that Philip Roth had written about and conjecturing that maybe she had a complaint, too. Naz had found this especially amusing and, it being one of my good days, I had expanded upon it a little, adding that, judging by her perpetual scowl and her irritable moods, I was quite sure that her particular complaint just had to be haemorrhoids. I'd known, of course, that I'd put my foot in it right away. I'd felt her presence hanging over me like a storm-cloud and turned as best I could to find her standing directly behind me. Naz had rolled his eyes and turned away, sniggering, and I had muttered something about now having to suffer her Roth—another joke that she didn't seem to particularly appreciate. With only a sniff, however, she had moved on, not saying a word but storing this newly acquired information away for a later date... for all those times when she could remind me by her actions who was in charge here.

"Is there something you would like to share with us, Mr. Grantham?" she now said.

Naz groaned beside me and buried his head in his book. I heard him say—Johnny-like—something to me about not rising to it, but I really wasn't in the mood for taking advice—however good it might have been.

"No," I said. "There isn't."

"Then please be quiet and stop disturbing the rest of the class."

"I wasn't aware that I was." I looked around at my fellow students. A number of them shrugged as if to say, *You're not bothering me, mate.* The majority, however, followed Naz's lead and avoided eye contact of any kind.

Mrs. Portnoy's gaze was steady and unyielding. I got the impression that she intended it to be intimidating, but it wasn't. I was beyond being intimidated by someone like her—someone who claimed a position of imagined authority. Feeling the tension building in the room, my fellow students either thoroughly enjoying the conflict or concerned about where it might end for me, I found that I couldn't have cared less. I didn't like the woman and it was suddenly very important to me to again let her know that I wasn't in the least bit impressed by her. Waiting for her reply, whatever it might be, I breathed steadily and held her stare, tired of her sarcastic comments—of the way in which she told me to "get the notes" every time I returned after a bout of illness, with a certain disdain, with the clear impression that I had not really been ill at all.

She took a breath and I prepared myself. *Polite,* I thought. *Remain polite but don't budge an inch. Give her hell, just like Johnny would have.*

"Well you'll just have to take my word for it, won't you?" she said. "You were disturbing the class."

"You seem to be the only one that thinks so," I told her.

"I beg your pardon?"

"I said, you seem to be the only one that thinks so."

"Yes, thank you, Carl, I heard what you said perfectly well. The point I'm making is that I'm surprised that whatever the consequences might be for you, you still seem quite happy to contradict."

"That's only," I said, "because I think you're wrong."

"That much I'd gathered. But I'm afraid that on this point, at least, we are going to have to agree to disagree."

"You still think I was disturbing the class?" I said.

"Well if you weren't, you certainly are now, aren't you?"

"Now isn't the point. I asked you, do you still think I *was* disturbing the class?"

"I'm not going to play these silly games with you, Carl. Either be quiet and get on with your work, or leave the classroom."

Christ, she was fat. I thought that now might be a good time to tell her that—recommend, perhaps, a good calorie controlled diet, one that didn't *heavily* feature burgers and fries. But I managed, barely, to control myself and instead said, "If you want me to leave the classroom, I will. I'd rather get on with my work and let everyone else do the same, however, without any further disturbance. But I will make my point again, before you decide what I should do. I wasn't disturbing the class. Naz thought I looked unwell and asked me if I was all right. I replied to him, that's all."

"That's true, Miss," Naz said. "If you've got a problem with anyone, it should be me."

"That's not what I meant, mate," I said to him.

"I know—but that's how it is, isn't it? If anyone was disturbing the class, it was me."

"That's the point," I told him. "*Nobody* was disturbing the class until..." I very pointedly looked at Mrs. Portnoy. I didn't need to say any more. She knew what I was getting at. She'd have to be very dim not to.

"What are you getting at?" she said, and I couldn't help but smile.

"Absolutely nothing," I said—my fatigue and depression suddenly weighing down on me all the heavier. This was a battle that would be best won by an early retreat, it suddenly seemed to me. Ignoring her response, virtually deaf to it, I returned to my logic network, knowing that the confrontation would earn me a few sharp words from my tutor the following morning but plenty of backslaps in the common room that afternoon. I wanted neither. This was not me. I was not this kind of person. Confrontation... I didn't go looking for it; it was not something I desired. Yes, I would face it when need be (and this was certainly one such occasion), but I didn't have it in me to enjoy it. Not really. The pointlessness of it all was virtually overwhelming. It was not a conflict that would go down in the history books. Nothing would be changed, for good or bad, by it. It was a petty exchange, nothing more. An obstinate youth who didn't much care anymore facing down the ridiculous authority figure who, in real terms, was nothing more than a self-inflated ego that didn't know when it was making itself look ridiculous. There could be no benefit to either of us. I, at least, understood that.

As I was leaving at the end of the lesson, she caught me by the door and said, "That was very grown up of you."

I was immune to her sarcasm. I'd been well and truly inoculated against it.

"You were wrong," I told her. "I had a good reason to be speaking and I was speaking very quietly. Nobody was bothered by it—except you."

"I've had enough of your cheek for one day—"

"A twelve-year-old gives cheek," I said. "Whatever you think to the contrary, the same can't be said of a nineteen-year-old." I looked up at her. "Can I go, now?"

While she was thinking of how best to answer me, I went, anyway. There would be consequences. I really didn't doubt that. But they meant nothing to me. I would take whatever was thrown at me and laugh it off—not because it was without weight, but simply because I had known much worse.

"You're the talk of the staff room," Gail said to me later that morning.

I was sitting in the corridor just outside the common room, by the radiator—trying to keep warm. Looking out the window, I saw it was raining again... the kind of rain that threatened to turn to sleet, slightly too substantial for mere drizzle and, yet, not quite ready to be considered anything more. The heaviness in my limbs that I had experienced in computer studies was still with me, but it now seemed somehow appropriate. Under the circumstances, given the day, taking into account my mood and outlook, this was the only way for me to feel.

"I am?" Of course I was. After my encounter with Mrs. Portnoy, it was inevitable.

"You are." She paused for a moment, looking out the window with me, seemingly trying to see whatever it was that I was seeing. She was wasting her time. I could have told her that. "What were you thinking, Carl?" she finally said.

"What do you mean?" I wasn't being deliberately obtuse. For some reason, I couldn't quite grasp just what she was getting at.

"Taking on Portnoy like that. Why would you even consider doing such a thing? You know she doesn't especially like you."

I shrugged as the drizzle turned to sleet turned to snow. "Maybe that was why," I said. "She doesn't like me and..." another shrug... "it just seemed the right thing to do. Under the circumstances."

"Under the circumstances?"

"She was being her usual bitch of a self. She needed taking down a peg or two and it seemed that I was the only one willing to do the job."

"You do realise that she won't just let this one go, don't you?"

I realised. I had realised at the time, so how could I now not? Truth be known, I think I'd deliberately set out to put myself in this position—to bring the consequences down upon myself like Samson in the temple (sort of). What could she do to me? What could any of them do to me? They were powerless. That was what Gail—what *all* of them—didn't really understand. As far as they were concerned, I was subject to their whims, their menstrual cycles and predilections. If they said "shit", I got on the pot. That was how they viewed our relationship. But they were wrong. I could do things that they would never even begin to believe or understand, whatever the personal cost. If they wanted a quiet life, if they wanted to dictate their terms without fear of contradiction, they could no longer count on me to be complicit. I would do what I felt I had to do, whatever effect that might have on my place here at the college. It was not a passive aggressive attempt at getting expelled. That was not what this was about. Rather it concerned the difference between right and wrong. I was not a superhero making a stand. I had no real sense of having a moral obligation. I just didn't like or want Mrs. Portnoy thinking that she could get away with whatever she wanted to get away with. Sitting in the classroom I'd realised, I told Gail, that something had had to be done. I'd understood completely that I would be in bother. But I had a good case to argue, and so I was content to take whatever they thought they could throw at me.

"She made it sound as if you were really offensive," Gail said. "I didn't recognize the Carl she was talking about. Was it as bad as she makes out?"

"Probably not," I said. "I was pretty direct and firm with her, but I don't believe I was over the top. I suppose it depends on what you mean by 'really offensive', though, doesn't it?"

"You didn't swear at her or anything, right?"

"Is that what she's saying?"

"Not that I've heard. But it wouldn't surprise me if she said something along those lines, just to give it a little added weight."

My response was fairly indifferent. As far as I was concerned, she could do or say whatever she bloody well pleased. Frankly, I told Gail, I was past caring. "I mean," I said, "just look at the place. It's not as if they've bent over backwards to make this easier for me, have they? I'm back and forth through that bloody car park Christ knows how many times a day, freezing my bollocks off just to be talked to like I'm a piece of shit by the likes of Mrs. Portnoy. What she says is up to her, I couldn't really give a flying fig."

Gail looked down at me. I was still staring out of the window, so I couldn't actually see her do this—but I could nevertheless feel her eyes on me as I listened to the silence drag out between us. I liked Gail. I always had. From day one, she had been someone I had respected simply because she had, without any effort, seen me as an independent, individual human being. Her humour and the compassion that never became patronising or condescending had been a constant throughout my time at East Park. She was dependable. She was funny. She was a friend—and I now realised more than ever that I didn't want her thinking badly of me. She knew I could be pig-headed. I'd revealed that very early on in our friendship. But I didn't want her to think I was some mouthy, argumentative, disillusioned yob. Under the circumstances, however—feeling the way I felt and knowing the things I knew—I thought this might be a distinct possibility. In Gail's eyes, I'd probably gone too far. I'd overstepped the mark, and I doubted that anything I could say or do would rectify that.

"What's wrong, Carl?" she said, ever so softly.

"I don't know what you mean."

"Yes you do. What is it?" She'd seated herself on the window ledge beside the radiator and was looking at me, now, with very genuine concern. "You aren't yourself. You don't normally take risks with your education like this. Someone like Mrs. Portnoy... they aren't important and you'd usually understand that. So why have you let this become such a big deal. What's going on?"

I would have to talk about it sooner or later to someone. If it wasn't my parents, who were more concerned than ever about my now obvious decline, continually encouraging me to eat, happy to let me take as much time off as I wanted, it would be Gail or someone else close to me at college—Naz, perhaps, though that didn't strike me as very likely. But *I didn't want to talk*. I didn't want to have to admit that this hadn't worked for me, that, like Johnny at his college, I hadn't been able to cope. All this time, on some level, at least, I'd believed myself superior. I'd thought that I could succeed where others had failed—prove myself, let everyone know that I could compete on their terms, playing by their rules and showing myself to be better equipped than they. But I'd been deluding myself. I couldn't do it this way. I still didn't want to actually say it out loud, but it was true. I could see it now. The Mrs. Portnoys of this world, as Gail had pointed out, weren't important. None of this was—because it was not the way for me. I couldn't do it. However hard I tried, I just... couldn't... *do it*. I had never wanted to be inspirational—*please God, don't ever let me be inspirational*—I had simply wanted to succeed in my own way. But I hadn't even managed to do that. I had failed. I was not superior. I was not even average. This place was for others, but it wasn't for me.

"Nothing's going on," I told her, my voice drab and unconvincing.

"Carl, don't be silly. You only have to look at you to see that you're struggling. Admit it... you can't go on like this."

I wasn't about to admit it. Not yet, anyway. And so I once again said what was fast becoming my mantra. "I'm fine," I told her.

Mr. Fitzpatrick called me into his office the following morning. The head of the Upper Sixth, I had only rarely spoken to him in the past—our paths only crossing on the odd occasion. He was a gentle man. Small and frail, with a redundant-looking moustache, he actually made me feel fit by comparison. He always smelt of Polo mints, the usual teacherly attempt at disguising the smell of cigarette smoke, and it was all too easy for me to imagine the cancer already well-established in his lungs, spreading with a glee and passion that Mr. Fitzpatrick himself would never know.

It was good that it was him, I thought. He was reasonable. One who was prepared to listen, I knew that I could depend on him to give me a fair hearing. His health almost required it.

"You, of course, know why I asked to speak to you today, don't you, Carl?" he said, leaning forward over his desk with his hands clasped together on his blotter.

"I have a good idea, yes, sir."

"Mrs. Portnoy is... well, she's a little concerned about your behaviour."

"The fact that I didn't happen to agree with her yesterday, you mean?"

Mr. Fitzpatrick smiled. He knew what Mrs. Portnoy could be like—all that transatlantic bullshit wrapped up in a parcel that, however big, still wasn't quite big enough. It got out, I was sure, in staff room situations as well as in the classroom, and I knew that someone like Mr. Fitzpatrick would find her brusque manner off-putting and abrasive.

"If you want to look at it like that, yes," he said. "Apparently you were rather rude?"

"Depends on where you were viewing the argument from, I suppose. Under the circumstances, I think I was very polite."

"I had a feeling you might say that—and, I have to admit, I have no real reason to doubt your sincerity. I'll be truthful with you, Carl, I've always found you, on the rare occasions when we have spoken, to be direct but polite. You're a decent chap—which is why I found Mrs. Portnoy's complaint—"

I bit my lip hard enough to draw blood.

"—rather perplexing. The way she described the conversation she had with you made you sound... well, very different to the Carl I know. Saying this, however, I'm not inclined to disbelieve her. I believe that she is as sincere as you when she makes this complaint. It stems from, if I am reading her correctly, a genuine concern for your education and well-being. Which is why I just had to speak with you today."

Sitting back in his chair, lacing his fingers together across his sunken belly, he eyed me over the top of his spectacles and inhaled a shaky breath before saying, "So tell me what this is all really about, Carl, old chap."

It wasn't possible for me to refuse this request. His willingness to listen to my side of the story, his gentle and accepting manner, drew me in in a way that I hadn't been prepared for. Where I had yesterday successfully refused to give in to Gail's attempts at getting inside my head, I today failed to resist Mr. Fitzpatrick. I started and I just couldn't stop. I told him all about the conversation with Naz, how lousy I had been feeling, and then moved on to the confrontation with Mrs. Portnoy. When I told him that I most definitely had not been disturbing the rest of the class, he nodded sadly, clearly believing my version of the story. But I didn't stop there. As he listened, I finally found myself admitting just how difficult I was finding life at East Park. I told him of the long treks through the car park, the toll that the protracted days were taking, and admitted that because of all the time off I had been forced to take I was now struggling academically.

"Sometimes... sometimes I feel as if I'm taking one step forward and five back," I said. "It's like I'm on... have you ever been to Blackpool?" He nodded tolerantly. "They have this walkway at the Pleasure Beach. Or they used to. It was like an escalator, only flat. I feel as if I'm on that, only going in the wrong direction. And I know I should probably get off—but I just don't know how to, or what awaits me if I do."

"You find yourself between a rock and a hard place?" he said.

"I do, yes."

"And your guidance counsellor had nothing to suggest?"

"Nothing that I especially wanted to listen to, no."

"Ah, yes." He nodded. "I remember Gail telling me that the two of you—yourself and the guidance counsellor, that is—hadn't especially hit it off. I believe you found her... patronising?"

"In part, yes. On the whole, though, it was more that her suggestions were simply unsuitable. She wasn't all that concerned with what I wanted to do."

"Which is?"

Shrugging, I wished we could move the conversation along. I was beginning to feel like a classic "difficult pupil", and that was not how I wished to be represented. "I wanted to work in computer programming or adaptive technology," I told him. "But that's all pretty much academic, now. I can't really see myself achieving that and... sometimes I wonder if it was the right career choice for me, anyway."

"I'm not sure I follow, old chap."

"I have an intuitive knack with computers. I'm not afraid of them and I like using them. But I'm no computer genius. People have always—well, for a few years, at least—gone on about my communication skills. Even my guidance counsellor mentioned it, though the related career she suggested was a bit of a disappointment."

"Something uninspiring, I take it?"

"A station announcer for British Rail."

"Ouch." Smiling, he sat forward again, folding his arms on the desk. "But you think these people might have had a point? That you should play to your strengths and do something that focuses on your communication skills?"

"Maybe. I really don't know."

"Certainly something worth thinking about, though, isn't it?"

Mr. Fitzpatrick held my eyes for a few moments, seemingly looking deeper into me than I ever would have thought possible. He nodded slowly, as if he had proved something to himself, and then continued. "Don't worry about the Mrs. Portnoy incident," he said. "Consider it over and done with. What you need to focus on now, Carl, is where you want to go next, and how you might achieve that. If you aren't happy talking to the guidance counsellor—which I can certainly understand—then please feel free to come to me any time. I do think you need to look at this realistically, though. Your health is suffering, old chap. I think you need to acknowledge that before you do anything else.

"So," he told me, getting to his feet. "Take a few days to mull it over, discuss it with your parents and then come back and see me. We'll have a coffee and see if we can find a solution to this little problem. How does that sound to you?"

"It sounds... very sensible," I said. "Thank you, sir."

"Good man."

The following Thursday found me alone in the common room. It was another cold and dreary day, the dampness all-pervading—seeping in through the windows, it seemed, passing through the very pores of the walls. Even in my jacket, Pierre Cardin scarf and fingerless gloves, I was perhaps as cold as I ever remembered being, and just when I was thinking that maybe I should leave the room in search of somewhere warmer—considering, even, the last resort of the study area—Carrie came strolling in wearing jeans and jumper, looking as if she had never been warmer in all her life.

The duffle coat he never got, I thought, before quickly dismissing the too numerous images this stirred.

Stopping melodramatically and staring at me before sitting down, she said, "You shouldn't be here."

A truer word was never said.

"You should be in physics or something, possibly maths—but you definitely shouldn't be here, that much I do know."

"Can't get anything past you, can I?" My voice was weak and croaky. It had been for the past couple of days. Whether it was another cold coming on, or just the result of fatigue, I couldn't have said, but there was just no shaking it.

Speaking with my parents the evening before, as Mr. Fitzpatrick had suggested I do before seeing him again, I had found myself repeatedly trying to clear my throat as I, for the first time, admitted to them that—as they had feared—I was indeed finding my time at East Park intolerably difficult. Patiently listening to me, I had seen the concern on their faces gradually transform into something that I thought was relief. Yes, we had discussed what other options were available to me, what I would do with my time—would I try to do something else or get my doctor to write me a sick note proving that I qualified for disability benefit?—and what would happen if I became bored or disillusioned, but by and large the main topic had been the clear benefits I would experience if I finished college. I would be healthy again. I had seen that right away, and so had they. I would not be ill every five minutes, forever taking antibiotics and expectorants. I would eat better, put on a little weight, even. Granted, the three of us had admitted, all would not always be rosy in the garden—and maybe this would not be a long-term solution, simply a way for me to build myself up and prepare for whatever it was I decided I wanted to do next—but I could not go on the way I was. It was the only sensible choice to make.

"You're going to get in such deep shit," Carrie said, sitting down on the armchair to my right. "Have you attended any lessons at all this week?"

"One or two," I told her.

"Christ, Carl."

"What?"

"You really have to ask?"

"I really have to ask."

She shook her head despondently. I was a lost cause, that shake of the head said. There was nothing that could be done for me and all her best efforts would be futile. But she couldn't just leave it like that. In her way, Carrie was as concerned as anyone.

"I thought this was important to you," she said, quietly. "I thought you wanted to get on and achieve things."

"I did." It wasn't the time for dressing things up. Not now. I had gone beyond that. "I still do, but... I just can't do it anymore, Carrie."

"That bad?" She looked up at me, the softness around her eyes telling me that she'd known this all along.

"You could say that."

"It isn't school, is it?"

I shook my head and sighed. "No," I answered. "That was difficult, but this... this is far worse."

"Would you want to go back to the way it was at school, though?" she asked me, like this might help somehow.

"No. Absolutely not. I had no choices, then, and... well, I promised Johnny I would never go back, anyway."

"I remember Johnny," she said, smiling. "Do you still keep in touch?"

I'd thought she'd known. It seemed ludicrous that anyone who had even remotely known Johnny could be unaware of what had happened to him. "He died whilst we were still at school," I told her. "Not long before we left."

"No."

"I'm afraid so, yes."

"That's awful. I didn't realise. You must have..."

"I got by. We'd all been expecting it—Johnny included."

"Nevertheless..."

"All you can do is remember the laughs and the promises to be kept." I was in danger of waxing lyrical, I knew, so I forced myself to be quiet.

"He didn't want you going back there, then?"

I nodded and swallowed hard, trying to get my throat working a little better. "Johnny was a year ahead of me," I told her. "So he left the year before I did and went on to this... well, they called it a college, but it wasn't. Not like this place, at least."

"But that doesn't make sense," she said, confused. "I remember seeing him in the Resolution in our final year..."

"That's right. He couldn't cope at the college. It was all too much for him and so..."

"... they took him back to the Resolution?"

We both saw how soul-destroying it had to have been for Johnny to return there. It must have been, Carrie said, the straw that broke the camel's back—the proof that he probably didn't need that there was no future for him. "Everything was in his past," I agreed. "Like you say, he had nothing to look forward to except... well, death and half-forgotten memories."

"Couldn't they have found somewhere else for him to go?" she said. "Somewhere that wouldn't have made it seem quite so obvious?"

Shrugging, I said, "When you can't cope at college, there are only so many options available to you."

Carrie was a lot brighter than some people gave her credit for. She knew right away that I was no longer talking about Johnny.

"You've come to a decision, haven't you?" she said.

It would not be like that for me. Remembering Johnny in those final weeks, facing an eternity of closed doors, any hope he might have had—however delusional—finally and completely banished, I made up my mind that I wouldn't let it be that way with me. On my final day at school, Mr. Dixon had again spoken of his egg, the clumsiest of metaphors. "There are always other ways, Carl," he had told me—and how right he had been. Granted, they weren't obvious. Talking to the likes of Christine Northam would not reveal them. But there was a world of possibility out there and, suddenly filled with energy and optimism, I thought that there just had to be a way that would better suit me... a way that only I could discover, a way about which those around me as yet knew nothing.

"Yes, I think I have," I told Carrie.

"What'll you do?" she said.

"I don't know. Get myself well again, I suppose. That's the main priority."

"A good start," she agreed.

"Then... like I say, I don't know. I'll find a way of learning the things I want to learn, I suppose." I shrugged and smiled (my first genuine smile in what seemed like a very long time). Thinking about Johnny again, about the adventures we had shared, the subtle humiliations we had suffered, I said, "I might even write a book. Maybe about Johnny."

"You'd be good at that."

"My communication skills are, apparently, quite impressive," I said with a smile.

"So you're leaving? You're really leaving?"

"I think I have to, don't you?"

~

There was no more for Carl to tell. I sat with him in the living room and my overriding emotion was one of relief. Carl had reached the end of this part of his story and had made the right decision. When the time had come he had, as I saw it, no doubt as his parents, Carrie and everyone around him had seen it, understood that really there was only one sensible thing for him to do. In order to live, in order that he might stand any chance at all of making something of his life, he had had to leave. Looking at him now, lightly tanned, thin but healthy after his struggle with pneumonia, his eyes behind his glasses as alert as his very capable mind, I could only think that he had done the right thing. What choice had he really had, after all?

"So did you ever write the book about Johnny?" I said.

"I tried," he told me. "I tried a few times, in fact, but I've never been able to get it quite right. I wrote one called *Even Dreamers Die* that came close—but I was only in my early twenties at the time and... I don't think I had the required perspective."

"But you wrote other books?"

Smiling a little wistfully, he said, "Oh, yes. I've written... well, a lot of novels—and some of them very nearly sold. If I'd been writing the way I am today twenty years ago, when the industry wasn't quite as hostile as it now is to new authors, I'd have probably been published. As it is, it's been one near miss after another."

This had the feel of a well-rehearsed speech. It was disconcerting, a little offensive. It told me what he had experienced but not how it made him feel. I was about to tell him all this, to ask him whether he thought our friendship didn't deserve a little more honesty, when he looked over at me with a slightly painful expression on his face.

"I sometimes wonder why I bother," he told me. "Oh, don't get me wrong, I know I've achieved a hell of a lot. I am a good writer. I have a readership, even though I'm not published—my blog is becoming more popular every day—but that... as wonderful as it is, it isn't what I set out to do. I have something to *say*, something valid, something that can change the way people think... something that, I sometimes kid myself, might actually help people. It's frustrating. I mean, I've been doing this for over twenty years. You'd think I'd have taken the hint by now, wouldn't you?"

"You couldn't stop writing any more than you could stop your heart beating," I told him.

He wasn't all that convinced, I could tell, but at least he was being honest with me again. "If I thought there was another way," he admitted, "I think I could give it up tomorrow—as long as with the success came the same degree of satisfaction I get from writing a novel. There are a lot of questions that need to be answered," he continued. "But before they *can* be answered, the questions have to be asked. That's what I consider my job to be. Sometimes it's a thankless task, but what can you do?"

"You can try again," I told him.

"Write another novel?"

"No. Write a book. An autobiography, a memoir, whatever you want to call it. Write about Johnny again. Write everything you've told me over the past month or two. Tell them how it really was, Carl. For Johnny. For you."

Epilogue—They Knock Them down, But We're Still There

We drove from one spot to another and it would have been so very easy for me to have felt alienated, to have not felt a part of this journey and to have found myself lost in the memories, in the solidity of a past of which I supposed I still only knew a little. But I was as involved in this as my fellow travellers, now. Sitting beside Carl in the back of the car, Sonia in the passenger seat, Bob driving, I saw that I had been the catalyst. Without me, had I not started visiting him in the hospital to discuss my now almost forgotten dissertation, he would not have revisited those times again, not in such detail and certainly not with so much promise. I had marked the beginning for him and I had marked the end, and in so doing I had allowed him to find the perspective he needed.

Bob pulled the car over to the curb. Carl was staring out of the window at some shabby looking council houses set back from the road. They looked as though they were no more than ten years old, but already appeared neglected.

"Well there it is," Bob said, his arm across the top of the steering wheel, looking in the same direction as Carl. "Sunnyvale School in all its glory."

"The area is at least as rough as I remember it," Carl said.

"That's where it used to be?" I asked, confused.

"It's hard to tell," Carl answered. "Everything's changed so much but, yes, that's pretty much where it used to be. Hard to believe, really. I've never been over here since I left all those years ago and... well, you just sort of think that everything will still be the same."

Sonia had been quiet up until now. Not her usual self at all. Now she spoke, tenderly and considered, barely controlled emotion weighing down her words even as it lent them added force.

"That first day was horrible," she said. "I can remember it like it was yesterday—taking our little Carl into that place and having to leave him there. It was the worst day of my life. Everything about it just felt... the people were nice, don't get me wrong. They were kind and understanding and helpful. But it all felt so *wrong*. He shouldn't have been there. That was how it felt to me. He shouldn't have been there but there was no other option. *This is where he has to go.* That's what we were told. And we could see no way around it. Either we did what they told us was the right and only thing, or we didn't."

"Though even that wasn't really an option," Bob pointed out. "If we hadn't let him go to Sunnyvale... I'm not sure how these things work, but I doubt they would have just sat back and let us make that decision without a fight."

Carl didn't want to revisit the Resolution, Swallowfields or the Almsby Comprehensive. When Bob suggested it a few minutes later, he simply shook his head and turned away. Now, as I listened to Bob repeating one of Carl's favourite phrases (something about human dignity being a matter of social permission), Carl still staring out of the window at the place where Sunnyvale School had once been, I thought how strange and touching it was that he still intended to keep that promise. Returning to the Resolution, and, by default, because they were so close, Swallowfields and Almsby, even after all this time, just wasn't something he wanted or was prepared to do. He had told me the evening before as we had watched a film together that he wasn't afraid of the memories. He never had been. The process of talking about those times, of writing about them, even, had not been cathartic because, he insisted, there was nothing to heal. That had happened a long, long time ago. It was more that he was afraid that the present might somehow infect the past, reduce its importance, dilute what it had been with what it had become. "I want to remember it how it was, without fictional flourishes," he had said. "Warts and all. If I don't... it isn't just that it would feel like a betrayal, it's more that I'd feel as if I was letting go of something important, something unique. If we are lucky enough to have something like that, however dark, we need to keep hold of it— especially if it's taught us something of value."

And so the three schools were off the list completely today. I promised myself that, someday soon, I would visit them myself. See if I could recognize any of the places Carl had spoken of. But for today, at least, they would have to remain a partial mystery to me.

East Park Sixth Form College had also been flattened long ago, modern, moderately expensive private housing built in its place. Smiling wryly, Carl admitted that, yet again, it was difficult to say, exactly, where the college had been. The whole geography of the place had changed and the specific became a general, virtually unidentifiable.

"They knock them down," he said, wistfully. "But we're still there."

I nodded, but didn't quite know what to say in reply. I thought I knew what he meant, but sometimes it was difficult to be certain with Carl. He had his own unique way of seeing things, and when confronted with a statement like this I generally found that I preferred to simply listen.

"More places to live," he added. "But fewer places to learn... if we ever really learned anything, anyway."

"You learned plenty there," Bob said.

"True. Just not in the classroom."

"That was the beginning, really," Sonia said. She could be as cryptic as Carl, when she wanted to be.

"What *are* you on about?" Bob asked good-naturedly.

Chuckling, Sonia said, "That's when he started to be the person he really wanted to be... he became the Carl he used to be. Happy and positive, again."

I looked at Carl. The two of us were grinning. I'd thought that this afternoon might be a little dismal and sad, but it was turning out to be quite the opposite.

"Happy and positive?" I said to him. "I really hate to contradict you, Sonia, but that doesn't sound like him at all."

"She's like one of those mirrors you see at the fair," Carl explained. "She reflects well enough, it's just that she tends to distort the image a bit."

Sonia was laughing, too, now. Nodding her head in agreement. "I don't suppose I can argue with that," she said. "What can I say? I'm a mother."

We spent the rest of the afternoon at Whitby. It seemed right, somehow, that we should finish up there. The summer season was over and we managed to find a parking place down in the harbour, overlooking the moored boats, the Abbey up on the East Cliff before us. It was cold, but whilst Bob and Sonia went for a walk together, Carl and I were warm in the car, looking out over the water, peaceful, quiet and strangely soothing. The gulls swooped low, one landing on the roof of the car at one point, clip-clopping back and forth briefly before flying off again, and Carl and I didn't speak for a very long time.

The silence, however, was not uncomfortable.

"Penny for them," I finally said, when the time seemed right.

He was smiling again, looking up at the Abbey and the church. I felt him shrug as he allowed me to take his hand in mine. "I don't know," he said, his usual way of prefacing something he *did* know. "I was just thinking—maybe, just *maybe*, I'm finally ready for another adventure."

Printed in Great Britain by
Amazon.co.uk, Ltd.,
Marston Gate.